Jane Rawlinson  a convent schoo... University. Her... Kenya; her seco... revolutionary Ira... paperback from Paladin. Jane R... lives in Scotland with her husband and four children.

JANE RAWLINSON

Cargo

PALADIN
GRAFTON BOOKS
A Division of the Collins Publishing Group

LONDON GLASGOW
TORONTO SYDNEY AUCKLAND

Paladin
Grafton Books
A Division of the Collins Publishing Group
8 Grafton Street, London W1X 3LA

Published in Paladin Books 1988

First published in Great Britain by
André Deutsch Ltd 1987

ISBN 0-586-08718-4

Printed and bound in Great Britain by
Collins, Glasgow

Set in Baskerville

All the characters, incidents and islands in
this novel are fictitious

To my family

Contents

DAY ONE
Monday Island

'They chewing gum, we chewing it faster. Remember how we use to turn up noses at roti? The Yankees come and say it too nice. So now roti in every social fete. Is that kind of people we are, yes.'

David Lowenthal,
West Indian Societies

A few Carib Indians skulking in the coconut groves feel their gastric enzymes flow as one meal after another staggers over the treacherous, icing sugar sand. Tin foil has not yet been invented but here comes the next best thing, a portable, sealed system of armour plating which allows none of the succulent juices to escape.

Christopher Columbus, medium rare, feet gently broiling in a salty marinade of sweat and seawater, staggers up the beach with the traditional rolling gait of the old sea dog. With great ceremony he plants a flag (the sugar cane comes later) then stands for a moment in a halo of singed hair under a helmet that is rapidly poaching his brains. Surely there was something else he had to do? Ah yes. A name. The island must be given a name.

'What day is it?' he asks one of his companions.

'June the twenty-first, fourteen ninety-three.'

Christopher Columbus takes out his pocket missal. It is the feast day of the Apparition of Our Blessed Lady of Córdoba and Seville.

'Too long,' he says, mindful of all those reports that will have to be submitted, all those centuries before the invention of duplicators and photocopying machines.

'It's Monday,' says his companion.

'Aha,' says Christopher Columbus in Spanish, quite forgetting in the heat of the moment his promise to name his very first island after the saint who had cured his grandmother of gout.

So Monday Island it became, with all the connotations of a stale, post-weekend feeling of exhaustion and despair.

This is too much for the Caribs, who step out from among their coconuts not with the show of humble servility and gratitude that might have been expected in the face of their forthcoming civilization, but with a hail of poisoned arrows.

Christopher Columbus notes that the natives are hostile. The natives resolve that next time these beings with small hairy faces and pallid complexions, which remind them of nothing so much as their own wild pigs, will not get away without supplying, literally, the meat for the feast.

(Or did the Spanish introduce the pigs who afterwards ran wild? History abounds with such chicken and egg questions.)

Of course the exact spot where Christopher Columbus landed is no longer an idyllic sandy beach, but an evil-smelling passage between the customs house and the weighbridge, commemorated by an inscribed stone which any smiling official will be happy to dust down and point out to you in anticipation of good American dollars. Such is the path of progress. The coconut groves have been replaced by a jungle of concrete sheds, the sparkling golden sand by concrete jetties, and the crystal clear waters now support more than their fair share of oil slicks and garbage. The Caribs ate their last white man four hundred years ago and then defeated their conquerors by choosing extinction rather than slavery.

At about the same time that Columbus arrived by sea, an alternative method of traversing great distances was devised by one Leonardo da Vinci. But many, many years were to pass before such a means of transport became feasible here, and even when commonly accepted throughout much of the globe, the mountainous terrain of Monday

Island, whose volcanic peaks rise steeply from the sea bed, continued to defy the flying machine.

Today, there is a small airport located on the leeward side of the island between the village of Sugar Bay and the island's capital city, Soufrière. It consists of one bright blue wooden hut and a single strip of tarmac on a spit of land constantly eroded by the tides, but at a quarter of a mile wide the nearest thing on the island to the geographical phenomenon known as a coastal plain.

In accordance with the strict security demands made by international airline companies, the area is surrounded by a two-metre chainlink fence and the gates are locked at night when the customs officer and the immigration official go home.

There are as yet no facilities for night-time flights but the airport must rank among the busiest in the Caribbean in terms of the number of take-offs and landings per daylight hours, when the whine of small aircraft is as familiar and persistent as the drone of the mosquito at night.

The commercial planes, twin engined, sixteen seaters, follow a timetable no less erratic than that of the old sailing ships badgered by the trade winds and the weather. They come when they come and park with engines running, while those who want to disembark do so in a flurry of red hot wind.

Ophelia, regal in pink silk under a large black umbrella, led the procession down the road towards the airport. She increased her pace as the buzz of a plane came over the water. Behind her was her mammy, Portia, with the scarlet suitcase balanced on her head. Next came Aunty Gladys, Portia's sister, with a handkerchief to her nose into which she blew repeatedly.

'I pray that the good Lord take care of Ophelia,' said

Jancis, nodding her head earnestly to comfort the older woman. Jancis had known Ophelia since their schooldays.

Behind Jancis came Ophelia's brothers and sisters, then her seven male cousins, Aunty Gladys's children, all grown-up and strangely subdued, whether because of the imminent parting or the pain of sunlight on water after the party the night before.

They reached the airport at the same moment as the plane, which made conversation impossible. The goodbye hugs and kisses took place in a passionate silence. Then Ophelia was gone, in one end of the blue shed, out at the other, but separated now from her family by the fence. She turned to wave.

'Phelie,' groaned Portia, face squashed flat against the mesh. 'Oh my God, Phelie.'

Gladys stood silently, arms outstretched against the wire as if crucified. 'Write me,' she called out.

Jancis's head was bowed so that the tight curls of her head bulged through the diamond spaces like brillo pads. Ophelia could not tell whether she was crying or praying.

The cousins stood absolutely still, hands in their trouser pockets. Expressionless. Only Ophelia's younger brothers and sisters were carried away by the excitement which Ophelia felt. They leapt up and down with their hands over their ears, squealing.

Ophelia crossed the tarmac briskly. She climbed up the two steps into the plane, ducked her head and was gone. She saw the faces of her relatives scream past and then she was up in the air, watching her home, the school, the church, the village and finally the island itself shrink and blur and then vanish in a blue haze behind her.

Christopher Columbus was looking for gold. Adventurers still come, say the tourist brochures, seeking gold, but of a different kind – the golden glow of the sun and the golden tan it so freely offers.

Christopher Columbus anchored the fifty-foot *Santa Maria* out beyond the surf-line of the reef, and came ashore in a rowing boat. His ship would have fitted comfortably into the second-class cinema of a modern cruise vessel. One such, the *Dream of America*, cast its six hundred and eighty-nine foot early morning shadow, not just over Monday Island's deep water harbour but over the road beyond, and the single-storied houses beyond that, over the rust red corrugated iron roofs and up the hill to the farthest suburbs of the capital.

The shadow is a welcome phenomenon: to the taxi drivers and the stall holders laying out their bead necklaces and steel drums along the quayside; to hotel touts and to the forklift truck operators dashing back and forth with cartons of milk powder, cheese and corned beef; to the stevedores whom it protects from the glare of the sun as they attach steel cables to the containers and signal with yellow gloved hands to the crane operators who hoist them out of the hold of the cargo ship; to the hucksters loading their small vessels with fruit and vegetables for the neighbouring islands; in fact to all the locals who anticipate with greedy excitement the tidal wave of dollars which is about to break upon the shore.

Two of the fourteen hundred passengers, Harry and Betty Stillman, stood among others, side by side, on the top deck of the *Dream of America*.

'You want to go look for some parrots today, Bet?' asked Harry.

Betty looked down at the docks. The gangway was now in position.

'I might just take a quiet day on board,' she said.

'But Betty, you've been looking forward to seeing this island.'

Betty shrugged. After a week on cruise she was a seasoned traveller. She had visited three islands and knew that if you'd seen one you'd seen them all.

'But Betty,' wailed Harry, 'this island is British and you know how you love anything British.'

'I'd really rather stay on board.'

Betty was surprised to hear herself say any such thing. A week ago it would have been unthinkable. To stay on board when there was a chance of getting off?

Betty, newly embarked, closes her eyes against the terrible inevitability of the skyscrapers of New York receding until they become as flat as a theatre backdrop. She murmurs faintly to Harry that she must go and unpack. It is suddenly immensely important to find her cabin, a place where her cosmetics and hairbrush and her nightdress under the pillow will proclaim to the world, just as Christopher Columbus's flag had done, that this is the territory of Betty Stillman.

Betty marches bravely down the nearest corridor, finds a plan of the ship and looks up B deck. Two flights down but she won't use a lift. Oh no. She has avoided lifts ever since that film where someone was trapped in one and burnt to death. She finds the black tiled stairs and knows from the click of her heels that she's really there. Now down to A deck, past the muster station (what is a muster station anyway?), blue carpet with red and yellow swirls. Click clack, another staircase, B deck, yellow carpet with red and blue swirls.

Down a corridor, endlessly long, chrome strips gleaming like Harry's teeth, slightly uphill and lined with so many doors, so many numbers that they cease to register at all. Falls flat on her face at the first watertight door – all part of safety regulations, madam, but a real nuisance believe you me – picks herself up, and at the next watertight door steps high like a race horse. She can't be caught twice, not Betty, that's what everyone says.

Suddenly she stops. She has forgotten her cabin number. All Betty can think of is finding Harry. She starts back for the staircase. But which deck did she leave him on? She walks up and down the staircases examining the swirling carpets, until she begins to feel sea sick. If she can only get outside she will be all right. She sees a wooden door, and beyond it, through the glass panels, the Statue of Liberty. Betty flings herself at the door. It doesn't give an inch. Beside it is a notice. IN THE INTERESTS OF ALL PASSENGERS PLEASE KEEP THIS DOOR CLOSED.

Betty stands like Alice in Wonderland, nose pressed against the glass, and watches Liberty glide smoothly astern.

'You wanna go out?'

Betty jumps. Her right hand clutches at her artificial pearls.

'It's on account of the air conditioning,' says the other woman. 'You just have to push hard.' And she pushes very hard with one bare, brown, bony shoulder. 'Your first trip?'

Betty nods.

'I go every year. Same trip. Same cabin. You get attached, know what I mean?'

Betty nods. She certainly knows. Half an hour later when she leaves Sally's cabin she is much more knowledgeable about cruises. And there is no problem about finding her cabin because, as Sally pointed out, the number is written on her ticket which is in her handbag. B deck. Number 2137. As if she could ever forget, but just in case, Betty has written 2137 all over her cigarette packet during her third highball, until the whole carton is covered in a hieroglyph of twos, ones, threes and sevens.

She finds B deck – yellow carpet with red and blue swirls – sees a bench and sits down. Takes out her cigarette packet but can't make head or tail of where one number begins and the other one ends. Gives up and lights a cigarette and waits for Harry to find her.

By the time she gets on to her third cigarette she has the feeling that he isn't even trying. She looks at the cigarette packet again. She would never have thought that one number could have so many possible combinations. She adds them up to see if they come to a lucky twenty-one. They don't. Whichever order she tries, they still come to a decidedly unlucky thirteen. At which point Harry appears.

'Where the heck have you been?'

Betty turns very white but puts on a smile for the benefit of the other people in the corridor. 'I guess I got lost.'

Harry turns to go. Betty trots behind. After what feels like a long time, she says, 'I'm sure I recognize this bench.'

'Don't be ridiculous,' snarls Harry.

'But look, honey,' Betty peers into the ashtray, 'I smoked those three cigarettes while I was waiting for you.'

'You're not the only person who smokes on this goddamn ship.'

'But Harry,' Betty takes out the cigarette packet from her handbag, 'this was a new packet, three cigarettes have gone.'

'Betty.' Harry speaks very slowly. 'Three different people could have smoked those three cigarettes, or one person could have smoked two and . . .'

'Harry, I know those are my cigarettes.'

'I am not interested in those cigarettes. I just don't care about those cigarettes. What's the number of the cabin again?'

Betty holds out the packet.

'What the hell am I supposed to make of that?'

She shrugs.

'If I hadn't had to come and look for you there wouldn't have been any problem.'

Betty sits down wearily.

'My feet are killing me, Harry. I'll just sit here and you come and tell me when you've found it.'

Betty sits and thinks of her new friend Sally. After a few minutes she begins to feel impatient. She wants a shower and a change of clothes, in a cabin like Sally's with a sea view and decorated like a bridal suite. Betty sighs. If only she were thirty years younger and here with anyone but Harry.

However, Harry is her husband. If he can't find her, it is her duty to find him. Perhaps the Captain would call for Harry over the loud speaker system above the orchestrated versions of pop songs of the sixties. 'Will Mr Harry Stillman please call at the Captain's office to collect his wife.' Harry would be furious.

Then she remembers her ticket. Cabin number 2137. She turns right left right and as if by magic finds herself outside it.

The door is locked. Betty puts her ear against it and hears snoring. She'd know that snore anywhere. She raps with her knuckles.

'Harry,' she calls.

The snoring continues. The fat pig, she thinks.

'Honey. It's me.' Raps louder. Hates him for keeping her standing there in the corridor, locked out of her own room. 'Harry dear, it's Betty,' in well-modulated tones. To think of him lying there with both keys in his pocket. Thunders with both fists. The snoring stops. She hears Harry's slow footsteps. The door opens. She almost falls inside.

'Nice, isn't it?' says Harry. 'Just like new.'

But all Betty can see are the stains on the carpet, the cigarette burn in the mahogany veneer of the dressing table. She doesn't say anything.

She notices that the closet is larger than the bedroom and shower combined and spreads out their clothes to make it look full. She manages to say, 'There's no window,' and her voice comes out high and brittle.

'What do you think we are?' asks Harry. 'Millionaires?' But a week later on the top deck, faced by yet another day of sunshine, Betty looked down at the dock and the upturned black faces and longed for a day in the seclusion of her very own cabin, especially if Harry was on shore.

'Betty, how can you do this to me?' He was talking loudly. People were taking notice.

What a silly thing to say, thought Betty. Typical Harry, as if every action was directed at him. She laid a hand on his arm.

'It's okay, Harry. Of course we'll go look for parrots. I've been looking forward to it.'

Harry flung his arm round his wife's waist and kissed her cheek. In public he was sometimes given to these wild displays of affection which were sadly lacking in private.

Betty disentangled herself as soon as she reasonably could and took out a mirror and powder compact to repair the damage. Exposure to the sun caused skin cancer.

Behind her Sam and Louella laughed indulgently.

Sam and Lou, Betty and Harry had become a regular foursome. Betty enjoyed their company much as she enjoyed the company of anybody who spared her from being alone with Harry. Harry enjoyed all company, though any new acquaintance enjoyed him only until boredom set in. Ten days was an ideal length of time for friendship with Harry, which could then be terminated without regret amid protestations about keeping in touch.

Now they stood together at the top of the gangway, making way for the first rush of people, so that they could disembark in comfort and, Harry hoped, at not a little financial saving as the souvenir sellers and taxi drivers lowered their prices in a last ditch stand for customers.

Betty hesitated at the top of the death-defying slope to terra firma. Sam and Lou stepped on to the gangway. Still, she stood there.

'Oh c'mon,' said Harry. He pushed past her, barely fitting between the two metal poles.

Betty looked down the narrowing perspective of the passageway and imagined the awful possibility of Harry firmly wedged at a point somewhere between the ship and the land. Then taking a deep breath she followed.

At every step taken by Harry, the gangway shuddered and bounced and Betty in her open-toed, high-heeled white sandals clung to the flimsy ropes on either side of her, feeling them vibrate like the strings of a violin.

At the bottom of the gangway stood two officers, one on either side, to help passengers down the last two steps.

'Gee, thanks,' sighed Betty as she was swung off her feet. For one brief second she was young again, not in the one horse town of her childhood, but somewhere in the deep South whirled in white muslin like a dandelion clock beneath a tropical moon, in the arms of a newly arrived subaltern with the face of Rhett Butler. Or Clark Gable.

'They sure must have thought you were some old crock,' chortled Harry, as she landed.

Betty thought of the opening sentence of *Gone With the Wind*. 'Scarlett O'Hara was not pretty.' Ah, but she knew better than the author. She'd seen the film. She opened her eyes to the sun and sea and sky and the sensation of being free to go wherever she liked, until she was engulfed in a tide of coral necklaces, coconut fibre hats and painted shells. 'Harry,' she called, fearing she might drown. But Harry was nowhere to be seen. Panic stricken she turned back towards the ship and there, just in front of her, was the small doorway from which members of the crew disembarked.

Betty almost called 'Thomas' when she saw her cabin steward step out of the ship. But behind him came another black man, then another and they all looked just the same. But although Betty could not tell Thomas apart from the others without his trays of coffee or piles of clean laundry, she knew that he was bound to recognize her.

Smiling grimly, she looked straight in the eye of every man who stepped ashore. They looked not just at her, but through her, as if she wasn't there.

The last crew member stepped ashore and the door clanged shut behind him. Betty with the strength bred of despair called softly, 'Thomas?'

Thomas nodded. He seemed taller off the ship, dignified and good looking. He carried a large bag.

'These people are troubling you, madam?' he inquired.

'Oh no,' said Betty. 'I've just lost my husband.'

'They are ignorant country people,' said Thomas. 'Follow me.'

The crowd parted willingly enough for Thomas, and Betty followed close behind.

Harry stood impatiently by the taxi, one foot on the running board, elbow on the roof. He stared at Thomas blankly.

'It's Thomas,' said Betty. 'Our cabin steward.'

Harry was instantly all smiles. 'Say Thomas, I didn't recognize you. You going some place? Want a lift?'

Betty thanked God that Sam and Lou were already in the taxi so that she wouldn't have to be the one sitting in the middle this time. She straightened the fur fabric cover and plonked herself down. Harry shouldn't offer lifts when there obviously wasn't room.

'Move over Betty, will you?' said Harry.

'Harry, we're squashed already back here,' said Betty. But Thomas had one leg in the door and his hip was sliding down the length of Betty's left arm.

'Lou can sit on my knee,' said Sam.

Betty wished she was physically more like Lou, the type of woman who could sit on a man's knee without crushing him. At the same time, there was something dry and brittle about Lou, though how that could be so when she was rarely to be seen without a drink in her hand, Betty could not understand.

Thomas humped his bag on to his knee and slammed the door. Betty thought she would faint with the heat. Thomas's bag was sticking into her. She was going to suggest that Harry had it on his knee in the front, but wasn't sure whether it would fit between his stomach and the dashboard. She thought of all the things that had gone missing, and had a sudden vision of Thomas's cabin as an Ali Baba's cave of looted treasures, half-used bottles of perfume, broken necklaces and not quite finished whisky bottles.

Thomas saw her looking at him and smiled such a lovely, open smile that Betty was ashamed.

'You going home?' she asked.

'To visit my girlfriend.'

'That far from here?'

Thomas shook his head.

'Ask that driver. He know my girlfriend house.'

'What's her name?' asked Betty as the taxi drove off.

'She Ophelia.'

'That's a lovely name,' said Betty.

'Shakespeare, isn't it?' said Lou.

Thomas shrugged.

'*Hamlet*,' said Sam. 'She drowned herself when she thought that Hamlet didn't love her.'

'You take care of her, Thomas,' laughed Harry.

Betty tried to imagine anyone drowning themselves for love of Harry.

'I show you the island?' asked Thomas.

'Well . . .' Harry was immediately suspicious, thinking of his dollars.

'That would be lovely, wouldn't it everybody?' Betty turned to Sam and Lou for support. What a tale to tell everyone back home.

Harry opened his guidebook. The whole point of having spent fourteen dollars fifty on a guidebook was that it saved you the expense of a guide. Thomas probably knew nothing about the island's history anyway.

Harry read loudly, '"Monday Island, discovered by Christopher Columbus in . . ."'

'The hospital!' said Thomas. The taxi driver swerved left through a gate, tore up a drive and spun round a small roundabout planted with bougainvillaea. Dust sprayed over a line of people queuing at a door marked OUT PATIENTS ONLY.

'What the day today?' Thomas asked the driver.

The driver tilted his cap with the scarlet pompom on to the back of his head. 'Tuesday, man.' Behind them, the dust-coloured people coughed.

'Sure it's Tuesday, so what?' said Harry.

'TB clinic today,' said Thomas.

Harry read on. '"Area thirty-two square miles, population 50,000, average income per capita per annum eighty dollars US, capital city . . ."'

'This a city?' asked Betty.

'Betty,' explained Harry, very patiently, 'I already told you that this island is British, and in Britain if anywhere has a cathedral, it's a city.'

'That a fact?' asked Sam.

Harry nodded.

'"Capital city, Soufrière,"' he continued, '"a name as

unfortunately applicable today as it was at its foundation in 1625 as the port where slaves were unloaded for work in the plantations. See the ancient steps, leading from the former high water mark up cathedral hill, one for each colony of the British Empire. At one time a team of slaves was kept occupied dressing stone to keep up with the British policy of expansionism. The slaves coming ashore were forced to walk up this staircase, which could not have failed to impress them with the magnitude of what it meant to belong to a nation at its greatest, the British Empire, on which it was later truly said that the sun never sets."'

'Sounds kind of interesting,' said Lou.

'Let's go there,' said Betty. 'You know this, uh, staircase, Thomas?'

'Everyone on Monday Island know it,' said the driver.

Betty sat and watched the two black men and wondered what they would have talked about had they been on their own.

The answer is: Ophelia.

'"Due to the earthquake in 1843,"' Harry read, '"the staircase is now some fifty feet above the sea, and far exceeds in height the original slope up which it was built. The visitor who makes the climb finds himself at the top of a dizzying precipice which affords a fine photographic viewpoint of the capital."'

Betty, who had been wondering why anybody should bother to climb a staircase which led nowhere, now understood. She would gain far more pleasure from the views shown on the screen in the living room, in the company of say the Smiths and the Bernsteins over a supper menu that was not yet clear in her mind, than she ever would from the real thing.

The taxi stopped abruptly. There to their left was the

imposing pile of granite blocks, imported from Dartmoor as ballast for the ships returning to the West Indies after depositing their cargoes of sugar and tobacco.

Harry heaved himself out of the car, cameras clunking together. The sight of Harry's cameras embarrassed Betty. Because of his large paunch they swung around the level of his navel, whereas most other men's cameras, she noticed, hung neatly somewhere between waist and ... she pulled herself over to the door and clambered out. Sam stood easing his legs, Lou with her hands clasped and eyes sparkling exclaimed at how exquisite everything was. Thomas and the driver were already halfway to the top.

Betty breathed in deeply. The air was no longer fresh but hot and heavy.

The four tourists paused often in the full glare of the sun, ostensibly looking at the broadening panorama of rusty roofs and squat wooden shacks.

'There's our ship,' called Harry at last, and indeed the ship was the only beautiful thing within sight, white and graceful as a swan on the bright blue water, towering over the island and its capital city. 'Isn't she a beauty?'

Betty hated the way he referred to the ship as female. Harry insisted this was correct, but she didn't know anyone else who referred to the *Dream of America* as anything other than 'it'. Looking up, Betty saw Thomas and the driver, dark silhouettes against the dazzling sky. Sam joined them, then Lou. Like Marilyn Monroe, thought Betty, although it was only the fluttering dress which gave that impression. She could have filled it out better herself. Then Harry arrived, pear-shaped and strutting.

At the top Betty grasped his arm as she saw the immense drop before them.

'Careful,' he growled. 'I might have fallen.'

'Oh.' Betty looked down. Was it high enough? She tried to imagine Harry spreadeagled on the dusty ground below.

But he would be sure to survive such a fall. Not, God help her, even as he was now, but in a wheelchair whining and petulant – 'Sweetheart, would you just fetch me this' or 'Sweetheart, just run upstairs and bring me that.' At least at present he took himself out for a good twelve hours a day. Harry housebound was a formidable proposition. It was the bedpans that finally decided her against toppling Harry off the top of this glorious monument to the British Empire. She looked out beyond the harbour to the airport, where the wings of the small planes shimmered in the sun.

'Betty, I don't want to have to read this twice.'

'Sorry, Harry.' Betty sat down safely away from the drop.

' "The spire of the cathedral owes its present tipsy state, not to the common local affliction of white lightning, but to the same earthquake of 1843. An interesting feature of the building is the old cast iron pillar lying on the roof, said to have been deposited there by the hurricane of 1887. Certainly there is no reason to imagine it having been put there by human hand, and its presence has been faithfully recorded by many eminent historians and predates the arrival in the island of the first crane." Betty, you're not even looking.'

'Oh I am, Harry, I am.' Betty turned again to face the view.

' "The pillar, identical to those which support the roof of the old slave market, caused considerable alarm to the church-going Mondegians, but as weeks and then years passed without mishap, there was no reason to suppose that God and the ancient roof would fail to hold it up for a good many years to come." '

Betty took from her handbag her own, abbreviated version of Friedman's guide, turned to the pages on Monday Island and was relieved to read that the historical sights could easily be viewed in under two hours. Monday Island, it appeared, had little to offer the discerning tourist.

Which is something that worries the three-man Department of Leisure and Tourism. Gone are the days when ships could be forcibly brought to port by seamen engaged in a shady business somewhere between defence of the realm and piracy. They have to be enticed by means which are at the same time legitimate and cheap.

The sun is free and the beaches, thank the good Lord, are free. But whereas the sun is as golden as on all the other islands, the beaches suffer from the misfortune of being labelled 'black'. Not, it is fair to say, as black as the darkest skinned inhabitants, but dark enough to detract from their appeal. Not even the seven hundred and thirty rivers, two for every day of the year, can wash the beaches whiter than white, though they try hard enough at certain times of the year to wash the whole island into the sea in a furious lather. And while the Department ponders inexpensive ways to whiten the beaches, the ladies of the island apply the equivalent brainpower to the lightening of their complexions.

'Now there's something to think about,' said Harry on the way down.

Betty stood still to see what Harry was pointing out. She was afraid to move without watching her feet every inch of the way. An enormous billboard stared at her.

SMALL MINDS DISCUSS PEOPLE
AVERAGE MINDS DISCUSS EVENTS
GREAT MINDS DISCUSS IDEAS.

Harry aimed his camera, focussed. Click.

'Whoever put that up there?' asked Sam.

'Government,' grinned Thomas.

As the taxi sped through narrow streets shaded by the overhang of wooden verandahs, Betty, sitting there next to a black man, was entranced by everything she saw in spite of the discomforts of the crowded back seat.

Thomas suddenly gave a loud whistle and the taxi screeched to a halt.

'You wait,' he said to the carload of tourists. 'I see if my wife here.' He disappeared into an alleyway.

'Goddamn cheek,' said Harry.

'That his business,' said the driver, pointing upwards to the sign that read TELE-TAXIS.

'You mean he owns this taxi?' asked Harry.

'He have four taxis all with radio.'

'Will he be long?' Betty wondered whether it was worth moving along the seat for a few minutes.

'He just see if his wife she up there.'

'His wife?' Betty was surprised. 'I thought it was his girlfriend. Or has he got a wife as well?'

'Wife, girlfriend, is the same thing. They have two little boys.'

Betty watched a dumpy figure, in a button-through white cardigan and a flowery bundle of a cotton skirt, trudge slowly along the sidewalk towards the car. Just as she drew level with it, she turned right into the alleyway in Thomas's footsteps.

'Hey,' Betty leaned forward, 'is that Ophelia?'

The driver slapped both hands hard on the steering wheel and yelped with laughter. 'You ain't never see Ophelia?' he asked in disbelief.

Betty shook her head.

'That only Jancis,' he said.

* * *

Jancis was functioning at half speed today. She had watched Ophelia's plane climb safely into the sky and then, wanting to be alone, she had walked slowly into town. Even going down the street wasn't the same without Ophelia. It was not Huntingdon's dramatic courtship of her friend which provided such excitement, but Ophelia's way of making everything she did into a drama.

Ophelia's progress down the street is slow and stately. She wears heels so high that her hips swing from side to side as she walks and her tight, broad gold belt pivots up and down.

For Jancis the street is simply a means of getting from one place to another. Ophelia has made walking down the street a work of art. She greets and is greeted by everybody, she smiles and laughs with her head thrown back and her hair bouncing and her teeth shining in the sun.

She stops at every stall turning over goods and asking prices. If she fancies a mango it is given for the pleasure of seeing her eat it. She tries out slides and combs and make-up and the old stall holders clap their hands and say, 'That look good on you, darling.' She seldom buys anything, and as she wanders along she suddenly says to Jancis in a casual manner, 'Today Huntingdon ask me to marry him.'

And Jancis, soft-soled at her side, frowns and worries.

'What you say to him then?'

'I go think about it.'

'He have a wife already.'

'You want to shock me dead, Jancis? You can't never do that. I know he have other women but is me he want marry.'

'That woman in Nelson's Look Out, she born his baby last week.'

'Huntingdon is a man,' says Ophelia. 'He have money.'

Ophelia pauses to buy kenibs. 'They sweet and juicy?'

'You try, darling.'

Ophelia bites into the small green fruit. She spits angrily. 'Why you pick the fruit when it ain't ready?'

Jancis is embarrassed and leads Ophelia away. 'She only a old woman, why you have to speak like that?'

Ophelia is angry. 'Look, Jancis. If I sell something, is because it is good. I give value for money.'

'Perhaps she need money and her kenibs are not ripe?'

'She a dirty old woman. You want ice cream instead?'

Jancis shakes her head. 'I don' have money.'

Ophelia clicks into the ice cream bar, leans against the counter, tapping the formica top with a coin.

'Yes, darling. The usual?'

Ophelia lays her hand on his arm. 'This is my friend.' She indicates Jancis, trying to make herself invisible in the doorway.

'When you go marry me, Ophelia?' asks the man, handing over two enormous cones.

Ophelia shrugs and holds out coins which the man waves away.

'It does do me soul good to see you,' he says.

Ophelia gives him a big smile and goes outside where Jancis, perched on the window ledge, frowns into the dust.

'Why you always have to worry 'bout money, Jancis?' asks Ophelia. She hands one of the cones to Jancis who licks it suspiciously.

Ophelia takes large bites, squealing as the coldness hits her teeth.

'Come. Today we go take a taxi,' says Ophelia, stepping over the gutter into the street.

A large blue Cadillac stops inches from her pointed toes. 'You want a ride?'

'Huntingdon! You got a new car?'

Huntingdon gestures with his hands to indicate that he could have a new car every day if he felt like it.

31

'You wanna lift?'

Ophelia would love to get into the shiny new car, but she shakes her head. She has to collect the boys from the nursery.

'No, I taking a taxi,' she says.

Huntingdon shrugs. His smile fades. He presses the button that closes the electrically operated windows and accelerates away showering the remains of Jancis's ice cream with dust.

'Huntingdon, you are a pig,' Ophelia screams after the car.

Jancis dragged herself up the office stairs, eyes never raised higher than the hand rail. Thus she failed to register Thomas inside the maroon sneakers and crisp blue denims that bounded past several steps at a time in the opposite direction. It was only when she looked through the office window down into the street that she realized who he was.

Though she rapped on the glass and called out, and even waved Ophelia's letter to attract his attention, Thomas got into the car, which promptly moved away.

Thomas might have noticed Jancis at the window, had he not been talking to Betty, who still could not see that a wife and a girlfriend were the same thing at all.

'You have two little boys, Thomas?' she persisted.

Thomas ignored her and spoke angrily to the driver.

'We go look for her at home.'

'What's up, Thomas? She playing tricks on you, eh?' laughed Harry.

'I'd like to send something for your, er, wife,' said Betty. She opened her handbag. Thomas stared at the gold watch which Betty took out and held in her hand. Nothing else seemed to interest him.

'Ophelia haven't got no watch,' said Thomas.

'I don't wear it because of the heat,' explained Betty.

She didn't like to admit how much her wrist and ankles had swollen during the holiday. She put the watch back. There was nothing that seemed a suitable gift for Thomas's wife but she did find a small packet of barley sugars for the children. She never went anywhere without her barley sugars but today she'd manage. Thomas put them in his pocket without enthusiasm. The taxi stopped.

'Which house?' asked Betty.

Thomas gestured vaguely with one hand. Betty looked at the wooden shacks stacked like packs of cards on the mountainside.

'The turquoise one?' she asked.

Thomas smiled and nodded.

The houses were all painted the same peculiar bluish green that was echoed nowhere in the landscape, sky or sea. But Betty knew which house she meant, the one at the top which would have such a delightful view. She was happy to think of Thomas and Ophelia sitting together on the verandah. It was all so romantic.

Thomas got out of the car and hoisted the bag on to his head.

'Doesn't that hurt you, Thomas?' asked Betty.

Thomas grinned and raised a hand in thanks.

'Say, can I take a snap?' asked Harry, winding down his window.

Thomas moved off up the hill. Betty couldn't take her eyes off him – the long loose swing of his hips, his easy grace. She would have liked to see him dancing.

'Where to, sir?' the driver asked Harry.

'Le, er, Perokay,' said Harry.

'Where that?' asked the driver.

'You're the goddamn guide,' said Harry. 'Le Per-row-kay.' He spoke very slow and loud and jabbed at the guidebook with his right index finger.

The driver scratched his head. Ah. Le Perroquet.

'You want taxi for the day?'

'No, no,' said Harry, 'we can easily get another one back.'

'Le Perroquet is in the rain forest. No one is there to bring you back. Is better you hire me for the day.'

'Sure,' said Sam. 'We hire you for the day. No problem.'

'Wait a minute,' said Harry. 'What's it cost?'

'You my friend,' said the driver. 'You only pay one hundred dollars.'

'US or Caribbean?' asked Harry, piggy eyes squinting.

'How I can give you that price Caribbean? One hundred Caribbean ain't enough for the petrol, sah!' He started the engine.

Harry fanned himself with the guidebook.

'Betty, shut that goddamn window.'

'Sorry, dear.' Betty shut the window and perspiration trickled down her forehead.

'You turned on the air conditioning?' Harry asked the driver.

'With air conditioning, a hundred and fifty dollars,' said the driver. 'US,' he added.

'Jesus H. Christ,' said Harry. 'That's robbery.'

'It's not bad for a whole day out,' said Sam.

'We don't even know how far it is,' said Harry. 'We might be there in half an hour.'

Betty eased herself forward on the furry seat lining.

'Cheaper to open the windows,' said Harry cheerfully. Betty held her breath. 'You got your window open yet, Betty?'

Betty's hand simply flew to the handle and wound round and round at the speed of light. 'That too windy for you, Lou?'

Lou, pinned between Sam and Betty, smiled serenely. Nothing ever seemed to bother her.

'I'm fine. Just fine,' she replied.

Betty gulped at the air streaming past the window.

The house which awaited Thomas at the end of the zigzag path up the hill belonged to Ophelia's mother, who had inherited the land on which it stood from a paternal aunt who had taken a liking to her as a child.

The Lapierre residence with its numerous doorways and levels resembled a rabbit warren. The central building, quite outstandingly modern compared with the other houses in the village, stood firm on concrete foundations, though the rest was made of wood painted the colour that had caught Betty's eye.

On closer inspection it could be seen that many additional rooms were stacked one against the other on the precarious slope. In these rooms lived the older children of Portia Lapierre. The rooms were made of odd sheets of corrugated iron and planks, or stones from the sea shore, roughly cemented, nailed or propped together. The removal of any one item would be sufficient to send the whole lot toppling down. The house spread its eaves over these fragile constructions like a mother hen spreads its wings over its chicks.

Ophelia always went home, not by the pathway which Thomas now climbed, but following the contours of the ravine itself, from the bridge over the road by the bus stop. The ravine was not particularly beautiful, but it did provide a convenient garbage disposal area which was flushed out regularly in the rainy season. Flash floods swept the morass of excrement, tins and bottles, bones, dead animals and old furniture out to sea where they bobbed on the surface in a huge and expanding circle of refuse. But it pleased Ophelia to come home by a different path as if she lived apart from her family.

Since her room was the latest addition to the house so

far, Ophelia was fortunate in having better ventilation than several of her brothers and the room was pleasantly shaded by an old breadfruit tree. However, she only had to open any magazine to know that anyone who was anyone didn't live in a wooden house at all, a deficiency she had remedied by nailing roofing felt on to the outside walls and then painting it a deep brick red with bright white lines. It was scarcely noticeable in the shade of the breadfruit tree that she had run out of felting some three feet short of the eaves, but by then Ophelia was in any case more concerned with the interior decorations.

Thomas approached Ophelia's house in some discomfort. Over the years he had become used to an air-conditioned life and walking up a steep hill in a temperature of ninety degrees with a bag on his head was not as easy as it once had been.

'You want Phelie?' someone asked. 'She ain't there.'

Even when he saw all the closed shutters, Thomas was not worried. If Ophelia was at home and ill she could easily pretend to be out so that nobody disturbed her. Another possibility also occurred to him. This time he had written to say that he was coming. On most occasions he simply turned up, assuming that Ophelia would have seen the announcement of his ship's arrival in the paper. Perhaps Ophelia had taken the day off work and was there, in the darkened room, waiting for him.

Thomas found the front door locked. He felt for the key under the anthurium in the milk powder tin and unlocked it. His bag wouldn't fit past the large new green fridge.

Huntingdon had had the fridge delivered the day before the party, together with a new radio cassette recorder for Ophelia. If she had had any doubts about his honourable intentions towards her, these were surely now set at rest.

Huntingdon insisted that the fridge was nothing. It had been damaged in transit and was unsaleable, but the small dent faced into the kitchen rather than towards the door, so visitors did not see it.

Portia had considerable difficulty passing between the sitting room and the kitchen. She eased herself in sideways uttering little squeaks of 'Oh my God' and 'Lord bless us' as she disappeared from sight.

Nelson and Napoleon thought the fridge was wonderful. They stood for hours opening and shutting the door just to see the light come on and go off as if by magic.

'I beat you Nelson, I beat you Napoleon, you hear?' Portia screeched from somewhere amid the greasy clouds of frying garlic and chilli. But the boys were safe because in the time that it took their grandmother to squeeze out of the kitchen, they could be miles away.

The stale smell of spirits, cigarette smoke and sweat hit Thomas as soon as he stepped indoors. He knew that on the island such a party meant one thing, and one thing only. Leaving.

Ophelia flops down at Aunty Gladys's feet.

'It hot for so,' she says, pulling her dress away from her skin, her face radiant, reflecting the admiration she knows she is arousing in this largely male party. Aunty Gladys's seven sons stand around her in a semicircle.

Aunty Gladys lays a hand fondly on Ophelia's head.

'Why you leaving us, child?'

Ophelia shrugs.

'Don' you have 'nough food to eat?'

Ophelia nods.

'Don' you have nice clothes to wear?'

'Yes, aunty.'

'Don' you have a nice house to live in?'

Ophelia nods again.

'Well, why you want to go somewhere else?' Aunty Gladys laughs comfortably, confident that she has made a point which Ophelia cannot answer.

'You remember, aunty,' says Ophelia, 'when I was little and Portia bring you that red dress?' Ophelia had never seen her aunt as magnificent as she looked in that scarlet tricel.

Gladys nods. 'I remember, child. Why you asking me?'

'And I asking you, why you didn't keep that dress for best, aunty?' Ophelia hesitates, remembering her aunt walking into the mountains every day with an axe and a cutlass balanced on her head, until the scarlet faded to the same dust colour as the rest of her clothes.

Gladys laughs as she did on hearing the question the first time, rubbing her palm against her nose.

'Now I see,' says Ophelia, 'that you never did need clothes for best.' She rests her head on her aunt's knee.

Huntingdon in his dark suit stands behind the settee on which Aunty Gladys sits. None of the cousins are quite at ease while he is there. They cannot dance with Ophelia and joke with her as they would like to.

Aunty Gladys leans closer to Ophelia and whispers. 'Phelie, why you don' stay here and find a good good man?' She clearly means someone other than Huntingdon.

'Aunty,' Phelie laughs, 'you already done take the only good man on the island. What you have left for me?'

Ophelia stands up and drags Uncle Remus into the small clear area in the middle of the room to dance. The cousins stand miserably around. The only other girl to dance with, other than children, is Jancis.

Ophelia has been irritated by Jancis all evening. She had thought her friend might enjoy an outing, but she seems to be making no effort even to look as if she is. Ophelia tears herself out of Uncle Remus's embrace.

'You want more drink?' she asks Jancis.

Jancis sits neatly on a hard chair with her ankles crossed and a glass which once held Coca Cola on her knee.

Ophelia goes over to the drinks table, squeezes in among the cousins. 'Why you invite her?' one of them says.

Jancis sits entirely alone in her best cotton dress and newly whitened tennis shoes.

'She is my friend,' says Ophelia. She pours a large measure of rum in the bottom of Jancis's glass and winks at the cousin. 'In ten minutes why you all don't ask her to dance?'

The cousins laugh. 'But we all waiting to dance with you, Phelie.'

Ophelia swaggers back across the room to Jancis with exaggerated courtesy.

Jancis gulps at the drink like someone dying of thirst. 'It have a nice taste,' she says. 'Where you buy it?'

'In the supermarket. Is American,' says Ophelia.

Jancis nods. Now she understands the difference in flavour.

'You come and meet my Aunty Gladys,' says Ophelia.

Aunty Gladys makes a space for Jancis next to her on the sofa.

'Now you tell me, Jancis,' she says, 'why it ain't have no office on Monday Island good enough for Phelie.'

'Oh aunty, I want to see the whole world.'

'You take care, child. That island you going to visit is a wicked, wicked place.'

'I go take care, aunty.'

'What time you going, girl?'

'Eight o'clock.'

'I go only be happy,' says Aunty Gladys, 'if I come and see you safe in your seat.'

'You upsetting that girl with all your questions, Gladys.' Portia brandishes a tumblerful of whisky. 'You leave she to enjoy she party.' And to forestall further conversation Portia turns a cassette on full blast.

The whole house shakes. Ophelia grabs the nearest cousin and begins to dance. As she passes the armchair where Nelson and Napoleon are fast asleep, she hauls them to their feet.

'Why you sleeping at my party?' she asks. 'You come and enjoy yourselves.'

She gives them a shove in the direction of the table laden with food and sodas. 'Hey, Etienne,' she calls to the eldest cousin, 'give them boys a cake and a drink. This is a party not a funeral, man.'

While Ophelia dances, she keeps her eyes on Aunty Gladys, and envies her, not for the life that she leads, but for her capacity to be content with what she has.

Thomas hurried outside into the dazzling sunlight and ran round below the verandah to Ophelia's door. The padlock was big and shiny, but the wood of the door so soft that he soon wrenched it off with a stick.

It was dark inside Ophelia's bedroom, rich with the warm sweet smell of her perfumes and powders. Thomas flung open the shutters. He dragged open drawers and cupboards, pulled aside the curtain behind which she hung her dresses. Everything was empty.

Ophelia's new room sparkles and dazzles from the vinyl wallpaper and gleaming paintwork to the new furniture. With the curtain drawn to shut out the breadfruit tree in the yard, she can almost imagine herself in a penthouse in New York.

The furniture caused considerable problems since the village carpenter took one look at the designs she had in mind and pronounced them unsound, offering her instead the traditional items that would still be as sturdy for her granddaughter's children as they would be for her own. Ophelia cannot see any point in planning this far ahead. Fashions will change and she will change with them. She is depressed by this incident so typical of the narrow-mindedness of the average islander.

She goes instead to the island's only department store and demands to see the manager. They spend a couple of hours after closing time exploring the comforts of every settee and bedroom suite in the shop, after which the manager, an almost white man, personally sees to the installation of one white settee, a cocktail cabinet and a large double bed in Ophelia's bedroom with very modest terms of repayment. Various other display items afterwards find their way into her room, from the oblong of white nylon carpet on the floor which is ruined by mudstains during the first rainy season, to the alabaster cherub holding a light bulb aloft. The little boys Nelson and Napoleon are forbidden to stroke it, even for the soft white powder which it leaves on their small dark fingertips. Ophelia still awaits the electricity supply that will enable it to shine with its full glory, but the Mondegian Electricity Board has proved disappointingly incorruptible and she has been relegated to the waiting list like everybody else.

Thomas went back outside and up the steps on to the verandah from which he could see as far as the coast road and the sea. He was breathing fast. He fumbled in the breast pocket of his shirt for his cigarettes, struck a match, changed his mind and flung it and the cigarette over the verandah railing.

'Where Phelie?' he roared into the heavy stillness that approaches midday. The village was practically deserted. The young were at school, the able-bodied at jobs or in the fields, only the old remained.

'Where Ophelia gone?' screamed Thomas, heedless of who would know that he had been abandoned.

Up the lane on the top of a rock, enjoying the warmth of the sun on his old bones and the enamel bowl of gruel on his lap, an old man was sitting.

'*Petit maman, petit papa,*' he sang over and over rocking back and forth in his trilby hat and old grey suit. He didn't hear Thomas's howl of grief, so wrapped up was he in his own thoughts.

It was to him that Thomas rushed in his anguish. He took hold of the old man's shoulders and shook him roughly.

'Papa,' he said, 'tell me, tell me where Ophelia going.'

'Ophelia? She have a big party and she going,' and he resumed his singing and sucking.

'Was that the whole of the city?' asked Harry in disbelief as the last house vanished into the clouds of dust behind the taxi and its corrugated iron roof was a mere glint through the haze.

'Yes, sah, that's Soufrière.'

The road wound for a while along the coast. Betty closed her eyes and turned away from the sharp drop down to the sea below. No coconut palm would be strong enough to stop the car once it started rolling down the cliff, not with Harry inside.

The road veered sharply inland, and began climbing.

'Bananas,' said the guide cheerfully, waving one arm out of the window.

'Gee, just look at those flowers,' said Harry.

Betty thought they looked quite obscene. Harry insisted on stopping the car and taking a picture. They all got out. By the time Harry had finished lining up his shot of the swollen purple tip of the flower and its surrounding fringe of small green fruit Betty was past feeling anything except

hot. Then she noticed someone below them in the plantation, who appeared to be washing the bunches of bananas
with a sponge on the end of a bamboo pole.

Betty willed herself to ask an intelligent question, if only
to prove to the others how much she was enjoying herself.

'What's she doing?' she asked the driver. It was a pity
that the woman was wearing nothing more picturesque
than jeans and wellingtons.

'She deflowering the bananas,' said the driver.

Harry laughed until his teeth rattled.

Then they all collapsed into the car and drove on
through a small village consisting of six wooden shacks and
three churches, one Catholic, one Revivalist, one
Moravian.

Higher and higher they went into the hills following a
narrow river valley whose cliffs rose sheer on either side,
then abruptly the car stopped.

'Here we are,' said the driver.

'Didn't I tell you?' said Harry. 'One hundred US for half
an hour.'

Betty flinched.

'Where are we?' she asked, seeing nothing but greenery
all around.

'Le Perroquet,' said the driver.

'Not a bloody parrot in sight,' said Harry.

The parrot question is one that has also bothered the
Department of Leisure and Tourism for years, since parrots
and rain forests are very promotable in terms of the tourist
industry. The Minister has been driven to consult various
ecologists and ornithologists on this very question, but he
might have got further with his research had he consulted
the local practitioners of creole cookery, the hardworking
mothers of larger than average rural families or the res-
taurateurs of Soufrière. For the simple answer is that most

of the parrots went into the cooking pots, and a very rich and satisfying meal they made too.

But let us return to that time when little was known about the island, before it was so miraculously discovered by Columbus. The Caribs, lolloping naked through the forests with their poisoned bows and arrows can be imagined, with the gorgeous plumes of these birds used as body ornaments, but equally it is hard to imagine that, even during bad days when little in the way of human flesh was available over the counter, the Caribs ever constituted any serious threat to the species as a whole. Indeed, the few primitive etchings left here and there on rock faces suggest that the parrot enjoyed a near god-like status at that time.

The rot set in with Columbus, who could not resist catching a few of these wonderful birds and sending them home in glory to Queen Isabella. The birds became quite the thing in Castilian society and seemed to adapt admirably to the change in climate, whereas the shipload of Caribs which accompanied them quickly perished.

The English were slower to catch on to the commercial potential of the parrot, and finding them nasty biting creatures wanted as little as possible to do with them alive. The sight of a pirate or buccaneer with a stuffed parrot on his shoulder so common in pantomime testifies to their having better sense than the Spanish, with whom they were so constantly at war.

The wholesale slaughter of the parrot began primarily as a means of recreation for the planter and his family and in response to the fashion industry of Paris. The fabled Père l'Abattoir borrowed from the buccaneers the habit of meat boucané. After days of indiscriminate slaughter in the forests, the planters were joined by their wives and children and numerous slaves in some idyllic forest grove to eat and drink themselves into that state of stupefaction which alone made life in the West Indies bearable. Carcases of oxen were stuffed with anything that moved or flew, together with limes, mangoes and the wild herbs of the islands, and slowly barbecued.

The American War of Independence struck another blow against parrots. While the citizens of America repudiated their mother country, the disruption of imports to Monday Island, which at the time produced only sugar, was such that ten thousand slaves died of starvation and the parrot population dwindled alarmingly.

There are rumours that one or two parrots still lurk in the depths of the rain forest. One or two witnesses have, in the past fifty years, testified to flashes of brilliant plumage among the dense vegetation, but whether this constitutes a viable population only time will tell. The government has set up a programme in schools to discourage the primitive and short-sighted attitude of some locals, 'If I catch I eat.'

Harry and the taxi driver walked up the uneven, moss-covered steps.

'No bloody parrots on the island for fifty years,' said the driver, 'but my grandmother she eat.'

'They must have been lovely birds,' said Harry, leafing through his guidebook for a picture. 'Look at those colours.'

'Le Perroquet,' said the driver, 'it just a name. Is French.'

Harry realized that Betty was not with them.

'C'mon, Bet,' he shouted. 'What's keeping you?'

Betty still stood by the car. There was no sign of a restaurant anywhere and she could just imagine the head-lines. THE WORM IN THE APPLE, they screamed. FOUR TOURISTS FOUND DEAD ON PARADISE ISLAND. It was the sort of thing that would make Harry chortle into his breakfast. Only he wouldn't of course be there to read it.

Slowly she followed up the steep gravel track, slithering

one step back for every two forward. The restaurant was so well camouflaged that she found herself on a stone verandah set with tables and chairs almost before realizing it.

The trees formed a dense canopy overhead, which filtered the sunlight in beams and lattices of a rich lime green. The trees were immensely tall, each trunk thickly layered with moss and each branch laden with orchids and ferns. From Betty's left came the sound of running water, and peering over the stone balustrade she saw the hot springs bubbling in a series of waterfalls, which fell steaming and tinkling into the garden below.

Betty held her breath. There in a spotlight of sun hovered a tiny, iridescent humming bird like some Tinkerbell in sequins. In this cathedral of warmth and greenery, Betty felt happier than ever before in her life.

'You look like you seen a ghost.' Harry slapped her on the back. 'The walk too much for you, eh, honey?'

Betty hated him. His voice, his presence violated this place. She walked to the opposite end of the terrace, as far away from him as possible, and leaned against the balustrade.

'Say, Bet, you'll get your slacks dirty,' called Harry.

Betty turned and looked out into the forest. She closed her ears and closed her mind to Harry.

Over the past five years, Betty's desperation has led her to regular consultations with an analyst. She has learnt that her 'cure' depends on herself, and particularly on her own ability to be herself. In the consulting room, it all sounded so absurdly easy, but of course Dr Greenberg had never met Harry. If he had, Betty felt that he would admire the single-mindedness with which she was now pursuing the only avenue left open to her. Getting rid of Harry altogether.

Betty was not a violent person. She imagined a gentle, almost pleasurable end for Harry. A low ship's rail, an almost imperceptible nudge and a drunken Harry falling over the top in a series of graceful turns, each one bringing him closer to the moonlit mirror of the sea. On Harry's face was an ecstatic grin – awkward, pompous Harry at the last transformed into a swan calling out in wonder, 'See me, Betty? I can fly!'

'Goodbye, Harry,' murmured Betty, and even went so far as to blow him a kiss before he disappeared with scarcely a splash.

Betty did not in the least consider herself a murderess. She only had to think of how she felt about children and animals to reassure herself on that point. She preferred to think of it as a judicial execution. He'd asked for it. Her only regret was that the act itself would leave no room for Harry to say to her afterwards in open-mouthed astonishment, 'Honey, I'd never have thought it of you . . .'

'Who's for a drink?' Harry the jovial host slapped his hands together, too thirsty to wait any longer for Sam to buy the first round.

Betty turned away. Well, let Harry enjoy himself. There were only six more days on this trip and she was determined not to take him back home with her.

'Say, what's your name?' he was shouting.

'Churchill,' the driver replied.

'Well, I'm damned,' said Harry.

'Say, that's a fine name.' Betty was anxious to make up for Harry's rudeness. 'A name to be proud of.'

Churchill gave her a shy smile.

'My name's Betty,' she said. 'I'm pleased to meet you.'

Churchill took off his hat and scratched his head.

'You want see the Falls?'

'Let me just look that up.' Friedman gave the all-clear and even went so far as to describe Britannia Falls as a mighty cataclysm of nature. Betty wasn't quite sure what a cataclysm was but it sounded spectacular. 'Sure I'll go,' she said.

Sam and Lou, already well into their whisky sours, declined the invitation. Harry clambered after Betty and Churchill for a few hundred yards before collapsing on a rock.

'Count me out,' he said.

'You be all right here?' asked Betty. The restaurant was already swallowed up by the lush greenery.

'Sure I'll be all right.' Harry was red hot. 'What sort of fool d'you take me for?'

They left him fanning himself with his hat. Churchill offered Betty his hand. She accepted gratefully and he hauled her over some loose rocks towards him.

'You have a lovely body,' he said.

Betty blushed and snatched her hand away. 'Gee, er, thanks.' She looked nervously over her shoulder. Harry was out of sight.

'Is a good thing I here with you, Mrs Betty,' said Churchill.

'Oh? Why's that?' Betty paused to get her breath back.

'The last white person who come here on his own, they chop him up into sixty-five pieces.'

'Sixty-five? You sure it was sixty-five?'

'Well, so many they can' find them all.'

Betty imagined sixty-five polystyrene trays in the supermarket refrigerator. Each packet neatly labelled, weighed and priced.

'Is my husband all right back there on his own?' He of course wouldn't make supermarket grade. He'd be rejected because of the fat content.

'Mr Harry?' Churchill shrugged and laughed. 'We go see when we get back.'

Betty was sweating heavily. 'Is it far?'

'We nearly there now. You don' hear the water?'

Betty stood still, but all she could hear was the blood drumming in her ears.

Harry was still sitting on the rock, waiting for the fire in his lungs to die down. Self-control was all that was needed. Harry took a deep breath and counted to three. One, two, three . . .

Harry – for the moment just call him Gary – swaggers down a Mexican street under the noonday sun, expecting at any moment a knife in his back. He sweats under the black stetson. Chews gum. Feels under his armpit the comforting metal shape of the latest in electrical hardware, an avocado-coloured toaster. Eyes crinkled against the heat and dust. Bow-legged. Hey, Harry, where's your hoss? Harry snorts.

In the middle of the deserted street of this ghost town, he stops. Sump'n sure is strange about this hick town. Snaps his fingers. Got it. There ain't no electricity. Might as well try to sell a toaster on the moon. Has a vision of a toaster in the Sea of Tranquillity endlessly popping slices of golden brown toast up into space.

Cackles. Finds himself back in Georgia. Noon? Yes. Hot? Right again. A deserted street? You got it. Electricity? Well . . . why the hell have they sent him to this goddamn place?

Madam, would you like an electric toaster to stand on your sideboard? We do a lovely line in toasters. What, none of your neighbours have one? This is your big chance, Mrs Jones. Be the first. Beat them to it. Impress them. Look on it as an investment for the future. Prices can only go up.

On the moon, the slices of toast are projected in unending succession into orbit.

These your children, Mrs Jones? Well, I declare. Aren't

49

they cute! Harry's hand refuses to pat the children on the head fearing perhaps the abrasive touch of steel wool. The door slams in his face. Manners just aren't what they used to be.

Harry tilts his stetson on to the back of his head. Swaggers back down the road to his clapped-out Ford. Slumps into the driving seat with his trouser belt like a vice and his kidneys spilling out over the top.

Betty aimed her small instamatic at the Falls.

'Well, that's really something, Churchill,' she said.

They were standing on a wooden platform built out from the cliff. Betty didn't look over the edge, though she did momentarily regret Harry wasn't with her as she stepped back from the flimsy railings.

Further down the valley the flux from the falls, an unattractive brown due to the force with which it struck the rocks below, merged with another river in an explosion of foam. Within the angle of the junction was a wide, flat rock.

On the rock two naked figures were dancing together. Betty could just hear the steel band from their radio. She raised her camera. Click. Feels she has got the one shot that will prove how close she got to the real life of the islanders, living naturally as God intended, just as in those days before Christopher Columbus discovered them.

'Caribs?' she asked hopefully.

Churchill laughed. 'That man a civil servant and she his secretary. They come every Friday lunchtime to same place and make love.'

Betty blushed. Oh God. How could she ever collect the slides from the chemist. He would be sure to have looked through them all. She couldn't send Harry for them either. She could just picture him and the chemist revelling in them together. But one thing was certain, she would never allow those naked bodies six foot high on her living room wall. Whatever would the Smiths and Bernsteins think?

Thomas stood by the tarmac road leading through Sugar Bay. The sun was hot but if he stepped back into the shade of the mango trees he might miss the chance of a lift. He watched some chickens pecking in the road and kicked out at a bony dog that sniffed at his shoes and then threatened to cock a leg against his new denims.

He wondered where to go for information about Ophelia, whether to Nelson's Look Out where her mother still tended the family land, or to the offices of Midwestern Electricals and tackle Huntingdon. The latter was the most promising course of action but he feared the confrontation and preferred to put it off for as long as possible.

Since there was no bus service up into the hills, the quickest way to get there would be in one of his own cars. He thought of going back to Ophelia's house and ringing for the Mercedes. Then he remembered. If Ophelia was not in the office there was no way of contacting a car without going into the office and using the radio telephone himself. Which brought him once again into dangerous proximity to Huntingdon.

Thomas's taxi business is operated from an office set between Midwestern Electricals, owned and managed by Huntingdon, and the headquarters of the Church of the Little People of God. For over four years Ophelia has been poised, as it were, between the Devil and the deep blue sea. Her right ear is being constantly wooed in a spiritual sense – 'Why continue to roam when God is calling you home' – while Edward Sparrow and his cronies insinuate themselves into her left ear with an appeal for more satisfaction, via Midwestern Electricals' demonstration stereo units.

Ophelia spends many hours at her desk looking through

51

the glass doors at the waxen leaves of the mango tree that grows in the courtyard below. At a certain time in the year it plops its ripe fruit on to the verandah which provides the only access to the offices on the first floor.

During the day, Ophelia sees many visitors and few customers. There are occasional phone calls from the tourist hotel which she attempts to relay to the drivers, only to find they have turned off their link with the office in favour of the local radio station. They prefer to cruise the street picking up fares as they can.

Working for God is the girl who used to be at school with Ophelia. Jancis Sheraton, if questioned about her ancestry, will tell you that she is descended from the famous furniture maker of that name, one of whose distant relatives sought his fortune in the Caribbean. There he pursued the native women with the same intensity as he pursued the native mahogany and other hard woods which the island so abundantly provided. Some of the family skill has persisted through the generations, though now sadly diluted. Jancis's father, retired, once called himself a roofer, and specialized in hammering nails into the sheets of corrugated iron which have long since replaced the hardwood shingles of days gone by. Jancis owes as much to her negro as to her European lineage. From the Sheratons she has inherited her build, but her features are obstinately negroid.

At school Jancis was never close to Ophelia. She was one of those plain stocky girls who hover around the more popular girls without ever being acknowledged.

Ophelia has always been naturally and, at one time, unselfconsciously beautiful. In the playground she attracted girlfriends as she now attracts men.

Since finding themselves in adjacent offices, the girls have become quite friendly. On Ophelia's side this is due to boredom and her need for an audience. Jancis provides unstintingly of her love and admiration, asking in return only to be used and allowed to remain in the presence of one whom she has long worshipped from afar.

At first, Jancis had called each day bearing bundles of religious tracts. Now she has dropped all pretence of trying to convert Ophelia, and save her immortal soul. Although she never fails to invite Ophelia to all the church meetings and services, Ophelia's reply never varies.

'I busy, busy, busy.'

Which Jancis accepts, knowing that Ophelia has three children and from time to time a man. She envies this capacity in her friend to live the way she does and yet appear untainted. From her long and lonely studies of the Bible she has imagined that the effects of sin are physical and horrible. But Ophelia is as radiant as ever. It is Jancis who has developed permanent worry lines.

'What you need,' says Ophelia, 'is a man.'

Jancis shudders in self-righteous indignation, though it is what she wants above all else.

'Otherwise,' says Ophelia, 'you might as well be a nun.'

Jancis has never before looked at her own sexuality as something to be actively used or positively discarded.

'Soon,' says Ophelia, 'you go find it too late.'

This is also a reflection on the precariousness of Ophelia's own position. She is aware that she is at the peak of her charms, and that now is the time to opt for a safe and certain future.

Jancis is thrown into total panic by her friend's remark. Her ideal man already comes between her and God, lightskinned and beautiful, educated and Christian, but even if such a man could be found she could not afford to be like Ophelia. No man will marry her without children, and children without marriage means the death of her soul and the end of her job. Sometimes life strikes her as unfair, she who has studied through to sixth grade and passed all her exams, still to be outshone by Ophelia who left school at fifteen in a cloud of disgrace.

Ophelia tries to be encouraging. She inducts Jancis into the gentle art of make-up but Jancis's missionary friends are scandalized, and Jancis discovers that the wages of this particular sin is a skin complaint that takes weeks to heal.

Ophelia suggests a clothes peg on the nose to narrow the nostrils. Jancis suffers agonies every night. She develops little red pits each side of her nose which after a few weeks fail to vanish even by tea time. She dreads the agonies of the coming night and her parents complain that she has started to snore.

Her elderly parents are both more or less bedridden. Ophelia visited them once, a couple of years ago, and they have talked about her visit ever since.

For Ophelia the whole visit was so shocking that she has never been back. She watched while Jancis bathed them and fed them and read them the Bible, and then got away as soon as she could. The cries of 'Come again, darling' followed her out into the garden where she paused, gulping in the fresh air to cleanse her lungs of the stale smell of the house. To her mind there were no two ways about it. She would rather be dead than live like that. But the experience made her look at Jancis differently, and she resolved to be kinder to her, even to the extent of attending one of her church services.

At the church, Ophelia at once found herself the focus of attention. Among the 'saved' she stood out like an orchid among daisies. The women were not quite as open and friendly as the men, but nevertheless, at her first service, Ophelia felt moved to stand before the whole congregation and appeal to God to have mercy on her, a sinner, in a voice that left not a dry eye in the church. Even God himself could not have been deaf to the plea of such a voluptuous supplicant. She vowed to cast out the devil and take Jesus into her heart. Never again Lord, never again would she stray from the paths of righteousness.

There were snags however, not least of which were her three children. The church elders were disposed to overlook previous lapses but to continue with her present union was quite unacceptable in the eyes of God.

Young men of the church there were plenty, who would have been only too happy to lead her to the altar and to God, but Ophelia stood firm and Jancis watched aghast as her friend turned down proposal after proposal.

Today Jancis enters the office, ever so humbly, clutching an envelope. She knows what it contains, and so does Ophelia, and both prepare themselves for the usual outpouring of righteous indignation.

'Sister,' says Jancis, for she still lives in hope that Ophelia's conversion might not be a mere flash in the pan. 'Brother Solomon send this letter for you.'

'What he want? I busy, can' you see?' Ophelia runs a hand over her forehead, then takes out her powder compact in case of any damage. She sets aside the pile of papers on her desk and looks at Brother Solomon's envelope.

'Why this man always bothering me?' she asks Jancis.

Jancis shrinks towards the door.

'All work have to stop because this man pestering me?'

Ophelia picks up a paper knife, points it towards Jancis.

'If he ask you, say I never go marry him. My heart is engaged and that is why I does live in sin and damnation.'

She opens the letter and begins to laugh.

'"My darling Ophelia" – who he think he is, eh? The cat's pyjamas? Why he call me his darling?'

Jancis shrugs and begins to feel breathless. When Ophelia tosses the discarded epistle towards her, she reads it avidly.

Ophelia sits back and picks her teeth with a matchstick.

'You want me to take back an answer?' asks Jancis hopefully.

'Never,' says Ophelia. 'Never. I could never reply to this man.'

Jancis sits down heavy-hearted.

'You think Thomas going to marry you?'

'No,' says Ophelia cheerfully. 'I wouldn't marry him if he ask. Which he don't.'

This news shocks Jancis, who saw Thomas as the only stumbling block to her friend's salvation.

'You not marrying Thomas?' Jancis wants to be sure she has heard right.

'I want to be free. I want to have fun. After, I go marry. I have meh children, I have meh job, I have a nice house, why the dickens I go get married for?'

'Baby baby baby, I need you . . .' the record player in Midwestern Electricals blares out.

Ophelia knows the message is meant for her. Sure enough it is only seconds before Huntingdon appears at the door.

Still by the roadside Thomas looked at his wrist watch and saw the precious hours of his shore leave tick past. He was hot and thirsty and couldn't decide what to do next. Just as a bus came towards him along the road, Thomas turned, jumped over the storm drain and crossed the pavement into the nearest rum shop.

Martha Johnson, licensed to sell alcoholic beverages and liquors, greeted him literally with open arms. Everybody loves a sailor and Thomas was also her second cousin by her stepfather's outside wife.

In the darkened room with the shutters down to keep out the glare of the sun, into the even darker bosom of Mrs Johnson, licensee, Thomas poured out his woes. Mrs

Johnson consoled him in the best way she could, with the bottle of rum ever open by her elbow.

The hum of flies was louder than the conversation around the bar. The men were anxious not to miss one syllable of Thomas's story, nor did they fail to offer advice which ranged from 'Women don't know what good for them' or 'I kick her all the way from here to Soufrière' to 'There plenty more arse on the island, man.' Thomas bought drinks all round and the men were soon united in a strong brotherhood of love and commiseration.

Betty and Churchill were almost back at Le Perroquet.

'He's not there,' Betty said, indicating the empty rock where they had last seen Harry.

Churchill didn't seem at all bothered, but Betty stopped just long enough to make sure that there were no pieces of Harry scattered around.

When she reached the terrace, she realized how silly she had been to worry. There in the thermal pool sat Harry. His stomach overflowed his swimming trunks in waves like congealed dripping. He wasn't even looking at the view, but sat facing the steamy grotto, from which the sulphur springs bubbled. The surrounding rocks were stained in varying shades of yellow, from pale custard to a rich, brown caramel.

Each time Harry breathed, a wave of water sloshed across the stone floor. It slopped into the toes of Betty's high-heeled sandals so that she staggered drunkenly, her toes slithering inside the wet leather.

Thomas, in the back of an open truck, leaned against the cab and stared listlessly at the dazzling expanse of cobalt blue which widened at each hairpin bend until the horizon danced to the rhythm of his flickering eyelids and the potholes in the road.

On the floor of the truck loose coconuts rolled front to back, side to side according to the camber of the dirt track. Thomas swore and kicked out at them as they clattered against his ankles. At last he closed his eyes and slept to the gentle clonking of the nuts as they bumped one against the other like the thwack of bat on ball, that sound so dear to his childhood. Thomas had once nurtured dreams of playing for the West Indies although nowadays he has switched his allegiance to American football.

If Thomas had been less drunk and more comfortable, his subconscious might have given him hints as to Ophelia's whereabouts which his waking self totally repressed. Via the Huntingdon connection he might well have worked out, from his own experiences as a seaman, just what had happened to her.

With the help of an airways timetable he could even have pinpointed the exact position of Ophelia's plane which, at the time he slept among the coconuts, had just carried her within sight of Sint Jan.

From high in the air, the island appeared like a child's sandcastle beleaguered by a tide which sometime soon must surely dissolve the whole fragile construction. Ophelia saw the dark ribbon of road and whole towns which would fit into the palm of her hand.

She pressed her fingers into her ears and laughed at the sensation as the plane began its descent. Down they plunged until she could see the white crest of every wave and cars like silverfish on a pantry shelf. The plane was haunted by its shadow, a monstrous bird shape passing over the scrublands to her left where miniature goats scattered in panic. Lower and lower they went until she saw washing hung out to dry and plants on windowsills, then suddenly they were lower than the tops of the trees. A violent convulsion shook the plane as it landed and shuddered to a halt.

Ophelia let out her breath in a loud sigh and smiled. She had arrived in Sint Jan. Stage one of her journey was complete.

Thomas was rapidly approaching Nelson's Look Out. The village had taken its name from the original house on the site where officers of the Royal Navy could enjoy a weekend on shore, high above the mosquito-ridden coastal plain and pampered with all the specialities the island had to offer by way of mountain chicken, land crabs, fruits, vegetables and girls.

Little remains of the historic house itself, other than a few grass-covered mounds and some stones now incorporated into local dwellings, but the name has lingered. From what was once the verandah, there is a fine view of the brilliant blue of the Caribbean sea framed by the V of the surrounding hills. Thus, Ophelia's grandmother told her, officers had an advantage over their men down in the harbour, in that they had prior warning of the approach of a foreign ship.

An unkinder interpretation has also been put on the fact that most of the road which zigzags tortuously up from sea level is visible from this same spot. Portia was of the faction which insisted that the reason for the name Nelson's Look Out stemmed from the Admiral's disastrous marriage to one Frances Nisbett, daughter of the governor of the nearby island of St Kitt's. With his wife installed in a small house near the harbour, Nelson himself retired to the more rarefied atmosphere of the hills with a sentry posted on look-out duty to give warning should Fanny chance to come looking for him.

Thomas, like every other Mondegian, is well acquainted with an island saying which refers to giving someone

'Fanny's welcome'. A visitor arrives by the front door to find a house inexplicably deserted and the back door left wide open as if the occupants had fled into the bush. But Thomas, arriving to find Aunty Gladys's house empty, knew on this occasion that he only had to go as far as the cucumber patch to find her.

He heaved himself over the side of the truck and swayed dizzily in the heart of Nelson's Look Out. It was not only the sun that dazzled so soon after waking, but also the brilliant shrubs and flowers. Everything seemed to flourish here and the houses were half submerged under blossoms of scarlet and orange, yellow and purple.

Thomas's bladder ached as much as his head. He peed into a hedge of scarlet bougainvillaea while he shouted greetings to the family gathered on the verandah beyond, eating their lunch.

'Thomas man, how you going?'

'My head hurt like hell. You seen Gladys?'

'Sure, sure. She up in the garden. The notice come in to pick the grapefruit. The boat coming Monday.'

'Phelie up there too?'

'Phelie ain't been in no garden since she grandmother dead.'

'That true, man. I think perhaps she visiting.'

'I ain't see she this twelvemonth gone, but Gladys she up there.'

Thomas zipped up his trousers and trudged unsteadily towards the small hut at the top of the hill.

'Thomas man, what wrong?'

'You look like something happen to you.'

Ophelia's cousins, lolling on empty grapefruit crates, were eating hot vegetable stew from enamel plates.

'You want lunch?'

Thomas shook his head.

'I looking for Phelie.'

'She not here, man.'

'Where Gladys?'

Winston jerked his head to indicate that his mother was somewhere down the slopes. Thomas was reluctant to go down and look for her, since that would mean climbing up again.

'Gladys,' he bawled over the ridge of the mountain towards the distant horizon of sea. 'Gladys.'

A few minutes later Gladys appeared from among the grapefruit groves. She walked up the steep dirt path testing each step carefully as she went. On her head was a black plastic crate set on a cushion of banana fibre. Her face was dripping but still she smiled and raised her left hand to Thomas in greeting. Remus followed close behind bearing a crate marginally less full.

'They say the grapefruit boat coming Monday,' said Gladys.

'I looking for Phelie.'

Gladys laid a hand on his arm and looked into his face. Then she patted him and turned into the hut.

Her seven sons watched her. One of them let out a large belch.

'Why you all let the fire go out?' asked Gladys with a smile. 'How your father food go keep hot?' She looked at each of the boys in turn, and with a swift movement lowered the crate off her head and on to the ground. Then she began to split planks from a pile of broken crates with her cutlass.

'Phelie she lef' the island,' she said to Thomas.

'That old man tell me but I don' believe until now.' Thomas squatted next to the dying fire, feeling suddenly cold. Gladys fed wood chips into the embers.

'You have a drink and eat some food,' she said to Thomas, peeling a grapefruit with her cutlass and squeezing it into a plastic bowl. 'You go feel better with food in the stomach.'

'Why did she go?' whispered Thomas.

Gladys touched him gently on the shoulder.

'Phelie not like me. She not like any of us. All her life she wanting to go 'way.' Gladys ladled food on to Remus's plate, rinsed another plate in the bucket of water she had carried up from her house, filled it and handed it to Thomas.

'You eat.'

'What 'bout you?'

Gladys shook her head. 'I go eat later. Just now I too hot.' She wiped her face with the hem of her cotton dress, then fanned herself with the crown of banana leaves.

'Why she leave me?' moaned Thomas.

'Is not you only she leave.' Gladys indicated everyone present. 'Is me. Is she cousins, she uncle, she daughter, the little boys. She gone because she have to.'

'But I looked after her,' said Thomas. 'I treated she good.'

'You only treated she good,' said Gladys, 'when you were here.'

Thomas put down his plate and left the hut. He went and sat at the top of the track and looked out over the mountains, ridge upon ridge fading blue into the distance. Behind him Gladys collected up the plates and spoons, and clattered them in the bucket. He heard the soft monotone of her conversation and the answering grunts of her menfolk. She stepped by him, lightly touching him on the head, on her way for another load of fruit. She always insisted that Remus took a rest after eating. Thomas sat hunched with misery. Then he went to look for Portia.

'You havin' a good journey?'

Ophelia had just collected her case off the conveyor belt.

She vaguely remembered Marianne from meeting her once at a disco in Soufrière.

'It all right,' she replied.

Marianne took the case from her. 'How things on Monday Island?'

'Okay.'

'You ain't got no more luggage?'

Ophelia shook her head. She was bound for the huge shopping precinct known as the USA. 'I ain't stopping here,' she said.

The two women walked across the vast, gleaming airport building.

'Huntingdon say you catching the boat in the morning. It leaving early, man.' Marianne held open the swing door.

'We taking a taxi?' Ophelia didn't want another long walk in her black patent shoes.

'What for we wasting money, eh?' Marianne put two fingers in her mouth and blew.

A truck drew up. Ophelia dusted down the seat and climbed in.

Thomas crossed the patch of land belonging to the absent uncles and spied in the distance the large posterior of Ophelia's mother Portia, bent over her weeding. He would on other occasions have skipped merrily enough across the field to greet her, but today the first Portia became aware of him was as a dark shadow across her line of work. She glanced up.

'Eh, eh,' she said and turned her eyes back to the soil.

Thomas took out a cigarette and lit it. He leaned against the trunk of a mango tree and waited.

Portia hoed in a straight line right across to the other side of the clearing and back again before she stood up, leaned on her hoe and wearily scratched her head.

'Where Ophelia gone?' Thomas ground the butt of the cigarette into the soil.

'They say the grapefruit boat coming Monday,' said Portia. She looked across towards the sea as if it might already be in sight. 'At the weekend the children coming to help me pick.' Her forehead creased. 'You taking the boys with you?' she asked in a flat voice.

Thomas shook his head.

'Your mother?'

'She too old to cope.'

'And I so young and strong, eh, boy?' Portia sighed.

Thomas took a wad of notes from his back pocket, counted some out and handed them over.

Portia counted the notes carefully. Frowned with concentration.

'How I know you coming back in a month?'

Thomas shrugged.

'And the school fees? How I go pay the school fees and take the boys to town each day?'

'I go pay the school fees direct. One of Ophelia's brothers can take them.'

'You think I here to spend my whole life minding your children?'

Thomas began to walk away.

'You think I have nothing better to do than cook and clean and wash all day long?'

Thomas walked faster.

'You want to know where Phelie gone, you go ask Huntingdon.'

Thomas almost ran from the field. It was the last thing he wanted to hear.

Portia stuffed the notes down the front of her dress and slashed at the ground with her hoe. Tears of rage and self-pity were pouring down her cheeks. Just as she had got the twins off to school, there she was landed with Ophelia's small children. Then there were Francine and Angèle, both nearly teenagers, and the whole wearisome business of babies would start all over again.

Portia knew what it was that Ophelia was trying to escape but could see no reason why she should be left behind to clear up the mess.

No vehicles went down from Nelson's Look Out into town in the heat of the day. Those which arrived in the early morning remained until evening, almost too hot to touch in the sun. Thomas, filled with a self-righteous anger which gave him the courage to face Huntingdon, strode down the hill.

An hour and a half later he arrived at the coastal road and there caught a bus into Soufrière.

'Mr Jackson has a client with him at the moment, sir,' said a coffee-coloured secretary, barring the way into Huntingdon's office.

Thomas sat in the cool office and stared at his feet. He saw his maroon trainers shabby against the silver grey carpet and looked from the secretary's crisp white blouse to his own sweat-stained shirt. He hooked his key ring on to his finger and jingled the keys impatiently.

The secretary frowned.

Thomas glared back. Who'd want a sallow-skinned woman like that anyway? He crossed his legs and jiggled his free foot up and down and thought back to his first meeting with Huntingdon – which was also Ophelia's. It now occurred to Thomas that the meeting need never have taken place; if he had not overslept that morning and been forced to take the Cortina instead of the Mercedes; if Ophelia had not insisted on the outing to Bournemouth; if he had not taken shore leave to spend some time with Ophelia and his infant son Nelson in the first place. Or was it the first place? The chain of cause and effect seemed to stretch back for ever, back to Ophelia's birth and beyond. But it was that fatal two weeks on shore which stuck in Thomas's mind.

Thomas arrives at the Lapierre house when Nelson is six weeks old, pushing a large shiny pram containing his own suitcase and an enormous pink teddy bear.

Ophelia's anger at not seeing Thomas before is forgotten. She removes the teddy bear from the pram and replaces it with Nelson who is of a much more manageable size. Together, Ophelia, Thomas and son take a stroll along the road.

'I lose the job,' Ophelia points out once the initial surge of happiness is over.

'I on holiday. I go find something for you,' says Thomas, his arm heavy on Ophelia's shoulder as if she were a walking stick.

Ophelia brushes his hand off, pauses to adjust the hood of the pram and shade Nelson's eyes. 'And what 'bout the baby?' she asks.

'What you have a mother for?' Thomas is surprised.

'She say that now her children done big, she ain't staying home with mine.'

Thomas looks worried. He has never envisaged that looking after a baby could be a problem.

'What 'bout the nursery?' asks Ophelia.

'How much that cost?'

'It not too much, man.' Ophelia puts the brake on the pram and leaves it by the roadside. Thomas takes off the brake and wheels his precious son off the tarmac and under the coconut palms.

Ophelia walks ahead of him across the soft sand towards the sea. Her high heels sink into the sand and she kicks them off. Thomas runs after her, takes her hand and they race into the surf at the water's edge.

Thomas and his suitcase are sent away for the night. As Ophelia points out, they are not married and it wouldn't be right for him to spend the night in her house. Thomas goes to his brother's and arrives back at Sugar Bay next morning somewhat late and dishevelled, and driving the red Cortina since his brother took the Mercedes before he was awake. Ophelia declines to go out with him. How, she asks, would they ever get the pram into *that*?

But she is at last coaxed into the Cortina and the boot tied up with string so that the pram doesn't fall out. Nelson is safely stowed in a cardboard box on the back seat together with the bag of bottles, tins of milk powder, bottom wipes, tissues, creams and powders, and they set off for their day in Bournemouth.

'These roads full of potholes, man,' says Thomas as they judder along.

Ophelia is surprised. The roads have always been like this.

'In the States, man,' continues Thomas, 'the roads they all smooth like glass and it have three four lanes of traffic going each way like a race course.'

Ophelia looks at Monday Island's coastal road, every inch hewn or dynamited from the volcanic rock which rises sheer from the ocean bed, and is ashamed of its meanness.

'Thomas,' she asks, 'you take me to the United States?'

'How I can take you, Phelie? On the ship I must work work work, and you know what the plane costing.'

Ophelia shrugs. 'My Aunty Celie, she want to take me to Birmingham England.'

'Birmingham England is not like the US, baby. I see Birmingham England with my own eyes. It shit, man.'

Ophelia tries to imagine a place more wonderful still than Birmingham, because she has heard from her aunty just how marvellous it is. 'My aunty's factory, it big like ten cathedrals.'

'Ain't nothing, man. In the US those factories so damn big you have to travel from one end to the other by bus.'

Ophelia is silent for a while.

'Look, Phelie, you don't need to go to no US, I looking after you, ain't I? You ain't got no problems here.'

Ophelia is about to reply that she would be quite happy to have problems if only she could get away from Monday Island, when the car breaks down.

'Shit.' Thomas gets out and opens the engine and peers about. Ophelia does her hair in the driving mirror. Several cars pass, skittering gravel against the driver's door.

Ophelia gets out, leans one elbow on the roof of the car and gazes out to sea. Instantly there are offers of help. Thomas is surrounded by a crowd of expert mechanics, who suggest everything from a new clutch to petrol in voices increasingly loud to attract Ophelia's attention.

Except for one man, in a brand new silver Mercedes, who makes no pretence of knowing anything about car engines, but simply walks up to Ophelia and offers her a cigarette. He is wearing a dark suit and dark glasses so that Ophelia cannot see his eyes, but only her own reflection twice over. When Nelson starts to cry, he drives Ophelia and the baby to a hotel just up the road where they can be cool and comfortable.

Some two hours later, the red Cortina limps into the forecourt. Thomas gets out, oily, dusty and tired. Nelson is asleep under a palm tree. Ophelia and Huntingdon lie side by side on loungers by the pool. They are the only black couple there, but such an exquisite pair that the management rejoices in their presence. They are living testimony to the Tourist Board's insistence on the racial harmony of the islands.

Thomas feels uncomfortable. He declines to change into

his swimming trunks but sits hunched on the edge of a sun lounger. He downs his beer and makes his excuses, anxious to start what promises to be a long, slow journey back to town.

Huntingdon is a charming host. He orders lunch for the three of them. The steak and kidney pie enchants Ophelia but reminds Thomas not too pleasantly of ship fare – alternate nights West Indian and English menus.

Over lunch Thomas learns that Huntingdon and Ophelia have been talking about his taxi business. Huntingdon cannot do enough to help.

'What you want, man, is to think big. Set up a proper taxi service, radios, offices, the lot.'

Thomas laughs. On his salary?

But Huntingdon, it seems, not only has office space to let, but he has contacts in banking should a loan be required.

When his leave is up, Thomas rejoins his ship, mortgaged up to the eyeballs, but owning three cars and employing two drivers in addition to his brother Henry, one of whom is Churchill, Ophelia's friend from her factory days. Ophelia is installed in a modern office with a telephone, whence she will co-ordinate and organize the business.

If Thomas has any misgivings about Ophelia's proximity to and reliance on Huntingdon's expertise, these are far outweighed by entrepreneurial greed. He sees himself already as a tycoon, and his son makes the whole enterprise worth while on a long-term basis.

It is not long before Thomas, with further ideas of expansion, leaves the banana business and lands himself a higher paid job on a cruise ship, a second son and a fourth taxi.

Ophelia becomes a commuter. She takes Nelson, and later Napoleon as well, into town each morning on the bus.

She leaves them at the nursery, then straightens her clothes, checks her appearance in the small mirror that she carries in her bag, combs her hair and click clacks down the street to the office. Her traditional hourglass figure has been enhanced by the birth of her two sons, which has resulted in an explosion of bust and hips, which she emphasizes with tight wide belts, tailored skirts and seamed stockings. Meticulous in her time-keeping, she unlocks the office door at precisely two minutes to eight each morning, so that she can be seated at her desk at eight, waiting for the phone to ring. For this rare event she has cultivated a low fast talking voice of infinite weariness which implies she has no time to waste.

Ophelia lives for her work. Life ends each day when she locks the office door, collects the boys from the nursery and returns home on the bus. She leaves Nelson and Napoleon on the verandah waiting for their tea while she goes to her room, puts in her curlers, hangs up her working clothes and in a loose cotton dress polishes her already gleaming room. She then lies down, leafing endlessly through the same five-year-old French magazine until her mother appears at her room door with a plateful of hot food. Ophelia only has to look at Portia, standing there in the doorway, weary from the day's gardening and cooking for ten, to know how far she has come. Her life will never be like that.

Thomas sat in Huntingdon's air-conditioned anteroom until his body cooled, and with it the fire of his anger. Well before Huntingdon was free to see him, Thomas was left nursing the cold ashes of his rage. When he heard Huntingdon push back his chair in the neighbouring room, Thomas got to his feet and fled.

He discovered the keyhole of his own office door was blocked by another key on the inside. Stranded in the corridor, in full view of his rival, Thomas rapped on the glass. He could see the cleaner sitting in Ophelia's chair with her feet up on the desk, talking on the telephone.

'What the hell you doing?' asked Thomas as she let him in. He stormed through the reception area into the safety of his own office and slammed the door.

The cleaning lady, going out, met Jancis coming in.

'Mr Jefferson here?' asked Jancis.

The cleaning lady nodded. 'He vex like hell.'

Jancis paused. Though she has long been in the position of delivering Ophelia's billets doux, she has never yet faced a task like this. She murmured a few prayers, then tapped on the door of Thomas's office.

Thomas sat slumped at his desk. 'What do you want?' he asked.

'Phelie, she send you this letter.' Jancis stood watching anxiously.

Thomas slit the envelope with the small silver paper knife he kept on his desk.

My dear Thomas,
    I afraid this letter go cause you pain. Only believe me my dear that I am truly sorry, but I have lost my heart to another and now I must leave Monday Island for a situation abroad without seeing you to say cheerio. Nelson and Napoleon your two sons are well and I pray that the good God keep them that way while I am gone. As for money you can leave that with my mother Portia Lapierre, she have need. When it come to you my dear husband, I pray also that Jesus keep you in his care and loving tenderness and that if God willing, we go meet again one day in the brotherhood of his heavenly love.
                            Yours sincerely,
                    Your true friend Ophelia Lapierre

Thomas noticed that it was typed on the office note-paper, probably in the little room next door. He flung the letter on to the table and buried his face in his hands.

Jancis picked it up and read it. She was very impressed with the turn of phrase and the sentiments expressed. 'I think Jesus will bring her safely back,' she said.

Next door, Huntingdon turned on the stereo. 'Baby baby baby, I need you . . .'

Thomas put his hands over his ears as the whole room vibrated with the rhythm.

'That man's a shit arse,' said Jancis.

Thomas picked up the paper knife and flung it at the partition wall. Seconds later, Huntingdon hurled through the door.

'All you mad in here or what?' he screamed. 'Why you throw knives at my good wall, eh?'

Jancis shrank back into the corner. Her lips moved audibly in prayer.

Thomas stood up.

'I go throw knives in my office as I fucking want.'

'It not your office. It mine. And I go tell you something else. You better get your arse out of here at the end of the month.'

'What make you think I want to stay in this stinking shit-hole?'

'What you calling a stinking shit-hole, man?' Huntingdon plucked the knife from the wall. 'You want me to call the police, eh? Is that you want?'

'Where Ophelia?'

'Ophelia? She have a better job now than you could ever give her.'

'She working for you?'

Huntingdon nodded. 'She peddling she arse out there and earn more in one day than she get polishing your chair for thirty years.'

Jancis put her hands over her ears.

'I kill you, man.' Thomas put up his fists and moved towards Huntingdon.

Huntingdon held the knife in front of him. 'You take care, man. I call the police. I have a hundred witnesses to swear you threw the knife first.'

Thomas was frightened.

'You trying to threaten me with this knife, eh?' Huntingdon was smiling confidently.

Thomas looked round. Huntingdon stood between him and the door. Thomas clenched his fists.

'You want a fight?' Huntingdon moved closer, the knife still in his hand. 'Sure we'll fight.'

Thomas moved round keeping the desk between them, then bolted out through the door.

Huntingdon laughed out loud. 'You want something, boy, you have to fight for it.'

Thomas slammed the outer door so hard that the glass shattered. He screamed through the jagged pane. 'You ain't nothing but a jack arse.'

The sound of Huntingdon's deep rich laugh followed him down the stairs.

Jancis, at the window, watched Thomas as he made his way down the street. Her heart was beating fast. Nothing like that ever happened in church circles.

She put a foot on the windowsill and tightened the lace of one tennis shoe. Then the other. She folded her cardigan neatly over her arm and followed in the direction Thomas had taken.

The locked doors on which Thomas hammered led into the only state-run pre-school centre on the island. The door was kept locked between ten and three-thirty in the interests of safety.

When Thomas finally stopped to listen he heard small voices all around him coming from the open windows, 'A, b, c, d, e, f, g, h, i, j, k, lmnop.' There was no other sound than rote learning. Such discipline pleased Thomas, who had not been favourably impressed by some of the young Americans he had met on the ship.

Looking up, he saw a number of children on the balcony, gripping the railings and pushing their small dark faces between the bars. On another occasion, Thomas might have stuck out his tongue to make them laugh, today he shouted, 'You all stupid or what? You go fetch your teacher.' He glared up at the children wondering whether Nelson might be among them. And Thomas remembered.

One sunny morning his ship docks in the deep water harbour, and Thomas, carrying a carton of duty-free champagne in anticipation of a happy event, staggers on shore.

'Hey, Thomas, man,' shout the stevedores. 'You hear the news?'

'What news, man? I just get off the boat.'

'You is a father.'

'Listen you guys, I already a father these past eight years.'

'A real father this time, man.' The stevedore climbs out of the forklift truck. 'You see what it say.'

Thomas screws up his eyes against the glare of sun off the white paper.

To Thomas Jefferson and Ophelia Lapierre, a son Nelson, at the Queen Victoria Hospital, Soufrière. With grateful thanks to the staff and doctors.

Thomas blinks back the tears. 'She make me a son,' he shouts, unable to believe his luck. 'Those other women just ain't no good, all they born is girls, every last one of them.'

Thomas unwires the cork on the first champagne bottle. It shoots up into the cloudless sky followed by a foaming jet of champagne. Thomas takes a long swig then hands the bottle to his friend.

They are rapidly joined by the customs officers, the weighbridge officials and the policemen on guard duty. The birth of Nelson is an event talked about for many days.

'You hear that, Phelie?' says Portia to her daughter. 'That man happy for so that you make him a little boy. He so damn glad he drinking eight bottles of champagne down at the deep water harbour and then he spending a fortune in the rum shop so everybody else on Monday Island happy too.'

'But why he ain't visit me yet?' wails Ophelia, sitting in the hospital bed in her best nightie with her hair freshly combed and her lips bright red. 'I waiting all day.'

'Now the ship gone,' says her mother.

Ophelia begins to cry.

'You dry those eyes, girl.' Portia has no time for displays of emotion. 'He done lef' you a whole heap of money. Lawd bless us if you don't know when you well off.'

'I never want to see him again.'

'Don't make me vex, child.'

'But why he don' come and see me and the child?'

'Is not like for a woman. He happy he have the child, but all babies look the same to a man.'

Ophelia wails loudly. 'My heart breaking,' she shrieks.

'But he dead dead drunk. He don' know how to put one foot in front of the other, girl. They carry him back to the ship like he is a newborn baby self.'

If Thomas is going to make Ophelia suffer, the whole island is going to hear about it. She tears at the bedclothes. She flings things off her bedside locker. 'My heart!' she screams.

Nelson in the cot next to the bed, wakened by the rumpus, wails loudly. Portia snatches him up, out of the reach of her mad daughter. She runs from the ward yelling for help. Legend has it that it took four nurses to hold Ophelia down while the doctor administered a sedative.

While Thomas waited, outstretched hands gripping the metal bars like a figure crucified, he felt a touch on his shoulder. It was Jancis. He grunted and turned back to face the courtyard again.

He heard the click of heels and a lightskinned woman wearing a string of pearls, with a white cardigan flung over her shoulders, came smiling towards him.

'Yes?' she said, unlocking the gate.

Thomas, instantly at a disadvantage, glared at the woman and indicated that he wanted to come in. He was inclined to be stiffly formal on such occasions to hide his discomfiture. For Thomas, in spite of all the efforts of his mother who had insisted that he was bright like a shining star man, and had diligently applied all the ointments and prescriptions of the local obeah woman, had failed to get into secondary school.

He shut the barred gate behind him, excluding Jancis. It was none of her business.

'I am the father of Nelson and Napoleon,' he announced.

'Oh yes, Mr Jefferson, won't you come this way?'

Thomas followed her into a large whitewashed room, cluttered with papers. The woman sat at a large desk and moved one pile so that she could see Thomas in the chair opposite.

'You want to see the boys?'

'I've come to pay the school fees.'

The woman took out a large red book, then she laughed. 'That's very good of you, Mr Jefferson, but they've already been paid up until the end of this quarter.'

'Phelie – the boy's mother, she pay?'

'Oh no. They've been paid by those dear old ladies, the

Misses Simpson, in fact they've been paying them for a whole year now.'

Thomas, who had been counting out a wad of notes, stuffed them back into his pocket and stormed out of the office. He got as far as the gate and found himself locked in.

'Wait and see your boys, Mr Jefferson,' the principal insisted, and she called up to a teacher on the balcony.

As the two little boys came down the stairs, Thomas knelt down and held out his arms. The boys shrank back behind the principal who yanked them forwards. 'You all not saying hello to your daddy?' she asked.

Thomas felt in his pockets and found Betty's barley sugars. He held them out and the boys came shyly towards him.

'You can' remember your own daddy?' He grabbed Napoleon and crushed him in his arms so that the child cried out in fear and fought to be free.

'You go give your daddy a big kiss,' the principal ordered Nelson. He obeyed, keeping as much distance between him and the man as he could.

Since Thomas had been away at sea when his sons were born, he had left the naming of them to Ophelia. Searching for something a bit distinguished, she settled on the name of her grandmother's village, Nelson, for the first son. She had studied European history, 1790–1850, while at school, and named her second son after another hero of the time, without realizing that there could be anything contradictory in naming the second after the man who had deprived the first of an eye, then an arm, and ultimately of his life.

Whether because of the names or because of a natural antipathy, from a very early age the boys showed every sign of becoming totally incompatible.

Ophelia did her best to correct this unfortunate development, firstly, by the removal of anything which might possibly be construed by either child to be personal property, and secondly, by treating them both exactly the same to the extent of punishing both of them if either did wrong.

The elder boy Nelson was of delicate build, and though shy and withdrawn had a will of his own. Napoleon by contrast was short and sturdy and of a passionate but more pliable nature. Home and school have conspired to produce two model children who have not, as yet, seen any reason to modify the good behaviour which attracted their mother's capricious hugs and kisses.

Ophelia, who had that morning dressed her little sons in their yellow shirts and bright green shorts, kissed them on the top of their curly heads and propelled them in through the school gates with a sharp spank on the bottom, had then rushed home to finish her packing confident in the knowledge that she was doing entirely the right thing by them. The financial advantages of her new occupation would enable her to offer her sons opportunities previously beyond her wildest dreams. Already she envisaged them as doctors or lawyers, and though this required her physical absence, this was a sacrifice she was prepared to make.

Thomas, still holding out the packet of sweets to Nelson, had his patience rewarded as the boy inched towards him and finally tolerated Thomas's arm about his shoulder.

'Your daddy's got to go back to his ship now,' he said at last, not knowing how to talk to these boys of his. The principal let him out.

They stared back blankly and sucked at the strange sweets. But neither looked back as they were led away with their little legs running to keep up.

Thomas walked fast. Jancis stepped out from the shade where she had been waiting and trotted alongside.

'Where they live?' asked Thomas.

'Who you talking 'bout?'

'Those ladies. Miss Simpson.'

'Boules.'

'You know the house?'

Jancis nodded. Thomas hailed one of his own taxis and they both got in.

Boules was another major colonial legacy to Monday Island, although the area was no longer what it had been. At its centre was a patch of wasteland known for its dead cats and dogs, tin cans, courting couples and impromptu games of cricket. This ugly patch of scrub was said by locals to be haunted by white gentlemen in knickerbockers with ghostly pie frills round their necks.

Popular folklore gives credence to tales about a certain Sir Francis Drake who was once laid up on the island with a severe bout of malaria. During a period of convalescence in which boredom drove him nearly to distraction Drake ordered the construction of a bowls pitch on which to finish the game so rudely interrupted on Plymouth Hoe by the arrival of the Spanish Armada. Sir Francis lay in his litter (of a different kind from that which so distinguishes the area nowadays) and supervised the laying of the foundations and the covering of turf and used his full naval powers to requisition some four or five slaves too incapacitated to perform the arduous tasks required by the sugar industry, but able to manicure the pitch to a state of perfection.

Once again the Spanish were to prove his undoing. Hardly had Sir Francis taken up his first boule than the Spanish treasure fleet was sighted. Whereas the proximity of the Armada to England's south coast had immortalized his pronouncement of first play and then fight, the lure of gold to one living on the perilously low income of an admiral in Her Majesty's navy was sufficient to make him forget his malaria, fling his boules over his shoulder and sprint for his flagship.

It is said that he pledged to return and finish the game, but after a dramatic show of fireworks out at sea followed by three weeks of contrary winds, the disgruntled planters returned to their sugar and their mistresses, and the pitch was abandoned. Rumour has it that the boules were left in position, though excavation has revealed nothing beyond a large flat surface, one Elizabethan silver coin and a few empty bottles of cheap Spanish wine. The episode was perhaps emblematic of the generally pessimistic view of the average Mondegian that nobody who has visited the island once ever goes back.

The decline of the centre of Boules into wasteland has been gradual. There were days when it was a park and the surrounding houses with their gardens and gardeners, bougainvillaea and frangipani, were desirable residences. Now behind yellowing lace curtains lurk equally yellowing spinsters, relics of one of the more sordid aspects of slavery, the white creole's outside children.

The Simpson family is one example of a once great, plantation-owning dynasty, now shrunk to three spinster ladies, last of their line, one blind, one deaf, one bedridden. Ophelia has visited them every Tuesday since she was a small child for the ceremony of afternoon tea.

It was now Thomas, with Jancis in tow, who thundered on the Misses Simpson's door. If his sons received a good education it would be because he paid for it himself. Thomas would accept charity from no one, least of all three elderly, almost white ladies.

Jancis giggled at the shrill twittering from upstairs. Thomas scowled. At last the eldest Miss Simpson could be heard tap-tapping down the stairs with her white stick then fumbling at the lock, as she gave a running commentary on what she was doing for the benefit of her sisters upstairs.

'Sisters sisters I am opening the door and then I shall see who is there.' She opened the door.

'Well who is there sister who is there?' the other Misses Simpson squealed.

'I don't know. How can I see who is there when I can't see anything at all?'

'It's Thomas. Phelie's husband.'

'What can I do for you? I can't ask you in because my sisters are in bed. They've been in bed for the last thirty years because they are not well otherwise I would ask you up but it wouldn't be proper because they are lying there in their beds and you are a man.'

'I've come about the boys' school fees.'

'Oh yes the boys' school fees and how are the boys getting on at school such dear little boys we are very fond of them and very happy to be paying the school fees.'

'I don't want you to pay the school fees any longer.' Thomas shouted out the words.

Jancis giggled with embarrassment.

'Nelson and Napoleon are my sons and I paying for them school fees myself.'

Miss Simpson turned her back on him and relayed the news up the stairs. 'And he says that Ophelia has gone and she has left the island and those dear little boys and he will decide what is to be done for them from now on.'

'Ophelia has gone and left the island? She has gone where has she gone and why has she left?' came the cries from upstairs.

Miss Simpson turned back to face Thomas.

'Where has Ophelia gone?'

Thomas clenched his fists as if he would strike the blind old lady. Jancis clutched at his arm.

'She's gone abroad to work,' he shouted. 'You know what that means?'

Miss Simpson stared blankly in front of her.

* * *

'I'd like to take your photograph if I may,' said Betty. 'Here on the verandah with that wonderful view.'

'Sure.' Churchill half turned, leaning against the stone balustrade.

To get both him and the view in the picture, Betty was forced on to her knees. It was late afternoon and the sun was dipping towards the horizon so that she saw Churchill only in silhouette. Against the sheen on the distant surface of the sea she couldn't make out his face at all. She pressed the button.

'I'll send you a copy,' she promised, 'if you give me your address.'

Churchill took a card from his trouser pocket. Thomas's office address.

'But I don't know your second name.'

'Just Churchill will do. Everybody on the island know me.'

'I can't send it to your home?'

'Is better you just use the office.'

Betty disliked business cards. She had been misled before. Harry had given her one on their first meeting, which at the tender age of nineteen impressed her tremendously. Harry Stillman, representative of Midwestern Electricals. Had she been more worldly-wise, she might have realized that the reason Harry said 'Call me any time at the office' was because he had no telephone at home.

Betty had known very little about Harry right up until their marriage some five years later. During that time, his card lay forgotten in her handkerchief drawer while she failed in almost everything she tried. She was the sort of girl that boys dropped after two or three dates when the stock of small talk was exhausted. It was no consolation when she narrowly missed going to college or was short-listed for a job which subsequently went to somebody else.

Though feeling that it was somehow beneath her, she finished up as a window dresser in a large department store. Like Harry, she used the euphemism that she was 'with' Mansfield and Grantley.

Window dressing had, if nothing else, left Betty with an eye for the visually dramatic. Harry in his youth had a certain appeal with his own very passable shop front line in smiles and chocolates. Their wedding, thanks to the generous discount allowed to staff, was twenty percent more glamorous than anything else seen in their home town that year.

Betty has often wondered what made her remember Harry's card after all those years. The responsibility for meeting him again fell squarely on her shoulders, since she had the feeling when she phoned him that he didn't remember her at all.

She knew when she arranged the rendezvous that her job could not possibly last much longer. The management wanted new young staff with new young ideas and Betty at twenty-four was beginning to feel lacking in both respects. She had already been moved from the windows fronting North Central Street to the side windows of the delicatessen, then to smaller ones overlooking the parking lot which advertised credit and loan facilities. It was clearly time to move on or be moved on and since she had neither qualifications nor contacts, marriage seemed the only way out.

Never having been the type to pursue leisure interests, Betty had made no friends since leaving school other than those she met in the course of her work. Now, since social contacts assumed a new importance, her thoughts reverted to her school days. She leafed through an old copy of her school magazine, picking out any names that still meant something to her. She called up one or two only to find that they had either moved away in pursuit of their careers, or had remained and were now married with an average of one and a half babies a piece. Except for Harry Stillman.

At the time, Betty tried to think of anything that might distinguish Harry from other boys of her year. Though she could think of nothing, she supposed that the same applied to her. They were both nonentities.

Their first meeting had gone well. Betty had dressed with care, looking nice but not threateningly so. Harry had made her laugh a lot, and even when doubts crept in on subsequent meetings, Betty firmly repressed them and nurtured the image of Harry that evening in the Trocadero. It was a picture constantly reinforced by her friends who had only experienced him in company.

Betty was not alone in requiring a knight errant to rescue her. Ophelia, five years earlier, aged sixteen and a half to Thomas's twenty-two years, was in a similar dead-end situation.

Imagine Ophelia, employed in a factory which produces grass mats for tourists. She kneels on a wooden floor for eight hours a day, with grass fibre eating into her knees and her sinuses permanently irritated by dust, as she stitches the mats together by hand.

Thomas has been at sea since he was fourteen. His family have been seafarers for generations though none in such luxury as his present employment allows. His father was a huckster, plying his own small craft between islands selling the fruit and vegetables which his wife, Thomas's stepmother, cultivated on their plot of land. When a violent squall deprived Thomas of both his father and the boat which was his only means of earning a livelihood, Thomas was fortunate in finding a job on a banana boat of the Fyst Line. On the *Fyst Bay* he made regular trips to Avonmouth whence after their meeting he never failed to bring Ophelia a gift, whether it was something to wear or a souvenir such as a snowstorm scene of the Tower of London.

Thomas appears at the door of the grass mat factory about once every six weeks. Ophelia can feel he is there even before she looks up through the soup of dust-clogged air which is stirred constantly by the large paddles of an electric fan.

He stands in the doorway like a god with the blaze of sunshine behind him.

'You lose me my job,' she jokes, sitting in the passenger seat of his car as they leave the town and speed along the coast road towards the deserted beaches of the north coast. 'Then what I can do?'

Thomas laughs and strokes her arm, confident that she will come with him whatever the cost. 'Then I go look after you,' he says.

Ophelia tilts the driving mirror towards her, combs her hair and adds fresh lipstick. She smooths in the lipstick with the little finger of her right hand. Thomas takes her hand and kisses the finger which leaves a small circle of red on his lips. Ophelia laughs and wipes his mouth with her hanky.

'How long you have today?' she asks.

'Until six o'clock.'

At ten in the morning that feels like forever. There is time to lie on the beach and make love, and dress and go into town and buy accra and drink beer, then return to the beach again.

On other occasions Thomas might have a mere hour on shore and then there is only time for love without the trimmings, in the dingy flat belonging to Thomas's half-brother Henry in Cardigan Drive. On those days Ophelia does not go back to her work in the factory, but stays there in the crumpled sheets on Henry's bed and dozes through the heat of the day dreaming of Thomas.

The days of love and picnics are few – perhaps only three or four in all. Thomas, who should have shore leave one voyage in three, has opted instead to work overtime. It is his ambition to own a fleet of taxis. Whatever the attractions of his newfound love, Thomas knows that this will only be achieved by hard work and a good injection of steady cash. While he is offshore, his brother Henry drives his red Cortina as a taxi. After a few trips, Thomas acquires a second car, an elderly Mercedes, from an expatriate who is forced to depart in a hurry after the discovery of some irregularity in his business affairs.

Ophelia, who is becoming noticeably larger each time Thomas sees her, finds the Mercedes by far the more comfortable car of the two. She now prefers driving about the island where she will be seen, rather than picnicking on isolated beaches where she will only be seen by Thomas. This causes their first argument.

'Every day I on the floor in the factory busy busy, until my fingers hurt like hell and my knees are sore. When I have holiday I want just to sit in a comfy chair and not feel like I still working.'

Thomas parks the car by the side of the road and stalks off towards the beach. Ophelia tilts back her reclining chair and sleeps, until he returns bringing her a fresh coconut to drink. Thomas looks down at the sleeping Ophelia and for the first time thinks about her life while he is away.

Now it was Thomas who had been left behind.

He stormed through the tables and chairs straight up to the bar. The barman hissed, 'What you come here for, Thomas, with no tie on?'

'Just give me a drink.'

'How I go serve you dressed like that?'

'Look man, you just give me a drink, eh?'

The barman gave Thomas a double rum.

Jancis, rather more self-conscious, approached the bar, and stood next to Thomas.

'She with you?'

Thomas shrugged.

'What the arse wrong with you, man? You want me to lose my job coming in here like that?' The barman refilled Thomas's glass and held the bottle towards Jancis.

'She don' drink,' said Thomas wearily.

The barman sighed and handed Jancis a pineapple juice. They were the only black people in the room.

'Look, man,' said the bartender, 'you have your drink and go. Don't make no trouble for me, okay?'

Thomas tipped back his head and felt the rum burn down his throat. He peeled off a forty-dollar note and stood up.

'Keep the change,' he said as he walked out.

While Thomas drank on Monday Island, Ophelia was perched beside Marianne on the verandah railings of a hostel on the outskirts of New Amsterdam, on the island of Sint Jan.

Ophelia and Marianne were drinking Pepsi out of cans, ice cold from the fridge. They both had their hair in curlers and had changed into comfortable cotton dresses. Some of the children from the hostel were playing football in the yard. They used an old squash bottle for a ball.

'You got your children here?' Ophelia asked.

'Perhaps later I'll bring them,' said Marianne. 'Just now they with my mother.' She tipped up the can and swallowed. 'I does send her money.'

'You been here a long time?'

'Four five years.'

'And you visit home every year?'

Marianne nodded.

'Why you ain't going no further?'

'Here is happy. Like home.'

This was the very thing which had struck Ophelia, and a good reason in her mind for not staying. 'But I just going for a little while, then I going back home to marry Huntingdon.'

'What shit he been telling you, man?' Marianne laughed. She took out a cigarette and offered the packet to Ophelia.

Ophelia laughed comfortably.

'You ain't meet Gloria yet?' Marianne screwed up her eyes against the smoke and looked closely at Ophelia, who was new to the business.

'I hearing 'bout her.' Ophelia was not in the least ruffled. She had unshakeable faith in herself. It was perfectly obvious to her why Marianne had got no further than Sint Jan. Marianne was pretty but she lacked style and ambition. Ophelia drained the can and flung it into the middle of the football pitch.

The two girls laughed as the game divided over the choice of footballs. A kick sent the can into the air spinning over and over, flashing sparks of reflected sunlight like morse code.

Thomas was not to be distracted by anything. He was oblivious to the presence of Jancis, who sat in the front passenger seat giggling nervously. Thomas headed for the centre of town, aware only of the need to deaden the pain of Ophelia's betrayal.

He braked hard outside a small local bar. Slouched at a table, he drank steadily. From time to time a friend passed, and patted him on the shoulder in silent sympathy. By now everyone on the island knew about Ophelia.

When the music started Thomas rose unsteadily to his feet and beckoned to Jancis to partner him. He didn't so much dance with her as lean on her. Jancis knew that if she tried to move away he would fall over, that was one of the evils of drink. Thomas was uncomfortably heavy on her shoulders, but she had never been so close to a man before and imagined that this was what it was all about.

After two or three dances crushed in his arms, she was beginning to enjoy herself.

'You're a good dancer, man,' muttered Thomas, his chin hooked over Jancis's shoulder. She tapped on his back to show she had heard. When he announced, 'Let's go,' Jancis allowed herself to be led from the room and back to the car.

She could see that Thomas was quite unfit to drive, but as she couldn't drive herself, she could only sit helplessly while he fumbled with the ignition and then lurched down the street.

Though Jancis had never visited the flat in Cardigan Drive which Thomas shared with his brother, she had heard about it from Ophelia, and when Thomas abandoned rather than parked his car somewhere in the vicinity, she assumed that was where he was going. She got out of the car and followed him up a flight of stairs.

'Anybody there?' he called.

They stood for a while but no answer came. Thomas felt his way along a corridor into a bedroom and Jancis followed.

Ever afterwards she was to believe that Thomas had made love to her. It was an act that he never remembered, and would certainly not have called love. But it was Jancis who lay there unresisting in her crumpled flowery skirt, and who afterwards delivered Thomas back to his ship and ship mates, only minutes before sailing time.

The relief Betty felt when the taxi drew up on the dockside in the shadow of the *Dream of America* was similar to the relief which flooded her on seeing her mother's front door on her return from her honeymoon thirty years ago, even though now, as then, there was no respite from Harry.

While Harry paid Churchill, Betty watched Sam and Lou climb the gangway with their bulging shopping bags. After a long day in the heat, Lou looked as crisp as ever whereas Betty felt as if she'd spent a week frying doughnuts.

Harry handed over the money bill by bill as if every dollar pained him. Betty willed him to go on above the agreed amount, to give Churchill a generous tip, but he counted up to exactly one hundred and walked off.

Betty called after Harry. 'I'm just going to do a bit of shopping, dear.'

'Well, don't spend too much.'

She stepped up to Churchill and touched him on the arm.

'I'd like to thank you,' she said and pressed twenty dollars in his hand.

Churchill looked offended. He closed her fingers around the money. 'You my friend,' he said.

Betty was lost for words. She patted him on the shoulder and hurried away.

'Remember the photo,' Churchill shouted.

Betty waved in acknowledgement. She looked at the stalls but there was nothing she wanted. It was the same on every island. Out of habit she picked up a few necklaces, asked the price and put them down without waiting for the answer.

At the far end of the stalls a woman sat alone on a wooden stool with a pile of palm fronds on the ground beside her. Betty perked up immediately. She loved anything to do with real crafts.

'Hi,' said Betty. 'You sure look busy. What are you making?' She spoke very slowly and clearly.

'Hats. Like those.'

'Why are those brown and these green?'

'That's when the palms dry out.'

'Have you been in the States?' asked Betty, puzzled by the accent.

'Yes dear. Thirty years in Brooklyn.'

'Well,' said Betty. She would have to buy a hat now.

She picked one up and tried it on.

'Sure is nice and shady,' she said, since it was neither flattering nor comfortable.

High above her she could see Harry, looking down at her waving. She felt annoyed, him standing up there like God the Father watching every move. Though she would have liked to talk to the woman some more, she couldn't, not with Harry watching. She paid and walked self-consciously back to the ship.

'You give that fellow money?' he asked as soon as she set foot on the deck.

'No, I didn't, Harry.'

'Huh!' Harry flicked his cigarette over the side of the boat into the water. 'And what for Chrissakes have you bought now?'

He picked up the hat and twisted it round. It smelt faintly musty. 'What's it supposed to be?'

'A hat.'

'And who for heaven's sake has a head that shape?'

'I thought it would make a nice fruit bowl.' She turned it upside down and imagined it filled with oranges and tangerines at Christmas.

'A hat is a hat, Betty, and a fruit bowl is a fruit bowl.' He stumped off down the gangway.

'Where are you going, Harry?' Betty looked at her watch. The ship was due to sail any minute now, she hoped, without him. But as the sailors made to withdraw the gangway, Harry came panting up. On his head he wore a large wooden bowl upside down, with the brim shading his eyes.

He executed a few dance steps just to make sure everyone noticed him, then announced loudly, 'My wife just bought a hat for a fruit bowl, so I've just bought a fruit bowl for a hat.'

Betty leaned over the boat and waved to her friend on the quayside as the ship moved slowly away. She thought that Churchill waved back, but she couldn't be sure because of her tears.

Harry remained on deck while the boat sailed. The ship's hooter was primitive and compelling like the call of an ancient hunting horn. Harry's chest swelled. Like a man-size statue of Liberty he held the fruit bowl aloft and the breeze lifted the few hairs on top of his head. For Harry, each episode of departure was significant. He was divided from those left on shore by a gulf immeasurably deeper than the widening strip of black water. It proclaimed that he, Harry Stillman, had arrived some-where, and he towered above the little harbour, the little island, waving the bowl for anyone who cared to see. He was proud to be on the ship, proud to be American, proud to be Harry Stillman, moving on to still greater things.

Betty's only thought was to escape from the sun and she found her way to her cabin ignoring all signs, carpet colours, even the numbers on the doors, following only her homing instinct. She looked forward to a cool shower and a glass of iced tea.

Thomas burrowed his head under the pillow not willing to admit where things had gone wrong. All the stories he had heard about Huntingdon's courtship of Ophelia were no longer funny, now that he had lost her.

'If she go by bus, Huntingdon is there,' Jancis had told him. 'He blocking the way of the bus with the Cadillac and it must stop. "Jesus Christ," say Ophelia, "who that man think he is?"' Jancis spoke with awe of the way Ophelia spoke to Huntingdon. 'The other passengers they laughing and the driver waiting to see what happen next.'

'And what Ophelia do?' Thomas had asked.

'She vex. "Get out of my fucking way, you bastard," she say.'

Sunset on Monday Island, where the call of frogs and lizards superseded the sounds of the day and the sky flushed with a colour fit to grace any tourist brochure.

Nelson and Napoleon played on the verandah with a three-legged frog brought in by the cat.

'Nelson, Napoleon, go wash the hands.' Portia's voice was harsh when she spoke to the little boys.

Nelson stamped on the frog and ran across the yard to the tap.

Napoleon paused for long enough to copy his brother, then walked after him with the funny feel of squashed frog under his shoe. Portia stood in the doorway framed by the light from the kitchen, holding a wooden spoon.

'Show me the hands.'

The boys held out their hands for inspection.

Portia brought the spoon down hard on Napoleon's right hand.

'You call that clean, eh, boy?' she screamed.

Napoleon cradled his hand to his breast and stared up at his grandmother.

'When I tell you wash the hands you wash the hands,' said Portia.

Napoleon trotted back to the tap. Portia pushed Nelson after him. 'Go help your brother.'

Napoleon held his hands under the tap while Nelson scrubbed at his palms with some grass. From the kitchen they could hear Portia dishing up their supper on enamel plates.

'You boys too too troublesome,' she said as they came back. 'What your mammy go say, eh?'

The children sat with their supper on the verandah steps looking out towards the sea and the orange sky. They spoke not a word to one another, just ate spoonful after spoonful until their plates were empty.

Portia took the plates away without comment. 'Bed,' she said.

The little boys stripped to their vests and underpants, scrubbed their teeth, and holding hands ran past their mother's dark room to pee in the ravine. They came back and walked silently through the living room between the television and the circle of watching adults.

'You boys ain't got no manners?' said Portia.

They stopped in the bedroom doorway and turned to face her, hand in hand.

'Good night, Granma,' they said together.

Portia sat chewing a chicken bone. 'And don' peepee in the beds,' she shouted as they closed the door behind them.

Their father Thomas sat on the edge of his bunk, his head in his hands. He tried to stand up but it was no good. He groaned and lay back.

'Shit, Johnson,' he said. 'I'm buggered, man.'

'Take it easy, man, take it easy.' Johnson covered Thomas with a blanket. He was shivering in the air conditioning. 'You sure tied one on, man.' He sat on the bunk next to Thomas and lit a cigarette. 'You want one?'

Thomas put his hands over his eyes.

In the pink black darkness of his palms he sees a dusty roadside stall. Beside the stall on a three-legged wooden stool sits an old woman. She cackles as the young girl bites into the mango. The girl bends slightly forward so that no juice dribbles on to her dress, chin out, eyes closed in concentration.

A car pulls up. A red Ford Cortina. At the steering wheel sits a young man, very dark, hat on the back of his head. He watches the girl.

She finishes the mango, then very precisely licks each of her fingers, one after the other and shakes her hand in the sun to dry it. The young man gets out of the car and offers his handkerchief. The girl laughs and wipes her fingers. The young man offers to pay for the mango. The old woman laughs and brushes the money aside. The young man picks up a scarlet hair clip and fastens it in the girl's hair.

The old woman is clearly delighted at the effect and again refuses any money. She takes the young man's right hand and the girl's left hand and joins them together. Then she opens her hands like a priest giving his blessing and laughs until her earrings dance and sparkle in the sunshine.

The young man and the girl get into the car together and drive away.

Thomas let his hands fall limply between his knees.

'This time', said Johnson, 'I go cover up for you, another time you do the same for me, okay?'

'I feel like death, man.'

'You be all right come morning.'

Johnson leaned over and turned off the light over Thomas's bunk.

'You sleep, man.'

'She leave me, Johnson.'

'She's a bitch, Thomas. What else you go expect?'

Johnson went out leaving Thomas alone in the darkness.

Napoleon lay down, his round face and dimpled legs and arms still those of a toddler. He lived entirely in the present, and for now that meant bed and sleep. He curled up and put his thumb and first finger in his mouth and sucked noisily.

Life was not quite so easy for Nelson. Nelson at four and a half was aware that Ophelia was not there. He lay and wondered whether she would be back in the morning when he woke up. He sat up and thought about going to ask Portia, then thought better of it. He looked at his brother in the other iron bedstead. Napoleon was only a baby, it was no good asking him.

Nelson stretched out on his side, arm extended above his head, cheek resting on his arm. He shared a bed with two of Ophelia's brothers, whereas Napoleon still slept with the girls. Nelson had learnt to sleep in this elongated fashion so that he didn't disturb his uncles. His mammy had told him that she was going far away on a plane and then in a ship. His daddy was a sailor, perhaps they would be together.

Jancis washed the greasy supper plates outside under the cold tap. Her mother lay on her bed, her eyes following every movement.

'The plates go on the top shelf,' she said.

'I move them so daddy could reach them at lunchtime.' Jancis did not look at her mother as she said this. 'You want me to move them back?'

'You doing the work now. Is not up to me.'

Jancis helped her father out of his chair and over to the other side of the double bed.

'You want to sleep now, daddy?' she shouted, with her face close to his. The old man nodded.

'You'll be late for prayer meeting,' said her mother.

'I'm not going tonight.' Jancis concentrated on her father's shirt buttons. Her mother was shocked into silence.

'I too tired,' explained Jancis. 'Instead I'll read the Bible to you.' Perhaps tomorrow she could go to prayer meeting. Today she couldn't face it.

Although Thomas hadn't said when he would next be on the island, she knew she would wait for him if it took a hundred years. Jancis's hands trembled so, the old man brushed her away. He tried unfastening the buttons himself while Jancis wondered how she could ever give up the prayer meetings and Brother Solomon, the hymns and the dancing, all for Thomas. She knew he could never be hers in the eyes of God, since it was Ophelia whom he loved.

She slipped off her father's shirt, and eased his arms into his pyjama jacket. Then she pulled back the covers, lifted her father's legs on to the bed, and hung his stick over the bed end. Then she took down her Bible from the shelf and opened it at random to see what words God had to say to her today.

Harry strode into the dining room, calling for the waiter as he went. There was no sign of Sam and Lou, but an empty seat caught his eye. Harry plonked himself down.

'What'll you all have?' He rubbed his hands together and beamed around the circle.

'Excuse me, but my husband . . .'

'Don't worry about your husband, lady, you've got me!' Harry flung an arm along the back of her chair, and ordered approximately the right number of drinks.

Betty, upset by the fact that a strange cabin steward had caught her in her bath robe, arrived some minutes after Harry. She hoped that Thomas would soon be better since she had come to take him for granted. His background presence was now essential to her precarious sense of well-being on board ship. She entered the Ritz Room not feeling in the least like a midnight buffet but afraid that Harry would be annoyed if she just went to bed. He would accuse her of not enjoying herself. As she stood in the doorway, trying to pick him out, she saw the statue. It stood, ice cold and glassy in a bed of tropical fruit, a life-sized girl with a pitcher of water held on her shoulder. Betty had seen pictures of ice statues in the brochures but the real thing took her breath away.

'Hey, Bet!' Harry didn't get up to attract her attention, he just yelled. She hurried over before he could shout again but by the time she reached his chair, he was already deep in telling a story. She plucked at his sleeve.

'Just find yourself a chair, honey.'

Betty looked around the circle. There were no spare chairs.

'I guess I'd better find one someplace else,' she said uncertainly, mortified by Harry's behaviour.

Harry apologized to his audience and turned to face Betty. His eyes narrowed and she could see the veins standing out on his neck.

'Can't you even find a goddamn chair for yourself?'

'I'm sorry, I didn't mean to interrupt.' Tears sprang to Betty's eyes. All she wanted to do was sit down and not be noticed.

Harry despised tears. But he didn't want to make a scene and spoil the punch line of his story.

The wine waiter returned. Harry saw to the allocation of the drinks, signed the chit and ordered a chair.

Betty sat down quickly on the far side of the circle. She was glad nobody had noticed she didn't have a drink. She was eating and drinking far more than was good for her.

'Since we're shipmates,' Harry was saying, 'we might as well get better acquainted.'

Betty was surprised that after a week there could be a whole group of people that she didn't even recognize.

'I'm Harry and this is my wife Betty.' He waved his glass in the general direction of Betty, who fixed the appropriate 'pleased to meet you' smile on her face. She realized that it looked odd, their being the only couple not sitting together.

'Harry and Betty Stillman.' He took a swig at his beer and got out a large cigar.

Betty steeled herself for what always followed.

'Stillman as in stillborn,' he added lighting up, but not, Betty saw, passing the packet round even though they were duty free. The other members of what Betty now had to concede must be thought of as 'their party' for this late-night session, laughed at Harry's remark. Betty wished she had a drink after all.

'It's all we've managed to produce, ain't it, Bet?' Harry laughed at his own joke but Betty felt sick as if she had been punched in the stomach. He had never gone quite that far before.

When another couple joined the group Betty somehow finished up next to Harry in the reshuffle, but since there was not quite space for the two of them they were forced out of the main circle. At least she was; Harry managed to edge forward and cut her out completely. She caught the odd snatch of conversation and by watching those faces she could see, she laughed when they laughed, and inwardly mourned her stillborn babies.

Betty had seen at a glance that Harry had chosen to join a party of A deck passengers. Though the more subtle aspects of social life on board ship were quite beyond him, Betty had learned from Sally on her first evening that there were certain distinctions to be observed. It was nothing so obvious as dress. Betty prided herself on being able to hold her own with anybody, from the state cabins to B deck, but there were certain people one didn't try to mix with and certain things one did or didn't do.

The most obvious thing about the passengers in the central, lower, windowless cabins was that they spent very little time in their cabins. They took their cocktails in one of the public bars, or strolled on deck with drink in hand insisting on their love of fresh air and sunshine.

The B deck passengers could not afford to be quite as casual with their clothes as those in the higher walks of life. They carefully spread table napkins over their laps at meals and dusted their deckchairs with a handkerchief before they sat down.

Betty had discovered that the higher the cabin number, the lower the status and there was only one couple with a number higher than theirs. Once she had got over the shock Betty went out of her way to be nice to Mal and Ida and invited them for a drink. Ida had insisted that she and Mal had come on the voyage as a last-minute whim, and had been lucky to get a cancellation, but Betty had not been fooled. Unlike Ida, she accepted the status quo. Little things like Sally's avoidance of her after the initial gush of friendship were hurtful however, and she preferred to avoid situations which might give rise to any unpleasantness.

As soon as she could reasonably interrupt Harry's flow of stories, which were being heard in an increasingly frosty silence, Betty leaned forward and tapped him on the shoulder.

'Why don't we go get something to eat?'

Harry leapt to his feet and patted his stomach. 'That's the best idea you've had all evening.'

Betty walked towards the buffet and the statue. Behind the lobsters and prawns, the crabs and fruit and salads, the chefs stood waiting to serve them. Betty looked along the row and tried to guess which one made the statue.

'Well, are you eating or aren't you?' Harry nudged her.

'It seems such a waste,' murmured Betty, picking up a stuffed egg then putting it down again.

'We've paid for it, haven't we?' Harry shovelled food on to his plate so fast it was hard to believe that he had already had three cooked meals that day.

'I don't mean the food. The statue.'

'Plastic mould made in Hong Kong, frozen by courtesy of Midwestern Electricals.' He put a prawn into his mouth. 'Say, they're good.'

'I think you're wrong, Harry. There was that picture in the brochure showing a chef chiselling at this huge block of ice.'

The tail of the monster prawn quivered out of the side of Harry's mouth. 'The trouble with you, Betty, is that you're so easily taken in.'

Harry set off back towards his chair with a mountain of food on his plate. Betty picked up one stuffed egg and followed. She felt vaguely disloyal, as if the meagreness of her helping only called attention to Harry's greed, but all this extravagance grieved her. She sent little contributions regularly to the Third World.

'Harry,' she asked, 'what do they do with the leftovers?'

'Fling them into the sea, I should think.'

'In plastic bags?'

'Bet, please, I am eating. I would rather not think about garbage.'

Betty supposed that the barracudas would eat up the scraps. But what about the statue? Would that be classified as garbage, or returned to the deep freeze and brought out again on the next voyage. She mashed up her egg all around the plate and watched the effect of the hot room on the ice figure. The fingers became short and stubby, the eye sockets deepened. It made Betty think of Greek statues she had seen in museums, but never before had she witnessed such a dramatic demonstration of the process of decay. It was like having a bird's eye view of a thousand years of history all in the space of one hour. As the slender neck narrowed, Betty clutched her hands to her mouth.

'You all right, Bet?'

Harry's plate was empty. Bet realized that most people

had gone and yet the buffet table looked as if it had scarcely been touched.

'I'm tired, Harry,' she said and stood up.

'I won't be long myself.'

Betty left Harry making a return journey to the buffet table.

Jancis awoke in the middle of the night, longing for Thomas.

The longer she lay watching the moonlight move across the lino the more restless she felt. Then she realized what caused this feeling. She had quite forgotten to pray for Ophelia. Jancis knelt on the cold lino and prayed for her friend. The prayer did not help. With the thought of God came the thought of her own fall from grace. She felt cold and alone. She had given her body to a man who, to all intents and purposes, was someone else's husband, and whether that mattered or not to Ophelia, it mattered to Jancis.

It was such a lovely night that Betty took a turn about the deck, enjoying the reflection of moonlight on the water. She leant on the rail at the stern watching the propellers churn the water and the widening fan of waves in the wake of the ship.

It was then that she heard voices on the deck below, and saw a white shape flung overboard. Her first instinct was to call for help. Then she realized it was the statue. It bobbed up and down in the wake of the ship, gleaming green in the moonlight and shrinking rapidly, until like Hans Andersen's mermaid it was no more than a patch of foam on the surface of the water. A real body would of course be more difficult to dispose of.

* * *

Harry, who had fallen in with a group of B deck passengers as he emerged from the midnight buffet, had been sidetracked into a visit to the late disco. It was a wonderful finale to a very successful day. He had a few more drinks and felt the calypso beat throb through his body, transporting him into a darker self which he had never experienced before.

No longer aware of his body, Harry stepped outside and saw the vast orange of the Caribbean moon. He stretched out his arms and saw his shadow as clear as a cross upon the deck. A surge of feeling flooded his soul and for the first time for years, he thought with some degree of passion of his dear wife waiting for him down in Cabin 2137.

Harry floated down the staircases. He tapped briskly on the cabin door, called out 'Guess whooo?' and popped his head round the door. Betty was sitting up in bed, in curlers and a chiffon scarf. Her eyes peered small and piggy through a thick white face pack, while she downed a glass of bubbling liver salts.

The smile froze on Harry's face.

DAY TWO
Saint John

'It is enough that they show us what we have made of them for us to realize what we have made of ourselves.'

Sartre,
Preface to *The Wretched of the Earth*
by Franz Fanon

'he quickly saw
that home was a dry river bed;
he knew he'd have to run away, again,

or stay and be clawed to death'

Andrew Salkey,
Dry River Bed

In the crook of the elbow of the Antilles festers what is known in travel agents' jargon as International Pleasure Island. Depending on the sector in which they have the misfortune to be born, it is known to the locals variously as San Juan, Saint John, Sint Jan or Saint Jean. The name (let us for the moment stick to Saint John) was of course conferred by the redoubtable C.C. after the beloved disciple of Jesus Christ. The voyage from Spain had proved unusually tedious. The crew had endured the usual hardships of disease, boiled rats and leather and had been forced to consume more alcohol than water, since the former was well casked whereas Spain had problems in paying for the importation of sufficient hard wood for the latter. The crew of the *Santa Maria*, before they went on to discover greater glories, were prepared to embrace the island with brotherly love. It was only afterwards they realized its lack of attractions in comparison with the other islands; the natives were unusually bellicose, gold was non-existent and fresh water hard to come by. They made no great efforts to keep the island under the Spanish flag, nor were other nations tempted to seize it, for precisely the same reasons.

But what in its history has led this postage stamp land to become the cesspit of the Caribbean? Of course as soon as the Spanish managed to get a few fields of tobacco growing along came Sir Walter Raleigh, who stopped off for long enough in his search for El Dorado to put to the sword those few Spaniards not yet barbecued by the Caribs. And once England had got her foot in, the French as a question of honour felt bound to drive them out.

Later Oliver Cromwell needed a place, where at the pull of a plug he could flush away the refuse of unruly Britain, the rebellious Scots and Irish, the Presbyterians and the Quakers, the royalist captives from Monmouth's rebellion and anyone else whom he didn't fancy living in close proximity to himself.

But it was the Dutch who put the greatest effort into making a go of Sint Jan. They quite simply needed more salt, and saw in the inshore lakes of stagnant water a cheap method of collecting this substance so vital for food storage before the advent of the freezer. It required only the capital investment of a few wooden poles dotted around the salt ponds, and a few boatloads of slaves to scrape the accumulations of brine off the poles. No doubt also, the very flatness of the island appealed to them, being a sort of home from home.

The settlers were in general by this time quite removed from the hostilities of their various mother countries. While their navies and a handful of militia slogged it out at sea and in the immediate vicinity of any forts, the planters plugged away at what they knew best. Planting. Naturally enough, the small groups of foreigners tended to crystallize into ghetto-like areas, for who abroad does not welcome the opportunity to relax with fellow countrymen? After three hundred and fifty years of constant governmental bickering, this informal division of the island was at last formalized and agreements drawn up between the powers of France, Holland, Britain and Spain. Saint John, in the fashion of the time, was hung drawn and quartered, and any chance of developing as a homogeneous entity finally destroyed.

After the emancipation of the slaves (and a weary lot

they were since the island was riddled with malaria and the only survivors were the West Africans with sickle cell anaemia), things went from bad to worse.

Tourism was the only industry which the island as a whole saw fit to promote, which did nothing for the locals who simply sat back and subsisted like leeches on the backs of the foreign-owned companies, seeking solace in the duty-free drink under whose influence they still talk maunder-ingly of 'home' whether it be Europe or one of the other islands of the Antilles.

However, it is towards this little patch of land which, apart from the central massif, scarcely raises its grey and dusty surface above the brilliant blue of the sea, that the *Dream of America* has been steadily steaming while its passengers slept. For the compilers of tourist literature, Kubla Khan could have decreed nothing better, although he himself might have eagerly anticipated the day when this gigantic supermarket cum pleasure dome would sink beneath the wake of its own enjoyment.

Sixty girls saunter along the dockside of New Amsterdam, capital of the Dutch segment of the island. It is a pleasant place to be, with the sun dancing on the water and the early morning air fresh with the sparkle of champagne. The local port officials turn a blind eye.

On the verandah of a restaurant overlooking the port, one of the cheaper places off the usual tourist beat, visiting seamen enjoy their breakfast. The outlook is captivating, but not so much in the long sweep of the bay as in the bevy of lovely creatures with their bags and bundles, and aura of cheap cigarettes and sweet perfume. For these girls are an essential part of the island's assets, no less important to the balance of trade than gambling and prostitution or the sale of whisky and sunshine holidays.

Ophelia, who has said goodbye to Marianne at the dock

gates, sees the containers stacked neatly in rows like giant building blocks. Anticipating some mild degree of discomfort during the two-day boat trip, she has packed the rose-coloured silk and wears instead a pair of jeans so new and stiff that she can feel them crack as she walks.

Like a conjuring trick, in the time it takes the waitress to bring a new pot of coffee or the Senior Port Official (sick in bed this morning) to wash down two aspirins with a glass of water, abracadabra, in the twinkling of an eye, sixty girls vanish into thin air.

The only sign of life now on the quay is a single man. Just as a guard at a railway station slams the carriage doors and waves his flag, he slams the doors of a particular container labelled Midwestern Electricals, then waves his hands (gloved to keep them clean) to indicate that this one is ready for lift off.

Betty awoke with a sudden ping of her eyelids which was startling. Her head throbbed from the combination of aspirins, liver salts, alcohol and sun which had left her totally disorientated. She looked at her bedside clock but it had stopped. She couldn't even tell if it was morning or night.

Harry was snoring loudly. If the whole night was going to be like this she would have to take a sleeping tablet or she would look terrible in the morning. If it was still night. The confusion all stemmed from Harry's meanness. Even the tiniest porthole would have told her whether to get up or go to sleep again.

Then Betty had an inspiration. Harry's twenty-four hour, digital wrist watch. And to think that in those far-off days when she lived a life ruled by sunrise and sunset, she had despised such things. His arm lay neatly on top of the bedclothes. Betty put on her glasses and crept closer. Twenty-nine nine for godssakes. Whatever did that mean?

* * *

Harry is in heaven. Bronzed and slim he lies by the swimming pool. Next to him, the chaise longue is occupied not by Betty, but by a sun-tanned apparition with long blonde hair. Harry keeps his cool. Tosses a few remarks oh so casual out of the side of his mouth. The blonde looks puzzled. Harry's eyes focus on the few inches of material and the surrounding glow of skin. The girl smiles and concentrates so hard on what Harry is saying that the corners of her mouth pucker. She puts a hand on his arm, looks up into his face. Harry rolls towards her . . .

Betty leapt back.

She decided to take one of her sleeping tablets. The bedside drawer where she kept them was empty apart from a Bible. She flipped through the pages as far as Proverbs and a slip of paper fell out. It assured her of the services of the cabin stewards at any hour of the day or night.

She rang Thomas and ordered a tray of coffee and toast. She was starving. Then she whipped off her chiffon scarf and took out her curlers. She was still combing her hair when Thomas arrived. When he uttered the magic words 'Good morning', she could have hugged him.

Portia up in her garden had on the boil a vast iron pot of assorted vegetables and turkey gizzards spiced with chilli and lime juice. It was her turn to cook for Aunty Gladys's family, in return for which Gladys's sons were picking grapefruit ready for the boat on Monday.

Portia carried the full crates up the hill to the shed. On each trip she stoked the fire and stirred the stew with the end of her cutlass. And all morning Portia thought about Jancis's offer to look after Nelson and Napoleon.

'What you think, Gladys?' she asked her sister, over lunch.

111

'If it for their education,' said Gladys, 'I think you should agree you know.'

Nelson, in the pre-school class, spent much of his day at his desk, not all in pursuit of academic excellence though, since social education also ranked high on the list of priorities.

Today the lesson was on the wonders of the modern bathroom. The teacher held up a small book with an even smaller picture of a w.c.

'What is this?' she asked.

All hands were raised.

'Yes, Nelson?'

Nelson stood up. 'That is a w.c., Miss.' He sat down again.

'Very good, Nelson. Now, who in the class has a w.c.?'

The children looked round at one another, but not a hand was raised. In accordance with the precept of learning by doing, the teacher led the class off to the toilets and back again.

'Now children, what do we say if we want to use the w.c.?'

Hands waved like sugar cane before a storm.

'Yes . . . Errol?'

'Want a piss, Miss.'

'No, Errol. Any other ideas?'

This was too much for the children. Suggestions came at the teacher loud and fast.

The teacher closed the book and waited for silence.

'We educated people,' she said quietly. 'We ain't savages living in the jungle. We using the correct terminology, the correct word, to urinate. Please repeat after me . . . '

Roly-poly Napoleon, perched on his blue potty like an elephant on a bun, has been in the potty training class for a year now. Soon he will move on to greater things. From time to time, when his hair was pulled exceptionally hard by the little girl on the pink potty next to him, he burst into tears.

'What the matter, Napoleon, what wrong with you now?' The nursery assistants didn't look up but continued to exchange gossip and knitting patterns.

Napoleon did not know that he was missing his mother, but he did know that his routine had been upset. There had been no time for breakfast today. Huntingdon had not called for them in his car as he had promised he would, and no mid-morning break had been put in his little school bag. Napoleon, hot and hungry, has been easily upset. When the little girl behind him reached out and drew her nails hard down his neck, Napoleon screamed. There was bedlam as all the other children started yelling too. The assistants came to life, bottoms were wiped and the children taken outside for a period of free play. Napoleon, issued with a headless doll, drooped by the verandah railings and slowly chewed off its toes, one by one. The assistants were perplexed. Napoleon was not usually so troublesome.

'Jesus Christ, Betty,' said Harry, 'why didn't you wake me?' He yanked his shorts up fast.

'I'm sorry, Harry, I didn't know you wanted waking.'

'But I'm down for putting practice.'

Betty poured her third cup of coffee and spread butter and honey thickly on her toast. 'No point in rushing, honey, you've missed the whole class.'

'Shit.' Harry stripped off the shirt printed with GARY PLAYER'S THE GREATEST, and started flinging other shirts out of the drawer.

'What're you looking for, Harry?'

'It's clay pigeons now.'

'Why don't you wear the aertex, it's cooler.' She hated

113

Harry in printed T-shirts. 'Or why don't you just come and sit here and we can plan the rest of your day.'

'Huh.' Harry plonked himself down on her bed.

'I always think that if you oversleep it's because the body needs it.'

Harry snatched the programme out of Betty's hand. 'Jesus, Bet, it's the Fancy Dress tomorrow.'

'I hadn't forgotten.'

'But what about our costumes?'

'We can choose them tonight.'

'I might just go and see about mine now.'

'But Harry, there's only an hour until we go on shore. Why not go and have a nice swim and a sun.' Betty was enjoying lying in bed when she should have been at an 'Exercise for Beauty' session. She knew that no amount of bending and stretching would ever render her sylph-like.

'What about you, honey?' Harry crammed his feet into a pair of trainers.

'I might just be a bit lazy,' confessed Betty.

'No good sitting around doing nothing, is there now, Bet? I brought you here to enjoy yourself.'

'But I am enjoying myself.' Betty loved her honey really thick.

'What about a quick game of squash?'

Betty, thoroughly alarmed by the energy and hatred he put into every shot, had vowed never to play squash with Harry again. 'Kill the ball,' he said, and looked as if he meant it

'I might just take a quick workout in the gym,' said Betty comfortably, with no intention of doing so.

Harry took off his tartan shorts right there by Betty's bed.

'Er, why don't you change in the bathroom, honey?' She was after all having her breakfast.

'Why?' asked Harry.

Betty dabbed her upper lip with the white napkin. 'Someone might come in.'

'Only Thomas,' said Harry.

He put on his swimming trunks, flung a white towel round his shoulders and feeling just like a sports ad, headed for the pool. By the time he arrived he was sweating profusely and ordered an iced lager, with not too much ice. He collapsed on a sun bed. If only everyone in the office could see him now. He took off his canvas shoes and socks and sniffed appreciatively. Must be years since he sweated like that. Harry anointed himself with sun oil and lay back.

Betty, not far behind Harry, picked up a deck chair from a stack near the pool and climbed up the staircase to the compass deck. It was here she was most likely to find some privacy. What had at first seemed a virtue in the ship's design – that not a centimetre of space was wasted – had over the last week begun to seem like a curse. Thirty-seven thousand tons of boat, six hundred and eighty-nine feet long and nowhere to hide away and write her postcards. The only quiet spot she could find was a small patch of shade behind the funnel, but the heat from the metal was stifling. When she tried to put up the deck chair it collapsed in an untidy jumble of wood and canvas. She gave up; she would never get it right now, and walked on without it.

Coming to the pool end of the compass deck, Betty paused and looked down. There was Harry, getting up from his sun bed. He tightened his trunks and waddled towards the water.

He hesitated, looking around to see if there was anyone he knew. It was a pity, he thought, that Betty didn't enjoy sport as much as he did. There was something about her that was, well, dull. That was it. She didn't hold him back, but she didn't inspire. With or without her, there was one thing Harry was determined to master this holiday, and that was swimming.

The scene around the pool was as close to Dante's Inferno as anything Betty could have imagined. She had taken one look at the close-packed, near-naked figures on their first day out and had never been back. Though she would have loved to find herself down there, in the water, she knew she would only make a fool of herself. She would appear just what she was, a fleshy, middle-aged woman whose only pretence at dignity lay in her clothes. One look at Harry confirmed that she was right.

Harry still stood by the pool, his belly a fiery volcanic red. Then he lowered himself to a sitting position and shuffled forward until he plopped heavily into the water at the shallow end. Now he cornered a small boy to whom he demonstrated a few strokes so that onlookers could take him for a fond grandpa teaching the lad to swim. But suddenly the boy dived under and bobbed up at the deep end where Harry could not follow.

Stranded and conspicuous, Harry launched himself forward, churning the water to a froth with his clumsy strokes, but slowly and inexorably he sank.

Betty, looking down, was speechless. How could she have been married to the man for thirty-two years and not know something as basic as the fact that he could not swim? Poor, poor Harry. To think that all these years he had been making excuses like 'It makes me feel nice and cool just watching you' or 'I think I've got a cold coming on'. But she was his wife. He should have told her. And who in their right minds would go on a cruise if they couldn't swim? Harry overboard took on a new light.

Betty's feet were killing her. She slipped off one sandal and immediately burnt the ball of her foot on the deck. She would have liked to dangle her legs over the edge of the ship and trail her swollen feet in the water. She had not imagined that from a ship the sea could be so inaccessible. She hobbled over to the rail and looked at the sparkling water far below. The ship cast a huge black shadow over the sea bed like some enormous fish cruising below them. She saw the lifeboats slung on the ship's side, and thought of the cool dark space beneath the canvas covers. She read the lifeboat drill and wondered whether she would ever have the courage to jump on to the green canvas taut as a trampoline. Axes hung ready to cut away the ropes. She imagined the boat plummeting down with a tremendous splash. A few tins of bully beef and some ship's biscuits and she'd be fine.

The sun was making her head ache again. Betty sat on the deck in the narrow strip of shade provided by the gymnasium, and worked out that she had precisely twelve minutes of privacy before the class ended. She drew her knees up under her chin to get her feet into the velvet shade and took out twelve identical postcards of the *Dream of America*.

She marked a cross on the card where their cabin must be, only of course you couldn't really see it. Dee would think that the porthole nearest the cross was theirs. She tried to correct this impression by adding a note under the mark, but the pen wouldn't write on the shiny surface.

Now she searched through her purse for some stamps. Harry had said there was no point in buying foreign stamps when they could post the cards tomorrow on an American island and save their foreign currency. Betty thought this was rather a pity as the card wouldn't look as though it had come from anywhere foreign. She wrote Dee's address which she knew by heart and then tried to think of something original to say. Something like 'Wish you were here' and then in brackets 'instead of me', but then Dee would never say anything so disloyal about her own husband.

117

A seagull perched on the railing not far from Betty, beak facing into the wind. Then it was off again, wheeling high above the ship. Betty was just wishing she were a seagull when plop, it deposited a large lump of guano in the middle of the postcard. 'That's what the gulls think of us,' wrote Betty, and signed off.

Harry had had his swim and earned his drink. He leaned back with both elbows on the bar and his stomach thrust out before him, eyes creased against the sunlight, studying the women round the pool. He drawled an order for a cigar out of the side of his mouth like John Wayne gone to seed. He has long been a devotee of Westerns and could list you every one made in Hollywood since *High Noon*.

He lit the cigar with studied nonchalance then gripped it between his teeth while he puffed steadily, thumbs thrust in the gun belt of the drawstring of his trunks. He stood with his legs slightly apart, swaying to the barely discernible bucking of the ship.

In spite of his willingness to stand drinks and play the clown Harry has become the best known, least sought after person on the voyage. Of course he laid any social failure squarely at Betty's door. She just wasn't a very exciting person. He hadn't liked to tell her so plainly, but the programme he had devised for her for the duration of the voyage was carefully aimed at her improvement. After all these years she might be able to play bridge well enough not to make a complete ass of him. Already he imagined the casual invitation – why not drop round for a few hands, but Harry we didn't know you played, oh yes, I've bin playing for years, but now my wife has learnt – and the drinks on the sideboard and the little crustless sandwiches. She must surely have picked up enough tips in the cookery line over the last week.

The thought made him hungry. He and Betty had made

a pact to miss out on breakfast but that couldn't apply when he hadn't had an early morning coffee tray for himself. Harry ordered a king-size jumboburger from the bar, which was somehow different from a sit-down meal in the dining room, and didn't feel as if he was cheating at all.

Betty looked up at what she took to be Saint John appearing on the horizon. She was not specially looking forward to visiting yet another island but land was land, she told herself. It would be good to stretch her legs, and if Harry were in a good mood there were still several little presents she wanted to buy.

She was changed and ready before Harry came down to the cabin with a bright red band across the top of his stomach as if he had been lying under a grill. She left him in the shower and stood in the doorway of the linen room chatting to Thomas to while away the time.

'She left you, Thomas? Gee, I am sorry, I don't know what to say.' Betty was genuinely upset. 'Didn't she leave a note or anything?'

'Oh yes, she lef' the note.'

'But what did she say? Hadn't she given you any warning?'

'She say she have los' she heart to somebody else.'

'That's too bad, Thomas.'

'And that she have a job in another country.'

'Where?'

Thomas shrugged.

'You mean she could be just anywhere?'

Thomas felt inside his jacket which was hanging on the back of the door.

'I go show you a picture.'

Betty took the photo, and stared at it. 'She's very beautiful.'

119

'This is meh children, Nelson and Napoleon.'

'What's happened to them?'

'They staying with Ophelia's mother.'

'She'll look after them, just like that?'

'But yes.'

'Well, I'm glad she didn't take them with her when she went.'

Thomas took back the picture and replaced it carefully in an envelope.

'I just don't know what to say, Thomas. Is there anything I can do to help you find her?'

'If you see her, you write me.'

'What's this, Bet, eh? Secret assignations?'

Betty turned to go. She couldn't talk to Thomas with Harry around.

'I'll see you later,' she called back. If someone could walk out on a nice guy like Thomas, what was she doing stuck with Harry? It just didn't make sense.

It didn't make sense to Thomas either.

But Thomas has only known Ophelia for five years.

He met her when she had already spent one year making grass mats.

He never knew Ophelia at fifteen.

Ophelia at fifteen is like a fledgling bird, poised on the verge of flight, not quite knowing which way to turn. She is a shy and lovely creature, the personification of all that is good on the island, from the warm daytime glow of the sun to the night-time fragrance of the ginger lily. Any earlier awkwardness is gone and she unfolds like the flower of the hibiscus, which awaits the kiss of the hummingbird. But there are no hummingbirds left, not in the towns or the villages or any of the places which Ophelia frequents.

Ophelia is in the factory which makes grass mats, five

days a week from eight until four, and a half day on Saturdays. She sits at a sewing machine and takes a large bundle of plaited grass, coarse and smelling like hay, and creates little rosettes, starting from the middle of each one and stitching round and round.

Ophelia sews and yawns and scratches her ankles where the grass fibre irritates, and counts the minutes until the lunchbreak. It gets hotter and hotter in the building as the day progresses and the pace of work becomes slower.

When Ophelia has completed a pile of rosettes so high that it threatens to topple over, she stands up, straightens her skirt, puts on her shoes and click clacks over to the girls who are hand-stitching rosettes together to make a large carpet. The management are proud of their carpets, one of which was once presented to a visiting member of a royal family.

If the work fails to inspire, at least it is work, and work is necessary to make money, for Ophelia is ambitious. She sees her present employment as a necessary evil – something to be endured only until something better comes along.

Ophelia was recommended for the job by one of the nuns at the convent. Indeed the atmosphere in the factory is similar to that of a nunnery, perhaps because its workforce consists entirely of ex-pupils of St Dominic's. There is only one male employee; this is the van driver and his appearances are greeted with much giggling. His name is Churchill.

Today he staggers into the building with an armful of plaited grass, flings it down in a corner, then stands picking needles out of his skin. Like a visiting bishop he is overwhelmed by offers of help, but there is no touch so tender or welcoming as that of Ophelia.

Ophelia frowns with delightful concentration as she uses

121

her long polished nails, thumb and forefinger, like pincers to extract the prickles from Churchill's bare arm.

He groans but the sound contains more of ecstasy than agony. 'Ophelia, when you go marry me?' he whispers.

Ophelia slaps his hand and the game is at an end.

'Churchill,' she orders, 'you go buy me a hot bread. I too too hungry, man.' She clasps her hands to her stomach.

Churchill is gone like the wind leaving the grass stalks fluttering and the girls on the floor coughing under a shroud of dust. But Ophelia gets her hot bread and Churchill sits on the edge of her table while she eats.

'You wanting a piece?' Ophelia holds some out to Churchill.

He will accept neither bread nor payment. It is enough to be allowed to sit and watch her.

When the bell goes at midday, Ophelia doesn't rush outside like the other girls. First she retires to the ladies' room where she removes from her clothing every evidence of her employment right down to the very last stalk. She straightens her seams, combs out her hair, and dabs a layer of pale powder on to her dark cheeks. Then she is ready to face the world.

Churchill waits outside for her with the van.

'We go take a drive today, eh, up in the hills?'

Ophelia laughs and walks past him. Churchill starts the engine and cruises along next to her.

'What you doing today, eh? Why you ain't want to come with me?'

Ophelia rubs her hand through his hair as if he was a child, then she bangs on the roof of the car by way of farewell and turns up a narrow alley where he cannot follow.

At the far end of the alley is the Monday Island Secretarial College, established 1924. The approach is unpromising – dark, rubbish strewn and stinking of urine.

The staircase is bare and the walls covered with graffiti. However, the two upstairs rooms which comprise the college are pleasantly flooded with sunshine and there is a fine view of the deep water harbour. It is here that Ophelia has spent five evenings a week for the last year, sometimes typing diligently about lazy dogs and quick brown foxes, at other times watching the boats come and go and imagining her own departure to the United Nations Headquarters in Geneva.

Ophelia makes her way through the jumble of desks and bags, abandoned for the lunch hour by the full-time students, and goes up to the noticeboard. She is anxious to know whether she has passed her final exam.

She doesn't need to look far, for there is her name at the top of the list. Ophelia Wellington, ninety-three per cent. She gets out her handkerchief and blows her nose hard, then stands by the window feeling for the first time that the end of her dream is in sight.

'Well, you'll be leaving us soon, man,' is Churchill's only comment.

'But I'll keep in touch,' Ophelia promises him.

Six months later she is still sitting at her sewing machine. Churchill is more sympathetic in the light of her failure. He often sits on the edge of her table chewing at a grass stalk and expressing his horror at the ways of the world and the island.

'The United Nations say', reports Ophelia, 'that they do not recognize the Monday Island Diploma in Stenography.'

'What that is?' asks Churchill.

'Typing.' Ophelia carries another pile of rosettes over to the girls on the floor.

'So', she says on her return, 'I apply to the foreign firms here. Same answer.'

123

She slumps down in her chair. 'They ask me, what this Monday Island Secretarial College is? And I say, it run by Miss Bertram, an English lady, but they say, it is not a recognized qualification.'

Churchill whistles in sympathy. 'What you go do now?'

'I ain't giving up,' says Ophelia. She combs her hair and her smile returns. 'I go write to every firm in the book. Fifty letters I sending until somebody make me his secretary.'

'You wasting your money, man.'

In her lunchtime, Ophelia sets about writing her first letter. First she goes to the nearest corner store and purchases one envelope together with one sheet of writing paper. Miss Bennett wraps it up carefully in brown paper. Ophelia buys one biro from a general merchant then goes to the post office where she sits at the heavy wooden table overlooking the sea. After much chewing of her pen she composes to her satisfaction a letter to one Mr Jolly, of the Seaborne Shipping Agency.

To her surprise, she is summoned to an interview the following week. She rings Mr Jolly to explain that she is unable to attend for interview during work hours because of her present employment. Mr Jolly, whom she can just make out in his third floor office on the other side of the street from the phone box, is most anxious to accommodate. He will see her the next day, after work.

So as not to arrive flushed and overheated, Ophelia arranges a lift with Churchill in the factory van. This unfortunately undoes all the good work carried out in the ladies' room before she left, as the van is full of grass dust. However, Churchill brushes down her back while a shrieking Ophelia flicks specks off her front, shakes out Aunty Celie's little black hat and repins it firmly on her head.

Apart from Mr Jolly, the building is deserted. Everyone else has gone home. Ophelia has some difficulty finding the right office and it is, in fact, Mr Jolly who finds her, having heard from his office the sound of her heels in the corridor.

He beckons her into his room where he sits down behind the biggest desk Ophelia has ever seen in her life. Ophelia, only fifteen but looking at least twenty, stands in front of his desk like a schoolgirl.

Mr Jolly indicates that she should be seated and to put her at her ease he comes round to the front of his desk and offers her a cigarette. He then insists on lighting it for her, holding her hands in his and drawing her face towards him.

Ophelia begins to dislike Mr Jolly.

'You want to see meh typing?' she asks, taking her diploma and a sample page from the *Encyclopaedia Britannica* out of her bag. Mr Jolly laughs pleasantly, and tosses them on to the desk. He asks her to walk over to the window and back, then suggests continuing the discussion over dinner.

'My husband he waiting for me in the car,' says Ophelia. With great dignity, she pulls on her gloves, retrieves her certificate and walks out of the office. In the van she confides to Churchill, 'He ain't want a good secretary he just want a good fuck.'

Churchill finds this terribly funny, but Ophelia is indignant. Her next lunch hour she spends purchasing another sheet of paper, another envelope and another stamp and writing a letter to the local newspaper, a letter which she is subsequently delighted to see in print, under the title

WHAT HAPPENING ON THIS ISLAND?

What happening on this island that a honest woman can't apply for secretarial work in safety? Who these men think they are so that when a secretary come with good papers they not even looking at the papers but all they interested in is she figure? What we qualified women go do?

And she signed herself 'Disgusted'.

Ophelia sets loose a maelstrom in the press. The newspaper office is besieged with so many complaints of a similar nature that she knows at once that there is no point in writing to any of the other forty-nine firms on her list. Her fingers lose their intimacy with the keyboard and her sinuses become solid with dust.

Right up until some six months before she meets Thomas, life brings little by way of surprise to Ophelia, either at work or at home. She is in danger of falling into a rut, but some instinct for survival and a hopeful nature come to her aid. She attends to her personal toilette as rigorously as ever, bearing in mind the dictum of her beloved Aunty Celia, 'If you dress like money, money come to you,' but sometimes the wait seems eternal. The only excitement comes from her stormy relationship with Portia. One particular eruption conspires to give Ophelia what she has long wanted: separate accommodation.

At this time Ophelia still lives in a room in her mother's house. She pays Portia a small amount towards board and lodging and a weekly sum to Aunty Gladys who has adopted her baby daughter Estelle. The rest of Ophelia's salary, though not large, is entirely her own.

Her room, little bigger than the iron bedstead, one small dressing table and a space scarcely adequate for dressing or undressing, is her sanctuary. It is the one place where she can be alone and relax – for Ophelia the two are synonymous. In the ill-fitting drawers and in Aunty Celia's old suitcase under the bed, Ophelia keeps her treasures, her make-up and the clothes handed down along with the suitcase.

She keeps her room padlocked every day while she is at work. Not for fear of outsiders breaking in, since such a thing is unheard of in Sugar Bay, but to keep out her younger brothers and sisters; and her mother.

Ophelia arrives home from work one day, walks across the sitting room with the key to the padlock already in her hand and stops in front of her bedroom door. A feeling of outrage quite takes her breath away. The lock has been levered off, the door is open and her room is in utter chaos.

Among the ruins are her twin brothers, Harrison draped in Aunty Celia's nylon underwear and Bentley covered in peach blossom face powder.

Ophelia steadies herself against the door frame, takes a deep breath and screams, 'What you all doing in my room?'

Portia comes running from the kitchen, wiping her greasy hands on an old shirt.

Ophelia picks up her little brothers one after the other and flings them out of the door.

'Now I ain't giving them the titty no more,' shouts Portia, 'they sharing your bed not mine.'

In neighbouring houses, women down their cooking utensils to listen. Some emerge on to their verandahs for better hearing. News of the row spreads to the very outposts of the village, from the ravine on one side to the church on the other, from the cliff to the north to the sea-shore on the south.

'This one is my room,' shrieks Ophelia, 'and those boys ain't coming in here no more.'

A small crowd gathers in the street beneath the unglazed window. Every word will be remembered and chewed over in the bar and by the women washing clothes in the river.

'This my house and if you ain't liking it you just get out,' bellows Portia. 'You hear me, eh?'

The crowd grins with satisfaction.

A heap of Aunty Celia's dresses tumble into the crowd like a rainbow from the sky. Ophelia's screams are deafening.

'You going crazy, woman?' Ophelia has recovered her

powers of speech. She is seen climbing on to the windowsill to make her escape. Portia drags her back by the hair. The house walls shake as Portia thumps heavily against the windowsill.

'This one is my room,' squeals Ophelia. 'I paying you for it.'

People look at one another. This puts a very different complexion on matters. Portia is clearly in the wrong. Her new husband, Henzel, summoned from his shoe-making, bounds up the steps and into the house. The neighbours pile in after him to help tear the women apart.

Though the episode is concluded with tears, rum, and protestations of love between mother and daughter, Ophelia no longer feels safe. She decides to build her own room. Aunty Gladys agrees to provide a tree, and her seven cousins offer their labour and undying love. Churchill promises to arrange transport.

The very next weekend Ophelia sets off with her work force into the rain forest, where a fine old mahogany tree is chopped down and sawn into planks by one cousin at each end of a two-handled saw. Ophelia provides lavish quantities of coconut punch which does nothing for the regularity of the planks but works wonders for the morale of the working party.

While the menfolk work, Ophelia sits with Gladys and Estelle, who was the cause of Ophelia's early departure from school and her subsequent employment in the grass mat factory.

Ophelia, seeing her baby daughter for the first time for some months, is almost seduced into motherhood. Estelle is now an enchanting one year old with her head covered in white ribbons like a cloud of butterflies.

'You want to take her home with you?' asks Aunty Gladys.

Ophelia watches Estelle taking her first unsteady steps,

and is tempted. She lies back among the bamboos and watches the tall slender tips flash like gold spears across the blue sky.

'Aunty Glad, why you not letting me live with you?'

'Eh, eh, Phelie, you think you would be happy here?'

Estelle plonks herself down by Ophelia's side. Ophelia traces with her fingernail the dimple just above the elbow of the toddler's arm. 'Sometimes I think I would be happy.'

'And you go work in the field with your old aunty?'

'No way. I go just lie in the sun like this.'

'This ain't no life for you, chil'.'

Ophelia in her new white slacks and a scarlet blouse, her sunglasses stuck on the top of her head, gets up with the basket of coconut punch on her arm. 'I go see if they thirsty,' she says.

'Make sure you don' give them too much,' advises Gladys, ''cos they can' work after that.'

'They done happy already, aunty,' says Ophelia. 'Listen.'

They hear the rasp of the saw and the rhythm of sticks banged together and one of the cousins singing calypso. Ophelia dances over with the punch and the thermos of ice.

By Sunday night the planks are loaded into the van. Estelle is tired and grizzly and it is easy for Ophelia to decide that the best place for a child is up in the hills where there is fresh fruit and vegetables and a cool breeze at night.

Her departure is tinged with sadness as the seven male cousins hang suspiciously around the van.

'Who go share your room with you, Phelie?' they ask.

Ophelia laughs. The cousins reluctantly make way to allow Churchill into the driving seat. Ophelia opens the window and leans out blowing kisses and shrieking goodbye long after the van is out of sight.

The second weekend there is a party down in Sugar Bay. Ophelia provides food and drink and enough batteries to keep the transistor radio going full blast for two days. In return she gets a room, and settles into a way of life whose predictability brings a certain satisfaction at the close of each uneventful day.

Every evening after work, Ophelia strolls to the bus stop. She never accepts a lift from Churchill which might imply that she is prepared to devote her out of work hours to him as well. Every day he hovers by the factory gate, ever hopeful, always with the same smile, and every time receives the same dismissal. 'G'night, Churchill. See you morning.'

And Ophelia wanders through the streets which are packed with office workers, factory hands, shop assistants and schoolchildren, all of whom spill as if by magic into the streets on the stroke of four. Now is the hour to meet friends and acquaintances, and the journey which might take Ophelia only five minutes in the mornings can take up to an hour and a half.

She sees her fellow classmates of days of yore, in their green gym slips and white ankle socks. She by contrast is resplendent in a shiny black tricel number with gold and scarlet triangles which wink at the sun.

'What you all do in school today?' she asks, and they cluster round, anxious to give her every detail.

Jancis is always there, too shy to push forward, her face pitted by acne and her hair short like a boy's.

Ophelia stops to take out a cigarette, causing ripples in the green and yellow tide like a boulder in a river. She crosses over to what has become known by convention as the boys' side, and there among the schoolboys looking absurdly mature for their shorts, she looks for someone with a light.

'Hey, Michael, you got a match?' The cigarette bobs up and down between her lips as she speaks.

'Why should I have matches, Ophelia, when I am in uniform?'

'Just because you dressed up like a little boy don't mean nothing.'

'You want to get me kicked out?'

Ophelia giggles and puts a hand into Michael's pocket. 'You just say I a friend of the family.' She lights her cigarette and replaces the matches.

'You come to the disco tonight?'

They turn and stroll together towards the bus ranks.

'Why you going dancing? You must work work work, man.'

'The exams aren't for another two months.'

'And what you go do when you don' get the scholarship?'

'I staying here and marrying you.'

'It better you go to Barbados and be a doctor. Then you sen' for me.' Ophelia dismisses Michael with a cheery wave, and turns into a newsagent for this week's copy of *True Love*. She reads by the kerbside waiting for her favourite bus driver to come along. She is in no hurry to get home. Nor is she too absorbed in her reading to notice everyone who passes, though she doesn't care to greet them all. She doesn't need to look out for her bus. Caesar will stop for her and open the front passenger door so that she can sit next to him rather than in the back.

Caesar is handsome, large and rising forty. In his younger days he was an ardent Rasta man until the sect was outlawed and his family commitments forced him to find some means of earning a living which was more reliable and less dangerous than the illicit sale of ganja. Though the form of his life has become entirely conventional, Ophelia admires him for preserving, outwardly at least, the symbols of his independence. He still sports dreadlocks and a crocheted beret, necklaces and bracelets and has cut himself off from the world in a drugged haze.

Even so, he notices Ophelia on the corner and slams on the brakes. Ophelia climbs in, and the bus proceeds to the legitimate stop some ten yards further on. Any lack of enthusiasm in Caesar's touting for business is more than made up for by his bus boy, who swings back the minibus door and is on the pavement in one easy movement scooping up bags and parcels, whose owners are forced to follow.

Ophelia enjoys the journeys. She likes to talk to Caesar and knows from the expressions that float across his face that he is hearing and yet not hearing her.

Today she opens her magazine at the horoscopes. 'It say', she reads, 'that this evening there is romance in the air. What you think that means? This evening I ain't planning nothing. I go home, do my hair, take a bath, eat my tea and go to bed. Where is romance?'

Caesar pulls up at the next stop. Ophelia quietly locks the door next to her. She doesn't wish to be crushed.

'You having romance in your life, Caesar?'

Caesar smiles a mysterious dreamy smile.

'You lucky lucky, man,' Ophelia sighs. 'Where I find romance this evening, eh? For me, it have only one romance, to get right 'way from this bloody island.'

She looks at Caesar and can tell from his expression that he is already far away.

As they drive into Sugar Bay, Caesar hits one of the chickens picking in the dust. The hen bowls over and over in a blur of feathers.

'Stop, man,' says Ophelia. She opens the side window and leans out. The chicken staggers to its feet, runs round and round in circles then regains its sense of direction and bolts into the scrub. 'You lucky that time, Caesar,' she says. 'I getting out here. I go visit my friend.' She opens the door and jumps down. 'See you morning,' she says as she turns to pick up her bag. 'Take care.' Caesar indicates he has heard by lifting one finger off the steering wheel then letting it fall again.

Ophelia ignores the voice of her stepfather Henzel inviting her into his shop.

'You wanting shoes today, Phelie?'

She wouldn't go into his shop if he paid her.

'I go make for you,' he calls after her.

His shop is dark and dirty, his shoes heavy and old-fashioned, and she doesn't want to feel beholden to him in any way.

'I go make for you shoes that last ten, twenty years,' he shouts.

Ophelia is not interested. In ten or twenty years she might be dead.

She skips down the steps of the house next door. 'Sadie,' she calls. 'You there?' There is no answer. Ophelia follows the sound of the sewing machine into the back room where Sadie sits with her back to the door by an open window dazzling with the blue of the sea beyond. Ophelia goes right in and puts her hand on Sadie's shoulder.

'Ophelia,' she shrieks. 'Oh my God, you frighten me. I didn't hear nothing with this machine going.'

'What you making, man?'

'A dress for Miss Charleston up at Bournemouth.'

'It old fashion like hell, man. Is cotton!'

'She done old, Phelie. That's what she use to.'

Sadie gets up from her chair and stretches her arms above her head. 'My shoulders aching, man.'

'You got any new patterns?'

'Sure. My sister send some last week.' She indicates a pile of battered magazines on a chair. 'You want some?'

Ophelia nods. 'Meh dress too old, man.'

'It still looking good on you.'

'I want something sharp, Sadie.'

Sadie nods. 'You take the book, Phelie, but right now I done busy.'

Ophelia tucks the book under her arm and leaves.

Back home, Ophelia doesn't open the magazine right away. She hangs her dress on the rail behind the curtain, then stands in front of the mirror and puts in the curlers which will remain until she goes to work the next day. Now she sweeps the wood-patterned lino and shakes out her white rug; she dusts the bedhead, the shelves, and the two ornaments sent by Aunty Celia from Birmingham England: a rabbit tucked up in bed and a little white boy and girl kissing. Next, she ties a scarf around her curlers, takes off her underwear, wraps herself in a towel and heads for the yard where she kicks a few hens out of the way and yells, 'Mammy, where the bucket?'

The bucket is by the back door full of dirty clothes. She tips them out, carries it back to the tap, rinses it out and fills it with clean water.

Ophelia hangs her towel on a nail in the trunk of the breadfruit tree, lifts the bucket and tips it over herself. Then she rubs the hard green coconut oil tablet over her body. After she has rinsed herself and wrapped the towel round her like a sarong she catches sight of a man at the window of the house next door.

'Hey, Benson,' she shouts, 'you ain't have nothing better to do with your eyes than watch me bathe? Why you don't wash yourself, you dirty 'nough.'

The face vanishes below the level of the sill. Ophelia, refreshed and smelling of coconut, returns to her room. She slips her feet into high-heeled white towelling mules and flops on to the bed.

The magazine Sadie has given her is a mail-order catalogue five years old, dog-eared, and called *La Femme*

Fatale. All that matters is that it was bought in Paris, a guarantee of being genuinely chic. Ophelia spends the hour until dark thumbing through the pictures. By doing a simple calculation Ophelia works out that by asking Sadie to copy this or that design she not only makes a huge saving on the price of imported clothes, but even undercuts the price she would have to pay for them in France.

Ophelia's fancy settles on a somewhat oriental design with a tight skirt, slit up the back to above knee level, and a demure high collar. Sadie runs it up in a brilliant turquoise imitation silk, with tiny fluorescent gold butter-flies. It proves an invaluable investment. It is on the first occasion that Ophelia wears this dress, that she stops at a certain mango stall on her way home and the promise of romance in her horoscope is belatedly fulfilled.

The dress, the time of day, the angle of the sunlight could have been responsible for the event which saves Ophelia from making grass mats for the rest of her life. But what was a girl of Ophelia's intelligence doing at the factory in the first place, when the rest of her friends had their sights set firmly on higher things in the shape of certificates and qualifications?

When Betty came up on deck, she realized how far offshore the ship was anchored.

'We're to go all the way in that, Harry?' She pointed to the lighter bobbing up and down on the water.

'It's because of the reef, honey.'

Betty looked at the rocks, like teeth breaking the surface. 'Well, if you're sure it's safe. I'm glad I can swim though.' She realized as soon as she had said it that she shouldn't have. She looked at Harry to see if he knew that she knew.

'If it were me,' said Harry, 'I'd get a stick of dynamite and blow the whole goddamn thing up.'

'But the reef's so beautiful, Harry,' Betty said as they

sped through coral outcrops as spiky as a shark's jaws. 'Look at those colours.'

'Can't see a goddamn thing.'

'Come further forward.'

'I'll just stick, thanks.' It was too hot to move.

Betty leaned over the edge and dangled her fingers in the water.

'Look out for barracudas, Bet,' called Harry.

Betty snatched her hand in, and concentrated on the fine Dutch architecture of the old buildings surrounding the jetty.

'Jesus,' Harry interrupted her thoughts, 'that rusty old can doesn't even look as if it will float.'

Betty turned away from the gabled roofs of the old town and looked in the direction Harry was pointing. A huge old cargo ship was moored at the commercial docks and a crane was loading containers from the dockside into the hold.

'It makes me dizzy just to watch,' said Betty, gripping the railing of the ship's lighter. 'Just imagine being spun around like that.'

Harry laughed. 'Bet, you sure get some funny ideas. People generally go on passenger liners. Only things go into cargo ships.'

The crate revolved slowly at first, then faster and faster. When it was fully wound up, it began to unwind. At the end came the sickening lurch and violent reverse motion that Betty remembered so well from her swinging days. At last it hung still and square in the bright sunlight.

'Why, Harry,' Betty clutched her husband's arm, 'just look at the name on that crate.'

Harry, reluctant to wear glasses during his leisure hours, raised his binoculars. He smiled smugly.

'Didn't I tell you that we had interests all over the Caribbean?'

'I thought you were joking, Harry.' Betty stared at the

136

container, at the letters printed large on the side for everyone to see. MIDWESTERN ELECTRICALS. She nudged Lou who was sitting next to her. 'Look,' she said. 'That's Harry's company.'

Lou told Sam. Sam told his neighbour.

The news spread like wildfire.

'That's Harry's company.'

'Harry who?'

'That Harry. In the sunhat.'

'With the binoculars.'

'Harry Stillman.'

'That Harry?'

The other passengers looked with new respect, not at the dull brown crates being loaded, but at Harry who turned a terrible shade of puce beneath his white sunhat.

To say 'Harry's company' could be interpreted in several ways, and if Betty realized it was open to misinterpretation, she certainly wasn't going to put anyone right. Nor was Harry.

When he is not on a cruise, and this is Harry's first cruise in his fifty-six years of almost living, Harry's day runs much as follows. Gets up early. Fixes on his smile as he fixes his teeth. For a door to door salesman this is part of the act. He smiles as he goes into the kitchen for his coffee and bacon and eggs. He smiles at Betty throughout their wordless sojourn at the breakfast bar. Slamming the front door behind him is the last thing that is needed to ensure the ghastly inflexibility of the lower part of his face. Armed only with his smile, Harry steps out to face the world.

The worse Harry's day, the harder he smiles. He was told to smile when he first joined Midwestern Electricals on leaving school. He has been obediently smiling ever since, all through the steady and almost imperceptibly downward trend of his career. He sometimes wonders why life has treated him so unfairly when his performance has been so flawless. Perhaps if he'd got these new teeth earlier on, so much more distinguished than the genuine article, which had become higgledy piggledy and nicotine stained. If only Betty had told him sooner, she was a woman, she ought to have noticed . . .

Betty had thought that nothing could be worse than Harry's own teeth. She was wrong. The sight of the brilliant white set grinning at her every night from the bathroom shelf (Harry, so proud of them he didn't bother about the box, said seeing them there gave him a boost for the next day) was so hideous that if she didn't manage to get into the bathroom before him, she found herself cleaning her own teeth (thanking God that she still had her own roots, fillings and crowns) with her eyes shut.

Now, Harry feels good enough to be a film star. He grips the ship's rail and drives through an imaginary salesman's utopia in a Buick convertible. Past trim new houses with lace curtains, brass doorknockers, double garages and television aerials. He selects one at random, stubs out his cigar, marches smartly up the garden path and raps on the door.

Harry smiles at the pine front door, at the exact spot where a face will appear. The door swings open. Jeez but this dame is tall. Harry stares at the hollow at the base of the most flawless throat he has ever seen. Gaze swivels upwards, meets cool grey eyes. Blonde hair. Oh God. A Swede.

'Yes?'

Harry produces credentials. Finds himself indoors, seated on a black leather settee in front of a glass coffee table through which he is uncomfortably aware of his dusty shoes. While the lady makes coffee, Harry polishes up his toe caps on the bright green carpet. He realizes as she returns with the tray of coffee, apfel strudel and cream, that she has nothing on under her housecoat. Asks whether she has a toaster and his palms begin to sweat.

Hang on, Harry. How do you know she has nothing on under her housecoat?

Harry laughs till his new teeth rattle like tin cans in a back alley.

'You all right, Harry?' asked Betty.

'Sure, honey. Just look at those boys.'

Small boys swarmed up the anchor chain on to the prow of the cargo ship. They leapt down into the water, then up they came fast as ants up a grass stalk to dive again and again.

Harry, quickly bored by the proceedings, took out a map of the island.

Harry and Betty, Sam and Lou, had decided – or rather Harry and Sam had decided – that although they were landing in the Dutch sector, they would leave exploring this until last, as it seemed to offer the greatest possibilities in the way of shopping and entertainment.

'Let's get the tourist bit out of the way, eh?' said Harry. He rushed off up the quay towards the hire cars, leaving Betty piqued that he hadn't noticed her first perfect landing. She followed more slowly, having to negotiate the slatted pier in her heeled sandals. By the time she caught up with Harry everything was settled.

'Are you sure it wouldn't be more sensible to hire a car with a driver?' Betty asked.

'Nonsense.' Harry climbed into the driver's seat.

Sam got in next to him. Betty and Lou got in the back.

'But we haven't even got a map.'

'Jesus, Bet, will you stop worrying! Look up Friedman.'

Betty did. Friedman's idea of a map was a thumbnail

sketch of the island which showed one coastal road drawn round the edge.

'Uh, it doesn't mark any turn-offs,' she said.

'That's because there aren't any.' Harry turned the key in the ignition.

'How d'you know that, Harry?'

'I just know, that's all.'

'What if we get lost?' It didn't look the sort of desert island where Betty fancied being stranded.

'How can we get lost, Betty?' interrupted Sam. 'The island's so small that if we keep the sea on our left we'll end up where we started.'

'You've hit the nail on the goddamn head,' shouted Harry as they roared away.

ST JEAN. BIENVENU A LA PARTIE FRANCAISE, read the sign. TENEZ LA DROITE, said another. Cars coming from the Dutch sector were changing over to the right hand side of the road while those coming in the other direction reversed the procedure. The overall effect was that of an eightsome reel.

'Harry, you remember watching the Royal Tournament at Earl's Court on Channel 23 last year?' Betty leaned forward and spoke directly into Harry's ear. 'The bit where they all cross over . . . ?'

'I'm trying to concentrate,' said Harry. 'Anyway, that was with horses, not goddamn cars. They don't go as fast.'

'They can be just as dangerous.' Betty could remember horses. She had once, and only once, been for a riding lesson as a child.

'Now,' said Sam.

Harry pushed down the accelerator hard, then changed his mind and hit the brake. There was a scream of tyres behind, and a black man with a beret leaned out of a small lemon Citroën and swore in perfect French.

140

'You hear that?' asked Betty.

'Betty, I am trying to concentrate.'

Another car flashed across their bows. Harry jammed down his foot and shot into the space in front of him.

'Isn't this some place!' laughed Lou.

'How's your French, Sam?' asked Betty.

'Can't say I've had much practice since I left school.'

Betty was enraptured. Everything about the countryside proclaimed itself to be French, from the advertisements for Pernod to the men on bicycles with black berets on their even blacker heads, the stink of the sewerage carts and the neat little roadside shops with their signs BOULANG-ERIE and PATISSERIE.

There were even rows of poplars along the verges and Betty would not have been the least bit surprised to meet Renoir in a smock, carrying his easel.

They came up behind an ox cart – so picturesque with its double-yoked oxen pulling steadily along the middle of the road. Harry hooted and pulled over to the left. The cart moved over too. The driver looked back and grinned.

Harry pressed the horn long and loud, and pulled up to within centimetres of the tailboard.

The driver cracked his whip and the oxen lumbered into a canter.

Harry pulled further over, off the tarmac, and drew level.

Betty saw the driver jab the sharp end of the stick into the anus of the lead oxen. She shuddered. She just could not bear cruelty to animals.

'Harry,' she said, 'I think you should tell him not to do that.'

The oxen broke into a gallop.

Harry looked as excited as the driver on the ox cart who was now standing up, flapping the reins and hollering. Then Betty saw another vehicle coming towards them.

'Look out, Harry,' she called.

His foot was flat on the floor and the engine roared. With a final stomach-heaving kerflump he swung the wheel hard right and the car careered back on to the tarmac in front of the cart. He stopped abruptly. Got out.

Betty could hear the terrible sound as the oxen gasped for breath. She saw their rib cages pumping in and out, a dark streaky brown like leather bellows.

'I could report you for driving like that,' said Harry.

The driver grinned. 'Pa connay.'

'Don't fuck me about,' said Harry.

Betty leaned out of the window. 'Tell him those oxen need a drink.' But Harry, realizing the driver was about to try and overtake, leapt back into the driving seat and was away.

'God almighty, I hope he never gets a car,' he said.

The remaining few minutes into town were comparatively uneventful. BIENVENU A PARIS MATCH read the signs. Lou and Betty were enchanted. There were flowers everywhere, bougainvillaea purple, white and pink rampaged over every house, plumbago and jacarandas were in bloom. And then suddenly they were at the waterfront, where Harry parked the car and they strolled down a slatted sidewalk overhanging the brilliant blue of the Caribbean. In a small marina yachts rode at anchor and blonde girls lay topless, sunning themselves beside hairy-chested men burnt almost black by the tropical sun.

Harry proceeded crabwise along the sidewalk, eyes bulging. Serve him right, thought Betty, if he toppled in. She wouldn't lift a finger to save him. Harry's shirt was wet, clinging to his back, and his neck was chilli pepper red.

'You got your hat with you?' Betty asked.

Harry ignored her. He started to whistle, strolling along with his hands in his pockets ready to wink if anyone should catch his eye. The sea-side activity was, thought Betty, just like the scenes of Paris she had seen on television

– the artists, the displays of painting, the little groups of bearded intellectuals, only this was so much more beautiful. The Caribbean simply screamed its prettiness at you.

'Let's stop here,' she said, indicating a café on her right. *Café de Paris*, it said, in such lovely squiggly letters.

'Okay,' said Lou.

The men shrugged and followed them into a small courtyard banked with flowers and palms. The tables and chairs were of white wrought ironwork. On the chairs were pink cushions. Everything was pink and white, the striped awnings, the checked tablecloths, the table napkins, even the roses in the small glass vase in the centre of each table.

Betty sat down with her back to the Caribbean. After all she could see the sea when she went outside. Just for now she wanted to feel herself in Europe.

'You think we'll get to Paris some day, Harry?' she asked.

'Sure, honey, sure,' he replied, adding between his teeth to Sam, man to man, 'when we've finished paying for this one.'

Betty leaned back and closed her eyes. There was a slight off-sea breeze which jingled the rigging of the yachts and the temperature in the courtyard was pleasant. From the back of the café came the sound of an accordion. A lump came into Betty's throat. It was all too perfect.

'Que voulez-vous, madame?'

Betty jumped. Opened her eyes. Saw only a black waitress next to her and decided she had been dreaming.

'Que voulez-vous, madame?' came the voice again. Such a perfect accent. So cultured.

Betty looked around her.

'Madame veut quelque chose?'

Betty was dumbfounded. That dark dark woman speaking such perfect French?'

'D'you speak any English?' asked Harry.

The woman shrugged.

Harry and Sam peered at the menu.

'What d'you want, girls? Seems to be coffee. What about some croissants and gateaux, we know what those are, eh?'

The croissant was heavenly. It melted on Betty's tongue leaving a slight salty aftertaste which she washed away with coffee.

'C'est le café du pays,' the waitress assured them.

Betty smiled and nodded.

'How the heck', said Harry, 'do they expect to get more tourists if they can't even speak the lingo?'

'It's very romantic,' said Betty.

'Huh,' snorted Harry. 'Like that canned music . . .'

'Canned?' Betty couldn't believe it.

'. . . and the plastic roses,' said Harry triumphantly.

'Oh Harry,' she laughed, 'surely not.' She picked up the vase and found that he was right. She twisted round in her chair suspicious now of everything. The flowers in the flower bed were plastic. And the palm trees.

'I don't understand,' said Betty.

'It's the same in Los Angeles,' said Harry. 'And it didn't worry you when you came in.'

'But I know now, and it's not the same thing at all.'

'Sometimes I just can't understand you, Betty. Think of the trouble it saves. No gardeners. Flowers all the year round . . .'

Betty drank the rest of her coffee quickly. 'I'll wait outside,' she said.

Betty sat, oh so blissfully alone, on the sea wall and felt the sun beat down on her closed eyes and upturned face. That at least was real. When she opened her eyes, she saw all the beautiful people strolling past, bronzed limbs, gold bracelets, little fingers linked, and – she could have sworn – not a single one of them over thirty. Or thirty-five. They

144

were all gloriously brown, confident and relaxed. She sat there red in the face but basically white, clutching her purse as if her life depended on it.

Listening with closed eyes to the sounds all around her, she realized how dreadfully foreign this French sector was. She hadn't heard a word of English since she arrived. She felt paralysed at the thought of not being able to make herself understood. What if Harry were to suffer a stroke, or if the car had crashed during that race with the ox cart?

The sun was warm and she gradually relaxed. After a while she even felt brave enough to go a hundred yards along the sidewalk past the dusty chalk drawings of naked black women in crude imitation of Gauguin.

Leaving the sea, she turned into a shopping arcade where she saw windows such as she had never seen before – fantasies of colour and shape that awakened her long dead professional eye. If only at the age of twenty she had known of the infinite possibilities of her art, she would never have married Harry. If only she had had the courage to leave her home town and travel a bit, perhaps not as far as Paris, but to New York or Washington, anything that would have opened her eyes to the fact that there was more to window-dressing than twin sets on plaster busts.

She would have liked to buy everything, not to wear but to inject the drab sterility of her house with life-giving splashes of colour. However, since there was no way she'd ever get anything like that past Harry's eagle eye, she contented herself with a few postcards of Caribbean sunsets on indeterminate islands. It was only after she had selected her cards and the assistant obligingly wrote down the amount owed, that Betty realized she had no francs on her. Acting out in pantomime gestures that she would be back in five minutes, Betty hurried towards the seafront, running again the gauntlet of the shop windows.

But as she stepped out on to the sidewalk she stopped

dead. In front of her was that eyesore of a cargo boat cruising past the harbour mouth beyond the acres of pastel-coloured sails and the brilliantly painted sea. Ten thousand of Harry's cigars could not have produced the muck that gushed out of that rust-coloured funnel.

Outraged, she turned left and hurried back to the Café de Paris to find Harry.

Harry was on his second gateau. 'What you wasting money on now, Bet?' he exclaimed, rolling his eyes at Sam, playing the long-suffering husband.

'Postcards, Harry, that's all.'

'Mind if I join you, Betty?' Lou got up and the two ladies went off together.

'Women,' said Harry. 'Never happy unless they're spending.' He patted his stomach. 'Could do with some more coffee,' he said and burped loudly.

Sam, tall and lean as Gary Cooper at sixty, ordered a Perrier.

'We earn it, they spend it,' said Harry. He drank his coffee black and without sugar as part of his attempt to lose weight. Then he lit a cigar. 'To be honest with you, Sam, I didn't like to say it to Bet, but you know how it is, we've about as much chance of getting a trip to Paris as a slow boat to China, know what I mean?'

Sam nodded. Took another sip of water, swilled it around his mouth, then swallowed it. He was watching the waitress.

'Nice piece of tail,' said Harry. He leaned back and exhaled a cloud of smoke. 'Tell you the truth, Sam, I'm in a spot of bother myself. Well, the whole holiday was booked up and paid for so it seemed a shame to worry Betty, but you know, well, I just ain't got me a job to go back to.'

'That's too bad.' Sam spoke as if Harry had just lost a game of squash.

'How's the law?' Harry was anxious to pursue any opening.

'Can't complain. It's a steady line of business.'

Harry's eyes narrowed. There wasn't much change to be got out of Sam. He knew the type. They'd let the rest of the world go hang.

Sam tossed back his head and swallowed up the rest of his water like a dehydrated sponge. 'Let's go find the girls, eh?' Sam stood up real slow. He didn't appear to notice the bill.

Harry, wishing that the next four days would last for ever, took a handful of francs from his back trouser pocket and plonked them on the table.

The heat outside almost knocked him sideways. Fortunately the girls were easy to find. Betty had emptied her whole purseful of coins on to the counter, and was separating the guilders from the francs and the pesos, and the Caribbean from the US dollars. Lou was trying to help, blaming her awkwardness on having forgotten her reading glasses.

'Aren't these cute?' Betty held up a flower-shaped Caribbean fifty cents when Harry loomed out of nowhere.

'You leaving that money there for any Tom Dick or Harry to help himself?' He elbowed her out of the way. 'Well, here's the Harry.'

Let us return for a moment to the question of why a girl of Ophelia's ability should leave school without any qualifications whatsoever, only two years into her secondary education. It is the day on which her gym slip bulges over the top of the headmistress's desk, and on top of it, Ophelia, with her hair in green ribboned plaits, rests her Latin primer.

Ophelia's mother Portia is wedged between the plain arms of an upright wooden chair facing the Reverend

Mother. Her enormous stomach rests on her lap, on which she can feel the drumming of four tiny feet. She twists a handkerchief nervously between her fingers and stares sullenly.

'Mrs Lapierre,' begins the nun, 'what can I say? Indeed, what need is there for me to say anything?'

Ophelia rests her thighs against the desk edge and her stomach obtrudes even more into the Reverend Mother's line of vision. 'I have put off making a decision as long as possible in the hope that you would see fit to make alternative arrangements and avoid this very unpleasant interview.'

Portia stares blankly.

'Mrs Lapierre, haven't you even noticed your daughter's condition?'

There is still no response.

The nun coughs discreetly into her enormous sleeve. 'Mrs Lapierre, what arrangements have you made?'

'What you talkin 'bout?' asks Portia.

'Your daughter's pregnancy. Ophelia is going to have a baby.'

'Me too.'

'I can see that, Mrs Lapierre, but it is Ophelia with whom I am concerned. She cannot remain in this school a moment longer.'

'Oh, my God.' Portia blows her nose loudly. 'Ophelia, what you do, eh? Didn't I bring you up right? Didn't I do everything for you?' Portia's voice shoots up an octave and rises to a rapid crescendo. 'Why you shame me, eh, chil'?' Tears begin to pour down Portia's abundant cheeks. She rocks backwards and forwards and the small chair creaks with every movement. 'Sweet Jesus, ain't I always telling her to be a good girl? Ain't I always sending her to church on a Sunday? Oh my God.' Portia tears her hair and wails.

Ophelia stares at the photograph behind Reverend

148

Mother's head. It shows the entire community of ten nuns seated in the rose garden to the rear of the building. She loves every one of them.

'We had such hopes for you, Ophelia, you are a scholarship girl. And what will those dear Misses Simpson say, after paying your expenses for two years? Have you no idea how you are letting us all down?'

Ophelia hangs her head and lowers her eyes.

'But, Ophelia, do you know who you are letting down worst of all?'

'No, Reverend Mother.' Ophelia bobs a little curtsey.

'Yourself, Ophelia. You have allowed a moment of sin and weakness to rob you of your future.'

At this point, Ophelia breaks down. Her Latin primer is forgotten. She hurls herself on her knees with her face buried in her mother's lap and howls.

Ophelia's mother prays to Jesus and pushes Ophelia away as if she were the devil himself. She plays the role of shattered parent so convincingly that anyone ignorant of island conventions might be forgiven at this point for not divining that Portia herself has borne six children to four or more different fathers. The headmistress simply waits for the storm of Portia's emotions to pass before ushering mother and daughter out of her office and briefly wishing Ophelia good luck in the future.

Portia waddles across the school yard, followed by her daughter, who has by this time recovered sufficiently to wave to her friends watching from the classroom windows.

Five minutes later they sit side by side on the bus, chatting as if nothing at all was amiss, although Portia does consider that Ophelia could have made more of her life given the advantage of a convent education.

It is at Boules that Portia and Ophelia get off the bus, Portia having decided that confession and honesty are the best tactics. They cross the green, Portia belligerently to the fore, Ophelia trailing some way behind, and soon arrive at the house on the other side.

Portia and Ophelia sit on the horsehair settee while Portia breaks the terrible news.

'Today I go see the headmistress and she saying Ophelia must leave the school.'

'Ophelia must leave school? How old is Ophelia that she must leave school she is not old enough to leave school she should still go to school why should she leave school?'

'She making a baby.'

'She is making a baby?' asks the blind Miss Simpson into the silence. 'How is she making a baby when she is only a child? Sisters tell me is it true that she is making a baby and why have you not noticed before?'

'We did not notice sister we are sorry we did not notice now we can see that she is making a baby but before we did not notice.'

'Well!' The eldest Miss Simpson bangs once very loudly on the floor with her white stick. 'Come over here,' she says to Ophelia.

Ophelia walks over to the eldest Miss Simpson who feels her way over to her stomach.

The other Misses Simpson hold their breath.

'Sisters,' says the eldest Miss Simpson, 'it is true. I feel the baby moving in the stomach and now what are we going to do for Eugenia's granddaughter what can we do, we must pray yes that is what we must do, we must pray.'

Portia has secretly hoped for some far more concrete help, but knows that with the Misses Simpson anything practical can be a very long time in coming.

The first market day after Ophelia's expulsion brings an unexpected visit by Aunty Gladys. Ophelia is overjoyed to see her, but Portia less so. The two women sit at opposite

150

ends of the sofa and avoid looking directly at each other. Ophelia finds it hard to believe that they are sisters. Portia is obviously her mother's child in a way that Gladys is not. Portia was born some years after her brothers and sisters. Eugenia was, at the time of Portia's birth, such a size that no one other than herself anticipated the happy event, least of all the father. He was one Constantine Lapierre, who found that his belated offer of marriage to the woman he found one day suckling his child, was totally scorned. He was an attractive man, given half-heartedly to fishing and whole-heartedly to rum and dominoes. Though Ophelia's grandmother had briefly succumbed to the charms of the man, and a few idyllic moments of rum and love among the whispering palms, she had kept her head. She would have defended her dark little daughter with her dying breath, but saw no reason why she should support the father as well. She had brought up her four children singlehanded and saw no reason to disrupt her way of life now that a fifth had arrived.

Gladys was, by contrast, the living example of Eugenia having followed her own mother's advice to 'put a little cream in the coffee'. By the time Portia was conceived, Eugenia gave more attention to physique and charm than colour, hence Portia emerged to the comment from the midwife, 'Eh, eh, but she black like a telephone.'

'How the boys, Gladys?' asks Portia, stiff with formality.

'They very well thank you, Portia.'

'And the garden?'

Aunty Gladys becomes more animated. 'Everything growing big like this. The bananas high so and flowering now.'

'Everything growing,' says Portia morosely.

'You remember, Phelie, those little seeds we done plant, what you call them?'

'And what 'bout those little seeds your boy done plant in my daughter?'

Aunty Gladys's hands cease their fluttering and die in her lap. 'For true, Phelie?'

Phelie hangs her head.

Gladys turns to face Portia. 'I done ask the boys already who did this wicked thing, and they don' answer. Nobody saying no, nobody saying yes. What I go do now?'

'And what about me? You think I want to spend all my life looking after children?' Portia sits massive and sweating in an old nylon slip yellowing with age.

'One baby, what difference it make, eh?' Gladys moves closer to her sister, puts an arm about her shoulders. 'You making a baby too.'

'If I ain't have no man how I go feed the children?' Portia breathes faster. 'And if I have a man I does make babies.' Portia shrugs off Gladys's arm. 'But look what your boys do. Why they so bad they make a baby with my child?'

'Is Phelia too, Portia. Is she to blame too.'

'Why you keep her up there if you don' look after her, eh?'

'I does mind Phelie, but I don' spy every minute of the day asking Phelie what she doing now.'

Portia's reply is to lash out with one elbow and catch her sister on the nose. Blood spurts out in a great jet that trickles slowly down the front of Aunty Gladys's dusty dress.

'What you doing, Portia, you killing aunty.' Ophelia rushes over to her aunt who sits pinching her nose.

'Is true, Phelie,' she says wearily. 'Them is lazy idle boys, but they don' mean bad. They don' want to make trouble for you.'

* * *

'What you have?' asks the woman in the next bed.

'A girl,' replies Ophelia. 'What you born?'

'A boy.' The woman sighs.

An orderly pushes in a large trolley heaped with what looks like a pile of dirty linen, except that the noise and ripplings indicate that it must be animate.

'Eh, eh,' sighs Ophelia's neighbour. 'Babies is too troublesome.'

'Shoulda thought 'bout that nine months ago, lady,' says the orderly. He plonks a white bundle in Ophelia's arms then plonks his own white bottom on the bed next to her. 'He hungry,' he says, pointing to the baby.

'Is a little girl. Estelle.'

'You come with me, we go make a nice boy together, eh?'

Ophelia puts the baby to her breast and groans as the muscles of her cervix contract sharply.

'He is a bad man,' confides her neighbour. 'Already three nurses making baby for him. One nurse, she catching 'nother nurse's baby on the delivery table and she look like she born her own any minute. And he done carrying on in the corridor with another nurse, right there outside of the door.'

Ophelia's eyes grow wide with astonishment.

'He ain't have no shame at all.'

'Ain't nothing,' calls a voice from further up the ward. 'My aunty she come home from the TB ward and make a baby.'

'Like that man working in the TB ward too?' asks Ophelia.

'No, man. Aunty she done make a baby with a patient from the male ward. They meet in the corridor and have a little smoke together, then she go in the ladies' toilet and he follow she and them nurses they almost had to break down the door.'

Aunty Gladys comes in to visit Ophelia with the cousins in tow. She carries an enormous bunch of flowers from her garden which she swops for a cuddle with Estelle.

The cousins, one by one, kiss Ophelia on the cheek then stand around the bed looking awkward. Ophelia is radiant and quite aware of the envious glances of the other ladies in the ward.

'Portia done visit you?' asks Gladys.

'Nah. She too busy with the wedding.' Ophelia takes out a comb and mirror and does her hair. 'Why you all didn't tell me you coming?' she pouts, but she looks quite delightful having already carefully prepared herself before visiting hours, just in case.

'Phelie,' says Gladys, 'why you don' marry one of these?' She holds out her arm to include all her seven sons. 'Which one you want?'

'Oh Aunty Gladys, how I could choose?' giggles Ophelia. 'I want to marry all of them.'

Aunty Gladys, who had given up trying to find out which of her sons had fathered Ophelia's child, had hoped to make the forthcoming nuptials a double affair.

For while Ophelia lies on her hospital bed, Portia is literally sweating over the preparations for her own wedding. Though she sends a message begging Ophelia to come home and help, Ophelia sends a reply saying that the doctors have told her she must spend at least five days in the hospital. Portia, with her own confinement imminent and her ankles swollen with the heat, mutters about life being too easy for young people nowadays.

In fact, Gladys is doing most of the catering. She will slaughter a pig in honour of the great day. But Portia wants the house to shine as never before, so she scolds and slaps the children and eventually drives them out to sit as good as gold in her future husband's shop. Two of them are after all his, and if he was going to admit responsibility for them shortly, she reasons that he might as well start getting used to it now.

Portia goes to Sadie's for the final fitting and what she sees takes her breath away. The enormous folds of white more than fill the mirror and Portia feels that the dress is the ultimate accolade of her life. Tomorrow she will become a respectable married woman, wearing for the first time (legitimately) the gold ring on the fourth finger of her left hand. And having achieved such a solid state of respectability, Portia decides without hesitation that when the twins are born, she can safely have herself sterilized. She will have done her duty by providing Henzel with four of his own children, not to mention four of somebody else's.

The great day dawns with Portia resplendent in white nylon through which her black skin gleams. Oily with excitement and flanked by her six children, she marches with firm and heavy tread up the aisle.

At the altar stands Henzel, shrunken inside a large black suit and a shirt whose collar Portia has starched unmercifully in honour of the occasion.

With the twins concealed under the copious folds of her bridal gown, Portia takes Henzel for better or for worse, knowing the latter will never come to pass, since even if the business fails, he can still keep the family in footwear.

But it is Ophelia who really steals the show. She looks magnificent in the glowing pink silk suit which once belonged to Aunty Celia, but which now fits her to perfection. She wears a pink hat to match, with a black net falling mysteriously over the upper part of her face and a little pink roll of material on top like a chimney. She wears no blouse under the shimmering jacket, but has fastened a red velvet rose in her cleavage, made more pronounced by the recent inflow – and outflow – of milk.

For Ophelia has after one week given up breastfeeding.

'She not want the titty no more,' she confides to Aunty Gladys as they suck their fingers over the cracked crab shells of the callalou at the reception. 'The titty not satisfying she no more.'

'What she go have then?'

'Cow and Gate. Is all she likes.'

'That go make good fat babies,' says Gladys.

'You know Jeanette?'

Gladys shakes her head.

'Her baby done have one and a half years and she so fat she can't walk.'

'That not good, chil',' says Gladys.

'You want a chicken leg?' Ophelia gets up and fetches the plate. On her return she bumps into one of the cousins, who is drinking rum straight from the bottle.

'Heh heh, Phelie, you looking good, girl,' he calls out and twirls her around.

Ophelia giggles and fights to get away, with the plate of chicken legs crushed between them. 'Hey watch out, you spoiling my suit,' she says sharply.

'Why you don' marry me today?' asks the cousin as he lets her go.

'I not marrying. Ever,' replies Ophelia. She returns with the chicken legs to Aunty Gladys.

Her aunt has, during her absence, fetched the baby Estelle from the bedroom. 'You have a bottle?' she asks.

Ophelia fetches one ready made from the fridge.

'It too too cold,' says Gladys, and stuffs it down the front of her new dress to warm it up a bit. 'You know, Phelie, that baby the selfsame colour as me. You see.'

She puts her arm next to the baby's. Ophelia laughs, and picks up a roll of fat from the top of the baby's leg. 'She fatter than you, aunty,' she says.

'What you going to do now, Phelie?' asks Aunty Gladys.

156

Ophelia shrugs. 'I don't know. Portia says I have to look after all the babies when hers done born.'

Portia's twins almost fall out of her vast body. The first is born on the hospital steps. The second, also a boy, arrives when Portia is on a trolley with her head in the delivery room and her feet still in the corridor. She calls them Harrison and Bentley, and signs up for sterilization and a ten-day stay in hospital.

Ten days of being a mother and housewife is enough to convince Ophelia that she must get out. On the Saturday that Portia is still in hospital, Aunty Gladys visits on her way home from market. At the end of the afternoon she leaves carrying her niece cum granddaughter while Ophelia sets out for the Misses Simpson.

The outcome is, that by the time Portia returns home, Ophelia has been relieved of her baby and has a job in the grass mat factory, while Portia is left to look after her own little twins.

Harry turned off the engine, got out and slammed the car door. He was parked right in the middle of the Plaza Mayor at the heart of the capital of Spanish San Juan.

The car was dust-covered after the incident with the ox cart, which gave it a pleasantly battered look.

For want of a sombrero, Harry pulled his towelling sun hat square across his eyes, and leaning nonchalantly against the car, lit a cigarette.

All round the square were low white-washed houses. It was very hot and very still. There was one man in the whole square, ostensibly asleep under the only tree. He was propped up against the trunk, wrapped in a blanket, his sombrero tilted forward to hide his face completely.

Otherwise, there was not a sign of life. Not a bird sang. A child's cry pierced the noonday quiet like gunfire and was instantly silenced. Harry turned slowly around, surveying each mean house in turn. He knew that behind every shutter in every window the dagos lurked, watching his every move. The only thing was to play it cool.

Harry strode slowly and deliberately to the centre of the Plaza. The watching eyes struck him like daggers. He threw down the butt and ground it into the dirt with his heel, then cleared his throat, swilled a small globule of phlegm around his palate and spat with deadly aim. Okay. So let them come. If they dared.

Nothing happened. The sun beat down as before and the dead weight of silence increased. He too could play the waiting game. He turned round slowly again, just to let them know they couldn't creep up on him. There was no green in Harry's eye.

What did attract his attention, now that he had made sure there was no imminent danger, was the cathedral. The biggest goddamn building in the place. It didn't just tower over the pathetic hovels, it dwarfed the whole island.

Harry moved with a careless swagger over to the cathedral steps, grunted as he set his right foot four steps up, leaned his elbow on his knee and his chin on his hand and gazed up at the stone work above the west door. One hundred saints were depicted there, he'd read that in Friedman, one for every island Columbus had discovered in the Caribbean. Of course Harry knew that some of the islands were little more than rocks sticking out of the sea, but he appreciated the man's efforts to get to a good round figure. He often did the same thing himself with his accounts.

Betty looked up at the statues, shading her eyes against the sun. She tried to count them in the same way that she counted the steps every time she went up a flight of stairs. She got to fifty-nine before her eyes ached with the glare off the golden stone. Fine statues though, one or two would look real good in the shrubbery. Her neighbour's garden was full of plastic statuary but Betty wanted the real thing. They were quite wasted up there so high, you couldn't see them properly whereas at ground level . . . Saint John himself would look just stunning peeping through a few fronds of myrtle with epaulettes of moss.

'Well, are we going in or aren't we?' asked Harry. If he had to be a tourist he liked to get on and get it over with. The heat was killing him. He took off his sunglasses and let them flop around his neck as he stepped inside.

Betty, Harry, Sam and Lou instinctively lowered their voices. Betty wondered what it was about churches that made people go like that, as if overwhelmed by the centuries of accumulated awe. None of the four was a regular churchgoer back home, but then nothing could have prepared them for Gothic Revival architecture at its most extravagant.

Betty fumbled through her wallet for a few pesos and dropped them into the collection box.

'Honey,' said Harry, 'there's probably a whole heap of urchins outside that will grab the lot as soon as your back's turned.'

Betty shrugged. 'It's locked and chained to the pillar, Harry.'

'You think that'd stop them?'

Betty tiptoed to avoid the clack of her heels on the stones, right to the very centre of the building beneath the huge span of the transept. She bathed in the delicate rose and purple of the stained glass windows to the south.

'Where's the bones?' Harry joined her, massive on the toes of his sneakers, shoulders hunched as if waiting for the starting gun.

Betty handed over the guidebook and turned her back on him. She held out her arm to see the patterns dance on

159

her skin. Had she been on her own, she might have raised her hands above her head and pirouetted like a fairy.

Harry, Sam and Lou were gathered round a massive iron frame which enclosed a tomb. Betty moved across to join them.

'He's going to have one helluva struggle at the Last Day,' remarked Harry.

They all stood peering through the bars. *Hic jacet Christophe Columb*. Betty loved old graves, but this one was disappointing. She liked effigies, scenes from the life of, that sort of thing. Still it was nice to be able to tell the Bernsteins and the Smiths that she'd visited the tomb of Christopher Columbus. Or one of them. Like King Arthur the poor man seemed to have been buried many times over.

Bones done, they all trooped outside, back into the red hot car, off to the next item on the agenda, Carib's Leap.

Carib's Leap was a spectacular cliff on the most northeasterly point of the island, where the Caribbean clashed with the Atlantic and seas ran high all the year round. The name originates from the legend that after resisting the Spaniards for nigh on a hundred years, the Caribs took their cue from the citizens of Masada and chose suicide rather than subjugation.

The cliffs have several times been renamed, and become in their time Spaniard's Leap, when the British took over the island in 1763, Englishman's Leap when the French defeated the English some twenty years later, and Protestant's Leap when it was recaptured by the Spanish the same year.

It is curious that one name never caught on, the name of Slaves' Leap. By all accounts, sixty thousand of the hundred thousand slaves imported to work on the cathedral were still alive on its completion thirteen years after the foundations were laid. Obviously so many could not at once be absorbed by the plantation system and it was not economic either to export or to feed unproductive labourers. In the year 1585, after the healthiest twenty thousand had been set aside for agricultural purposes, the remainder were driven over the edge of the cliffs on to the rocks below.

Betty felt queasy. Perhaps she shouldn't have read all that historical stuff, not while the car was moving, but if she didn't she never got the chance. Harry monopolized the guidebook on all other occasions.

Harry parked at the end of the track where a fingerpost leading off into the scrub was painted TO CARIB'S LEAP. As soon as he opened the door, about twenty urchins materialized from nowhere. They clutched at Harry's clothing asking for pesos, begging to act as guides or to look after the car.

'Aren't they just beautiful?' said Betty smiling at them with her purse tucked tightly under her arm. But she couldn't resist them. She opened her wallet. The children milled around her grating 'Gracias, Señora' in hoarse voices.

'You pay them now, Bet, we'll find the car stripped when we get back,' said Sam.

Betty hesitated, but she couldn't stop now they had seen the money. She was rewarded by huge white smiles, and a small hand thrust into each of hers to lead her towards the cliffs.

Afterwards she remembered nothing about the walk except the two glossy heads at about elbow height. The children chattered, pointing out this and that while Betty silently dreamt of taking them both away with her. She had once broached the subject of adoption with Harry, but he had said that he wasn't sharing his house with any dagos. Betty would have welcomed any baby to still the aching emptiness of her womb.

Harry was entranced by the landscape. The earth was grey and gritty. There was not a blade of grass. There were no shrubs or trees, only species of euphorbia and cactus and needle sharp rocks. Now Harry knew a thing or two about deserts. This was the sort of countryside that separated the men from the boys. The children spoilt it a bit. He'd have dealt with them easily enough if it hadn't been for Betty's foolishness with the money. The trouble with Betty was she always acted on impulse, she was a prey to her own emotions.

All he needed was the rest of the Gunfighter's Club with him. The fights they could have staged. He whizzed round, forefingers blazing. 'Stick 'em up.' Sam and Lou were a few paces behind, Sam with his arm round Lou's shoulders.

'Harry, you startled me.' Lou's chin was slack.

Even Harry could see that she was near to tears. 'You want the car keys? You could take a rest.'

But the last thing Lou wanted was to be left alone.

Harry rode on, his horse's hooves silent in the dust apart from the occasional clink of hoof on stone. He held the reins loose and his head high and swayed gently from side to side keeping time with the movement of the horse.

'Whoa-ho, old Beauty,' he murmured as he suddenly came to the cliff edge and looked down. 'Ain't that sump'n, Bet?' he whistled.

Betty hung back in spite of the children holding her hands and urging her closer. They skipped around barefoot, completely confident. Without looking down she felt the immensity of the drop and heard the wash wash of surf tinkle the fragments of coral bleached bone-white on the rocks below. The numbers that had perished there defied thought, and yet when she opened her eyes there was no horror, just the endless blue of the sunlit sea stretching towards a calm and distant horizon. Then she noticed the plume of black smoke.

'See that, Harry?' she called out.

Harry raised his binoculars. 'Probably that old crate we saw this morning.'

'It's terrible. All that filthy smoke.'

'What's one ship, Bet?'

But she knew that if there was one boat that she could see, there were millions more that she couldn't. The smoke gathered in mushroom clouds. Betty turned away.

When they got back to the car, Harry was surprised to find it unlocked. 'Godammit, I know I locked it,' he spluttered.

His bag was gone from the back window ledge.

'Lucky it was only your bathers,' said Betty.

Harry turned purple with rage. 'It's all because you encouraged them,' he said. 'They'd never have hung around if you hadn't.'

Betty rested her hands protectively on the two small heads. At least they couldn't be blamed.

'Harry dear, you've got more bathing trunks on the boat.' She bit her lip to stop herself adding 'and anyway you can't swim.'

Lou got into the car and away from the children as fast as she could. This surprised Betty. Didn't Lou have four children of her own? Not that she ever sent them postcards or anything. Betty would have been writing every day.

Harry hooted impatiently. Betty hugged the children briefly and got quickly into the car.

They drove back through the city.

'Real Madrid?' said Harry. 'I thought that was a football club.'

'Real means "royal",' said Lou.

Harry went very quiet. Betty wondered how Lou knew that about the name. She wished she could come out with little facts like that. Harry drove fast through the town although Betty would have liked to linger and watch the old people in black, the handsome youths kicking tin cans around in front of the cathedral and the small white donkeys with laden panniers but she could see the veins standing out on Harry's bull neck, so she sat back and said nothing.

Early afternoon in the Caribbean. Not a palm leaf stirs along all those golden miles of sand. The waves slop listlessly on to the beaches of Soufrière alternately nudging and sucking at dead cats and broken bottles, scarcely disturbing the flies.

Jancis, in the shadow of the old slave market, ate a toasted saltfish bun. She ate, not because she was hungry but out of habit. Every day at about this time Ophelia used to tap with her ruler on the wall dividing their offices and call out, 'Hey, Jancis, you hungry?', at which Jancis would go out into the scorching sun and bring back toasted buns and iced Coke for lunch.

Today Jancis did not feel like eating in the office on her own. So she sat on the sea wall, and in her mind composed letters to Ophelia and to Thomas to inform them of the decision she had taken to look after the boys. It would be hard work, but she prayed to God to give her strength and already imagined Nelson and Napoleon, clean and scrubbed, trotting cheerfully into Sunday school. If she had lost her own soul, she could at least save theirs.

Huntingdon's lunchtime routine of sharing Ophelia's sandwich and Coke in return for a cigarette, had been no less disturbed. But he did not mope around on his own. Today he was at the airport, meeting Gloria off the plane from Paris. He could pick her out as soon as the passengers started filing down the steps, in her elegant two-piece and dark glasses. By contrast, Ophelia was simply a cheap imitation, but he'd give her time, two, three years maybe, to see if she'd make the grade.

Huntingdon wore a dark suit for the occasion. He believed in matching himself to his ladies. It also let them see in very obvious terms exactly what their contribution to his income was worth, and hence what they were worth to him. He intended to spend Gloria's holiday displaying their success to the whole island. He stepped through the door marked NO ENTRY FOR UNAUTHORIZED PERSONNEL and steered her luggage smoothly through customs.

Jancis, having chewed her way through the bun, went back towards the office.

'Where your friend?' somebody called out.

'She go work in the Newnited States.'

'Eh, eh. She go earn big money there.'

It was a dismal walk on her own. Soufrière was a drab place without her friend.

Napoleon sat on the bench with his chin just over the edge of the dining table. The assistants spun tin plates of mashed haricot beans and plantains down the table. Napoleon stood up, reached for one and pulled it close under his chin. The smell was so wonderful that he dribbled. But it wasn't time to start eating yet.

First came grace. Then the assistants began the feeding of the under threes. Feeding oneself was a social skill taught in the next class.

Napoleon dipped his little pink tongue in the pale plateful of mash. It tasted good. Feeling bolder he picked up a handful and crammed it into his mouth.

'Napoleon, what you do? Why you so troublesome today?'

Napoleon put his hands under the table and wiped the mess off on his shorts.

'What your mummy go say when I tell her you too troublesome today?'

Napoleon licked up the food still clinging round his face.

'Is only animals eat like that with no spoon.'

Napoleon did not have the vocabulary to say that at home he ate with a spoon and that if somebody gave him a spoon he could very well feed himself. As it was, he sat and waited while the assistants with their spoons worked their way down the table where the children sat like fledgling birds with their mouths wide open, gulping down whatever was shovelled into them.

Ophelia's daughter Estelle, nearly seven years old, walked slowly up the road from the primary school in Nelson's Look Out, through an avenue of poinsettia bushes. She should have been hurrying home for lunch but it was too hot.

Her footsteps dragged. She stopped altogether at the sight of a butterfly on a hibiscus flower, and would have happily stayed there until the school bell rang, even if she went hungry.

'What you doing, Estelle?' shouted a neighbour from her verandah across the street. 'Gladys be vex.'

Estelle moved on reluctantly. She arrived at the shed to find that Gladys had already eaten and gone back to the grapefruit picking. Portia handed her a large plateful of hot stew which Estelle pushed around her plate with her spoon.

'Something is the matter with the good food I giving you?' asked Portia.

'No, aunty. I done hot.'

'Then eat the hot food, child. Is good for the stomach.'

Estelle ate a few small mouthfuls.

'You eat the food the good Lord giving.' Portia squatted on the ground rinsing dinner plates in a bucket of cold

166

water. 'Every day we must thank the good Lord for his bountiful generosity, is not so?'

Thomas knocked on the door of cabin number 2137. He'd cultivated quite a brisk professional knock over the years which no inmate could possibly mistake for a friend. He paused, then lifted the bunch of keys tied to his waist and unlocked the door. The knock was perhaps a needless precaution as he had already said goodbye to Mr and Mrs Stillman when they went ashore after that nice Mrs Stillman had commented so kindly on Ophelia's photograph.

He pulled back the bedclothes with a flourish and stripped off the bottom sheet. Even if he had never seen them in bed he could have told you which of them slept where. Betty's bed emitted a pink sweet odour. Harry's was damp and salty. Thomas shook apart the cleanly folded sheets fresh from the ship's laundry and fluttered them evenly over the mattress.

There was a basic anomaly to Thomas's situation. As an average West Indian male he would not, at home, have dreamt of doing what he would have called woman's work. And yet his present job conferred on him enormous prestige in the eyes of his fellows. Thomas only knew that the basic pay was good and the extras considerable. He regarded himself as an entrepreneur would regard a business, purely in terms of whether he was viable financially. On the ship, during work hours, Thomas the man ceased to exist, except at very rare moments such as now when his whole body was filled with the knowledge that Ophelia was gone.

But what if he had given up his work, his income in good foreign currency and stayed at home to be a model husband and father to his two sons? There was little point in considering the proposition, since with no job and no income – at least until his taxi business was sufficiently prosperous – there could be no model life with Ophelia. He could not expect her to settle for half an acre and a pig and a new dress on Christmas Day. They both wanted more from life than that.

Thomas smoothed down the counterpane and plugged in the hoover. He picked up Betty's shoes from under the bed. They were too small and wide for Ophelia, had she been at home waiting for new shoes. But nice shoes all the same. He put them neatly at the back of the wardrobe. Turned on the hoover and turned it off again. Went into the bathroom and helped himself to a couple of aspirins from the jar on the washstand and looked through the other bottles. Vitamin B6 and Yeast-Vite. He took off the lids and sniffed but decided they probably wouldn't do anything for a hangover. Back in the bedroom he found an open packet of cigarettes next to Harry's bed and popped one in his pocket for later. He turned on the hoover again, and sucked up Betty's talcum powder which lay in a delicate film all around the dressing table leaving her two footprints clear in the middle.

Thomas neatly coiled up the vacuum cleaner lead. Took out his duster and flicked it idly over the bedside cupboards and the dressing table. Then the mirror.

He dragged Harry's hairbrush through his hair. It left a greasy feel. Thomas looked at himself and wondered what Huntingdon had that he didn't. In build they were similar. In colour Thomas had if anything the advantage in that he was marginally lighter. And though his nose was inclined to broadness, that didn't worry him either since Ophelia had never seemed to mind. Also he had more cars than Huntingdon, but then Huntingdon had never had to work for a penny of what he spent. His brother was the Minister of Education and Thomas had no connections whatsoever.

He gathered together the discarded sheets and towels, and left the room towing his vacuum cleaner behind him. Usually he stopped part way through his work for a bite to eat. Today he just wasn't hungry. His grief sat heavy in his stomach, solid as a sea-soaked sponge. He couldn't eat if he tried.

Harry swerved violently left on to the dusty verge. 'Jesus, Betty, why didn't you tell me?'

'Tell you what, honey?'

'Shit.' Harry mopped his forehead with a handkerchief. 'Don't you know anything, Betty?'

'I'm sorry, Harry, I really don't know what you're talking about.'

'That's what I mean.'

Sam and Lou were absorbed in the view from the window although Betty couldn't see anything to look at except more dust and stones and a scraggy goat nibbling half-heartedly at some spiky shrub.

Harry started the engine again. 'We're into goddamn British territory,' he growled.

'Already?' Betty laughed shrilly. 'We've only just left Real Madrid.'

'Betty, from Real Madrid it's only two and a half miles to the border.'

Harry turned the car back on to the tarmac and Betty saw the enormous sign. WELCOME TO ST JOHN, BRITAIN'S FRIENDLIEST CARIBBEAN ISLAND. Underneath was written in smaller letters PLEASE DRIVE ON THE LEFT. Since the tarmac was barely wide enough to be even single lane, Betty couldn't see that it made much difference.

'Look, Bet,' said Harry very slowly, 'if I meet an oncoming vehicle like that lorry back there, I have to pass on the left hand side.'

'On his right, you mean, Harry.'

'That's just what I said, Betty.'

'Harry, I heard you say distinctly, you have to pass on the left.'

'Are you so goddamn stupid you don't know your left from your right?'

Betty blinked hard to keep back the tears. She got out her hanky, blew her nose, and under its cover scrunched up a couple of aspirins. If Monday Island had felt hot, this was hell.

Sam in the front passenger seat yawned and stretched. 'Feels like lunchtime,' he said. 'Shall we be looking out for somewhere, Harry?'

'Could do with a bite myself.'

The car ground in and out of the potholes at the edge of the road, two wheels on, two wheels off the tarmac.

'Why don't you go on the smooth bit in the middle, Harry?'

'Jesus Christ, Betty, not again. It says drive on the left.'

'But we seem to be the only vehicle on the road.'

'Are you driving or am I?'

Betty blew her nose again. Her stomach was bouncing up and down inside her like an empty shopping bag. She looked at her watch. Two o'clock. On the ship they always ate at twelve-thirty.

'Look, Lou, those must be royal palms.' She touched Lou on the shoulder and pointed to the delicate fronds which shimmered against the deep blue sky. There was a whole avenue of the palm trees, at the end of which she could make out a small white blob.

WELCOME TO LONDON TOWN read a large, hand-painted signboard.

A few wooden shacks came into view. They made Soufrière, Monday Island's capital, look like downtown New York in comparison.

'I wouldn't hold out too much hope of a restaurant in this city,' laughed Sam.

170

'City?' said Betty. 'But Harry said yesterday that it could only be a city if it had a cathedral.'

'I was just joking, Bet,' said Sam.

Harry snorted and put his foot down and the car leapt through the palm trees towards the white blob which, as they got closer, turned out to be a statue. It was fenced off by iron railings like a row of spears, painted bright green.

As soon as Harry parked the car a policeman materialized.

'Sorry, sir, you are not parking here, sir.'

Harry looked round. There was not another vehicle, nor for that matter any sign of life at all in the whole sandblasted acreage of square. 'Am I in the way?' he asked.

'Is no parking area, sir.'

Harry turned the key in the ignition.

'There somewhere we can eat in this dump?'

The policeman looked puzzled.

'Food,' said Harry. 'You know, nosh.' He shovelled imaginary food into his mouth, chomping like a porker.

'Harry!' said Betty. She needn't have worried. The policeman doubled up with laughter.

'Oh no, sir, it have nowhere to eat in British St John.'

Harry got out the guidebook. 'It says here', he read, 'there is a good hotel for local food.' He turned towards the policeman and spoke loudly. 'The West Indian Tavern,' he said.

The policeman roared. 'The West Indian Tavern done close down when I a little little boy.' He indicated the size he was at the time, which Betty judged to be three or four years old.

'We are hungry,' said Harry.

'It ain't have no food in London Town. Only one bar.'

'We'll go to a bar then,' said Sam.

Harry backed the car around.

'You come back three o'clock,' said the policeman. 'Is the last post.'

The bar, when they found it, was dark and hot. Over the door was written MAMMY JOSEPHINE, PURVEYOR OF SPIRITS. Betty giggled. She had often wondered just from little things that had happened to her, whether she might not have psychic tendencies herself.

Apart from the darkness, there was nothing very spiritual about Mammy Josephine's bar. She offered a choice of tepid rum and, or, lukewarm Coca Cola. Betty opted for Coke, the others for the mixture. They sat at a chipped table, on metal chairs already warmed to blood heat.

'You want to eat, ladies?' Harry gestured towards the glass cabinet on the counter which contained indeterminate fried lumps.

'Fish or chicken?' asked Mammy Josephine.

Betty watched the flies buzzing inside the cabinet. 'I'm really not hungry,' she said.

Sam chose the chicken, Harry took the fish.

'You sure it's fresh?' hissed Betty.

'Sure,' Harry spluttered through a mouthful. 'Nowhere on this island could be more than two miles from the sea if it tried.'

'That doesn't mean it was caught today. It could be years old.'

'Tastes delicious.' Harry went back for more. Betty was sure he just wanted to spite her by making himself ill. Well, if he wanted to poison himself, that was his own lookout. She sipped her Coke. The sugary sweetness relieved her feelings of starvation while the caffeine, after the third bottle, made her feel pleasantly alert and clear-headed.

Lou drank one rum and coke after another with a novel open on the table in front of her. Reading, for heaven's sakes, thought Betty. How could she sit in this stinking, stuffy, godforsaken dump and read? She watched the flies on the fish and she watched Mammy Josephine, who leant on her elbows on the counter gazing out at the square beyond, where her satisfied customers dozed through the heat of the day under the royal palms.

A sudden commotion, the barking of dogs, the sound of muffled tramping, left, right, left, right, made Betty's eyes open wide.

'Harry,' she whispered, ash white. 'You think it's a coup?'

'For God's sake, Bet, who'd want to take over this dump anyhow?' Harry downed the rest of his umpteenth rum and Coke and walked unsteadily to the doorway. 'Come and take a look at this,' he called.

'Is the police force,' said Mammy Josephine.

'What're they doing?' asked Sam.

'Is the Last Post.'

The four Americans strolled outside. Five policemen in khaki shorts marched down the centre of the road, heading towards the faded flag which looked as if it was indeed dangling from the very last post at the end of the world. The flag was so thin that Betty could see the statue quite clearly through it.

'What's the flag anyway?' asked Harry.

'Oh Harry, that's the Union Jack, can't you see?' The cross of St Andrew was just discernible as a pinkish tinge, the blue of Wales had faded beyond recognition.

The sergeant roared a command as if he were in front of Buckingham Palace. His four companions stamped their feet on the spot and then were still.

'Gee,' said Lou, 'I just love these old British customs.'

The five policemen were drawn up in single file, facing the statue. Betty and her companions walked closer. It was only then that they could see that the statue represented a Highlander, complete with kilt, tam o'shanter and sporran.

Written on the plinth were the words 'They died that we might live'. There followed the date, 1939–1945, and two names, Jonas Barringford, 2nd Gordon Highlanders, and Moses Partridge, 3rd Scots Fusiliers. A pair of pigeons were mating on top of the tammy.

Then came a loud explosion at the far side of the square. Betty screamed and flung her arms round Harry. He brushed her off and pointed to an ancient cannon, with smoke curling sleepily from its barrel. A sixth policeman stood by, still holding a burning brand and grinning broadly. The gun had a magical effect. Along the entire avenue, people were clambering to their feet; children appeared from nowhere; and as a radio blared the latest cricket score, the policeman by the cannon got down on his hands and knees and wound up a gramophone. When he lowered the needle the cracked sound of a trumpet wavered through the smoke and dust.

The five policemen stood rigidly to attention swaying slightly. Betty wondered whether they might be drunk. All through the Last Post they fixed their eyes on distant and invisible glories while the sergeant lowered the flag inch by inch.

When the ceremony was over, Harry and Betty, Sam and Lou, followed on along the coast road towards the Dutch border. Since the island was almost totally flat apart from the central mountain, and since shrubs and trees were massed on either side of the road, there were no views at all.

Betty was reluctant to leave the British Sector so quickly, because she had read that the greatest sport was to be had swinging in an old car tyre from a manchineel tree at a certain spot which Friedman marked vaguely with a cross. She thought that Harry was just being selfish in not trying harder to find the place because he was still sulking about his swimming trunks.

174

But Lou, who was something of a botanist, pointed out that the tyre was probably a joke – a tourist trap in the real sense of the word, since machineel trees were poisonous, any contact with the bark or sap could produce a painful rash, and the apple if eaten, contained irritating hairs which caused constriction of the throat.

'You really want to go there, Bet?' asked Harry.

Betty sat staring at the back of Harry's head and wondered whether, like the original Eve, she could tempt him to eat of the apple.

Indeed a tree can be a dangerous thing. And not only a coconut palm in a hurricane, as the old adage has it. What seemed to Ophelia, at the time, the greatest blow of her life, was dealt by a tamarind tree, whose sweet sour fruit dangles grotesquely beneath a feathery overhang of leaves, like necklaces of drying goat's turds.

One exceptionally hot summer's morning, on the most beautiful and perhaps the only white beach on Monday Island, where the sea twice daily deposits its treasures of shells and coral with a sound like the tinkle of bells, Ophelia's beloved Aunty Celia is found dead.

A little boy comes with the news, hammering on Portia's front door. She flings back the shutters of her bedroom window and appears magnificent in her petticoat stretching and yawning.

'What going on out there?' she grumbles, scouring her face with her rough hands as if it was one of last night's saucepans. 'You making enough noise to wake the dead.'

But no amount of noise can ever again waken Aunty Celia.

Portia and Ophelia fling on some clothes and follow the fisherman's lad back to the beach. As they run through the streaked sunlight beneath the gently waving palms they know from the loveliness of the morning that there is some mistake. But as they approach the far end of the beach away from the bar and the car park they see the quiet, dark knot of people round the foot of the tamarind tree.

The tree is thick and its branches hang low. As they approach they see only Aunty Celia's feet pointing downwards like the toes of an invisible ballerina. Portia stops to wipe her sweating forehead with her handkerchief, but Ophelia speeds on.

Ophelia, a shy girl of thirteen, stops behind the little crowd of people and stands in silent appreciation of the untoward view of Aunty Celia's lace petticoat hanging limply around her stiff, straight legs.

It is Portia who bursts through the circle of onlookers shrieking, 'You ain't got no manners or what? Why all you stand gaping up a woman's petticoat, like you never seen no woman before?' Portia for all her size springs up the tree to cut her sister down.

The fisherman steps forward, grabbing at her ankles as she shins up the branches.

'Hey, sister, you leave she alone. The police coming to do that.'

'Ain't no policeman going touch my sister,' yells Portia swinging the cutlass hard at the scarlet patent leather belt from which Celia hangs.

Celia falls with a thump to the ground, scattering the crowd and sprawling awkwardly, her face down in the sand and her skirt rucked up to show her suspenders.

Portia springs down from the tree beside her. 'Phelie,' she calls, 'where you, girl? You going to stand all day while these worthless men staring at your aunty's underwear?'

Ophelia pushes her way through the crowd. Between them they make Aunty Celia look more respectable. Portia removes the terrible belt from round her sister's neck and absentmindedly loops it round her own.

176

'Shoulda cut down that old tree long long ago,' murmurs someone from the crowd.

To Ophelia at the time it seems a sensible suggestion. No tamarind tree, no dead Aunty Celia, for how could anyone ever hang themselves from a coconut palm in a slimline skirt and high heels? Which reminds her. She looks round but they are gone. 'Mammy,' she whispers to Portia, 'Aunty Celie's shoes.'

Portia is on her feet in an instant, brandishing the cutlass at a retreating circle of menfolk. 'You all thieves as well as Peeping Toms?' she shrieks. 'You even done rob a corpse of her shoes?'

Aunty Celia makes a brief star appearance on the front page of the *Monday Island Chronicle* with a picture taken of her council flat in England with a white poodle sitting at her feet. She is wearing a hat and gloves which everyone supposes to be quite natural since that is how the Queen is commonly photographed.

While a sudden squall hits the east coast of the island, and unnatural blue grey clouds bank on the horizon, Celia is hastily buried, and even the thunder of her death is stolen by another lady, ever afterwards known as 'Sylvia'.

Sylvia approaches from the east as a tropical storm sweeping towards Monday Island at the rate of twenty miles per hour, but with speed steadily increasing and winds rapidly approaching hurricane force. As Celia is lowered into her grave the first drops of rain lash the mourners who scatter in unseemly haste leaving Celia with a covering of earth which is barely respectable.

Portia, Gladys and the children scamper home to nail down the shutters and barricade the door against the force of the storm. Bent almost double against the wind, they stagger to the shelter of the concrete primary school in the

177

centre of the village, taking with them a few essentials such as blankets, candles, food and drink.

They are in the school for three days, while the wind prowls round the building. It is a time of singing and praying, and being together.

Portia and Gladys, with fifteen children between them, stake out their claim to a small corner in the infants' classroom. As the hurricane strikes with full force a darkness comes over the island. The single light bulb in the middle of the room flickers and goes out.

'Jesus save us,' calls out Gladys, 'dear Lord protect us.' The women cross themselves and mumble their prayers.

Portia launches into 'Onward Christian Soldiers' and soon all sixty people in the room are singing, clapping and stamping in time to the rhythm while outside Sylvia howls and screams to be let in.

'You know we love you . . .'

'Yes, Lord.'

'You know we your servants . . .'

'Yes, Lord.'

'We know you lead us out of the valley of darkness.'

'Amen, Lord, amen.'

'Sweet Jesus, if it is your will protect us.'

'Sweet Jesus.'

And Gladys with her eyes screwed fervently shut prays for Uncle Remus up there above Nelson's Look Out weeding the dasheen patch.

'Sweet Lord, keep my husband in your tender care,' she prays and her sons chorus 'Amen'.

'Where your man gone, Portia?' Gladys asks her sister.

Portia shrugs. 'Ain't seen nothing of him since Celia done dead.' She doesn't seem unduly upset. He had long since ceased to take any active part in supporting the family and she couldn't help thinking that she was better off without him. There was one less mouth to feed and once

178

word got about that she was a single woman once more, there was hope for a brighter future. 'He 'fraid Celia's jumbi come to haunt he,' she chuckled.

Ophelia and her cousins, her brothers and sisters doze and play cards and tell stories. During her first three days in the tomb, poor Aunty Celie is unmourned except by Ophelia. She keeps close by her Aunty Celie's suitcase containing all those wonderful clothes and hats, and the little pots of make-up and creams. The clothes are at present far too big but some instinct tells her how valuable they will be later on. Ophelia by candlelight, with a small hand mirror, experiments with the make-up and tops the whole effect by putting on one of Aunty Celia's hats.

'Why, child,' says Aunty Gladys, 'you too much like your Aunty Celie. Ain't she, Portia?'

Portia looks up from the kerosene stove where she is stirring peas and rice. 'Oh my God, I thought it Celie self back from the dead,' and she insists that her younger children take off their clothes and put them back on inside out as protection against Celia's ghost.

Ophelia keeps the hat on for the rest of that indeterminate day and flirts with the cousins in the way she has seen Aunty Celia flirt with the men of the island over the last few weeks.

By the third morning most of the food and drink is gone and the candles are finished. The excitement has worn off and the children are fretful and bored. The women scold and doze and look forward to getting back to normal life.

By evening the sky is lighter and the wind has abated, changing its tone from a high-pitched scream to a steady whine.

Two of Ophelia's cousins are sent out like doves from the ark. They come back wildly excited. People are about in the streets again and there is debris everywhere. The top floor of the school has been lifted right off and lies in a heap in the playground. They describe a world hit by a holocaust, not a blade of grass, not a leaf, not a building standing between the school and the sea. But, they assure everybody, it is safe to go home.

Gladys, desperate to find Remus, judges by the rows of twisted and overturned vehicles that there is little point in looking for transport, and sets off with her sons to walk to Nelson's Look Out. Portia and Ophelia take the children back to their own house. They search for it for a long time. The little wooden cabin has been torn from its foundations as if it were no more than a doll's house, then rolled over and over and smashed against the hillside.

Portia leaps on top of an old man carrying off half a plank that she swears 'the Lord God know it mine'. With half the houses in the village painted the same livid turquoise it is hard to see how she tells one plank from another, but she swears she knows every piece of wood in her house and there are few people in the village willing to argue with her.

Ophelia climbs higher looking for pieces of corrugated iron that have been ripped like tissue paper and flung all over the hillside. From far above Sugar Bay she can see the wreckage of the deep water harbour where huge twisted pylons rise from the sea bed like the ruins of Pearl Harbor. When she looks for the coastal road, it is not there. Both the road and the roadside houses have vanished without trace and the sea heaves, choked with unaccustomed debris.

She is not as expert as Portia at asserting her rights over the scraps of roofing, but she collects a modest bundle which she carries down to where her brothers and sisters are combing the ground for nails on their hands and knees. All about them flutter the sad remains of the villagers' lives, a scrap of curtain, or a dented saucepan clanking dully as it passes by.

They return to the school to sleep. An army Land Rover appears and scratchy Red Cross blankets are given out. Early next morning, Portia rouses the children and they walk the ten miles up country to Nelson's Look Out where she is sure they will find food and shelter.

She is quite wrong. Though Gladys takes them in willingly, into what remains of Grandmother's hut, she can offer them nothing to eat. There is not a tree left standing, not a cucumber gourd left in the ground. The bananas lie like drunken soldiers, snapped off at the base.

But Gladys is happy because she found Uncle Remus safe and sound. After the farm hut was lifted clean away above him he had rolled himself up in a foam mattress and lain clinging to the stump of a banana tree.

Gladys sends three of her sons and Uncle Remus to rebuild Portia's house and it is a matter of only a week before Ophelia and her younger brothers and sisters can return home.

'Why you don' stay with me, Phelie?' Gladys asks as she and her niece stand side by side slamming their hoes into the soil.

'Portia say I have to live there.'

'What you going to do down there all day, look after the children?'

'No.' Ophelia pauses to draw breath. 'I going to secondary school.'

'Who say that, Aunty Celie?'

'Aunty Celie say school is good. If I work hard, I go get a good job.'

They hoe in silence for a while. It is like being on top of the world up there, with the mountains all around, and beyond, the sea.

'I going to miss meh auntie,' says Ophelia suddenly.

'Celie?'

Ophelia nods and blinks back the tears. 'Why she do that thing?'

'That girl done los' she way long long ago, child.'

'She say she taking me to Birmingham England. She promise.'

'What Celie can offer you like this?' Gladys stands up straight and indicates the countryside and the sunshine and the dark rich soil beneath their feet. 'Why you think the good Lord done born you a Mondegian? Is because he love you, child. He want to bless you.'

Ophelia, back in Sugar Bay in the reconstituted house, dreams of nothing but Birmingham. On her bedroom wall she pins the newspaper article and the photograph of Aunty Celia. Ophelia knows that Aunty Gladys is wrong about Monday Island. She has heard from Celia's own lips about life in England, and knows that it was slavery and not God's blessing which has put her on Monday Island.

Though the coroner's verdict was that Aunty Celia took her own life while the balance of her mind was disturbed, Ophelia knows that Aunty Celia was the most beautiful and happiest person she has ever met. Why should she want to die with a suitcase full of beautiful clothes, half the men of Monday Island ready to fall at her feet and a return ticket to London Heathrow in her handbag? She feels that Portia must be in some way to blame since she remembers the quarrel between her mother and her aunt. She knows from experience the depressing effect of Portia's sour, black presence.

Soon after the hurricane Portia returns to work in the coffee-coloured suburb of town where the smart white bungalows, instantly restored, gleam high above the mangled wreckage of the town.

If Portia had to choose between work and home she would probably choose her work. After twelve years she can please herself, which is a luxury rarely offered to her at home.

Every morning Portia waddles up the steep hill. The buses do not climb to such dizzy heights. Each householder owns at least two cars and does not wish the suburb to be available to anybody who can afford a five cent bus ticket.

Hence each morning sees an exodus of shiny cars going down the hill, and a stream of domestics and gardeners trudging up it. Portia carries a bag containing her work clothes and her sandwiches since she receives drinks but no food as part of her salary. She ignores the greetings of the gardener, shuts the front door firmly behind her, and, alone in the house, helps herself to a beer from the fridge. She flicks the top off expertly with the wall bottle opener, kicks off her shoes and sinks thankfully into a large green leather armchair.

Ophelia at home with Portia's children (the only state secondary school having been swept away by Sylvia) sees Birmingham England receding into the distance. One day, in desperation, she retires into her bedroom whence she emerges not as a replica of Aunty Celia, but as a model schoolgirl. She polishes her old leather sandals until she can see her face in the toe caps, crams her feet inside and hobbles off to the bus stop.

At Boules she walks briskly across the green to the house of the Misses Simpson. It looks strangely denuded by the hurricane which has swept away the shrubs and litter from the garden and left the stone building looking like new.

Ophelia taps smartly on the door and causes the sort of commotion usually associated with a fox in a henhouse.

Tap tap comes the eldest Miss Simpson with her white stick.

From upstairs, the voice of the deaf Miss Simpson shrills

through the open window, 'Sister sister open the door hurry up or they will go away again whoever can it be.'

The white stick thumps twice on the floor, calling the deaf Miss Simpson to order. Then the door opens.

Ophelia faces the door with a winning smile, which is totally wasted. There is a short, unnerving silence before Miss Simpson speaks.

'Yes?' She stares into the sky over Ophelia's head.

'It Ophelia, Miss Simpson. How are you?'

'Oh I'm very well thank you and the other Miss Simpson is very well and the other Miss Simpson is very well too thank you but won't you come in it is such a lovely surprise to see you and my sisters will be so pleased and won't you come upstairs and have a cup of tea.'

Upstairs Ophelia sits on the horsehair sofa in her gym slip with the cracked leather scratching the backs of her knees, and dunks a biscuit in a cup of tea. The Misses Simpson can contain themselves no longer.

'You have been to school today Ophelia we have been so worried about you in that terrible weather and we wondered if you would be going to school.'

'Yes it was terrible weather and we prayed to God that it would soon pass and God heard our prayers and the storm passed.'

'No,' says Ophelia loudly, 'I have not been to school today.'

'Sister, you hear that?' screams the bedridden Miss Simpson. 'She has not been to school today and why has she not been to school today and what has she been doing in those clothes if she has not been to school?'

'Tell me tell me what she is wearing how can I know what she is wearing if nobody tells me?'

'She is wearing the green gym slip and the white blouse and the green ribbon in her hair and her white socks and leather sandals.'

'But she has not been to school today?'

'No,' says Ophelia again. 'The school has gone.'

'Where has the school gone to a school cannot move I went to school every day and it was always in the same place.'

'Sister sister that was St Ursula's perhaps the country schools are different perhaps they move.'

'Hurricane Sylvia she blow it away,' says Ophelia.

'Oh sweet Jesus oh dear Lord protect us the hurricane can blow schools away perhaps it has blown St Ursula's away and it is lucky we were not at St Ursula's today or we might have been blown away as well.'

'Sisters you were not in St Ursula's because you left school twenty-five years ago so even if St Ursula's blows away you are quite safe.'

'St Ursula's has not blown away,' says Ophelia loudly. 'It is the only school left on the island apart from St Dominic's.'

'If St Ursula's is still there,' says the eldest Miss Simpson, 'why doesn't Ophelia go to St Ursula's?'

'Yes of course she can go to St Ursula's she must go there this minute why doesn't she go now why is she just sitting there drinking her tea when she could be going to St Ursula's?'

'How I can go to St Ursula's?' asks Ophelia innocently. 'It cost money.'

It is only a few days later that Ophelia receives a letter from the bedridden Miss Simpson who, acting as scribe for her blind sister and for the one who cannot write because of her weak heart, wishes to inform their dear Ophelia that there is a place for her at St Ursula's convent, and that Mother Clare would be pleased to see both Ophelia and her mother at the earliest opportunity. Since Portia is tied up during her working hours, Ophelia attends for interview on her own.

Ophelia is a clever child. Her grandmother has instilled in her, as she did in Aunty Celia before her, the habits of diligence and perseverance. Ophelia is an attentive pupil, eager to learn, assiduous in her homework and attractive and pleasant to teachers and pupils alike. And she has before her the example of Aunty Celia's success to know that hard work pays. Why, then, do we find Ophelia expelled and pregnant at fifteen? Has she so rapidly forgotten all her grandmother's teachings?

The answer, as so many educationalists will be quick to point out, lies in the home not the school.

Ophelia catches the bus home each day after school, and it is now that she makes the acquaintance of Caesar who is a character quite unlike anyone she has ever met before. He dismisses her Latin with the comment 'It shit, man', a phrase he applies to every academic subject she mentions. Portia too has scant regard for learning although she does appreciate the job prospects at the end of the educational ladder. But in the meantime, Portia who has washed out her dusters and floorcloths and hung them out to dry, removed her overalls and walked home to save the cost of a taxi, is tired. Ophelia sometimes sees her mother as she zooms past in Caesar's bus, a heavy, slightly bowlegged figure with an enormous bag on her head, and ducks her head in shame.

She hurries up the hill, folds away her uniform and goes into the kitchen to peel the vegetables or set the fish to fry or a pan of water on the stove to boil. Nothing she does is right. If she helps, Portia says she is not doing it properly, if she does nothing she is told she is lazy. But though domestic life is a cauldron of discontent, Ophelia can switch off from these matters by retreating to her room with a magazine or going to join her friends on the beach.

One Friday after school, Ophelia's bus has not passed Portia on the road. Because of a traffic jam at the bridge, Ophelia alights later than usual, on the bend where Henzel the village shoemaker has his shop, in between the bakery and the post office.

Ophelia bends down to adjust her sandal. Possibly she has caught a stone in it during the walk from the convent to the bus stop. So she bends with her back to the bread shop and the shoemaker's, both of which are set below road level down a flight of five steps.

Portia, who has been feeling particularly sunny-tempered these days since she has borne the shoemaker two children and has reason to believe that marriage lies within her grasp, comes out of the bakery with a basket of hot bread just in time to see the look on the face of her beloved Henzel as he watches Ophelia. Ophelia has managed to get the forefinger of her right hand under the heel of her right foot feeling for the object which is causing her discomfort. At the same time she displays what Portia feels is an indecent amount of leg and worse. She swipes at Ophelia's green school knickers with a French loaf and Ophelia spins round and topples over.

'What you think you doing?' screams Portia. 'Showing your drawers to all the world and to some people who should have more manners than to look?'

Henzel, eyes on his last, knocks in nails at twice his usual speed.

'I see you, Henzel,' squeals Portia. 'You think I don't see you, eh?'

She hounds Ophelia all the way home with cries of 'Jezebel' and worse until the poor girl doesn't know whether she is coming or going. 'And you just get out my house,' screams Portia. 'I ain't having no scarlet woman in my house.'

Ophelia stands under the bedroom window and catches her belongings as they come sailing out of the window. She ties them in a large bundle, and with Aunty Celia's suitcase in the other hand sets off for Nelson's Look Out vowing never to return.

Ophelia, aged fifteen, arrives at Aunty Gladys's house in Caesar's bus, carrying all her worldly goods. Aunty Gladys, Uncle Remus and the seven cousins welcome her with open arms.

But by Sunday night, for the sake of her education, Gladys insists that Ophelia return to Sugar Bay. Ophelia returns bathed in the love and affection that have been lavished on her. Not even the discovery that Henzel has moved into her mother's room and that three sisters and one brother have moved into Ophelia's room can ruffle her. For Ophelia has over the weekend received from her cousins education in a field totally ignored by private school, and one which in nine months' time will have such drastic repercussions on her chances of academic success.

For the twenty-fifth time that morning, Thomas unplugged the vacuum cleaner. He looked at his watch. He'd get a couple of hours on shore. He tidied up his little kitchen, swallowed a cup of black coffee then hurried off to his cabin to change. From underneath his bunk he drew out a large cardboard box then made his way to the lifeboat station which served as an embarkation point for those wishing to go ashore.

'Where you going with that box, man?' asked one of the crew.

'The hostel.'

'You lucky, man. I gotta work all afternoon.'

Thomas shrugged.

'You give Rosie one helluva kiss for me, eh?'

The white officer got to his feet as the boat approached the jetty. The two black men fell silent.

Thomas scrambled out over the ropes at the bows to avoid the queue of white passengers. He walked along the jetty with the box on his head and cut across Fore Street into the less fashionable area to the west.

The hostel was famous throughout the island. Any inhabitant could have directed you there not because it was outstanding as architecture but because of the well-known charms of its inhabitants.

The building was unfashionable, but comfortable. Children played in the yard while their mothers folded linen or sat and talked on the verandah.

'Marianne in there?' shouted Thomas.

He waited in the yard with the cardboard carton by his feet.

'Who wanting me now?' A tall girl came to the front of the verandah. 'Thomas!' She swung her legs over the top of the railing and jumped down into the yard.

Thomas caught her in his arms. 'How you doing, baby?'

'What you bring for me today, Thomas?'

'Your mammy send avocado pears and mangoes and limes and I don't know what else.'

Marianne looked into the box.

'Rosie there?' asked Thomas.

'Somewhere.' Marianne squinted into the sun. 'Rosie.'

'Yeah?'

'Robertson send you one helluva kiss. You want to come get it?'

Rosie laughed. 'Tell him kisses ain't enough,' and she disappeared.

'You coming in, man?' Marianne picked up the box.

'Why you ain't working? It have a ship in harbour.'

'Later. You want a beer?'

Inside the hostel children were playing tag among the dining tables. 'All you get out,' shouted Marianne, clapping her hands.

'Is a happy place here,' commented Thomas.

Marianne brought him a beer. He sat staring through the window at a bougainvillaea that climbed over the windowsill.

'What wrong, man?' Marianne lit a cigarette and ran her hands through her hair. 'Tell Mammy thankyou for the fruit.'

Thomas nodded. Sitting at a table with another woman only emphasized his pain. 'Ophelia she done lef' me.'

Marianne patted Thomas's forearm and let her fingers lie lightly on his dark skin. 'It bound to happen sometime,' she said carefully.

'She done lef' the island. I don't know where she going.'

'She don't leave you no letter? No nothing?'

'She done lef' a letter, but she ain't say where she going.' Thomas tilted the beer bottle and took a long drink.

Marianne watched his Adam's apple jerk up and down as he swallowed. A slight dribble escaped at the corners of his mouth. She took out a handkerchief and leaned forward.

'True to tell, Thomas, Phelie, she come here last night.'

'Phelie here?'

'She done gone now. She lef' this morning.'

'By boat?'

Marianne nodded.

'You think she go stop on Christian Island?'

'Perhaps. I think she want to go to the States.' Marianne flicked the stub of her cigarette out through the open window. 'You wan' a next beer?'

Thomas held his hand out for the fresh drink. 'You think if I write she go come back?'

'Where you going to write to, man? Talk sense.'

'I going to find her if I have to search the whole island.'

'You going to force her to come back? She done lef'
because she want to. Phelie is a free person, man.'

'But I want she back bad.'

'You leave she, Thomas. One day she go come back.'

'I sick for so, Marianne.'

Marianne put her arms around Thomas and hugged him
close.

'Well, thanks, Harry, that sure was good of you,' said Sam
as they walked away from the car hire place.

'My pleasure,' said Harry, realizing too late that Sam
was not going to offer to pay even a share of the expenses.
'You going to explore New Amsterdam?'

Sam squinted up and down the street at the pastel
houses. 'Sure is pretty.' He put his hands in his pockets
and rocked back on his heels.

'Charged me eighty-five dollars,' hinted Harry.

'You got yourself a good deal there, Harry.'

They found Betty and Lou windowshopping. Betty was
pointing at a display of tweed skirts and Arran sweaters.
'All made in Scotland,' she was saying. 'You can't beat
that.'

'Makes me hot just to look at them,' said Lou.

Betty quite agreed.

Sam and Lou went next door into a liquor shop.

'Aren't you going in, Harry?'

'Not bothered.'

'But you always buy liquor on shore.'

'This time I'm not,' Harry snapped.

'Suit yourself.' She still couldn't get her mind off those
Arrans. 'Think I might just get me a sweater.'

'You cold or something?'

'It's such an incredible saving, Harry, and Arran sweaters never go out of fashion.'

'You want to break the bank, Bet?' He broke into a grotesque smile as Sam and Lou came out of the shop, two plastic carrier bags apiece, each bulging with bottles. Harry's eyes boggled.

'Guess we'd better see these safely stowed away,' said Sam.

'What're you two doing? Want to come back for a drink?' Lou was always generous with the drinks.

'No,' said Harry. 'We'll just take a look at the town.' He laughed, looking up and down the single street hemmed between the salt ponds and the sea.

'They alcoholics?' he asked, as Sam and Lou moved jerkily down the street.

'What makes you think that, honey?'

'You a complete moron?'

Betty didn't know Sam well enough to judge, but there was something about Lou which made her uneasy. There was a certain lack of co-ordination about everything she did. Nothing flowed. That was it.

Harry and Betty ambled along the main street in silence until the small pastel-coloured shops gave way to larger modern buildings, and Harry nudged Betty up the steps of the Grand Casino with his vast belly. She shuddered as she stepped out of the sunlight, and felt the first blast of the air conditioning.

Harry steered her deeper and deeper into the building. She was aware of being pursued by a nightmare of three Harrys, one behind her, and one in profile in the mirrored walls on either side. She made her escape into the ladies' powder room and stayed there a long time hoping he would have given up and gone before she came out. But he was still there, tapping his foot angrily.

Betty's soul gave a little tremor of delight as Harry ushered her into the Games Room. The inside was disappointing, an amusement arcade display of one-armed bandits. Harry got a pile of chips from the cashier and Betty followed him from machine to machine, as he pulled handles and cursed. When he got to his last chip he handed the plastic disc over to Betty.

'Well, let's see what you can do.'

Betty shook her head. She knew he wanted her to lose the last chip so that he could blame her for losing the lot. 'Harry,' she protested, 'you're the expert.'

'Bet, this is your big chance to make a million.'

Betty could tell from his tone that if she didn't give in he'd make a scene. In the interests of deferring present unpleasantness whatever the cost in the future, Betty took the chip, like a communion wafer.

'Uh, where do I put it, Harry?'

'Bet, haven't you been watching me?'

She looked vaguely at the machine. 'I just have to line up all those little bananas, is that right, Harry?'

'Or the pineapples, or the lemons.'

'Okay, okay. Don't rattle me.' Betty shoved in the chip and when the dials spun so fast that she couldn't see whether the pictures were bananas or rainbows, she pulled every lever in sight. The machine juddered to a halt. There was a ghastly clonking noise. 'Oh God,' thought Betty. 'I've broken it.' Suddenly the machine was spewing out chips. They came out so fast they flooded over her shoes and rolled away across the carpet.

'Jackpot,' screamed Harry on his hands and knees sweeping them up in armfuls. 'You've done it, Bet.'

Attendants came from every direction. Betty watched Harry watching them as they gathered up the chips in bundles of ten.

She sat in a quiet corner and lit a cigarette.

Some minutes later Harry came over, his eyes shining. 'Fifteen hundred dollars, Bet. You're a genius.'

'Fifteen hundred, Harry?'

'Oh God, Betty, when I saw you there with those things spewing out all over your feet . . . !'

'What'll we do with fifteen hundred dollars?' Betty thought of next year's cruise in a state cabin or perhaps a new three-piece suite for the sitting room.

'What'll we do with it, honey? You just watch.' Harry's eyes sparkled. 'I'm going to turn that fifteen hundred into fifteen thousand.'

'Harry, can I just have enough for an Arran sweater?'

'Sure, honey. Go treat yourself.' He peeled off twenty dollars.

'They cost fifty, Harry.'

'You kidding? For one jumper?'

Betty held out her hand. Harry handed the notes over one by one. Fifty dollars exactly. Betty stuffed the notes angrily into her wallet. 'And then I'm going back to the ship,' she said.

Harry went over to the roulette table. Although he'd never played roulette, he knew that James Bond had. The setting wasn't quite Las Vegas, no Pussy Galore here to bend over him with her milk-white bosom, he'd just have to play it straight.

His seat was right next to number twenty-one which seemed a good enough place to start. The croupier spun the wheel, the little ball clattered around, Harry's heart beat faster. He placed one hundred dollars on the red, number twenty-one. All the other bets placed were miserably small, but probably the big-time gamblers would only be along at night.

'All bets are closed,' announced the croupier.

The wheel was slowing down. Harry stood up. The ball clattered, then settled in a numbered slot. Harry craned closer. It was too goddamned close to be true. Right next door. On the red. Number eighteen. Harry grunted and sat down. The croupier reached out and scooped up the bets with his rake. With still more than a thousand dollars under his belt, Harry placed another bet. Seventy-five dollars this time.

Betty slipped a large off-white Arran over her head. Not only did it make her feel prickly all over, but she looked like a pregnant ewe. Betty dragged the sweater off again and went outside. Really, she had to admit that she preferred the little shops with their curious local handicrafts. The tablecloths embroidered with endless improbable flowers in lazy daisy stitch, crude pottery figures, painted shells and black velvet wall hangings with maps of the various islands worked in gold thread. Betty made a selection of purchases which would do as presents for anybody she might have forgotten. Then she wandered back to the jetty and stared at the tepid sea, waiting for the lighter.

Down to his last fifty dollars, Harry was sweating heavily and placing five-dollar bets on twelve numbers. He was on his last cigar and parched with thirst, but he didn't like to leave the table. Any minute now would come the big one.

Betty on the lighter hummed happily, heading home with her little purchases on her knee, home to the bliss of her cabin with Harry on shore.

Harry, down to forty-five dollars, placed five on half the board. He abandoned red in favour of black since black seemed to be having all the luck. The ball spun, the bets were closed. The winning number was red. With forty dollars in his pocket, Harry decided to cut his losses. He kicked back his chair savagely and walked out.

The sun was too bright, the sidewalks too narrow. When he stepped into the dirty street to move more freely, cars forced him back into the garbage-filled gutter. Harry hated every inch of this goddamn jaded, faded one-street dump. Two hours until the ship sailed and forty dollars in his pocket. God, he was dying for a drink but not in one of these tarted up places filled with dreary replicas of himself and Betty sipping those ghastly concoctions more like desserts than drinks. What he needed was somewhere to do a bit of serious drinking. Drink for the sake of getting drunk.

To hell with Friedman and culture. Harry turned up a side street away from the sea front. He didn't want to see the sea again as long as he lived.

The pastel house fronts were, it seemed, only a façade. Two paces off Fore Street, all pretence at gentility vanished. The houses were plain wood, brown and flaky, not a pavement in sight, and pariah dogs snuffled through the rubbish. It all suited Harry's mood perfectly.

In front of him now were the salt ponds, the flat heavy water separated by fences. Fences for godssakes? Sea birds were hunched on the rotting wooden poles. Harry turned right along what was called Back Street. Couldn't they even think up any proper names in this godawful place?

Harry flattened himself against a house wall as a car came dangerously close. At first he thought the driver was deliberately trying to crush him. There was no time to run and he wasn't Spiderman to shin up the wall behind.

As the car swerved away, Harry realized that the driver was simply trying to negotiate the ruts in the road. He drooped against the wall panting slightly, when he felt a tap on the top of his blue towelling sun hat.

'Mr Stillman.'

Harry looked up. Saw a black face. 'Yeah?'

'It's me, Mr Stillman.'

'Sure it is.'

'Thomas.'

'Why, Thomas. Good to see you. I'm just taking a stroll.'

'You want a beer, Mr Stillman?'

'Now you're talking sense, boy.' Harry turned round and saw that all he had needed to get out of the way of the car was to walk up two or three steps on to a ground floor verandah.

Thomas sat alone at a table, a bottle of rum and a bottle of beer in front of him. He was drinking alternately from both.

'Want some, Mr Stillman?'

'Sure could do with some.' Harry tilted his hat on to the back of his head, cowboy style. Thought of asking for a glass. Thought better of it and drank from the bottle instead. 'Shore leave?' he asked.

Thomas nodded.

'Christ, it's hot.' Harry took off his hat. Jesus, it was a dingy place. Dirty. Uncared for. Needed a woman's touch. Yet it seemed popular enough. Not there on the verandah, but indoors by the bar. Harry took another swig of rum. He felt it burn right down his throat and into his stomach. Sweat was pouring off him.

'I come here to look for a friend,' said Thomas. 'You want to meet her?'

'Girl in every port, eh, Thomas?' Harry soothed the rawness in his throat with a large mouthful of cold lager.

'Is not like that, Mr Stillman. Every trip I bring this girl a food parcel from her mother on Monday Island.'

Harry gave Thomas an enormous wink.

'Sure you do.'

'But I didn't find Ophelia.' Thomas paused. Shook his head. 'She was here yesterday, now she gone.'

'She sure gets around, eh?'

A pretty girl in a bright crimplene dress such as Ophelia herself might have worn, walked out of the bar and came and put her arm around Thomas's shoulder.

'Won't you introduce me to your friend?'

'Marianne, this is Mr Stillman.'

'Harry.'

'Pleased to meet you, Harry.' She sat down between the two men. 'What d'you think of New Amsterdam, Mr Stillman?' She picked up Harry's cigarette packet and turned it round and round as she spoke.

Harry saw that her nails were very red.

'Well . . .' He held out his arms in a gesture that could have meant anything.

'What d'you think of our clubs and casinos?'

'Matter of fact, had a bit of luck in the Casino.'

'I'm sure you deserved it.' Marianne laid a finger on Harry's arm. 'May I?' She indicated the cigarette packet.

'Sure. I just won fifteen hundred dollars on a fruit machine.'

'Fifteen hundred dollars US?' Thomas leaned closer.

'And lost it all at roulette.' Harry laughed as if it were an everyday occurrence. Until he remembered Betty and took another swig at the rum.

Thomas looked at Harry again, wondered if he'd summed him up correctly before. 'You got a friend for Mr Stillman?'

Marianne nodded. Beckoned to a girl over by the bar. She was small, Spanish-looking, very young. She sat in the remaining chair. Thomas passed the rum bottle around. Marianne fetched two glasses, one for herself and one for the girl.

'This is Dolores,' she said.

'Spanish?' asked Harry.

'From the Dominican Republic.' The girl had a deep, harsh voice and spoke with soft vowels, slurring the words together.

'What're you doing here?'

'At home there is no work.'

198

Harry liked the way she said that. Work, with the rolled 'r'.

The rum bottle was nearly empty. Dolores fetched another. A fight broke out by the bar and two men were pitched down the verandah steps. They staggered to their feet, cursing.

'Russians,' said Thomas.

'Really? No kidding?' Harry's eyes bulged. He watched the men help one another down the street.

Betty arranged her purchases on the dressing table. First the embroidered tablecloth, then the shells polished up with a hand towel from the bathroom. They were so shiny she wondered whether they had been varnished. She imagined them placed tastefully about the rockery. If she still had a rockery to go back to.

Of course she'd known all about Harry's job the day it happened, the day she was down at the supermarket, at the fresh fruits counter, and that terrible Mrs Cyprianou came up and said how sorry she was to hear about Harry.

'What'll you do now?' she had asked.

Betty had defiantly picked up a tray of fresh Californian peaches. There must have been twenty at least, she didn't bother to count. She simply laughed at Mrs Cyprianou. 'What do you think I'm buying all this for?'

Mrs Cyprianou stared. 'You aren't celebrating?'

Betty moved on to the meat counter. Picked up a dozen T-bones and smiled mysteriously.

Mrs Cyprianou manoeuvred her trolley alongside and picked up one miserable little tray of minced meat.

Betty sailed on to the liquor department. 'Red with the steak I think, don't you?'

The small Greek lady nodded feverishly.

At the check-out, Betty produced her American Express

card. She'd only brought enough in her wallet for one sliced loaf and a lettuce.

When Harry came home that evening with a grin even broader than usual, Betty could tell that something was up. She tried a little delicate probing, but Harry failed to take the bait.

Looking back, Betty could see that there were other things that should have aroused her suspicions that all was not well. Harry's announcement, for example, that the office were holding a party for him the night before they sailed. 'We'll only be gone ten days,' she'd said, and Harry had simply shrugged.

The other pointer was the car. Harry had walked home from the office on that last day. 'A new policy' was how he'd explained it. It would be used by one of his colleagues while he was away.

Now Betty arranged her little treasures and tried to calculate how long the fifteen hundred, hopefully by now fifteen thousand dollars would last.

Had Thomas been less drunk when Harry returned to the table, he might have been surprised by his comment, 'I can still do it.' Thomas would have been more surprised by the converse. Harry ordered a bottle of champagne by way of celebration. Thomas drank the bubbly liquid as if it were lemonade and heard not a word of Harry's garbled explanation.

Harry for once in his life bared his soul, and the confessor he chose was completely oblivious both of the words and of the honour. It had been fifteen years since Betty moved out of Harry's bedroom, as if once the attempt to conceive had proved blatantly impossible she had no further vested interest in him as a man. He had come home one day and found that Betty had moved into the spare room, which she said was perfectly natural now that they were both rising forty-five. Harry had not touched another woman before or since. Not that the inclination wasn't there, but his looks were against him and opportunities were few in their small home town.

Harry wiped his face with a handkerchief and poured more champagne. And with a black woman at that. A black woman for Chrissakes! At home it would have been inconceivable, but Harry was on holiday, and Harry waxed lyrical. 'Cry God for England, Harry and St George.'

Thomas beamed and clapped. 'You should be an actor, Mr Stillman.'

Harry hadn't felt so good in years. He was a god. He could do anything.

Except pay the bill. Shit, how could he have spent so much in so little time. He stood up and felt in the back pocket of his shorts. Empty. He fumbled around in the front pockets under the overhang of his belly. Oh Christ. Harry slumped down in his chair. Buried his face in his hands.

'Time to go, Mr Stillman,' said Thomas, lurching to his feet.

'Can't,' whispered Harry. 'That bloody whore. She's robbed me.'

Thomas sobered up in an instant and was in the bar yelling for Marianne. Harry drained the last dregs of champagne straight out of the bottle.

Thomas came back waving Harry's card. 'You dropped it, Mr Stillman,' he said. 'Down behind the chair.'

Betty, showered, changed and rehydrated, took a turn about the promenade deck. She paused to watch the lighters dashing to and from Saint John, ferrying passengers home. She tried to spot Harry's blue towelling hat, but even by ten minutes to sailing time, he still had not returned. She wondered whether to report him missing, or whether to let the ship sail without him. The thought was tempting, until she imagined Harry chasing after the *Dream of America* in a rowing boat like a speeded-up cartoon character. Harry would not be left behind without a fuss.

She was delayed on her visit to the purser's office, in helping a lady up one of the staircases. A stroke victim, Betty assumed as she first carried up the zimmer frame, then returned to help the woman whose mongoloid daughter beamed non-stop, but offered no practical help.

The girl must have been about twenty. Betty's daughter would have been the same age, had she lived. For there had been the one baby who had lived for four days.

In spite of her ill-health, the mother seemed cheerful. Looking at her, Betty thought that no price was too great for the privilege of motherhood. But without it? She took a deep breath and went to report Harry missing.

Had she remained just five minutes longer she would have seen the last lighter return and Thomas and Harry shuffle up the ladder. Harry was completely zonked by drink and sunshine. Thomas, with another crew member who came to his rescue, got Harry below decks and into bed. Thomas was back in his kitchen within minutes, in time to answer the call from the purser and report Mr Stillman's safe return.

Among the islands, little dramas of arrivals and departure are part of the pattern of life. Yet Ophelia never forgets Aunty Celia's return to Monday Island, some three months before her tragic demise. For Aunty Celia steps off the plane looking like a million dollars, and even Ophelia, who has never seen her before, knows at once who it is, poised there at the top of the three steps leading from the small twin-engined plane.

The sunlight flashes off Aunty Celia's sunglasses and the

patent leather shoes. Ophelia presses her face hard against the wire netting surrounding the airfield. Portia dabs her handkerchief against her sweating upper lip and murmurs, 'Oh my God, you see her, Gladys? You see our sister?'

Gladys, in a clean but faded cotton dress, leans against the wire with both hands high above her head in greeting, as if like a very lithe monkey she will suddenly shin up the netting. She smiles and shakes her head and chuckles 'eh, eh, eh' over and over to herself.

Celia walks across the sticky tarmac. For a moment it seems that she hasn't seen them, then just before she disappears behind the customs shed, she presses both her hands to her mouth and blows a kiss towards her waiting relatives.

'Celie,' screams Portia. 'Oh my God,' and bursts into tears.

Celia, in immigration, carelessly tosses her British passport on to the desk. The officer picks it up and slowly leafs through. He looks at the picture and looks up at Celia, but all he sees is his own reflection, twice over. He straightens his tie. Celia removes her sunglasses, slowly and deliberately.

'Derek,' she says.

The officer flings down the passport and leaps over the counter. 'Celie, how you doing, girl?' He swings her round and down and kisses her on both cheeks.

'Hey,' protests Celia. She straightens her little black hat and steps back.

'All ya see who here?' shouts Derek over the top of the partition into customs.

The customs officer abandons his suitcases and joins them.

'Celie man, you here for a holiday?'

The passport official nudges him.

'Oh, is your mother. I sorry to hear 'bout her, Celie.'

Celia blows her nose. 'Have my cases arrived yet?'

'Eh, eh, eh, you talking like a real English lady, Celie.'

And Celia finds herself in no time through customs and out the other side, protesting over her shoulder, 'Perhaps I got the crown jewels in there,' and into the bosom of her family.

Portia sweeps Celia right off her feet, crushing her in an enormous bear hug while Celia squeals with delight. Then on to Gladys who rests her head on her sister's shoulder and weeps. Celia shakes hands with Gladys's children. 'Why, your boys are quite grown up, Gladys,' she says and kisses Uncle Remus distantly on the cheek.

'This must be Ophelia,' says Aunty Celia, and, Ophelia, overcome by the occasion, gives a little curtsey as if she was meeting the Queen and says, 'Yes, ma'am,' in a voice that hardly comes out at all. Celia bends forward and kisses her. Ophelia gazes back with adoring eyes. 'How you've grown, child,' says Celia patting her on the cheek. 'You were just so high when I left.'

Aunty Celia speaks in such a funny accent. Her cheek is soft and smells of powder and perfume.

Portia looks at her sister somewhat more dispassionately and says, 'Eh, eh, Celie, you looking quite the lady.'

Then they all stand looking at one another, not quite knowing what to say or do next.

Aunty Celia burrows in her handbag. 'It's hot,' she says.

Ophelia can see tiny drops of sweat standing out on Aunty Celia's forehead on top of her face powder.

'You got a car now, Gladys?' Celia asks.

Gladys and Remus and the cousins shriek with laughter, as they form a long procession and set off for Sugar Bay, all dressed fit for a wedding. Portia goes first with one of the suitcases on her head, then comes Gladys with the other, then Aunty Celia in her pink silk suit and patent leather high heels. Ophelia comes close behind, shading her aunty from the sun with a large black umbrella. Portia's children follow, the older ones walking, the smaller ones hoisted on to the shoulders of the cousins.

The house has been scrubbed as never before, but as soon as Celia sets foot inside the living room, Ophelia can see that it won't do. In spite of the new plastic roses in the glass vase and the carefully dusted arrangement of seashells on the china cabinet, everything suddenly seems cheap and shabby.

Aunty Celia is sweating profusely by this time. Long streaks appear through the pan stick on her temples, which reveal the darker skin underneath. The base of her neck is quite moist.

Celia flings herself down on the vinyl settee.

'Now you English,' says Portia, 'I go light the charcoal and make you a nice cup of tea.'

'I'd rather something with ice.'

Everyone crowds into the small living room to watch Celia drink her mango juice. She drinks as if she will never stop and they stare at the green liquid vanishing down her throat and the ice cubes clunking against her lip.

'That's better,' says Celia, holding out the empty glass and laughing at everyone. 'This is a nice house you've got, Portia,' she says. 'Do you mind if I go to the bathroom.'

Portia claps her hands together, throws back her head, slaps her hands against her thighs and roars.

'What you think this is, chil'?' gasps Portia. 'This ain't no Hilton.'

'I go show you the toilet, aunty,' whispers Ophelia.

'Ain't the toilet I need,' whispers back Aunty Celia. 'Is a wash and brush up, I stink like a goat.'

Ophelia takes her aunt through to her bedroom, fetches a basin of water from the tap outside and passes it in through the window. 'You have a towel and some soap?' she asks Aunty Celia.

Aunty Celia shakes her head.

Ophelia reports back to her mother who grudgingly fetches a cake of hard green soap and half a towel from her own room. When Ophelia knocks and goes into the room Portia shoves the suitcases in after her.

'You can stay if you want to,' says Aunty Celia.

Ophelia sits on the edge of the bed and watches Aunty Celia while she arranges her jacket on a hanger and kicks off her shoes. Ophelia is alarmed to see that one of her heels is bleeding. 'I'm not used to walking in this heat,' explains her aunt. Ophelia realizes at once that the least her family could have done would have been to hire a car for the occasion.

Aunty Celia gently sponges the make-up off her face with tepid water. Then she dabs the flannel under her arms.

'They all still sitting out there?' she asks.

Ophelia opens the door a crack and peeps out. Everyone is standing in a semicircle about the room with their eyes glued to the bedroom door. Ophelia shuts it again quickly. She hears Portia turn on the television and the loud soundtrack of a Western.

Aunty Celie is slumped on the bed. She suddenly looks tired and breathes out loudly. 'What they all waiting for?' she asks angrily. 'I ain't no zoo animal.'

'They waiting for the presents.' Ophelia sits on the bed next to her aunt and rests her hand on her thigh. She has never seen such a white petticoat before. 'You want me to get you another drink, aunty?' she asks. Celia nods.

When Ophelia returns, stepping across the outstretched cousins sprawled in front of the telly, Aunty Celia looks brighter. She is applying a fresh layer of make-up in front of the triangle of mirror that Ophelia has propped on her windowsill.

Ophelia is fascinated. She picks up each article as her aunt puts it down and sniffs at it. When her aunt runs a comb through her hair, Ophelia would like to touch it. She has never seen such bouncy, shiny hair before.

'You got any plasters?' asks Celia.

Ophelia shakes her head.

Celia makes little pads out of coloured tissues she takes from a box in her suitcase. She forces her feet back into the high heels and groans. Ophelia hands her the silk jacket.

'All the presents are in that red suitcase,' says Celia. As she opens the bedroom door, the bounce returns to her step and her voice becomes bright. Ophelia follows with the suitcase.

A Fistful of Dollars just can't compete. The audience rating hits rock bottom. The cousins leap to their feet, the grownups sit more upright on the chairs, and all eyes are on the suitcase. Celia gestures for Ophelia to put it on the table.

'Does the fan work?' Celia asks. Portia turns it on grudgingly. 'It using electricity,' she points out. Portia is stripped to her petticoat.

Celia bends over the suitcase. There is a parcel for everybody, each one neatly wrapped and labelled. It is more like Christmas than a funeral gathering. Everyone squeals with excitement and exaggerated joy, and anxiously eyes what their neighbour has in his or her parcel.

Gladys has a tiny box which contains earrings so small and delicate she can only shake her head in wonder and know that she will never have occasion to wear them.

Portia is gratified to receive the largest parcel, the sight of which causes her to fall upon Celie's neck and weep. 'You bring this for me, Celie, eh girl, but you too too kind.' Inside is a magnificent crystal set of six tumblers and a punch bowl complete with glass ladle. Portia unpacks each item carefully, polishing it up with its tissue paper wrapping before she puts it in the glass-fronted cabinet with the other items for display purposes only.

The cousins try on their T-shirts printed with Union Jacks and pronounce them 'real sharp' which pleases Aunty Celia.

For Ophelia there is a small hexagonal jewellery box. When she opens the lid, music begins to play, so softly that she can scarcely hear it above the noise of the television, and a pink and white ballerina pirouettes slowly, reflected in a glass mirror on the inside of the lid. Ophelia is so overcome that she cannot speak. She goes outside and sits under the breadfruit tree and watches the tiny figure twirl round and round.

It is through Aunty Celia that Ophelia gets to know Monday Island. Celia, once Granma's funeral is over, wants to go everywhere and see everybody, and Ophelia scarcely leaves her aunt's side. They go to town and buy fashion magazines, then make a tour of the shops which sell materials.

Ophelia pauses by the gaudy sea island cottons that she usually wears. 'You like this one, aunty?'

Celia takes her elbow and steers her gently past. 'Phelie,' she explains, 'in England we do not wear cotton. Cotton shrinks. It creases and you look like a ragbag.' Celia crumples a length of the material in her hand. 'Now, you come and see this.' Celia goes over to the synthetic fibres, the crimplene and terylene, rayon and tricel. She screws up a little ball of material in her hand, then she unfolds it. 'Look.' It is like a miracle. The material lies as smooth as if it had come straight from the ironing table and gleaming with a faint sheen.

'But aunty, you done look at the price?'

Celia dismisses the price with a wave of her hands. 'If you dress like money, money will come to you,' she says.

Ophelia can see that Aunty Celia is a living testimony to the accuracy of this remark. Everywhere they go Celia is fêted and welcomed, by people she knows and by people she doesn't know.

Ophelia tries to imitate her aunt in everything she does, and is flattered when they are taken to be mother and daughter. Celia, after a quick look through Ophelia's wardrobe, dismisses everything and treats Ophelia to a new outfit from overgarments right down to lace panties and her first bra. They stroll through Soufrière as if they were in Paris. They drink ice cream sodas at a tourist hotel and Celia is amused that Ophelia attracts as many admiring glances as she does herself.

'Look, child,' says Celia, holding out her arm, 'you see how I changing colour here.'

Ophelia has indeed noticed how the sun has darkened her aunt whose skin now shines like the bark of a cherry tree.

'In Birmingham England,' says Celia, 'I going grey, believe me, chil', my skin go grey like a mouse.'

'When you going back, aunty?' Phelie asks.

Aunty Celia laughs and shrugs. 'I going back soon.'

'Take me with you.'

'What you go do in Birmingham England, Ophelia? This your home.'

'I could live with you and go to school.'

'How I go feed you and keep you?'

'But you rich, aunty.'

Celia looks down into her banana fizz. 'Every day, Phelie, I go work in the factory. But I ain't rich. I have a government house. But for everything else I have to pay. For heat, for light. It always cold, Phelie. Even in summer. And in winter the snow come everywhere and it all white. It white on top the cars and the roofs, on the trees and the dustbins, the pavements and all over the road. Everything is white. And when I waiting for the bus my feet hurt like hell. And I go inside into the factory and the heat make it hurt even worse.'

Ophelia sips at her drink.

'Why you don't work here, aunty, in the sweet drink factory in Sugar Bay.'

'Here,' says Aunty Celie scornfully, 'they ain't have the technology. If I work here, I only get one quarter of what I get in Birmingham England.' Celia pays for the drinks with a crisp new hundred-dollar note, and Ophelia knows that things in Birmingham England can't be as bad as Celia sometimes makes out.

On Celia's first morning back on Monday Island, Ophelia, who has given up her bed to her aunt, lies on the floor on a mattress not daring to move for fear of waking Aunty Celia up. Aunty Celie had remarked the night before that she needs her beauty sleep, and Ophelia would have hated to see her any less beautiful than she was the day before, still less to feel that she, Ophelia, was responsible.

Portia, up at dawn as usual, lights the fire and crashes in through the bedroom door without any ceremony and stands by her sister's bed.

'I go bring you some cocoa tea, Celia.' She shakes Celia's shoulder as she speaks.

Celia half opens her eyes. 'To boil up the blood, as mother used to say.' She struggles upright, leaning on one elbow in her nylon nightdress, and takes the cup and saucer with her free hand.

Portia goes out.

Celia winks at Ophelia. 'You had a good night?' She sips her cocoa tea. It is thick as semolina and sweetened as if Portia's life depended on it. Celia offers the cup to Ophelia. 'You want it?'

'Mammy go get vex if you don' drink it.'

210

'Phelie, I couldn't drink it if I tried.'

'What mammy go say?'

'Let's not tell her, shall we?'

It is the start of many little secrets they share together. Like the breakfast which follows.

Celia sits at the table, all alone. A place has been laid for her, set with a knife and fork and a mat. There is hot fresh bread under a napkin and a china pot of bush tea.

Portia emerges from the kitchen, smelling of hot fat, carrying a plate which she sets before her sister. Ophelia and the other children have already eaten, standing up in the kitchen or in the passageway leading on to the verandah. Now they all crowd into the doorway to watch Aunty Celie have her breakfast. Portia stands with arms folded, looking down.

'Well, isn't that lovely.' Celia looks at the plate of fried onions and corned beef swimming in a sea of chilli pepper and grease. She tastes just a fraction of the meat then takes a large mouthful of fresh bread. 'Delicious,' she says.

'What you does eat in Birmingham England?' demands Portia.

'Just a light breakfast. Cornflakes and a cup of tea.'

'Is not good all that tea you drink.'

'Cornflakes are very nice with fresh milk and sugar.'

'Where you get the fresh milk?'

'The milkman brings it every day to the door. In bottles.' Celia nibbles at a greasy onion.

'In bottles. Eh, eh.'

'You like English food?' asks Celia.

Everybody shrugs.

'Well, today I will cook for you English food. Ophelia will help me. First we will go to the supermarket.'

Portia goes back to the kitchen. The younger children lose interest.

'You want this?' hisses Celia.

Ophelia empties the plate quickly with her back to the door.

'We will go to the supermarket and we will buy baked beans and Irish potatoes and sausages and then I will buy all the ingredients for a cake.'

Celia and her niece spend the morning in town. They go to the biggest supermarket in Soufrière, but even this fails to impress Celia.

'It is very smart,' she says, 'but where are all the things I can buy at home? Where is the cheese and the cakes and pastries?'

Ophelia leads her aunt over to a refrigerator containing cheese, imported and processed. 'In Birmingham England we all too conscious of our health,' Celia sniffs.

It is only when they are back home and Celia is beating margarine and sugar to make the cake that the problem of the oven even occurs to her. 'Phelie,' she asks, 'where we go cook this damn thing?'

The only oven in the village is owned by the baker. When the mixture is ready, Celia and Ophelia trip down the footpath to the main road and cross over to the bakery.

Magnus is delighted to see them and only too happy to oblige. They are just in time to put the cake in with the last lot of bread for the day. He puts the cake on to a paddle and opens an oven door, which lets out a heat so ferocious that Celia steps back with her hands clasped to her cheeks.

'Oh my God, Phelie,' she says, 'that go be too hot.'

Sure enough, by the time the cake is cooked in the middle the outside is a cinder. They take the sad remains home and feed it to the chickens. But the potato chips are very popular. Celia stands over the hot charcoal and the boiling fat until her hair is lank with grease. She never offers to cook again.

212

One day after the funeral, after the uncles from Canada have come and gone, Celia suggests a swim. She and Ophelia change in their bedroom then slip on dresses for the walk down to the beach. Celia stuffs her hair inside an enormous yellow shower cap to protect it from the salt water. As they pass the kitchen door, Portia steps out, hands bloody from gutting fish.

'Where you going?'

'Sea bath,' replies Ophelia. She too has taken to tying up her hair in curlers and a scarf.

'You ain't going nowhere,' says Portia. 'It too hot. You go get ill.'

'Why don't you come with us?' Celia suggests, stepping between mother and daughter.

'And who go cook food?'

'We can help you with that later.'

'Phelie, you not going out, you hear me? You get back in the house.'

Celia puts a hand on Portia's arm. 'You don't really believe that it'll make her ill?'

'She go catch a chill.'

'That's ridiculous.'

'Is ridiculous, eh? You think you is she mother? Who go nurse Phelie when she sick? You going to Birmingham and leave me to make she better.'

'I'll see she doesn't get cold.'

'Don' make me blasted vex.' Portia turns back into the dark kitchen.

Celia takes Ophelia by the arm and leads her outside. 'She always vex,' she says.

The two of them set out into the sunshine, towards the sparkling blue glimpsed between rusty roofs. At the top of the sandy slope Celia hangs her towel and her dress over a branch, kicks off her high heels and runs down over the white hot sand towards the water.

'Hello, you all,' she calls out to the other bathers, splashing into the turquoise water, screaming at the coldness.

Ophelia follows more slowly, shy to be there on the beach in a new swimsuit and all the fishermen sitting under the palm trees, drinking and watching.

Celia is swimming out to sea. She doesn't need to swim towards other people, other people always come to her. A tall dark youth dives under the water and bobs up next to her.

'Hello, Celia,' he calls out. 'How you doing?'

Celia spins round and laughs, flicking water towards him with her fingers. He dives and comes up, this time behind her, catching her round the waist. 'Celia,' he says, 'why you don' marry me?' Celia, looking up, sees him only as a silhouette against the sparkling water and the setting sun. 'You too young for me, boy,' says Celia. 'Why you don' marry Phelie instead?'

'Who that?' Ophelia asks when she swims up.

'He call he self Thomas,' replies Celia. 'He is a seaman.'

'Why you don' marry him, aunty, and stay on Monday Island?'

'What for I go marry a sailor who spend his life at sea? Anyway,' and Aunty Celie looks sadder than Ophelia has ever seen her before, 'he too young. You know, Phelie, I thirty-eight, chil', I older than your mother.'

Ophelia looks at her aunt who is still so young.

'Why you ain't have no children, Aunty Celie?' she asks. 'You never been to see no doctor?'

'Child, the only reason I see a doctor is that I don't want no children. What I would do with my life if I had children? Then I would be like Portia, eh?'

After this outing to the beach, Celia goes out more on her own. Ophelia is hurt. She sits for hours on the bridge peeling guavas with her teeth and spitting the skins into the gutter, waiting for Aunty Celie to step off a bus or return from town, and dreaming of potato chips wrapped up in newspaper.

When Celie comes back she wants to talk about Thomas, but all Ophelia wants to talk about is Birmingham England. Celia is quite short with her niece and suggests that if she is serious about going to Birmingham England she had first better see about getting herself a good education.

Celia's holiday becomes so long that her straightening is growing out and still she makes no mention of leaving. In the evenings, Portia makes no attempt to listen politely to her sister's stories but turns on the television as loud as it will go. She starts to make remarks like 'Food cost money' and 'Some folks has to earn their living' and she refuses to lend Celia her clothes pegs any more.

Aunty Celia spends more and more time just sitting in the drawing room. When Thomas's ship sails she doesn't bother to get dressed and go out any more, not even with Ophelia.

'You ain't have no work to go to?' Portia asks one evening.

'How I go live if I ain't have work?'

'You got a man, ain't you?'

'Course I got a man, what 'bout you?'

'How you think I get eight children,' replies Portia indignantly. 'I ain't the blessed Virgin Mary.'

'I can see that.'

Ophelia's heart is in her mouth when she hears her aunt dare to make this last remark.

'Perhaps,' says Portia, very slow and deliberate, 'you ain't have no ticket to go home with?'

With great dignity, Celia opens her handbag and takes out her plane ticket, British Airways. She places the ticket on the display cabinet for everyone to see and walks out of the house.

Ophelia never sees her alive again.

Afterwards she sometimes thinks that if Granma hadn't died, Aunty Celia would still be alive and well in the Coca Cola factory in Birmingham England. But of course, if Granma hadn't died, she would never have met her Aunty Celie at all.

At the same time that Betty in cabin number 2137 poured cup after cup of black coffee in an attempt to sober up Harry, and Ophelia on the cargo boat put in her curlers for an early night, Jancis on Monday Island sat on the horsehair settee between Nelson and Napoleon. The blind Miss Simpson served the tea and the younger Misses Simpson were dipping their plain biscuits into their cups and sucking them noisily. The boys had each been given a glass of bright pink sarsaparilla with a straw. They sucked at the straws and gazed wide-eyed at the three sisters.

'I pray every night for my sister Ophelia,' said Jancis to break the silence.

'We pray too oh we pray yes we do we pray to God for her,' chorused the sisters.

'You see the lamp,' intoned the blind Miss Simpson, and she waved her white stick in the direction of a small red sanctuary lamp set on a shelf in front of a statue of Mary. 'We lit the lamp yesterday I fetched the lamp and the bottle of oil.'

'And I poured the oil into the lamp.'

'And I struck the match.'

'And then,' continued the eldest Miss Simpson, 'we prayed to God to protect our dear little girl Ophelia and we recited the rosary in front of the lamp and I can stretch out my hand and feel the warmth and make sure that the lamp is still burning and as long as it is burning we know God is looking after our dear girl.'

'And that He will bless and protect her little boys.'

Another silence ensued, during which the Misses Simpson sat and stared at Jancis, who, oblivious of their expectations, finished her cup of tea. It was nervousness, rather than the realization that she was now the chief bearer of news from the outside world, that prompted her to begin talking. But details of the youth fellowship and the Bible study group, Tuesday's choir practice and the forthcoming jumble sale, were tame affairs beside the diet they had come to expect from Eugenia and then from Ophelia. By the time she announced that subscriptions were now due for the monthly newsletter, one Miss Simpson in bed, the other propped on a chair, both lay back and snored.

Nobody noticed the trickle running down Napoleon's shorts and into his shoes except Nelson who nudged Jancis in the middle of the parable of the fig tree and whispered loudly, 'He urinate, Jancis,' which Jancis totally failed to understand. Instead she woke the two sisters with a spirited rendering of 'Onward Christian Soldiers'. The blind Miss Simpson beat out the rhythm on the wooden floor with her stick. The Miss Simpson with the polio clonked out a calypso rhythm with her teaspoon on the metal bedhead, and the deaf Miss Simpson clapped and sang loudly out of key and out of time. Nelson giggled and Napoleon clasped his hands over his ears and wailed. Jancis's first visit with the boys turned out to be a success after all.

After leaving the Misses Simpson, Jancis walked across Boules Common to the sea, where she stripped off the little boys' clothes, tucked her skirt in her pants and led them into the water. They both gripped her hands tightly and clung to her when the waves broke against their little stomachs and Jancis hugged them and laughed and was happier than she had ever been in her life before.

They wandered along the beach collecting sea shells until the sun dried the sand on their bare skin to a pale powder. They searched through the enormous red leaves along the beach edge, looking for almonds, and hunted for landcrabs in the shrubs behind the almond trees. Jancis carried Napoleon sun-warm and naked on her hip.

When she took the boys to her home, her parents were overjoyed.

'The sweet Lord know', said her mother, 'that if a angel child need a home my door is always open,' and the matter was settled.

The evening meal was divided into five rather than three, and everything that the boys said or did was a matter for comment.

Before Jancis tucked the boys one into each end of her bed, she taught them how to kneel and pray to God their Heavenly Father, with their palms together, fingers pointing towards heaven and eyes screwed tight shut. 'We thank you, God our Father,' said Jancis, 'for a lovely day, for the sunshine and for the good things you give us. We pray you to bless the mother of Napoleon and Nelson, our good sister Ophelia, and keep her safe in your loving arms, amen.'

Revived by several cups of coffee and a cold shower, Harry has ploughed his way through a five-course dinner, but Betty can tell he isn't happy. There was no sign of Lou and Sam so they had eaten alone which was unusual and Betty had not enjoyed the experience.

Now, as they sipped their liqueurs, Harry broke his silence by belching, then went on to tell Betty what was troubling him. He was worried about the Fancy Dress Ball, an event built up to be the orgasmic triumph of the whole cruise, before the *Dream of America* turned and sailed for home.

'But honey,' said Betty, 'if you were so keen to go as a cowboy, why didn't you bring your own clothes?'

'Fancy dress is different from the real thing.' Harry knew he couldn't go into that ballroom in his carefully stained Western clothes smelling of saddle soap and horse.

'But it's not as if you get them dirty, Harry. I mean you're only acting at the Club.'

Harry snorted. Clint Eastwood acted. The Rock City Sharpshooters were for real. Why, if she'd seen the way he'd dived over those hay bales into the saloon . . .

Betty gathered together her sequined evening purse, postcards, pen and address book, and stood up. Harry was being childish.

'If there are no cowboy outfits you like, you'll just have to go as something else.'

'You don't understand, Bet. I'm a real Sheriff now, I just got my promotion. I'm not going to that party with some kid's pistol stuck in a plastic holster.'

'Well, I'm off to choose my costume, Harry. Give me half an hour.'

Harry took out a cheroot. He looked utterly downcast.

'Harry, I'm sure you can find something else. Go on . . . surprise me.'

Harry puffed and thought. Surprise her? Well, how about it? If there wasn't a cowboy costume for him, he'd have to think of something else. Something really outrageous. He'd go all out for the Entertainer's Badge. As the ship changed course for home, he would be the life and soul of the party, so that ever afterwards people would say, 'You remember that man, Harry Whatsisname? Stillman. Harry Stillman. What a character!'

Harry was totally unaware of the quiet formation of parties for the following evening, which no one had invited him to join, but Harry was happy with his dreams. Why should he be confined to any particular group? He saw himself moving among his twelve hundred friends, stopping to pat someone on the back here, or to whisper suggestively into the ear of an attractive lady there. The whole ship was Harry's oyster.

Betty, down in costumes, had never seen anything more gorgeous. 'Er, d'you have a larger size?' she asked hopefully.

But no, there was no larger size. Betty flipped along the rack. There was nothing that took her fancy so much as this costume. Betty giggled. What would Harry say? His wife in scarlet satin and black lace.

'D'you think I'd fit?'

'We could try, madam.'

Betty was grateful for the tact of the wardrobe lady who made no comment as she fought her way into the glorious yards of material and emerged as red as the dress and gasping for breath. The effect was stunning. She kicked out with one foot and caused the whole skirt to ripple in flashes and rivulets of crimson fire. She risked looking up a little further. Why had Harry never told her she had such a magnificent figure? She saw her bosom straining beneath the black lace film and yearned for an orchid or a gardenia to offset its creamy whiteness.

'Not very brown, are you, dear? Don't go on deck much?'

'No. I don't like the sun. It gives me a headache,' Betty explained.

The woman arranged the puffed sleeves over the folds of flesh on Betty's upper arms.

'Will you be having your hair done, or would you like a wig?'

'A wig,' said Betty stiffly.

The wardrobe mistress hummed along the shelves and cupboards. Betty studied her reflection from the neck downwards and took a few experimental breaths, quick shallow puffs from the upper lungs, the only part of her rib cage that she could move.

'This suit you, dear, or this?'

Betty looked at the confections, white, blonde, brunette, black, loose or elaborately coiffed.

'That one, I think.'

Madame de Pompadour herself could not have looked finer. The wig added at least three feet to Betty's very ordinary height. It had the effect, she thought, of elongating her whole figure. But the costume had been made for someone slightly taller than she was so that the hem dragged on the ground. She would have to wear her very highest heels.

'Do you want to take it with you?'

'No, I don't want my husband to see.'

'Okay, dear, we'll leave it here until later. Number thirteen. I'll mark your name on the ticket.'

'Number thirteen?' Betty shivered.

'Something the matter, madam?'

Betty laughed. She must throw off all this small-town superstition once and for all.

Now it was Harry's turn. He stubbed out his cigar, put it into his breast pocket, and marched purposefully through the door. He intended to go down with a flourish if only in the photograph albums and memories of other people's holidays.

Harry knew he would never make the grade as Prince Charming and, recognizing his cultural limitations, ruled out the French courts. The rubber mask of President Reagan was tempting, but made him feel faintly uneasy.

221

Then, perched high on a shelf, Harry saw an enormous Mickey Mouse head. It appealed to him immediately and when the wardrobe mistress pointed out that he had the perfect figure for the outfit, Harry looked no further.

'I'll slip along for it later,' he said. He really wanted to surprise Betty. He imagined her peering around the ballroom, trying to find him, and mentally rehearsed his Mickey Mouse voice. He didn't want to put her out of her misery too soon. First, a few words as he whirled past with some Princess Diana look-alike. Poor old Betty at an otherwise empty table, fiddling with a glass which had once held orange juice.

Then at midnight, he could hear the announcement, 'The first prize is awarded to . . . Mickey Mouse,' cheers, laughter, and Harry whispering in the compère's ear, 'Harry Stillman, yes, Stillman as in Stillborn, from Rock City.' On the far side of the room, he could see the surprise and pride reflected in Betty's face.

Betty, up on the compass deck, felt nothing between herself and the stars. Though she laughed at herself now for her naïvety, this was how she had imagined the whole voyage, just herself on a white ship, small as a speck of foam in the vast expanse of ocean. This was how sailors must have felt in days gone by, setting their course by the glittering constellations above them.

Below was the black immensity of the water. She thought of Thomas and she thought of Ophelia, and was troubled. She would have liked to feel that everyone was as happy as she was.

She had never imagined that the moon could be so brilliant. Her shadow as clear as at noon. She leaned on the starboard railing, and thought of asking Thomas if he would mind bringing her bedclothes up here. But she could hardly do that after all she had heard, it might be misinterpreted . . .

In unspoken answer to these grosser thoughts, Harry's shadow clambered arm over arm up the railings beside her like some ghostly orang utang. Harry had a new jauntiness to his step and his cigar belched smoke like a factory chimney.

Betty coughed and waved her hands in protest.

Harry was too good-humoured to notice. 'I've got myself a costume,' he smirked.

'That's great, Harry.' Betty looked up and out to sea, away from him. 'You see that, Harry?' she asked. The cargo ship was there on their port side. Whereas the *Dream of America* skimmed effortlessly over the surface of the water, the other boat seemed to create troughs and crests where there were none. It wallowed and rolled from side to side under a thick black pall of smoke.

'Looks like a cargo ship,' she continued. It was the sort of remark for which Harry would usually have bitten her head off.

'Sure does, honey.' Harry was obviously pleased as punch about something.

'D'you think it's the same one we saw this morning?'

Harry shrugged.

'I'm sure it is, Harry,' said Betty with all the excitement of meeting up with an old friend. 'Only it left hours before us.'

'Honey, a ship like this could knock the shit out of an old crate like that.'

'I'd be ill if our ship rolled about like that.'

'I told you this morning, Betty, a cargo ship is for cargo.'

They stood and watched the ship slipping astern, until it was distinguishable only as a black shape defined by the sparkling waters all around.

A sudden breeze made Betty shiver. Goose pimples stood out on her bare arms, and a cloud obscured the face of the moon. 'Harry,' she said, 'I feel as if someone has just walked over my grave.'

DAY THREE
Christian Island

'We are deluged with facts, but we are losing the ability to feel them.'

William Shawcross,
The Quality of Mercy

'During the voyages I was frequently a witness to the fatal effects of the exclusion of fresh air.'

George Francis Dow,
Slave Ships and Slaving (1788)

As the ship docked, Betty experienced the usual feeling of relief at the prospect of going on shore, before her habitual panic induced by alien surroundings set in. Harry, by contrast, approached each island in the same spirit as Christopher Columbus, who collected islands much as an Indian collects scalps.

Columbus had named this island Santa Maria de los Angeles, or Holy Mary of the Angels. By that time he was so into the swing of bagging islands that he carried a piece of paper around in his pocket, a list, with names to suit every occasion. His initial experience of appropriation and christening on Monday Island, he now regretted. On reflection the name was pretty feeble but it could not be altered once the report to Queen Isabella had been filed. Like a housewife faced with an infinite number of choices, he realized that it was not always easy to make the right decision in the heat of the moment, and on this occasion he was determined to fulfil his promise to that formidable old lady, his maternal grandmother, who suffered from gout.

Over the next two hundred years, the island changed its name and its flag as often as some people change their underwear. Sir Francis Drake realized on annexing the property, as any good Protestant would have done, that to call the island Santa Maria de anything was to put his head, theologically speaking, on the block. The name he chose offered no insult to the mother of God, and could at the same time be interpreted as honouring his queen, since one reason for his despatch thither was to put malicious tongues at rest. He confounded his detractors once and for all by denying any carnal knowledge of his monarch and renaming this miniature Garden of Eden 'Virgin Island'.

The name Virgin Island was to the Dutch of the time like a red rag to a bull. So the British and Dutch fleets played tag among the Antilles until the British grew bored with the game and went off to chase the Spanish and French instead. Whereupon the Dutch, who had little respect for anybody who might be sitting upon the throne of England, virgin or not, chose instead to name the island after some seventeenth-century writer of hymns who has long since been forgotten.

From the top of the neighbouring island, the British looked comfortably down on the twenty square miles of flat parched land, and left the Dutch to sing their hymns in peace until another lowland people, the Danes, cast covetous eyes on one of the few islands they could even consider capturing since their soldiers were unused to hills.

Thus the Danes marched their twenty soldiers on to the island and after bitter fighting during which three members of the Dutch garrison of fifteen died of dysentery, they claimed the island in the name of the Danish crown. The conquerors, who had hitherto lacked the wherewithal to ice their pastries, settled down to a good solid hundred years devoted to the cane, but showed the same lack of imagination in selecting a name for their new territory as they did in the naming of their kings. Hence, Christian Island it became, after about the fifth monarch of that name, which went on to prove immensely flattering to the next ten in line of succession.

Betty, completely misled by the name (the first erroneous impression confirmed by the many spires thrusting skyward over the tops of the yellow houses), stepped on to the island as if she were on a pilgrimage. Harry, who had given no thought whatsoever to the name, was simply overjoyed to be once more on American soil. For the Stars and Stripes had hung limp in the steamy heat over Government House for nearly three quarters of a century, ever since an astute bargain in real estate had brought the whole island under the protective wing of the eagle. He stepped ashore with all the confidence of one going home.

Ophelia has no home, not in the way that America is Harry's home. Though the little island which saw her first draw breath has now spewed her out on to the sea of life like flotsam to be carried here and there at the whim of the tide, her estrangement from it began long ago. Then, just as one last violent contraction expels a child from its mother's womb, one dramatic event expelled Ophelia from the womb-like security of her early childhood.

Ophelia was twelve. She remembers it well . . .

Lying on her crumpled bed, she hears in the first chilly light of dawn the cocks crow all over the village. A child cries, a door slams and she smells kerosene and woodsmoke as a fire is lit outside her window. Ophelia closes her eyes again, but it is too late, the familiar weight of sorrow has returned. She is in a different bed in a different village and it is not Granma who grunts as she puts the heavy pan of water on the fire to prepare the hot drink that will boil up the blood for the day. Granma is in hospital.

Next door a radio comes on, then another. 'It's Radio Monday every day of the week.' She hears the weather forecast, which scarcely varies from day to day, and the island news and parliamentary report, both of which are brief. Then come the holy chords which herald the religious broadcasts for the day. The announcer's voice is charged with holy dread.

'We regret to announce the death of Eugenia Branston, of Nelson's Look Out.' Ophelia has surely misheard her grandmother's name, but as if there could be any mistake, there follow the names of her children, 'Gladys Dupont also of Nelson's Look Out, Celia Smith of Birmingham England, Cecil and Eisenhower Cotton of Montreal, Canada, Portia Lapierre of Sugar Bay. Miz Branston was also the loving grandmother of . . .' but the rest is drowned by Portia's shrieks. 'Oh my God. My mammy. My mammy done dead and lef' me all alone. Oh sweet Jesus,' and Portia who has seen her mother at most twice a year over the past twelve years thus announces from her verandah to the whole village that her house is a house of mourning.

But Ophelia, who has locked her sorrow away so firmly since Granma was taken into hospital six weeks ago, prepares for the funeral and the arrival of the relatives from overseas. She scrubs and cleans and bakes with eyes dry enough to sting.

She sees Granma's face in the black puddings that Portia makes for the party and wonders what Granma would say could she see the breadcrumbs added to make the recipe go further. She thinks of Granma lying there in a big fridge costing ever so many dollars a day to give her uncles and her aunt time to fly home, and her heart feels as cold as if it too were being slowly chilled.

Granma's house is the obvious place to put up the visitors now that it stands empty, but after living in Canada and England how would Uncle Cecil and Uncle Eisenhower and Aunty Celia manage? Quite apart from the long walk up the dirt track to Nelson's Look Out or the cost of a taxi, the house is not grand enough for such dignitaries. They will be more comfortable in Portia's house not ten minutes' walk from the tarmac and a bus stop.

For the same reason that Granma cannot be brought home to die, she cannot be brought home for the night before her funeral. No one is willing to carry her up the path from the main road. Ophelia is greatly relieved. She has been worrying about Granma lying in the living room like some monstrous black lollipop, slowly defrosting and beginning to drip.

So Eugenia Branston is refrigerated until the last possible moment then rushed via Sugar Bay to the Catholic church in Nelson's Look Out, in the back of a banana lorry, surrounded by her distraught relatives.

Betty was glad to step ashore. The sea this morning had lost its mill pond look and was decidedly choppy. The *Dream of America* was hardly affected, but the smaller boats anchored in the harbour tossed their masts in the wind.

'Quite a swell, eh, honey?' said Harry, every inch the sailor. Betty didn't know where he got these nautical terms from.

A large poster greeted them on the dockside. WEL-COME TO SMILE ISLE it screamed in capitals and underneath in smaller letters MORE SMILES PER MILE THAN ANYWHERE ELSE IN THE CARIBBEAN. The letters were printed in yellow across a black face with an enormous white smile. The teeth made Betty shudder. Smiles there were in plenty on the quayside but all of them framed by charmingly pink lips set in white faces. Betty relaxed. She could tell she was going to love Christian Island.

Betty and Harry picked their way across the quay towards the yellow ochre buildings beyond. Harry just didn't know where to point his camera first and Betty didn't help with her 'Look, Harrys' as she caught sight of yet another view more beautiful than the one before.

The houses were beautiful in the old Danish colonial style, all carefully tended, their gardens manicured and brilliant with colour. The town was teeming with tourists, and Betty felt comfortably at home. Little brick arcades were built out over the sidewalks and the windows glittered with displays.

She stood before the window of a shop called 'South American Emeralds'. She had never seen such big stones.

Could they really be genuine? A forest of ghostly plaster hands sported rings with gold settings as chunky as a cowboy's lassoo and every stone the size of a dollar piece.

In the next display case was a necklace which took her breath away. Betty, with her costume in mind, knew that it was just the sort of thing Louis XV would have given his mistress. It lay on its own, gently radiating the cold green glow of reflected sunlight on a cushion of black velvet.

Ophelia, not quite twelve, kneels on the floor next to Granma's bed and nuzzles into the dark, velvet skin at the crook of her elbow.

'Wake up, Granma,' she pleads.

She may as well ask a mountain to get up and walk, for Granma's self-inflicted remedies of egg white and flour and charms about the waist have failed. She lies like a beached turtle, weeping with pain and praying, 'Sweet Jesus, make my stomach better is all I ask this day.'

Ophelia does not hang around waiting for miracles. She runs out of the house and over the patch of ground laid bare by the chickens, screaming for Aunty Gladys. And it is Ophelia who runs the ten miles downhill to the coast road to catch a bus into town to find a doctor quickly quickly, because she fears her cousins may be too slow.

It takes Uncle Remus, five grown cousins and the ambulance driver to lift the blubbering mound that was Granma on to a stretcher and manoeuvre it down the rickety steps to the ambulance. Ophelia stands on the verandah and sees the door shut and the ambulance drive away. Granma has not said goodbye.

Ophelia shrinks back into the darkest corner of the verandah under the plumbago vine, where the shade is dark and warm about her shoulders, like Granma herself.

She hears Aunty Gladys calling for her in the house and by the pigsty, and she sees her cousins sent outside to look for her. She peers through the stalks and the leaves and the purple flowers and sees Aunty Gladys fasten a scarf tightly about her head and jam her straw hat on top of that and is sorry to make her aunt worried for she loves her dearly. Next to Granma she is the dearest person in Ophelia's life. But she is not Granma, and Granma is the only person who can comfort Ophelia now.

Granma's apron still hangs over the verandah railing. Ophelia sees the top of Aunty Gladys's head pass behind it. Then she pulls the apron into the shade and buries her face in the checked cloth. It smells of coconut oil and cinnamon, and Ophelia remembers . . . Ophelia stacks the dirty dishes on the draining board. Granma rinses them under the tap. A few grains of rice gurgle down the waste pipe and a squabble breaks out among the hens outside.

Granma and Ophelia lean out of the window to watch them fight. The cock flutters down the hillside and dives among the hens, who scatter, leaving him alone to snap up the last few grains.

Granma leans out and screams 'Go 'way' and the cock scutters off after his ladies. She will not rinse another plate as long as he is there. She stacks the rinsed plates under the running tap, picks up the scrap of cloth that was once a dress, and rubs it on the hard bar of blue soap. A cold greasy lather scatters the hens who have reconvened to peer eagerly up the waste pipe like astronomers looking for the stars.

When she has finished, Granma flicks her hands through the unglazed window and the hens run to the dark specks on the dry, hard soil. But there is nothing there. Granma dries her hands on the curtain and leads Ophelia on to the verandah.

She removes her checked apron and folds it over the chair back. She sits with Ophelia on her knee in the fading light and calls out greetings to neighbours returning from the fields.

'Good night, Etienne, how the grapefruit doing?'

'Good night, Miss Branston. They fine, thank you.'

Ophelia puts an arm round Granma's neck and rests her head on the well-padded shoulder. Granma croons a lullaby. Her mind returns to her own childhood and beyond, and she begins to talk with an excitement the child has never heard before. For Eugenia, in her eighties, feels a sense of urgency about everything she does. There is suddenly so little time left and so much to do, and one of the most important things is the passing on of the family history as told her by her father George. Eugenia can remember many an afternoon when he took her down to the sea, or sat her next to him on a wooden stool to watch a game of dominoes. It is in the drowsy warmth of her Granma's lap that Ophelia learns what Eugenia calls 'Real hist'ry. I ain't talking 'bout no corn laws, chil'. I ain't talking 'bout no William the Conqueror, I talking 'bout your relatives and how you come to born on this island.'

Eugenia tells her how she was born to her father late in his life with all the promise of a rainbow after the Flood. For George found himself at the turn of the century, rising fifty and with little to his credit except a string of illegitimate children whose numbers were reputed to run into three figures. George was a quadroon who went by the name of Branston. This name he inherited from his father Horatio who had in turn been given the surname by his mother Nell. Nell was a slave, who never found out the name of the sailor who deflowered her and left her pregnant, but who had discovered that the majority of the crew of the *Golden Fleece* were Devonians, in the fine seafaring tradition established by Drake and Raleigh. In the belief that Branston was a town in Devon, she named her son accordingly. The name appears on the island with an infinite number of spellings (such is the hazard of an oral tradition) but the name may well preserve some distant folk memory of the south Devon seaside town of Branscombe.

Like the proverbial grasshopper, George made his way through the spring and summer of his life by being both decorative and entertaining. From his paternal grandfather he inherited the honey-coloured skin and features which, though somewhat heavy in the cider drinking, agricultural mode, were nonetheless finer than negroid. From his mother Bessie, one-time dressmaker and lady's maid, he inherited a certain flamboyance, the flair for creating an impression. But all this was so much window dressing. He was a child born into freedom with neither the education nor the skill to enable him to make his way in the world by anything other than personal charm.

Hence his delight at the arrival of Eugenia, or more accurately speaking, at the arrival of her mother Alice on his doorstep some ten months earlier. George, opening the front door of the family house in Nelson's Look Out, rum bottle in hand, realized that there were alternatives to drinking himself to death with nothing but Bessie's jumbi for company.

Life began again. George took Alice under his roof and into his bed. Like Snow White she cooked and cleaned and tended the garden and even presented him with a baby daughter. George never quite conquered the demon rum and at that stage in his life it was too late for him to become a truly reformed character. But at her mother's skirts Eugenia learned a love of the soil and of God, which were, Alice assured her, the only two things that can be relied upon in this life. And from George, Eugenia learned a sense of fun and a zest for living which never let her down. She also learned George's own colourful version of the family history.

'Phelie!' calls Gladys gently, shaking the child's shoulder. 'Phelie, we been looking all over for you, child.'

Ophelia puts her arms round Aunty Gladys's neck and cries. It is the only time she weeps for her grandmother.

Afterwards Gladys leads her down to the tap in the yard to splash cool water over her burning face.

'You hungry, Phelie?' asks Gladys.

Ophelia cannot eat. Gladys scrapes the remains of lunch into the slop bucket and hand in hand they go out the back to the pigsties, where there are two porkers, one for Aunty Gladys's family and one for Granma. The pigs hurl themselves at the wooden fence and thrust their snouts through, squealing as loud as if the knife was already at their throats.

'Granma don' like pigs,' says Ophelia.

'For true?' Gladys looks surprised. 'Why she don' like pigs?'

Ophelia shrugs. It's hard to put into words.

'They just meat,' smiles Gladys. 'Soon they go get fat.'

And Ophelia wonders who will make the black puddings now with Granma gone . . .

Ophelia sits on the school wall in her long white socks, kicking her heels against the stones and eating her way through a lapful of guavas. She stares at her grandmother's pig, slung by its hind legs from the branch of a tree on the other side of the dirt road. Ophelia has hated the pig for such a long time that its squeals cannot now move her to pity, even when the metal stick is jabbed into its neck and the blood spurts out, and the pig screams and twists this way and that.

Ophelia has for as long as she can remember (to her it feels like forever) had the job of feeding the pig. She dislikes everything about it – the smell of the rancid leftovers, the stench of the pig itself stretched out in the sunshine in its own filth, and worst of all its small red eyes which light up with greed as soon as she opens the back door.

Granma is over by the big tubs of boiling water. She is anxious that the job should be properly done and the pig nicely scalded so that the bristles scrape off cleanly, leaving it as soft and pink as a newborn white man's baby. So she checks that the fire is well stoked and tests the knives on the butcher's table. She curses the last squirmings when a few drops of blood miss the bucket below, and heaves a sigh of relief when the pig is at last still.

'That damn pig awkward to the last, eh, Phelie?' she calls out.

Ophelia smiles back and carries on chewing, surprised to hear that Granma felt like that about the pig. She hopes Granma will not get another one, but knows she will, for there has always been a pig in the pen behind the house.

The pigs still waiting their turn grunt and squeal and sniff the air as Granma's pig is lowered to the ground, then humped upside down towards the tub of steaming water. But this pig is so big that it has to be scalded in two goes, first the hindquarters then the fore, with its legs sticking up in the air like snorkels.

'Eh eh eh, but that's a mighty fine pig,' chorus the men.

'He grow like the devil hisself,' chuckles Granma, thinking of the smoked pork and the salt pork and the black puddings. Ophelia is proud that her grandmother's pig is so large. The next one being hoisted into the tree is a mere runt by comparison.

For three or four days the whole village stinks of pig. In the back yard, Granma stands up to her elbows in blood and fat, salt and woodsmoke. The smell lingers long after the pig has disappeared.

Eugenia's black puddings are famous. People even come up from town. Ophelia stands on the verandah taking orders from the street below and relaying them into the kitchen where Granma sweats over an enormous saucepan in which the puddings bounce in the boiling broth. She wraps each one in a brown paper bag and Ophelia delivers it to the customers who loll against the verandah railings discussing the latest scores in the test match.

When at last Granma herself staggers out of the kitchen

with sweat oozing between the folds of flesh at the base of her neck, everybody knows that the puddings 'done finish'. And with a cheerful 'Good night, Miss Branston' the customers satisfied and unsatisfied take themselves off into the setting sun.

Then Granma sits down heavily on the verandah steps and her apron pockets rattle with money. She holds out a brown paper bag for Ophelia who laughs as she bites through the pig gut and feels the explosion of hot blood and chilli pepper on her tongue.

'What 'bout you, Granma, you ain't eating nothing?'

Granma shakes her head.

Betty peered at the price tag. Twenty-five thousand dollars.

'You figuring on buying something, Bet?'

'Just looking, Harry.' Betty was halfway through the door when Sally pushed past her as if she were the doorman and disappeared into the crowd before she even had time to say hullo.

'Are you out of your mind?' Harry hissed, following her in.

'I'm just looking.' Of course if she'd kept her little windfall from the fruit machines yesterday she might have been tempted. Not to the necklace in the window, but one of these little unset emeralds maybe, which lay about in sparkling mountains like illustrations for a fairy story.

Betty walked over to the necklaces.

'May I help you, madam?'

The sales staff were, of course, all white.

Betty pointed to the twenty-five thousand dollar necklace. The assistant unlocked the showcase, leaned forward and fastened it around Betty's neck.

Betty picked up the hand mirror. She could see Harry looking over her shoulder, his eyes standing out on stalks. She concentrated on the necklace. Since she'd avoided the sun her skin was still pleasantly creamy and the colour

238

looked just right. She undid the top button of her shirt and parted the collar slightly.

'For God's sake, Bet!'

Betty ignored him. It was a strange sensation to be trying on thousand-dollar jewellery, but it was the sort of thing some people did every day. Did the dress come first and was the jewellery just an accessory, or was it the other way round? She revolved slowly in front of the mirror. The back was as neat as the front. She was quite proud of her gently rounded shoulders. She didn't have a humped back like some people she knew. She took her hormone replacement compound regularly. She worried sometimes about any side effects, as her blood pressure tended to be high, but felt that on the whole Harry was to blame for that.

Harry was not exactly relaxed, but sufficiently in command of the credit cards to look about him equably. He judged the distance to the door and calculated how many emeralds he could sweep up with both hands before making a dash for it. 'Whadya think, Sundance?' he muttered under his breath and cocked the trigger of his telephoto lens in readiness. Outside in the glaring sun the trusty Silver hung his head, fooling anybody into believing he was half asleep. Only Harry knew that when he burst through that door with both guns blazing, Silver would spring into action like an arrow from the bow. Harry thrust his thumbs through his belt and chewed gum, real easy.

'It's not quite right,' Betty was saying to the assistant. 'Something slightly darker perhaps?'

Harry looked round the showroom. The place was dripping with emeralds – all identical in colour as far as he could see. Jeezus. He pushed his blue towelling hat on to the back of his head and scratched his scalp. Bet must sure have flipped her lid.

'Where Ophelia?' asks Portia who has visited Eugenia in hospital, and now stands in the doorway of Gladys's house.

'She in there.' Gladys indicates the bedroom. 'She sleeping.'

Portia is puffed from the walk up the hill. She perches on the edge of a metal chair and fans herself with her hand. 'I come to collect her,' she says simply.

'What you want collect Phelie for? She can live with me until mammy better.'

'She ain't never coming home no more,' says Portia.

Ophelia, disturbed by the voices, lies with her eyes closed, listening. She wonders who Gladys is talking to.

'They operate,' says Portia with relish. 'They take a lump from the stomach big like this.'

'Eh, eh, Portia,' clucks Aunty Gladys.

Ophelia slips from her bed and peeps round the door to see Portia sitting there, almost as big as Granma herself.

'It big as a baby,' continues Portia.

'Eh, eh.'

'Only it like a lump of blood and flesh.'

Ophelia tries to imagine the lump removed from Granma's stomach. Since her Granma is too old to make a baby, perhaps this is what women make after that.

'Then they sew up the stomach again. Just like a piece of sea cotton.'

'Eh.'

'And all the time Eugenia sleeping and she don't feel nothing at all. No pain. No knife. No needle. No nothing.'

'Eh.'

But Ophelia feels the knife and the pain and weeps at the thought of her grandmother being cut about and patched up like an old flour sack.

'You gone and wake up the child,' says Gladys. She beckons to Ophelia and pulls her close.

Ophelia looks from Portia to Gladys and back again. It is hard to imagine them both issuing from the same vast body even though they had different fathers.

Gladys's father, Granma was only too happy to admit,

was 'A bad man. No good.' He was half English and half West Indian and half-witted to boot. Though it is hard to imagine, he had apparently swept Eugenia off her feet when, as a young agricultural officer, he had advised her father of the benefits to his market garden of using artificial fertilizers. He had however gone on to leave undeniable proof that fertilization could still be achieved by natural means and left the island in some haste.

Ophelia's aunt was named Gladys after her maternal grandmother whose studio portrait, taken in the Liverpool pub where she worked, had aroused much admiration when passed around the rum shops of Monday Island.

Aunty Gladys was not quite like any of the other women in Ophelia's life. Whereas both Portia and her mother had acquired a comfortable accumulation of fat during their years of childbearing, Aunty Gladys had gone the other way. It was as if each child had sucked her drier than the one before.

Ophelia once inquired how she fed her children when she had no titties.

'Them children, they done eat me up,' laughed Aunty Gladys.

Thereafter, Ophelia looked with horror on her seven plump cousins with big round cheeks and big white teeth.

Though she was tiny there was nothing flimsy about Aunty Gladys. Ophelia watched while she lifted sacks of coconuts which weighed more than she did, and heaved them over the back of a pick-up, or walked home with two stems of bananas on her head and always the same angelic smile on her face and the same readiness to stop and talk cheerfully with a friend.

Her features were as fine as those of a Grecian statue, but it was her eyes which most attracted the attention. They were blue. Not the blue of the sea or the blue of the enamelled teapot that sat on the oilcloth on the table, but the startling pale clearness of a turquoise. Ophelia, who would have given anything to have blue eyes, assumed that it was because of these precious stones in Aunty Gladys's face that Uncle Remus had married her. Quite contrary to custom he had married Aunty Gladys when she was sixteen and a virgin, and again, unique among the other men Ophelia knew, he had remained faithful to her for thirty-three years during which he had toiled faithfully by her side on the land.

But why Ophelia as a week-old baby came to live with her grandmother in the first place is another story. All her childhood, Portia dreamed of getting away from Nelson's Look Out to the bright lights of Soufrière. Enter the Misses Simpson, who as descendants of the original white owners of Nelson's Fancy, still paid periodic visits to the school to distribute prizes to the Sunday School or to offer condolences on the occasion of a bereavement. In their youth, they were even given to picnics among the ruins of the Great House and local legend has it that one night they were seen, three pale figures wandering among the ruins in the moonlight. Other locals insist that the place is haunted and certainly Ophelia and before her Gladys and Portia avoided the place after dark.

Portia was born in the dark days between the decline of the sugar cane and the rise of the banana. Reasoning that, in the God-given climate of Monday Island which made clothing a luxury, where water poured abundantly off the mountains and where wood for cooking was to be had for the trouble of gathering it, the only thing that was lacking to enable people to live healthy, God-fearing lives was food, Eugenia concentrated on farming and showered on the small plot of land inherited from her father George the same devotion which she lavished on her fatherless children. The land responded to her touch and soon she had crops more than enough for her own needs.

When the time came for her children to go to school,

Eugenia was forced into the cash economy. She had to provide shoes and books, uniforms and pencils, all of which were reserved strictly for school and locked away in the living room cupboard at all other times. They stood in less danger of being worn out or used up by the children than by the assiduous attention which Eugenia paid them, washing and ironing, sharpening and dusting as if her life depended on it.

Driven by this need for money, Eugenia dressed one day in her Sunday best and proceeded to town. One inquiry sufficed to direct her to the house of the Misses Simpson in Boules where she found the three ladies quietly starving among their silver teaspoons. From then on, Eugenia visited weekly with fresh provisions and new-laid eggs, for she was a woman of deeply held Christian beliefs which she carried out in her daily life.

Her business expanded rapidly, first to friends of the Misses Simpson and then to friends of the friends. But right up to her death, she would never accept one penny from these women whose ancestors had once owned hers.

Portia was an indulged child, twenty-three years younger than Gladys, and the same age as her nephew, Gladys's third. So it was that Eugenia, in response to Portia's wish to escape, made a pilgrimage to Boules and asked for help in placing her daughter in domestic service.

Portia went straight from the country to a glittering middle-class housing development from which she was sent home seven months later considerably larger than when she left home, and without a clue as to who the father of her child might be. It was this fact rather than the pregnancy itself which distressed Eugenia, who though she never married, believed throughout her life in romantic love and in strict serial fidelity. Since the father of Ophelia was unknown, Eugenia called her granddaughter Ophelia Wellington to avoid the disgrace of unknown parentage,

Wellington being the name of the street in which Portia had worked.

Ophelia at the age of ten days was a built-in fixture of Eugenia's vegetable rounds, strapped on to a bed of mangoes under the shade of her grandmother's black umbrella, while her mother, thanks once again to the intervention of the Misses Simpson, took up a new and better position.

And so Ophelia grows until every Tuesday, in her Sunday best, she clutches her grandmother's hand and they cross 'The Pitch' together. On Granma's head is a basket of vegetables, from her own garden, and eggs for 'dose poor poor ladies' the Misses Simpson.

Ophelia stays very close to her grandmother in the house that overlooks the wasteland, while the eldest Miss Simpson – the one who is blind – serves them tea in porcelain cups so thin that she fears even the touch of her teeth might fracture them.

And with the tea are very plain, plain biscuits which the two bedridden Misses Simpson dunk in their tea and suck avidly.

The greatest mystery about the tea to Ophelia, is how the eldest Miss Simpson, being blind, manages to make it at all. She listens to the little crashes and tinkles from the kitchen and the continuous high-pitched commentary on what she is doing, which is frequently punctuated by shrieks of encouragement from the Misses Simpson in bed.

When Ophelia starts to giggle, her grandmother places a warning hand on her knee and continues to stare straight ahead as if nothing out of the ordinary was happening.

The two younger Misses Simpson watch the door; the one who is deaf with the weak heart begins to dribble. Then in comes the blind Miss Simpson, feeling her way between the furniture and water trickling from the spout so that Ophelia giggles again and is glad that the eldest Miss Simpson cannot see her.

'She put the teapot in the oven I think she did it on purpose so that we would not be able to find it what a hard thing it is to be dependent on a girl like that you can never trust anybody in this life but she's a good girl who else would look after three poor old ladies like us . . .'

And the other sisters chime in.

'Sister sister pour the tea the tea is getting cold and we don't like cold tea we like hot tea and the little girl is thirsty.'

'All right all right there's no need to rush me I am pouring the tea as fast as I can.'

'Stop stop sister the cup's full the cup's overflowing it will make the biscuits soggy.'

Ophelia's grandmother sits amid the chaos like royalty, in her white gloves and her best straw hat. Ophelia copies her every movement.

In the merciful silence occupied by drinking and sucking the blind sister sits down on the sofa next to Ophelia's grandmother and feels along the table top for her own cup.

Ophelia closes her eyes and tries to imagine that she too is blind until she drops her rich tea biscuit on to the floor.

'Sister sister she has dropped a biscuit on the floor,' screeches the sister by the window, 'and I hope she will find it and pick it up because otherwise the biscuit will be wasted and then afterwards the rats will come and eat it and I don't like rats and . . .'

'Where has she dropped a biscuit I don't see a biscuit,' says the blind Miss Simpson feeling around on the floor with her fingertips.

'I can't hear I can't hear what are you saying nobody's talking to me,' says the youngest Miss Simpson, which Ophelia considers equally strange but she doesn't like to say anything.

Ophelia's grandmother proceeds to give the Misses

Simpson a rough outline of the week's news which they receive with equal agitation and cries of 'Sister sister what will become of us' and supplications to God, whether each news item relates to a murder or an increase in the price of powdered milk.

They are surprisingly well-informed on certain matters due to the positioning of the elder Miss Simpson's bed next to the window above the back alley where she can hear the servants gossip as they hang out the washing and air their grievances.

When, at last, Ophelia and her grandmother step outside, the child hears the birds sing and feels the sun warm on her arms.

'Granma,' she asks, 'why they don' go to hospital?'

'Speak proper,' hisses Granma, 'if you want to get on in life.'

'Why don't the Miss Simpsons go to hospital and have theyselves made better?'

'It too troublesome,' says Granma.

Ophelia knows that if she were ill she would do anything to get better. Each bus ride home is like the shaking off of a nightmare. This involves asking her grandmother about those things which have most confused her during the visit.

'What Miss Simpson mean that if people don' look at her she can't hear what they say?'

Granma tears herself away from the news of the man in the seat behind her whose daughter has just given birth to triplets in Canada. 'Why you so troublesome today, Ophelia?'

'Why the deaf Miss Simpson say that if people don' look at her she can't hear what they say if she can't hear anyway?'

Granma laughs and relays the question to the whole bus. They laugh and slap their knees at the precocity of this child. Ophelia tugs at her grandmother's arm and looks up, waiting for a reply.

'Lord bless this child.' Granma wipes her eyes with the back of her white glove. 'She know what we say by the shape of the mouth.'

Ophelia sticks her fingers in her ears, watches the lips of the other passengers and cannot understand a word of what they are saying. She feels a new respect for the deaf Miss Simpson. As they near their own bus stop, Ophelia tugs at her grandmother's arm again.

'You making me vex with your questions.' Granma looks ferocious, but Ophelia knows her too well to be frightened.

'Granma, why does the oldest Miss Simpson say she can't see to find the biscuit on the floor when everyone know she blind and she feeling for it with her fingers?'

'She does just talk like that.' Granma resumes her conversation, leaving Ophelia with the conviction that she has not been told the truth. If the deaf Miss Simpson can hear with her eyes, it is surely not beyond the realms of imagination that the blind Miss Simpson who makes tea all alone in the kitchen can see with her fingertips.

But now Granma is not there to answer any more questions. Ophelia stands with her hand resting on Gladys's chair back and watches Portia.

Gladys serves glasses of sarsaparilla laced with rum. Portia drinks deeply and sweats even more. Gladys looks at her suspiciously.

'You making baby.'

Portia looks sulky. 'That is why I needing the child, Gladys.'

'She ain't lef' school yet. You wait till she finish.'

'What I go do when this baby done born?'

'Your man ain't have no mammy?'

'I ain't got no man.' Portia has had six children to her credit since Ophelia's birth. The latest lodger taken to her bed as a means of easing her financial situation has, as usual, compounded her difficulties by making her pregnant and moving on.

'Why you don' find yourself a good man?'

'You tell me where to find one.'

Gladys pours more drink. They sit and sip in silence.

'I taking Phelie with me.'

'You ain't taking that child nowhere, Portia. She staying with me until mammy come home.'

'Mammy no coming home no. I telling you she good as dead.'

Portia stands up, waddles belligerently towards Gladys and takes Ophelia by the hand. 'We go pack now.' Portia leads Ophelia next door into the house where she too spent her childhood.

Harry sniffed suspiciously at the bottle. Calvin Klein. The name was reassuringly masculine but Harry had never been one for cosmetics.

Betty was wandering along the perfume counters. The names reminded her of scented gardens peopled by beauties as exotic as the flowers among which they trod. But it was the tiny bottle labelled *Bal à Versailles* that she couldn't tear herself away from. An emerald necklace might be beyond her budget, but not even Harry could grudge her this small extravagance.

'Harry?'

He was preoccupied. He was beginning to wonder whether he was the only unscented male in the whole of the United States.

Betty paid for the bottle and hid it under her postcards. Harry would be sure to insist on smelling it, and she didn't want to give him any clue to her identity at the masked ball.

Ophelia watches Portia as she steps into Eugenia's sitting room. The clock on the china cabinet has stopped. Granma must have forgotten to wind it up last night. Perhaps she felt ill even then. Portia wanders around the room she has visited so seldom in the last eleven years. She picks things up and she puts them down again as if they hold no interest for her.

But Ophelia remembers . . .

It is night-time. Ophelia chews her pencil and gazes into the lamp, waiting for inspiration. Granma takes out a noisy oiled paper parcel which contains a crochet needle and balls of white twine.

'What you waiting for, child?'

Ophelia shrugs.

'You planning to wait for the end of the world?'

Ophelia smiles and begins to write: 'What I will do when the Queen comes to visit Monday Island.' She takes her ruler and neatly underlines the heading.

Granma casts on, and the white twine is stretched tight across her black knuckles. The needle flickers like a snake's tongue in the dim light. She works fast, making table mats, cushion covers and chair backs. However fast she works she will never catch up with the fashion of a bygone age, but she will not rest happy until every jug and glass, every shell and candlestick stands on its own delicate cobweb of threads.

Portia shoves a few glasses into her straw shopping bag and tosses the mats aside.

Gladys carefully gathers them together. 'Mammy ain't dead yet and you looking like you couldn't wait till she done dead and buried.'

Ophelia looks wide-eyed on this sacrilege. She knows what wonderful things doctors can do. What if Granma were to walk through the door this very moment?

She goes through into the kitchen and stands looking out into the yard. She can still see Granma there squatting over the washing, her head bowed under the cool water which runs off her coiled hair in big oily drops as if off a sheep's back. When her neck too burns in the heat of the sun, Granma drapes a wet towel about her shoulders. She spends two whole days a week washing for Aunty Gladys's sons. Afterwards the seven pairs of jeans hang on the rusty corrugated iron fence until the sun bakes them so stiff they could almost walk off on their own. Alongside are the shirts and the pants and Ophelia's school uniform and her grandmother's own pink bloomers and the huge flowing dresses of sea island cotton.

Portia picks her way through the contents of Eugenia's kitchen cupboards.

'She still using that?' asks Portia in disbelief, picking up the old charcoal iron and carelessly putting it back on its side.

'Of course,' says Gladys.

Ophelia stays by the door and hears night falling. The dusk is loud with the song of frogs and lizards. Thud, goes the iron on the sun-fried denim and Granma gives a small grunt as she presses down hard on the table. Ophelia closes her eyes. She can feel the presence of her grandmother as she moves from the fire to the table and back again, spit and test.

'What they teaching you at school today, child?'

'Eighteen twenty-four, the repeal of the corn laws,' replies Ophelia.

'Repeal of the corn laws,' chuckles Granma. 'You know what happen on this very island in eighteen twenty-four?'

Ophelia shakes her head.

'That is the year of the slave rebellion, child. Them poor black people don' want to wait no more for they freedom.' She slams the point of the iron into a small crease, then holds up the jeans and sighs with satisfaction.

The air in the kitchen is still peppered with curried cod fish and the smell of Granma's warm moist skin. Ophelia, eyes closed, sighs in the luxury of it all.

Her school shirt is next, crisp with starch. Granma shines the collar with the iron and Ophelia feels the agonizing stiffness of it about her neck. She puts her hands up to tear it away.

'Phelie, you sleeping right there by the door?' Gladys speaks gently, her hands on Ophelia's shoulders. 'Is time you go now. Uncle Joe bringing the lorry.'

Ophelia sits between Portia and Uncle Joe on the ride to her new home. Everything is happening as in a dream. More real to her is Ophelia the child, pinned like a rag doll on the wooden seat of the wooden cab, between Granma and Uncle Joe. Aunty Gladys sits in the back of the lorry, huddled against the cab among her sacks of dasheen, cucumbers and grapefruit, clutching at her bright pink cardigan and straw hat as the night wind whistles round her.

They are off to market. It is early Saturday morning. The lorry rattles along roads silent and perfumed by the ginger lily, its headlights scarce as bright as the moon.

The moon hangs on their right, sending a column of light across the sea towards them. The sandy beaches gleam and the palm trees rustle silver.

Granma's grass baskets scratch Ophelia's bare legs and the gear lever shudders against her right knee. But grandmother is there. The child rests her left cheek on the enormous biceps. She looks up through the brim of her grandmother's hat at the stars beyond the dark sphere that is Granma's face looking down at her.

It is easier to see Uncle Joe outlined by the glittering ocean, as he steers through the smell of dough from the bakery by the deep water harbour. Ophelia's stomach grumbles loudly, almost as loud as the deep chuckles that come like the rumblings of a subterranean volcano from Granma in response to Uncle Joe's continuous chatter. Ophelia does not listen to what they say. It is enough to be there, pressed against her grandmother, hearing her 'eh, eh, ehs' in the waking dream of moonlight and perfume which is the essence of her childhood.

At the market Ophelia is frightened by the bustle of trucks and people. Standing in the black moon shadow of the enormous building, she is afraid that she might be lost.

'You just keep close to me, child,' murmurs Granma.

She buys provisions, dasheen, yams and plantains, bunches of thyme and chives, parsley and limes.

They move out of the shadow of the building into the brilliant light of the open market at the water's edge where the sellers sit crosslegged, creating their own moon shadows, while they arrange pyramids of vegetables as silver as the gilded fruits on a Christmas tree.

'You all right, child?' Ophelia nods dumbly. The light in the east becomes stronger, to outface the moon which finally slinks unnoticed behind the horizon.

Immediately the market takes on colour. Bunches of lilies and dahlias and multicoloured daisies, vegetables and fruits glow richly as the rising sun strikes them with its magic wand.

Grandmother's baskets grow heavy.

'We going now, child,' she says and weaves her way among the mounds of fruit.

Ophelia and Eugenia sit on a boulder on the dry edge of the river bed and Granma pours strong black coffee from a flask. Ophelia unties bundles of thyme which release small explosions of fragrance.

'Like benediction,' says Ophelia, and Granma clucks her tongue in disapproval at such blasphemy.

Ophelia splits each length of banana fibre lengthways, then bites it in half while her grandmother divides the bundles into yet smaller bunches to sell in the open market at a few cents a time.

Granma overflows a rickety wooden-legged stool, which sways in time to her breathing. Ophelia leans against her, with one arm round her neck. On the ground in front of them, neatly arranged on a clean plastic sheet, are the tiny bunches of herbs, dasheen and green bananas. The vegetables gleam from their scrubbing in the river, and from time to time Ophelia runs to the public drinking fountain and returns with a plastic cup of water to refresh them.

Ophelia's grandmother half stands and moves her stool round so that her shadow protects her wares. But the sun rises higher and higher until it shines down through the brim of grandmother's straw hat and makes patterns of lace on her dark face. Then she opens her umbrella and a halo of colour surrounds her head. Ophelia nestles close under the riot of poppies and cornflowers.

If she possessed a watch, she would know that at precisely the same time every Saturday morning, her grandmother sighs, and the legs of the stool teeter and she speaks directly to Ophelia.

'This sun too too hot, chil'.'

Ophelia knows better than to rush the words which will come in Granma's own good time.

'Pass me meh bag,' she says, being quite unable to bend down for it herself. From it, Granma draws out a handkerchief. Wrapped in the handkerchief is a plastic bag containing her money. She counts out the coins carefully, while Ophelia tries to restrain her excitement.

'Ten, twenty . . .' says Granma counting out each coin.

Ophelia pretends that her feet are nailed to the ground. 'Thirty, forty . . .' Ophelia looks at the sky and whistles to distract herself. 'That you whistling, Phelie?' asks her grandmother, and Ophelia is instantly silent. 'Forty-five . . . fifty.' Granma carefully closes Ophelia's small fingers over the money.

'Now child, you go buy two snow cones, eh?' Granma speaks as if this is a special treat instead of a weekly occurrence, and Ophelia skips off to buy the paper cones of ice, more violently coloured than passion fruit ever could be.

And then Ophelia and her grandmother hug one another under the floral umbrella and lick until their tongues are redder than a Caribbean sunset. It is during one such interlude that they hear the ring of a hammer and see the billboard erected.

'Ophelia,' says Granma, 'my eyes too old. Tell me what it does say.'

Ophelia reads without expression or comprehension exactly what the poster says. 'Great minds discuss ideas average minds discuss events small minds discuss people.'

There is a stunned silence.

'Eh *bon Dieu*, but she's a good little reader.'

'It's a gift from God.'

'Be careful her head don't get too heavy for her neck with all this learning.'

Granma ignores all the comments but inwardly bristles with pride.

'Don't you forget that, child,' she says to Ophelia in the bus on the way home. 'It for true.' Ophelia, up since before dawn, drowsy with heat and exhaustion leans against Granma's shoulder. 'Great minds discuss ideas and you goin' be a great mind, child.'

Ophelia never forgets.

Betty and Harry staggered out of the shop. The crush in the streets with the arrival of yet more tourist ships was frightening. Betty shrank against a wall to get her breath back. Harry pointed to a sign above her head. NO LOITERING.

'But I'm tired, Harry,' she protested. Underneath, someone had written 'fuck off'. That was more like it.

He guffawed and focussed his camera.

'What's so special about that?' The buildings opposite made such a lovely picture.

'Let's try down here,' suggested Harry indicating the smaller, darker streets which lay on the other side of the shopping area, away from the hotels and the sea.

Betty felt a little nervous. Everyone she could see down there was black.

'Don't you think we should go back now, Harry?'

Harry tossed his head and strode on.

Betty followed. There were few shops – well, not what she would have called shops anyway, one or two clothes stores, and otherwise nothing but bars. They were not appealing, quite unlike the open terraced cafés with striped blinds and potted plants along the sea front.

'Want a drink, Bet?'

Betty shook her head. She was parched but she'd wait until they got back to civilization. She could just picture the dirty glasses. Hepatitis. Aids. She'd rather stay thirsty.

'It's cooler by the sea,' she ventured.

'But look at these prices, honey. No point in going back and paying double.'

Betty followed him in.

The shutters were closed and a fan revolved in the centre of the ceiling. Betty stumbled against a table. A couple of girls, perched on bar stools, wore tight skirts slit higher than she considered decent. One looked Spanish, the other – well, could have been from anywhere in the West Indies. Dark, but pretty. Betty smiled. They ignored her. She sat down with her back to them where she could see through the open door and out into the sunlight.

Harry, facing the bar, called for a beer. When it came it was warm. 'Got any ice?' he called out. There was no ice. Harry swilled the tepid liquid round his mouth and ogled the two girls. Pity Betty was there. He thought about yesterday in the bar with Thomas and the girl, and was tempted to tell her. She'd never believe him. She was such an innocent. He could tell from the way she greeted these girls that in her eyes they could have been the Bernsteins' daughters.

Betty sat until she could stand it no longer. One second more and she would melt. 'I'll wait outside, honey,' she said.

As soon as she was gone, the darker of the two girls moved to join Harry at his table. If he was sweating before, he felt now as if he was going to drip right through the perforated plastic seat. What if Bet were to come back now? Harry abandoned his beer and fled.

Betty, at the end of the street, surrounded by a reassuring number of white people, stood staring at the poster which said SMILE. And it seemed to work not just on her, but on everybody else as well. She had never seen so many happy people in all her life. Just as she was playing over the memory of a neighbour telling her that newborn babies could be conditioned to cry to show their pleasure, up came Harry with a grin like a slice of water-melon. A smile like that could only be genuine. Harry, God bless him, really and truly was happy. She was so struck by the smile that she failed to notice the T-shirt.

'Take my photo, Bet,' said Harry. He fiddled with the light meter, then passed her the camera and posed in front of the poster.

Betty lined up the camera.

'You got it in focus, honey?'

Betty twiddled the lens until the writing on Harry's shirt stood out clear as an optician's chart. NO FRIGGING IN THE RIGGING.

'You got yourself a new shirt, Harry?' Betty asked.

'Sure I did, hon. Cute, eh?'

'I think a close-up would be better.' She aimed for a head and shoulders shot.

'Not too close, Bet. I'd like you to get all of the poster in.'

Betty stepped back again. There was no escaping the printing on Harry's chest but at least she could spare herself the sight of his lobster-red legs emerging from the tight white shorts.

'You taking it today or tomorrow?' asked Harry.

'Just trying to line it up, dear.' Betty moved slightly to the right, and with a click Harry was immortalized. Betty could already hear herself saying as she handed round the canapés, 'Harry will have his little joke,' and the Bernsteins and the Smiths staring stonyfaced at the outsize image of Harry's T-shirt on the living room wall.

'I could do with a drink, Harry,' she said.

They made their way back to one of the sea front cafés but the tables were all taken, so they squatted on the sea wall and longingly read the all-American menu. Everything guaranteed flown in from New York. Fish, fruit, vegetables, meat and booze. Even the waitresses.

'Hi.' An intensely bronzed face with a patch of discoloured flesh on the bridge of her nose leaned towards them from the sidewalk.

'Hi there,' said Harry. He smiled as if he'd known the woman all his life.

Cancer, thought Betty. To her, the bared teeth seemed predatory.

'Care to take a tour?'

Harry looked at Betty. 'Why not?' she said. It might be her only chance on the island to get a seat.

'Name's Dodie,' said the woman. 'I'll be waiting for you right there at the end of the sidewalk.'

Everything was so relaxed, so friendly. So much so that they didn't like to keep Dodie waiting but set off after her at once.

Betty was dismayed at the size of the coach. 'I thought there'd just be the two of us, Harry.'

Dodie stood on the steps. 'Welcome aboard, you two.'

There was no escape now. They sat in the last spare seats, the doors shut, and they were off.

'My name's Dodie. On behalf of the Christian Island Society for the Preservation of Antiquities, welcome aboard!'

Dodie sat comfortably on the ledge at the base of the windscreen, swinging her legs and twining the wire of the microphone around her hand as if she were singing in a nightclub. She looked towards the passengers with a smile, and history flowed from her lips like cane juice from the mill.

'On your left is the old slave market built in the eighteenth century, which is now a cultural centre.'

The bus drew up for photographs.

'The market was restored ten years ago for the visit of Mrs Carter.'

In the centre of the slave market was a steel band hemmed in by tourists fighting to get under the shady overhang of the roof.

Betty was pleased to see everything and everybody looking so bright and cheerful, from the gaily painted pillars to the smiles on the faces of the musicians.

'Concerts are staged by the Ministry of Culture, every day on the hour,' said Dodie.

The slave market was of course central to the life of the town in the days of the plantations. Depending on the direction of the wind, the arrival of a slaver was heralded either by cries of 'A sail, a sail' from the fort on the hilltop above the town, or else, given a strong following wind, by the smell which permeated the island long before the ship itself hove into sight. It drove planters' wives to send servants scurrying for their smelling salts while the planters held out their feet for their riding boots to be dragged on by slaves who glistened as much as the polished leather.

The atmosphere at the market was like home from home.

A garden party perhaps, with the women in their prettiest dresses accompanied by their muslin-clad daughters and precocious sons and a retinue of slaves who had run the distance into town behind the master's horse or the mistress's carriage.

Bessie attends many such social occasion, three paces behind her mistress, keeping one eye open for any new ideas in fashion, and the other on the slightest disarrangement in Madam's dress.

'What are they doing?' asks the Mistress, twirling her parasol in a dizzying swirl of lace and chiffon which casts dimpled shadows on her pale cheeks. The ship takes so long in entering the harbour.

'Sluicing down, my dear.' Master twirls his cane and tweaks his moustachios.

'Sluicing down?' inquires the Mistress.

'Otherwise my dear, they'd stink out the whole island.'

And they take another turn about the harbour where the Master raises his hat to acquaintances and the Mistress drops a curtsey to the Governor, and Bessie stoops to straighten the Mistress's skirt should a breath of wind tweak the flounces astray.

'You see, child,' says Granma, 'those days was different.'

Granma is pounding breadfruit and plantains and dasheen to a fine mash. Sitting on the doorstep with the hollowed-out tree trunk gripped between her knees, she raises the wooden pestle high above her head, then lets it fall with a thud among the boiled vegetables.

Ophelia sits next to her, with one hand on Granma's knee. When Granma lifts the pestle, Ophelia dips her fingers into the warm mush.

'Your grandmother's great-grandmother, called Nell, was all polish up with coconut oil when she leave the ship and walk up the steps to the market. She so thin and weak she own mother wouldn't recognize she. She walk all that

way, and all the time she expecting them white gentlemen
to gobble she up.'

Bessie's Mistress still stands and watches.

'Why are there so many soldiers?' she asks her husband.
'They don't look as if they are going to run away.'

'Humph,' he says and takes a swig of rum, for the
tropical climate warms the extremities while leaving a
deadly chill within.

Bessie knows it is because the black bodies are too
valuable to be allowed to jump over the edge into the sea
and drown themselves.

She feels so superior there in her Mistress's best muslin
of five years ago with the big sash around her waist. 'They
ignorant savages,' she says as the slaves stumble ashore,
naked and terrified.

Her Mistress says, 'Poor things,' and holds out her hand
for a handkerchief to wipe away a tear.

In the market the calypso rhythms jangled irresistibly and
the younger tourists shuffled their feet in time to the beat.
Harry was taking the photographs of a lifetime. A painted
backcloth of palm trees and exotic flowers will convey to
those back home the popular image of a sleepy, colourful
place, with a steel band under every coconut tree.

Nelly, chained to her third partner, walks with the other
three hundred and sixty survivors of the voyage between
the lines of soldiers. She is not at present in the pink of
health, but she is young and resilient and breathes deeply
of God's wholesome fresh air. Her teeth are good and
strong, her hair no more louse-ridden than one would
expect, and her recent and painful attack of the flux has
been ingeniously halted by a plug of alum in the rectum.

She arouses considerable interest among the planters.
Now that the slave trade is illegal and slaves are hard to

come by, natural replacement of the labour force by means of reproduction has become necessary. Sold to the gentleman in the straw hat for twelve guineas. A bargain, had he but known it. Two for the price of one, though the fact is not yet apparent.

The coach had now left downtown Charlottested and was heading into those grey areas where black meets white, and the streets of two-storey houses gave way to high rise concrete flats. Washing hung over balcony walls and most of the windows were broken. The concrete acres were daubed with graffiti. BLACK POWER RULES OK. KILL WHITE PIGS. Then as the road almost ceased to exist, they were out into the open countryside.

Every hill was topped by a windmill like a flag on a sandcastle and every one of them, Dodie pointed out, was lovingly restored and converted by some member of the Society for the Preservation of Antiquities. The windmills now contained a variety of amenities from swimming pools to honeymoon suites, while the nearby plantation houses had become condominiums, hotels or sports clubs.

'Look, Phelie!' Granma lifts up a spoonful of sugar and lets it trickle slowly back into the bowl.

Phelie looks and the sugar sparkles in the sunlight like the foam of a waterfall.

'So much evil', says Granma, 'for that little bit of sweetening.' She stirs some into her enamel mug of tea. 'They telling you at school how they make sugar?'

Ophelia shakes her head.

'They burn the canes and cut them and take them to the mill. Two slaves stand there, one each side of the rollers, pushing the canes through until the juice run out.'

Horatio has been feeding cane into the rollers for ten hours. He sways on his feet, dizzy with the effort of staying awake.

But still the cane keeps coming, cartload after cartload. He leans forward resting against the wooden trough which carries the extracted juice down to the boiling vats. He can almost do the job with his eyes shut, such is the monotony of harvest time. Pick up a cane, push it between the rollers, pick up the next, discard the one that has already been through twice. When his right hand is only inches away from the rollers, his eyes jerk open and he snatches it back.

An hour later, he is still there. The overseer has promised to send someone to relieve Horatio, but the overseer is a busy man. The fires are stoked, the mill is turning, the ox carts keep arriving. Nothing can break the rhythm.

Nell brings Horatio his meals to the foot of the windmill where he snatches a few minutes' rest.

Another cane and another . . . and another . . . and Horatio is asleep. Forward goes his hand still gripping the end of the cane. His scream slices through the roar of machinery, the bellow of the fire. Horatio's fingers, knuckles, then his wrist vanish between the rollers and the overseer grabs the long-handled axe off the wall. As Horatio's right arm is crushed as far as the elbow, the axe flashes . . .

Horatio may consider himself lucky. On a conservative reckoning the life of one slave was sacrificed for every ton of sugar produced. Of course, consumption levels were nowhere near the twelve million tons consumed annually in Europe today. In those days the same amount sufficed for one hundred years.

The original Horatio of the West Indies, Admiral Nelson, would have despised anyone who thought the loss of an arm any impediment to a full and fruitful career. One eye was better than no eyes, one arm an infinite improvement on no arms.

* * *

Betty loved the idea of a honeymoon in a windmill. Not that she was in the least bit insensitive. She just didn't have a mind that could grasp even the basic principles of engineering. The mechanics of grinding were quite beyond her. Hence she could quite happily see at one and the same time the slaves, the sails turning, the honeymoon couple at the cobbled glass window and the end product of a packet of granulated sugar on her local supermarket shelf.

The only thing that didn't fit into her dream was Harry. She had only to look at him on the seat next to her, taking up a good bit of her seat as well, to be reminded that nothing could ever be romantic with him around.

Nothing could be more divine than the windmills, thought Betty, until she saw the plantation's Great House. It quite took her breath away.

The long, low, grey and white house rose like a ship above a sea of shimmering trees. It stood serenely in a beautiful garden separated from a new government housing scheme by a twelve-foot mesh fence. Betty watched the black children peering through and wondered why nobody had thought of the simple expedient of planting some sort of shrub cover to give the tourists a better historical appreciation of the Great House as it really was.

'That's where the slave huts used to be.' Dodie waved a hand in the direction of the housing estate. She led the party across a bridge over the moat. Overgrown with ferns, it looked pleasantly green and shady.

'The dry moat,' said their guide, 'was to provide ventilation and light for the store rooms.'

Betty could almost bring herself to believe the explanation, although everything she had ever read about moats had led her to believe that their purpose was purely defensive.

Dodie did not add that the year in which the Great House was built was the same year in which Louis XVI and Marie Antoinette lost their heads, and a time when the notions of liberté, égalité and fraternité permeated the Caribbean with all the persistence of the trade winds.

Betty's suspicions were aroused by one or two facts which Dodie failed to mention, such as the barred windows on either side of the bridge. Even if she could accept that they had been installed recently as a precaution against theft, there could surely be no doubt about the purpose of the loopholes. They were for cannon. Her heart went straight out to those frail and lovely ladies, marooned and hopelessly outnumbered by their work-force.

She was once more led to doubt her own judgement when she stepped inside the house. Certainly Dodie's explanation about ventilation seemed plausible. The air was so cool that Betty shivered.

'Besides the height of the ceiling and the directional layout,' said Dodie, 'the walls are exceptionally thick, and made of stone, cemented by a mixture of ground coral and molasses.'

It sounded as good as a gingerbread house. Harry rubbed one finger against the wall and then sniffed it. White emulsion. Dodie was talking a load of crap.

Betty drew his attention to a selection of prints. 'Wouldn't they make lovely table mats?' She forgot about the bars and the loopholes. The pictures showed negresses swinging jauntily along smoking clay pipes, rows of happy slaves with their picks perfectly synchronized, smiling overseers with idle whips, and a print of the inside of a mill where beaming black men cheerily fed cane into the grinders.

'Have to be careful about slopping the gravy, eh, Bet?' Harry drew his finger round the outline of a slave resting under a palm tree, like a darker version of Mata Hari.

Betty lapped up every detail of the tour, even the bit about the coconut husk mattress. Well, she supposed, it all depended on what you were used to, but it stretched the imagination. After all, coconuts were in her experience brown and hairy, and hard as cannonballs.

She moved on to the planter's chair with its gently angled back and its footrest, and the hole in the arm to hold a glass of punch.

'You want to try it out?' asked Dodie.

'I'd love to.' That chair was the most comfortable Betty had ever sat in. Its gentle creak took her right back to her childhood, and the sleepy afternoons in the town where she grew up.

Ophelia hears the creak of Granma's chair on a sleepy dusty evening. It is as if the chair breathes in time with Granma. There is no chair for Ophelia on the verandah. She either sits on the railings or on Granma's knee or plays marbles with small pebbles on the rough boards. She knows every knot in the planks, every cranny through which the ants trail and the different paths they follow to the larder. She sometimes places one of her stones in their way so that they have to divide and re-form on the other side.

The chair creaks and Granma remembers . . .

Nell, fourteen and pregnant, wears a faded cotton dress and works in the cane fields until something in the way she wields her hoe suggests to the overseer that she is on the way to doubling her worth.

She is put on to lighter duties tending vegetables, and when even that is beyond her she is promoted to the Watch Hut. This is the easiest time of her life, if only she knew it. She is well fed. She is clothed. Her standard of living is considerably higher than she could have expected at home and she is under no threat from tribal warfare. She has also had the opportunity to learn a second language.

The Watch Hut, stone built and brick tiled, is pleasantly cool and quiet. Nell, that pioneer of the crèche movement, tends the babies of nursing mothers who work in the fields. It is there with no other adult present that she gives birth to her son. The overseer, with reference to the fairly recent victory at Trafalgar and by way of tribute to the child's colour, names the child Horatio.

Of course malicious tongues will wag, but the Mistress knows that Nelly was only bought six months ago, and that anyway the Master had other irons in the fire at that particular time.

In any case, Nelly's appearance gives the Mistress no cause for suspicion. Her sea voyage has left none of the physical charms which once singled her out for promotion. She never bears another child, and she remains a field slave for the rest of her days. Though not unduly ill-treated, her health steadily deteriorates. But all in all she gets by all right, unlike some . . .

Granma's eyes flash. She leans towards Ophelia and her chair creaks ominously. Ophelia can swear she sees flecks of fire at the corner of Granma's eyes, and her nostrils flare like bellows.

'You know, child,' she says flinging away the newspaper with its headline captions of riots in South Africa, 'you know what they doing to them poor black boys?'

Ophelia shakes her head, cowers back against the verandah railing.

'They tying them to a pole and they roasting them slow, slow over a fire, with a gag over they mouth so that no screams don't disturb them white people food.'

Vomit clogs Ophelia's mouth. She feels dizzy. Everything rocks from side to side with the motion of the sea. She reaches out with her arms into the darkness. Her eyes are closed in terror. Sweet Jesus, keep my soul this night.

* * *

Betty went into the dining room where an enormous, oval mahogany table is laid for dinner. The silver is from Antwerp, the porcelain is Royal Copenhagen, the crystal is French, and the plastic fruit made in Taiwan. The mahogany, said the notice, was local, but the cabinet makers were imported.

Betty imagined sitting there, eating little delicacies in the heat of the day – the mousses and soufflés which required so much energy in the kitchen. She saw the master come in from touring the plantation, wearied with trouble among the slaves which his wife and daughters seek to dispel with the lightest of honeyed conversation . . .

Betty broke off as she heard the heavy, familiar tread.

'Soup tureens?' chortled Harry, who had just caught up with her. 'They look more like piss pots to me.'

Thomas, up on deck, was looking for the cargo ship. He carried a silver tray with a folded piece of paper on it held down with his thumb. It could just be a message he was delivering if an officer happened to pass by. Thomas's duties were strictly below decks.

'You see Mizz Stillman?' he asked Lou who was sitting at the poolside bar.

'I've an idea she went ashore.'

'I looking on the compass deck,' said Thomas bounding up the stairs to the highest vantage point of the ship.

His ingenuity was rewarded. He could not make out the ship itself, but the black smoke from its funnel stood out like evil in paradise.

Thomas whistled as he went back down to B deck.

As Betty got off the coach at the end of the tour, her pictorial guide to the Great House was carried away and out to sea by a gust of wind.

'Why didn't you put it in your purse, Bet?' whined

Harry. His cameras clattered together and his new T-shirt, cast adrift from his shorts, flapped like a spinnaker.

'I was reading it, Harry.'

'If you read it while you're walking along you're asking for trouble.' Harry indicated the waves slurping up underneath the sidewalk. Although the sun still shone the sea looked deeper somehow, and more sinister.

'I was just reading, Harry, that the original town was built out there somewhere.'

'Oh yeah?'

'Until it was destroyed by an earthquake in 1650 and the whole lot vanished beneath the sea.'

Harry shrugged. In the seventeenth century things like that probably happened all the time. Man didn't have control over his environment like he did now.

'People said at the time it was a punishment for the wickedness of the city.'

'Now how on earth did they know that, Bet?'

'People wrote that it was just like Sodom and Gomorrah.'

Harry snorted. 'You want something to eat?'

'Okay.' Betty was quite hungry.

'Same place we went to before?'

'Don't mind.'

Harry led the way on to the slatted sidewalk over the sea which was churning around like soup in a liquidizer.

'Where have all the boats gone, Harry?' The small harbour was strangely empty now.

'How should I know?' he snapped.

Betty hurried after him. It was so important to keep Harry well fed, like a small child. But she couldn't help wondering . . . the sea-side artists were gone too, and the sandwich boards advertising trimaran trips to the reef, and free champagne and cocktails aboard the *Saucy Sue*.

'Oh shit,' yelled Betty as a particularly large wave splooshed up through the planks and a jet like a whale's spout soaked her white jeans right up to the crotch.

Harry doubled up with laughter. 'Funniest thing I've seen in years, Bet,' he said when he'd recovered.

Betty moved away as fast as she was able, what with keeping her heels on, rather than between, the wooden slats, and the wet cotton dragging at her legs.

The restaurant, when they got there, looked as though a bomb had hit it. The tables and chairs were heaped up against the wall of the building as far from the sea as possible. Waitresses were staggering indoors with pot plants in macramé hangers.

It was then that Betty heard the roar of heavy vehicles and the tramp of boots like the sound effects from some Gestapo movie. Sure enough, some soldiers (fortunately white) burst out of the restaurant building on to the terrace.

'Look like some of our boys,' Harry said.

The soldiers began piling sandbags across the entrance to the terrace.

Harry raised his binoculars to the horizon, looking for conning towers. He knew all about warfare at sea. He'd sat through *The Battle of the River Plate* seven times. But there was nothing on or in the endlessly blue-grey sea except that rotting hulk of a cargo ship that seemed to be dogging them wherever they went.

'See that, Bet?'

Betty squinted. 'Is that the old tramp ship?'

'Looks like it.'

'You mean they'll let that in here?' She wouldn't have thought it, not with America being so pollution-conscious these days.

The black smoke was whipped by the wind into a long pennant fluttering behind the ship.

'Burning all that fuel, you'd have thought it would be dashing along, wouldn't you, Harry?'

'Looks kinda rough out there, Bet. Must be hard going.'

The sandbags were now waist high all around them.

'You expecting some kind of invasion?' he asked a lad in military fatigues.

'Not for another six hours.'

Further conversation was made impossible by the drone of aircraft. They whined overhead, all shapes and sizes from sea planes to a jumbo jet.

'Where're they going?' he asked.

'Take shelter down south. The airport's likely to take the worst of it.' He took a pocket radio from his belt, adjusted the aerial and spoke a few hurried words in response to an incomprehensible crackle.

'But what about us?' wailed Betty.

'Look, honey,' said Harry, 'he said six hours, didn't he? That's plenty of time to steam out of trouble.'

Betty wondered how he could be so sure. Probably the CIA were pretty hot on these things. Perhaps wars now began on schedule like TV programmes. She wished she had a flower to give to the soldier. That young man was as fine as any she'd seen back in '44 when her father went off to Europe. Vietnam had been different. There just wasn't the same enthusiasm. Of course, she'd been to see Harry off. She'd waved like mad. And then he was back in three weeks, with hepatitis.

When the sandbags were so high that Harry and Betty could no longer see over the top, they went into the restaurant. The waitresses and a handful of customers were gathered round a small transistor.

'This is Christian Island Radio . . . and here is an update on Hurricane Sophie . . .'

Harry looked at Betty and wondered whether he'd said anything to make a complete arsehole of himself. Betty tactfully said nothing beyond, 'Fancy that, Harry. A hurricane.'

Monday Island. Portia and Gladys were carrying boxes of grapefruit when one of the children came running up.

'Hurricane Sophie coming this way, mammy.'

'What you saying, child? Don't make me vex.'

'Is for true, mammy. The teacher hear it on the radio.'

Portia tipped her box of grapefruit into the crate and sat down. 'Dear Lord,' she said.

'Jesus will protect,' said Gladys. 'Put yourself in his hands.'

'You want to come to Sugar Bay, Gladys?'

'No, I staying here. Is better away from the sea.'

'Oh my God, Henzel' shop. You think he hear?'

'Everyone in Monday Island will get warning.'

'What we go do with the grapefruit?'

'What we can do? God will protect.'

'I gotta go, Gladys. Nail down the shutters.' Portia stood up wearily. Rubbed her back. 'The children go worry.'

'They say this Sophie is one bad lady. With a sting in she tail.' Gladys laughed but she looked worried.

Jancis, in the office of the Little People of God, was putting circulars into envelopes. The circulars were from Brother Benjamin to all the Little People. It was not often nowadays that he was moved to issue a letter but yesterday, after learning of Ophelia's departure, he had spent a sleepless night, as a result of which the duplicating machine has been working ever since.

The sheets of paper had to be folded into three to fit the brown envelopes. The first fold came at the base of Brother Benjamin's neck. Brother Benjamin's face was startlingly pale and his black beard fit to rival the pirate of the same name. There was a time when Jancis quite fancied Brother Benjamin although he was already quite hopelessly in love with Ophelia.

Brother Benjamin's turn of phrase still had the power to move Jancis. 'Come to me. Drink at my fountains,' she read. 'Abandon your vain ambitions. Rend your hearts.'

Jancis was grieved that he still suffered so much on

account of Ophelia and decided that she would go round to church that very night with the express purpose of offering her prayers for his comfort. Purely as a sister. For though her man was absent, he was still her man. Jancis would be faithful unto death.

Harry and Betty had still not managed to get any food when the ships first sounded their sirens. Betty clasped her hands to her ears as the noise rasped across the island. She and Harry were on their way in an instant. They had studied the safety rules and regulations avidly when they first went on board with no idea that they would ever be required to put them into practice.

The ships' hooters repeated their summons at regular intervals and soon the streets were jammed, as the day's quota of ten thousand tourists began making their way back to the harbour. They poured out of hotels and restaurants, bars, brothels and amusement arcades.

Although the shop windows were now boarded up or shuttered, in case of storm damage and looting, the shops inside were packed with people buying as if it was the last shopping day before Christmas. Then they too crowded out on to the pavements carrying packages like refugees.

Thomas sat on a bollard on the quayside of the commercial harbour. He too had noticed the black smudge on the horizon which heralded the arrival of the cargo ship from Sint Jan. He looked at his watch.

'What time you think she coming in, man?'

Jim, short for Jim Crow, the blackest of the dockers, pushed his hat on to the back of his head and scratched his scalp.

'I ain't saying nothing, man. All I saying is, look at them waves.'

They were soon joined by others, watching the waves break and splash over the top of the quay. Out at the reef the sea was at its fiercest and foam flew over the jagged coral outcrops thick as shaving cream.

'They ain't letting no more ships in today,' said another man gloomily. 'I going home for sure.'

Thomas watched the cargo ship now beyond the surf line, rising up and down like a horse on a merry-go-round.

'Ain't no point in sitting here no more,' said Jim Crow.

Thomas didn't move.

'Perhaps Sophie going pass us by.'

'You got to be kidding, man.'

The whole group turned to look at the thick curtain of cloud approaching from the east, high as the Tower of Babel.

Someone passed round a rum bottle and they all drank.

The cloud became livid like a bruise.

Out came the beer and the dominoes, and a bottle-opener with which Jim Crow drummed out a calypso rhythm on the metal bollard that set their feet dancing and their lips whistling.

It was when the cloud towered over them like some demonic volcano that the ships first sounded their hooters.

'That my ship?' asked Thomas.

'That all the fucking ships, man.'

It sounded like some orchestra out of hell, loud as the trumpets on the Day of Judgement.

Thomas got to his feet unsteadily.

'Hey, man, what you wanting off the ship? I go keep for you.'

'My wife,' hiccuped Thomas.

'Sure thing, man. I go look after she for you, eh?'

'There's Thomas,' said Betty.

'Where?'

'Over there.' Betty pointed. 'Hi, Thomas, you had a good day?'

Thomas joined them as they reached the gate.

'Not bad,' he said.

'I was kinda hoping you might show me round,' said Harry, giving Thomas a big wink. 'Like you did yesterday. Did I tell you, honey, that I met up with Thomas yesterday in Sint Jan?'

'No. Really?' said Betty.

'He showed me a real slice of local life.' Harry flung an arm round Thomas's shoulder and patted him.

Thomas swayed, ready to fall over if the density of the crowd hadn't supported him.

'I waiting for the ship,' he said, nodding in the direction of the old steamer. 'But it too rough.'

'It's not coming in today?'

'When Hurricane David come, he lift the boats right out of the sea and mash them up on the dock.'

'Really?'

'So now they all staying further out.'

'Did you see them loading yesterday at Sint Jan?' asked Betty. 'There were some crates there from Midwestern Electricals. That's Mr Stillman's company.'

'Huntingdon he working for Midwestern Electricals on Monday Island.'

'Who's Huntingdon, Thomas?'

'The brother of the Minister of Education. He want steal Ophelia.'

'That's just terrible.'

'Keep going, honey, or we'll never get there.' Harry held Betty in front of him like a battering ram. Thomas didn't seem to have the same trouble. Wherever he moved a small space appeared around him as if by magic. This embarrassed Betty who moved closer to him and away from Harry.

Once they had squeezed through the narrow aperture of the dock gate the crowd fanned out but the confusion became even greater as each person made a beeline for his or her own ship.

Betty, who'd been following Thomas, realized as they arrived at the gangway of the wrong liner, that Thomas didn't know where he was going or what he was doing. He had eyes for one thing only – the rusty hulk of the cargo ship on the horizon whenever it came into view between the passenger ships.

'This way, Thomas.' Betty put her arm through his and turned him in the right direction.

At the *Dream of America* people were massed in the shape of a Chianti bottle, bulbous at the narrow neck of the gangway.

Betty soon saw the reason for it. One third of the way up, pushing her zimmer frame in front of her like a lawn mower, was the woman with the mongol daughter. The daughter in a white fur hat and pebble spectacles kept turning to wave and grin at all the people waiting below.

'Chrissakes,' said Harry, 'people like that shouldn't be allowed on a cruise.'

'Really, Harry,' said Betty, who'd played such an active part with her collecting box during the International Year for the Disabled. 'They probably enjoy shopping and looking around just as much as you or I.'

'There must be eleven hundred people here, all held up by one goddamn cripple,' said Harry.

Betty was glad that the woman was in front. Otherwise like the cripple in the Pied Piper, she might have been left behind.

Betty had agreed to stay on deck while Harry changed so that their disguises would remain a complete surprise. She was so confident of the attractiveness of her own costume that she nurtured the slender hope that he might be drawn to her by some spark of the passion he had seemed to feel early on in their relationship. If this happened, the last thirty-two years had not been completely wasted.

In the Bar Napoli, where waiters in the guise of gondoliers served cocktails, Betty sipped her first colada and watched the sun set. Though the sky to the west bled orange, above her the normally clear blue was marred by something she had not seen before during the voyage. A solid, purple grey mass of cloud. Betty thought about Hurricane Sophie. With Christian Island shrinking on the horizon and no other land within sight, the *Dream of America* felt very small and vulnerable on a blood red ocean.

Betty ordered another pina colada – for courage, she told herself. After all, she was far short of her calorie ration for today. On the back of a postcard she noted down the ingredients. This recipe would just kill the Bernsteins. Ounce and a half of Cruzan rum. One ounce canned coconut cream. Well, somewhere in the whole of Rock City there must be canned coconuts.

Betty paused, trying to remember the next ingredient. Hotly pursued by the towering black cloud formation was the same rusty old cargo ship. Thomas had said that it would stay out at sea until all danger from Sophie was past. A ship like that in the harbour could be dangerous if it tore loose from its moorings and ripped into the old houses along the waterfront. Though she felt sorry for the houses, what about her and Harry and all the other eleven hundred passengers on board the *Dream of America*? For all their assurances, she could see the crew making preparation as if for war. The pool bar was closed for the first time, and she watched them dropping the sun loungers, tables and umbrellas into the water so that they wouldn't be carried away by the predicted hundred and fifty mile an hour winds.

Betty's fingers on the stem of her pina colada were white. With a trembling hand she continued her list of ingredients. Three ounces of pineapple juice. Chilled. Would the ship really be safe? Ships did sink. There was that Russian liner off New Zealand only recently, with eight passengers lost. She just knew that she would be one of the eight. What, she asked herself in a voice cold as her cocktail, would be the best thing to do in case of shipwreck?

Chappaquiddick came to her mind. If the boat actually sank like the Kennedy car, how did one escape the fate of Mary Jo? Lesson number one, she told herself, keep calm. Do not panic. Open the car window slightly so that the water level rises gently and evenly, keeping the head as near as possible to the roof where there is likely to be a pocket of trapped air. Secondly, open the door and swim to the surface.

Betty mentally rehearsed the procedure. She stood on her bed and heard the steady inflow of water down the staircase and along the corridor. It was somehow important that she was in her cabin at the time, surrounded by her own belongings. The water swished in through the cabin door and washed around the bed legs. Betty put on her new swimsuit for the first time this holiday. The one with the vertical stripes that the shop assistant had assured her was so flattering to the more generous figure. The water rose gently to her ankles, then her waist, then her neck. It was pleasantly warm. Thank heaven she was in the Caribbean and not the Atlantic. But what about the woman with the stroke and her mongol daughter? What, in God's name, about Harry?

Betty sipped her drink thoughtfully. A third of a cup of ice. She giggled. Must be getting drunk. She was on a ship, not in a car. Okay. Start again. The ship sank. Harry could not swim and she wouldn't go on a lifeboat, not after all the tales of cannibalism she'd read. She heard herself protesting, 'Harry first, he's much fatter than I am.' But Harry was a fast talker. He'd get out of that one somehow.

Her best bet was to remain in their cabin. People could be trapped in air pockets for weeks and survive. She'd seen it in a film – the people inside tapping on the hull and the divers outside saying, 'There's people still alive in there.'

The snag to this scenario was that their cabin was not

only removed from the hull by one whole layer of cabins to either side, but there were more above and below. Cabin number 2137 was like a cell at the centre of a beehive. However much Betty tapped with her nail file on the metal water pipes, would anyone be likely to hear her?

She drained her colada in one enormous gulp. Hiccuped. Whirled the ingredients in a blender, poured it into tall iced glasses, decorated with sliced frozen strawberries and carried the silver plate tray into the living room where Harry was setting up the projector ready for the slides.

She looked at her watch. She'd given Harry forty-five minutes to get ready. She turned her back on the approaching hurricane and putting one foot carefully in front of the other, went down to their cabin to change.

Hurricanes have always been one of the plagues of the West Indies. They have plucked and stripped the islands fairly regularly with all the efficiency of a beautician who removes not just the surface hairs but the roots as well. Through these unparalleled acts of violence, planters have been ruined financially and locals have been robbed of their lives. At sea, it will never be known how many ships and men have sunk without trace and founded with their rib cages of wood or bone yet another coral reef in the shimmering blue waters.

Nowadays, with efficient warning systems, there is no reason other than lack of foresight, and in some cases cash, why everyone should not be prepared, their houses made secure and adequate supplies of drink, corned beef, crackers and candles laid in.

Those on board ship are perhaps less fortunate, but smaller boats can for a price be hauled out of the water and larger ones can ride out the worst of the weather with few ill-effects other than the disruption of timetables and a fair bit of sea sickness. But snuggly battened down below decks, there is little to fear.

* * *

Harry hummed a tuneless little tune to himself and chuckled inwardly. Hey, not bad! He slapped his paunch and slipped a packet of cigars into his pocket. Then he pulled on the Mickey Mouse head. The radio sounded as though someone had abruptly turned down the volume and knocked the tuning knob.

He stepped briskly outside and slammed the door behind him.

Pink as a sweet pea, glowing from the shower, Betty heaved at the corset. She had not expected to need it at all during the holiday since daytime wear was cool and casual and current evening styles were loose and flowing. She'd packed it just in case.

The garment was a real son of a bitch to get on. She could quite see why all the best heroines had corsets which laced, only that of course required an extra pair of hands . . .

Adept in such matters is Bessie, Ophelia's great-great-grandmother, wife of Horatio, mother of George, the father of Eugenia. She was brought into the family in the dramatic circumstances which followed from the axe incident.

The year is 1830. Horatio, following the tradition set by his famous forebear, comes round on his mother's bed with the tarred stump of his right arm resting on a flour sack, and an ache somewhere level with his thighs where his hand should have been.

His mother Nelly wipes his forehead with a tepid cloth and moans and prays. When the bell rings she is gone with her hoe to the fields, leaving Horatio in a clouded state between consciousness and unconsciousness.

Enter Bessie, seventeen years old, lady's maid and dressmaker, sent by the Massa's wife with a bowl of broth. Not just one day, but every day for three weeks she is there, cradling Horatio's head to her bosom while she spoons in the nourishing liquid.

By the end of the first week, it is not just the broth that Horatio anticipates in his delirium. It is the light footsteps down the path between the huts, the opening of the door and the rustle of petticoats. Bessie in her Mistress's cast off silks is like an angel from heaven and the invalid delays picking up the spoon and feeding himself for many days after he was in fact capable of doing so.

Nelly, with the common antipathy of the field slave towards the coddled house servants, does not approve of the relationship. Where Nelly's life has left her as thin and tough as a cane stalk, Bessie is as soft and puffy as rising dough. Nelly believes that her son, especially with the handicap of his one arm, needs a woman of greater physical stamina.

But Horatio is passionately in love. One day, soon after he is able to get up and about, Horatio in his Sunday best presents himself at the Great House to see the Massa, and humbly requests the hand of Miss Bessie in marriage. The Master sees this as an answer to two problems. One, that he is becoming somewhat tired of Bessie's puddingy charms himself, two, what on earth is he to do with a one-armed slave who is no use to anybody? He can neither sell him nor afford to keep him, unless of course he can prove himself useful at stud.

There is something about Horatio's colour that suggests intelligence to his master. His features are good, having more of the European than the African in them, and the Master thinks again of ways to turn this liability into an asset. Horatio thus finds himself actually promoted by virtue of his accident to one of the most skilled jobs in the sugar-making process, that of assessing the moment at which the boiling sugar should be turned into vats to crystallize. It is a job which requires expertise rather than physical labour.

'Only let's not have you falling into any sugar vats, eh, Horatio?' laughs Master. And Horatio obligingly doubles up with mirth at the thought of himself sugar-coated.

There are two snags to the consummation of this love match, both severely affecting the Mistress of the house. She is loath to lose the skill of the only person who can lace her up to a neat eighteen-inch waist after the birth of her two children. Also, in her opinion, Bessie is one of the very best seamstresses on the island. Bessie has a flair for the dramatic – an eye for design which the Mistress has never encountered on the islands before.

When the Master points out that it is quite unreasonable to employ a full-time dressmaker when three or four dresses might be made elsewhere at a fraction of the cost, the Mistress suggests that Bessie double up as laundress in any spare moments she has.

And Bessie fosters her Mistress's notions of dependence. She does not in the least want to leave the luxury of the Great House and the casual embraces of the Master for the one-armed caress of a field slave.

Thus Bessie, whose opinion nobody has yet seen fit to consult, stalls on the question of marriage, though she attends church regularly in a whisper of silks and permits her one-armed lover to walk her home when the service is ended. For four years he carries her umbrella every Sunday. For four years he sits every evening on the back steps of the Great House while Bessie, her ankles neatly crossed, mops her sweating brow with a white lace handkerchief delicate as a snowflake. On the front verandah the violins play and her young ladies and the Mistress dance, until some necessary adjustment to their apparel sends them screeching through the house, 'Bessie, Bessie.' Horatio watches her through the open doors shiny and dark as a ripe cocoa pod amid the pale flutterings of her young ladies.

At night, Horatio returns to his hut, where Nell lies, now

covered in sores and wandering in her mind, raving about her childhood and her capture which in her madness are more real to her than anything that has happened to her in the twenty years since.

Horatio feeds and bathes his mother; he opens the windows and the door to try and clear the smell of her rotting limbs. He washes the flour sacks until they become soft like silk. But nothing brings Nell any relief until Bessie suggests laudanum. Since her Mistress has long been addicted, supplies come easily enough to hand. Horatio administers to his mother the doses of opium which Bessie prescribes and is overjoyed at the peace it brings her.

The merry bells of courtship chime for Horatio and Bessie until Emancipation strikes the death knell to the plantation system. One morning, they wake up with the amazing realization that they are free. Horatio joins his mates and gets drunk. Bessie in the Great House weeps with her Mistress and sees only ruin. They begin the packing, during which Bessie quickly sets aside her trousseau – not merely clothes, but also those generous gifts of pots and pans, furnishings and saucepans which her Mistress does not think worth the bother of shipping home.

'You free now, mammy,' says Horatio, sitting on the end of her bed, offering her a drink from the rum bottle.

Nelly stares at him blankly.

'You free,' repeats Horatio. 'Me, I free. We all free.'

Nell's eyes close again.

'What you goin' to do now you free, mammy?'

'Why you ain't working, son?'

Horatio takes another swig. 'Mammy, I ain't a slave no more.'

Nell lies, waiting for the bells and the footsteps. 'Is Sunday?'

'It ain't Sunday. We free. Massa day done.'

'Who going to cut the cane and boil up the sugar?'

'The Massa go have to do it hisself.' Horatio opens the door, lets in the brilliant sunshine, preens in its warmth.

'My medicine,' calls his mother. 'Where my medicine?'

Bessie staggers into the house with the first instalment of loot.

'Bessie?' calls the old lady.

'She bad today,' whispers Horatio. 'She not know what happening.'

'My medicine,' wails Nelly.

'The Mistress done gone,' says Bessie, sitting gently on the bed. 'Ain't no more medicine, Nelly.'

Bessie and Horatio go up to the house to fetch more of Bessie's belongings. While they are gone, Nell drags herself off the bed. Freedom? Hah. She struggles to the door, eases herself outside. She is free. Her life is her own. That's what Emancipation means. Half walking, half crawling, Nell drags herself to the highest point of the plantation, above the falls recently renamed 'Britannia' after the victory over Napoleon. There Nell exercises her freedom for the first and last time. She crawls forward into space.

Bessie moves into town. She rents a room opposite the former slave market and fixes a sign over the door: MRS BRANSTON, DRESSMAKER. She and Horatio never marry but Horatio lives there. It is only during the sugar harvest that his skills as tester are required. Between whiles he rests and drinks and plays dominoes, which with the decline of the plantations gradually matures into a full-time occupation.

Bessie sits in her doorway where the sun falls bright on her stitching, and there she is joined at regular intervals by little replicas of herself and Horatio. She sews and she talks to the passers-by and becomes a well-known and much respected figure among the townsfolk of Soufrière.

As the years pass peacefully by, Bessie becomes steadily more magnificent in figure – an amplitude which will be handed down to future generations in the shape of Eugenia and Portia. It is not until the youngest son George is a boy of ten that Bessie's sight begins to fail. She buys herself a sewing machine, but the damage to her eyes has already been done. She passes the machine on to Anastasia, the only one of her daughters who shows any aptitude for the craft (and through her line the same machine finishes up with another of Bessie's great-great-granddaughters, Sadie, the dressmaker of Sugar Bay). Now Bessie and Horatio take their son George back to the only other place in the world that they know. The former plantation at Nelson's Look Out.

The house itself had been abandoned in the years following Emancipation and in the lush tropical climate the land had quickly reverted to its wild state. They clear for themselves a plot of land and build a house. Horatio dies as George enters his teens, and poor sightless Bessie, who could so tightly lace a lady's waist proves sadly inept at keeping any control over her son.

No eighteen-inch waist for Betty. Scarlett O'Hara might have managed the tiny span of seventeen inches, but Betty, on her own, had to rely on will power and the illusion which she hoped would be maintained by a tight bodice and a very full skirt.

Although there wouldn't be anybody at the party creeping around with a tape measure, she'd get the goddamn corset on if it was the last thing she ever did in her life. She dragged the whole screwed-up affair as high as she could, and thanking God for her own good teeth gripped the top of the corset in her jaws and yanked the lower edge down. At last her suspenders dangled just where they ought to and the bra top pinged hard down on to her breasts. She sat weakly on the bed and waited for the quivering to subside.

While she got her breath back, Betty listened to the

radio. 'If I loved you . . .' She lit a cigarette. Plenty of time to relax. She didn't want to arrive early. '. . . words wouldn't count in the same old way. If I loved you . . .' Betty was as excited as if she were seventeen, getting ready for her first ball – only her first ball had been nothing to sing about. That drip Wayne Andrews whose father owned the grocer's store on West Eleventh. No flowers from Wayne, just a salami now and then. 'If I loved you . . .', life could have been so different. But it wasn't too late. Betty stubbed out her cigarette with resolve. It was never too late to begin again.

She stepped inside the scarlet dress just as the weather forecast came on. Hurricane Sophie eighty miles east of Christian Island travelling due west at twenty miles per hour. The clock said nearly eight. Sophie would hit at about midnight, or a few minutes after given the distance they had travelled from the island. Winds were forecast of up to one hundred and sixty miles per hour.

She shrugged her shoulders into the tiny frilled sleeves then put on the wig. The lady in costumes had said six pins would be adequate, but Betty, to be on the safe side bearing in mind the weather forecast, doubled the number.

She shook her head from side to side and nodded backwards and forwards. Steady as a rock. The pearls and little silver chains sparkled as they bobbed up and down.

Betty stepped into her high heels. If Wayne Andrews could see her now! She didn't fancy him herself, but she could never see what he saw in that Sheila from the leisure complex. She practised breathing in short little gasps. Swooning, like some eighteenth-century beauty was not an attractive prospect to someone weighing a hundred and sixty-five pounds.

It was only when she was ready to leave that Betty realized she was going to have problems getting out of the cabin door. Squeezing her skirts in at the sides as hard as she could, she lowered her head and burst through into the corridor.

The lift took her up towards the stars already reflected in her eyes. At the final ping of the doors, she stepped out into the foyer, spectacular for the occasion with palm trees and banks of hibiscus and orchids. Through the open door came the soft sound of violins. She took a deep breath.

'Madame la Marquise de Pompadour,' called the Master of Ceremonies.

Lowering her diamante butterfly mask over her face, Betty stepped into the ballroom.

A gorilla bounded up and she rapped it smartly on the nose with her fan.

'Betty, hey Bet, we're over here.'

Betty was astounded. She hadn't thought that anybody could possibly recognize her. Oh gee . . . she looked down at her costume and its splendour reassured her. It showered crimson sparks across the carpet as she walked.

'Hi, Lou. Hi, Sam.' Betty was pleased that Harry wasn't with them but she wasn't going to pretend that she hadn't recognized them. Not now.

'El Draqui.' Sam bowed deeply. 'Not quite of your century, but may I present my virgin queen?'

'El Draqui?' Betty was often lost when talking to Sam.

'Sir Francis Drake, scourge of the Spanish,' explained Sam.

'You look magnificent, Bet,' said Lou.

Betty wished she could say the same for Lou. She looked every bit the part – still, pale and flat chested. 'Should you two be consorting so openly?' she asked, settling back comfortably and unfolding the ivory fan.

'El Draqui was one of the early slave traders,' said Sam. 'What'll you drink, Bet?' With all the swagger of an Elizabethan gentleman, he headed for the bar.

* * *

286

Somewhere on the Gold Coast, Captain Henry Brown sits on a small, three-legged stool under a cinchona tree. His family claim kinship with the descendants of Drake, the famous gentleman adventurer, which it has been impossible to prove or disprove. However, Henry Brown believes himself to be following in the two hundred year old footsteps of his doubtful ancestor who, if gold was not to be had, was by all accounts equally unfastidious about any cargo provided it returned a handsome dividend.

Captain Brown is oozing from every pore, not because of the heat or even the potential danger of the situation since he has implicit faith in the superiority of his handful of armed men against a bunch of savages; he is sweating, while blood flows and the drums continue to beat, because he fears that not so much as a shipload of merchandise will be left and that he will have parted with his beads and materials for nothing.

For Captain Henry Brown of the *Golden Fleece*, 235 tons, registered in Liverpool the year of the fall of the Bastille, and a sailor of some repute, knows what it is to have a pack of hungry investors breathing down his neck. At the end of the day, he is a business man like any other, and profits must be made. He is the front man, the one who takes the risks, and this is a risky business.

His ship is one of about a hundred vessels plying the triangle trade. By the time Henry Brown came on the scene the trade had been well established for over a century, and carried, as every child learns at school, woollens, cottons and Sheffield wares to trade for slaves to trade for sugar. At the time we meet him he has been seasoned and hardened to his trade like a piece of mahogany, having survived all that the sea, the sky and pestilence of every description could throw at him.

But enough is enough. This is Henry Brown's last voyage, after which he plans to retire with his tidy little capital to a fashionable house in his home town, where he will live in the bosom of his family for the rest of his days. He has said the same thing every voyage for the last half decade, but his reputation is high among investors, his knowledge of the west coast of Africa and its tribes is rivalled by none, and he has developed an unequalled skill in selecting merchandise of the highest quality. His ship is eagerly awaited in all its regular ports of call.

And so he sits and yawns and waits through the mutilations and the ritual slaughters. He has seen it all before and simply prays that seven hundred prisoners of superior quality will be left to fill his hold. This is a point he has never managed to get across to these self-styled kings who think that just any old thing will do. Only Henry and his crew know the rigours of the voyage and that careful selection is therefore imperative. He has ordered and paid for one thousand slaves in the hope that two thirds will prove saleable commodities.

The King too is getting bored. Five executions can be exciting, but a thousand has the same effect as watching too much television. If one cannot switch off literally, one switches off mentally. Hence he wanders over to the Captain and indicates that the festivities are over.

Captain Henry bows deeply to the man who might otherwise become his own executioner and closely surrounded by his men, he marches to the holding pens by the seashore.

There are of course certain physical prerequisites for a good slave (as there are for an astronaut), and the ship's surgeon plays a vital part in the selection procedure. The six to ten week journey to the West Indies is exceptionally demanding. Health and youth is at a premium, teeth and hair are inspected, as are the private parts to eliminate those who suffer from yaws.

One successful candidate who passes all examinations with flying colours and elicits wolf whistles of admiration, is an adolescent girl who is named Nell (after she of the oranges) by the sailors for obvious reasons. She is one of two hundred women selected as good potential breeding stock. Even if they fail to survive the voyage they will provide one of the few compensations for life on board which offers little else by way of entertainment.

Betty sipped at her drink and watched the other guests arrive. There were several Lord Nelsons, at least one Napoleon, a couple of Dukes of Wellington and Spanish ladies and pirates galore.

The couple from cabin 2138 came and joined Betty, whereupon Sam and Lou made their excuses and left. Betty went out of her way to be especially nice, although why Ida had to come as a hula-hula girl with her spare tyre inflamed by the sun she couldn't imagine.

Mal had obviously never been to an occasion like this before. Betty and Ida watched the black tassel on top of his felt fez disappear in the direction of the bar as he went to fetch their drinks. Five minutes later he quickstepped past, not with the drinks, but with a sylph-like creature wearing little more than a sash embroidered with *Miss Dream of America*.

Betty recognized the girl. She was First Class. That was the wonderful thing about fancy dress. It was a great leveller.

Ida laughed and said, 'Trust Mal,' but Betty could see she was hurt.

'Let me get you a drink.'

'I think we can leave that to my husband,' said Ida.

Betty wasn't convinced. She hadn't even seen Harry since she arrived.

The music was now becoming too loud for conversation so Betty concentrated on looking serene instead. As if she were just getting her breath back between dances. Goodness, Ida was boring. She knew why Sam and Lou had moved on.

Mal eventually came back, plonked himself in a chair and took a big swig from his beer mug. He had nothing for the ladies.

'Am I sweating!' He took out his handkerchief.

Betty turned her chair away from Mal and Ida. Very discreetly so as not to hurt them but so that she didn't quite look as though she was with them.

Harry, from his position by the bar, had spotted Betty the second she walked in. After thirty-two years she couldn't fool him. He knew every ounce of her.

People patted him on the shoulder as they passed. 'Hey, Mick, how ya doing?' and he rewarded them with a clumsy little tap dance. He would have preferred to dance with a partner, but he'd seen Mal with that luscious *Miss Dream of America* and could tell that she was hating every minute of it. He had more sense than to go for a young girl like that.

He crept up behind Ida and gave a sly punch at her spare tyre with his gloved hands. 'Wanna dance, baby?'

Ida gave a little squeal, then giggled as she saw the grinning black and white face. She was up off her chair and away without so much as a word of apology to Betty.

Betty sat and flicked open her fan. Soon, she thought, there would hardly be room to move on the dance floor.

This feeling of being supported by other bodies in response to a common rhythm is one that is familiar to any tube traveller in the rush hour. Only Ophelia has never travelled on the underground. She has never before left Monday Island, and Monday Island has no rush hour, let alone any underground.

Ophelia, however, does not feel panic. She is used to the close, companionable feel of flesh and she is used to darkness, whether the darkness of her own skin, or the soft, velvet touch of the tropical night.

290

Likewise she has never been to a fun fair. There are no fun fairs on her island, so she has nothing against which to measure the thrill of the sudden soaring upwards on the crest of a wave (there is one hotel on the island with a lift, but Ophelia's friend who worked there told her that black people use the stairs) nor the swoop down at breakneck speed. Ophelia closes her eyes and waits for her stomach to settle in its rightful place, and feels not the warmth of these unknown girls, but the enveloping presence of her grandmother.

Granma is seated on the verandah, her upright wooden chair carefully positioned on the rickety floorboards. To move the chair an inch in either direction would be to court disaster.

Ophelia kneels at her grandmother's feet, her face buried in the checked apron that bulges over Granma's thighs, soft and warm and fat as twin bundles of sun-dried kapok. The next day is Sunday, and Granma, by the light of the moon and a single candle, is doing Ophelia's hair. With one end of the comb, she divides the scalp into a chequer board of dark squares divided by lines of skin that shine silvery grey in the moonlight.

Granma grunts as she leans over towards the table and the tub of vaseline. She rubs a blob of jelly into her hands, then massages it into the first spike of combed out hair.

'You keep still child, you hear me?' rumbles Granma, deep as summer thunder. She begins the first plait, right over left, left over right, her fingers fast as an ant with a grain of sugar. While her fingers are busy, nor is her tongue idle.

Granma remembers . . .

Nell, the never mind how many greats-grandmother of George, mother of Horatio. Of course she wasn't known by this name before . . . Nell is her God-, or rather sailor-given Christian name for reasons which were explained earlier.

The year is 1807. William Wilberforce and his cronies are patting themselves on the back for having at last abolished the slave trade. Such a move had awaited one thing, victory over the French at sea which freed the British Navy to enforce the prohibition. Nelson's victory at Trafalgar had consequences far beyond the balance of power in Europe.

An edict in Westminster to be enforced by a handful of rickety sailing ships was bound to fail. The trade was simply driven underground to become still more profitable. Gone were those wonderful government regulations in triplicate for the health and well-being of livestock in transit, which had produced the excellent result, statistically speaking, of a survival rate of up to sixty per cent.

Now the risks are greater, the profit must be higher and the cargo more efficiently stowed. The ships travel faster, threading their way stealthily up the jade necklace of the Antilles, hatches battened down and not a soul on deck except innocent sailors at their swabbing and splicing, or clinging to the rigging like monkeys.

But let us return to the story of Nell.

Nell, who has passed through the hands of the doctor and before the X-ray eyes of the Captain, sits in a small rowing boat fully expecting to be slaughtered and eaten by these strange pale coloured men. With a yo, heave, ho she is rowed out to where the *Golden Fleece* labours heavily at anchor. Not a breath of wind stirs.

As she steps on board, Nell is chained to another woman with manacles of the best that Sheffield can produce. She is then, according to witnesses, whipped or shoved below decks.

The lading lasts for two days. The heat is merciless. Nell obligingly lies on her side so as to make more space for her neighbours on either side. Before the two days have elapsed, Nell is surprised to feel that the back and buttocks of the woman chained to her are cold, in spite of the heat. Fortunately there is just time before the ship sails to replace her with a more talkative companion.

'May I join you?' asked Sally who sat down as she spoke.

Betty did not answer. She was reluctant to speak for fear of giving away her identity. Sally of the first class cabin had snubbed her often enough for Betty to want to remain incognito. On this occasion she needn't have worried. All that Sally wanted was an audience, and she neither knew nor cared who this was. She prattled like a wound up doll. At first Betty thought she was drunk, then she put it down to nerves. Nobody could help their nerves, she suffered that way herself.

While she watched the feathered headband toss like a palm before the storm, and the wrinkles break through the carefully applied layers of pan stick and powder, Betty preened herself. She had the good taste not to look like mutton dressed as lamb. She was a woman in her prime and had sought not to disguise her figure but to exploit it to the full and give expression to those smouldering passions that had long lain dormant.

'Cigarette?' Sally held out a packet.

Betty declined. A flapper with a cigarette in a long holder was one thing, but she couldn't imagine the Marquise de Pompadour smoking . . .

'May I have the pleasure?'

Betty was startled. She hadn't seen President Reagan approaching.

'I would have asked you before,' said the President, 'only the charleston didn't strike me as being your style.'

Betty was flattered. How could she refuse?

They dipped into the forward glide of the tango. 'I'm just an old-fashioned girl with an old-fashioned . . .' With Betty's left, and the President's right arm outstretched like the prow of a ship, they carved their way through the other couples until the boat gave a sudden lurch sideways. Betty and the President, wildly out of control, hurtled across the parquet floor and in that instant, Betty wondered just how many people could move to one side of the ship without tipping it right over.

The MC was instantly at the microphone. 'Looks like Sophie's a jealous lady,' he said. 'Doesn't want to be left out. Well, let's celebrate her arrival by free drinks all round.'

Already the waiters were moving smoothly among the tables, mopping up, collecting overturned bottles and glasses, reassuring the ladies.

The President returned Betty to her seat.

'I must go and find my wife,' he explained. 'She might be worried.'

Betty knew Harry would not come looking for her.

At the same sudden lurch, a roller falls from Ophelia's hand. She feels around the base of her suitcase and remembers the eldest Miss Simpson. But she cannot find the curler. She lights a candle and little flickers of light lick around her, dancing with the movement of the ship. She gets up to have a better look but cannot keep her balance. She sticks the candle in a pool of wax on the corner of her suitcase next to her and takes another curler from the bag. Rolls it up. In goes the pin. She looks at her watch. Ten o'clock. They should have arrived at Christian Island by now. Something must have gone wrong. She picks up another curler and remembers . . .

Granma blows up the charcoal until the coals glow like wolves' eyes in the semi-darkness. On the fire she places a cooking pot. In the pot is saltfish, rice, herbs and vegetables. As Ophelia kneels with her head on Granma's lap, the smell of the food floats warm across her nostrils. Granma pushes Ophelia's head hard down upon her lap.

'Don' make me vex, child.' She ties a neat green bow in the end of plait number six.

Ophelia imagines herself, not in the old skirt and blouse she is wearing now but tomorrow at communion in the pale green nylon dress with the silky underskirt and a large bow around her waist. On her head she will wear the new hat that Granma bought her in the market this morning. It is a wonderful hat made of yellow straw embroidered with luminous raffia daisies.

Ophelia fidgets. She thinks of herself having tea with the Queen in her new clothes. She feels under her cheek the hard bundle of keys in Granma's pocket. Keeping her head quite still, Ophelia's hand creeps up and holds them up to catch the last gleam of daylight. She is hungry. She puts one of the keys into her mouth. It is cold and hard. The smell of the codfish is making her dribble.

Granma reaches the end of another plait. She sees the keys in Ophelia's mouth. 'That dirty,' she says, snatching them away.

The key catches the corner of Ophelia's mouth, jerking her head back. She claps her hand to the place. When she takes it away there is blood on it.

'You too troublesome, child.' Granma dabs at Ophelia's mouth with her handkerchief. 'Why you eating keys when the sweet Lord Jesus put good food in the pot, eh?'

She kisses Ophelia on the cheek then flattens her head on her lap again. Granma begins another plait and another story.

Granma remembers . . .

Nell, below decks, has room to neither stand nor sit, but like any passenger of whatever class she is spared the labour of housework and food preparation. Her meals are brought to her where she lies – breakfast and dinner are both served in bed.

But Nell doesn't feel like eating. It is too hot. There is no air. The sailors who bring round the meals sensibly remove all their garments before entering the furnace of the hold. They ladle out the *soupe du jour* as fast as they can and escape through the hatches into the sunshine and the wind.

Nell doesn't want to eat. Food means life and she doesn't want to live. She doesn't even bother to lift her head when the tin mug is plonked down beside her. She closes her eyes and drifts into sleep.

Food is life and life is money in this business. If people are stupid enough not to eat they must be made to eat for their own good. Back come the naked sailors pale and clumsy as moths in the darkness, blundering over the bodies, collecting the empties. And what do they see? Nell has not eaten? They bluster and threaten and she lies uncaring. They unlock her chains and haul her up on deck where the coals still glow beneath the cooking pots.

Nell closes her eyes against the sunlight. She feels the red hot coal drawing nearer and nearer to her lips. She draws her head back and away until it can go no further and still the coal comes closer. Nell parts her lips in a scream and in goes the gruel. She gags and chokes but the thick slime keeps coming until she feels she will drown in it. And she dare not move for the embers scorching her eyelids.

Harry, who didn't mind Ida so long as she kept her mouth shut, twirled her round in a fast quickstep. Over his partner's shoulder he could see Betty sitting at a table glowing from head to toe. What a colour to choose at her age. He was so hot in that damned mouse head he could feel the sweat trickling down the back of his neck and inside his collar. He pulled the elasticated bowtie away from the shirt to let in a bit of air.

'That's cheating,' said Ida. She pulled the tie until it was taut like a catapult and then let go.

Harry yelped like a neutered cat.

'I can be a pretty mean mouse if I want to,' he snarled.

Ida looked into Mickey's permanently smiling face and laughed. 'Harry!'

'I need a drink,' Betty was saying.

'Get you one,' said Sally. Sally only had to lift one finger and the steward was there. Betty had noticed this before. First class one finger. Middle deck one hand. B deck stand up and scream.

She toyed with her fan. It would all be over soon, and back to a ten o'clock bedtime so that she could be asleep before Harry came in from the Sharpshooter's Club or bridge. Only Harry was going to be around all day. Every day.

If Sally wasn't drunk before, Betty reckoned that she was now. She slumped in her chair with her eyes closed, until a new lot of drinks arrived. The sound of ice chinking had an effect as immediate as plunging tired celery into cold water. As the drink went down, Betty watched the winding up mechanism set in motion.

Sally's back straightened, the veins in her neck swelled and her eyes looked like stuffed olives on the end of cocktail sticks.

Ida returned from her dance. Sat down exhausted and took her shoes off.

'C'mon, Bet. I'll give you three guesses. Who was I dancing with?'

Betty knew darned well it was Mickey Mouse. As if anyone could have failed to notice. But she'd humour her. 'Frank Sinatra?'

Ida frowned.

'President Reagan?'

'Betty, how can you be so dumb? I mean, who was inside the costume?'

Betty shrugged.

'Come on. I'll give you a clue. He's from your very own home town.'

Betty's heart sank. Someone from Rock City here on this ship, and only three days until everything she had said or done on board became common gossip?

'I just don't know where to start, Ida.'

'Well, I'll give you a clue. His initials are H.S.'

It took a while for the penny to drop. She looked at the ridiculous head bobbing obscenely over the dancers. Typical Harry. She might have known it. He could never manage anything dignified. She was only thankful that he was still keeping away.

'Now don't say I said so,' said Ida. 'Harry made me promise.'

But Harry found her all right. When Betty returned from the buffet Harry was plonked in the only spare seat, which happened to be hers.

'Excuse me, Harry,' she said coldly, all six foot six of her, wig and heels.

'How did you know it was me?' Harry shovelled a forkful of lobster mayonnaise into his mouth.

'Harry, how can you eat with that thing on?'

'No problem. It's a knack.' Inside the head, Harry's chin was beginning to itch in a sea of mayonnaise.

'Why don't you take it off for supper?'

'Bet, this is a fancy dress party. I don't want to spoil the fun.' The truth was he couldn't get the head off and he didn't like to admit it.

Betty was tired of standing there holding her plate. She was about to ask Harry for the second time if he would get out of her chair when she felt a hand on her bare shoulder.

'Where have you been all my life?'

Betty turned round, face to face with Louis XV who took her plate and put it down on the table. Betty was quite unable to speak. She had never seen anyone so handsome.

'I'm not used to dancing with kings,' she spluttered.

'Commoners are all the rage nowadays.' He gave her back a gentle squeeze and Betty's heart fluttered.

'I fell in love with the dress,' she confessed. 'It was so pretty.'

He spun her round in a tight circle. 'I think', he said, 'we may surmise that Madame La Marquise intended it to be more than just pretty.'

Betty looked down at her skirt. It looked very scarlet. 'I've always liked red,' she said sticking out her chin. She noticed for the first time the crow's feet around her partner's eyes.

'Red can be very suggestive.'

Betty blushed under the diamante butterfly. He was holding her uncomfortably close.

Ophelia wishes that she had her radio with her. It would be something to do. The other girls jabber in Spanish, and although she knows there are some girls from the British islands somewhere, it is too hot and stuffy to make the effort to find them and she doesn't feel like talking anyway. She finishes putting in her curlers and ties a bright pink hair net over to keep them firm. The hairpins dig into her scalp, and Ophelia remembers . . .

The pattern on Granma's dress. Her right eye is squeezed shut against Granma's knee, but her left eye, half open, follows the pattern of the material of Granma's skirt. The pattern swirls round and round in enormous circles, purple like the bougainvillaea over the porch, red as the flamboyant, yellow as the alamanda by the hen house.

Granma's dresses are enormous. Yards of sea cotton go into their making. They flow around her vast body like mist about the mountain tops in the early morning. If Ophelia stares into the circles she feels herself being sucked in and down as if she had fallen into a whirlpool.

Ophelia lifts her left hand from the cool floor and traces

the patterns on Granma's knee with her forefinger. Round goes her finger, faster and faster, twirling to the music which her toes drum on the planks . . .

While Granma remembers . . .

Out of sight of land, the hatches are unbattened, and the manacled slaves are brought up on deck. It is time to attend to personal toilette, health and beauty. A time to dance. A time to sing.

Nell holds her hands to her eyes, shutting out the unaccustomed light and the barren emptiness of the unending water. She leans against the railing and eases her cramped limbs.

Then the whips crack and she raises her parched voice to heaven in a wail of longing for all that she has loved and lost.

The last falls across her shoulders and she shambles with her partner about the deck, hands upstretched and the air all about her like the full glory of God's love.

Suffice it to say that Nell, who has been lying in obscurity below deck, here draws attention to herself even in the tortured grace of her movements, with a figure as yet undimmed by ship life.

Though her style of dancing goes unappreciated by the sailors little versed in the finer points of ethnic culture, they cannot fail to recognize that Nell, now twisting and turning in the spotlight of the sun, will provide a pleasing diversion amid the general squalor.

Instead of being returned below deck with her fellows, she is tethered above at the sailors' pleasure. She weeps at being thus singled out for special treatment but this extra ration of fresh air is probably just what the doctor would have ordered. And by the time she is returned to the hold later on in the voyage, the crush has been appreciably lessened, to which fact she may very well owe her survival.

* * *

Granma plaits Ophelia's hair so tightly that the child squeals with pain.

As the music stopped, Betty fought to be free of Louis XV's embrace. The large artificial flower was digging uncomfortably into her cleavage.

The party was definitely lowering its tone, thought Betty. She was feeling mildly drunk herself and the floor was gently rolling under her feet.

When the music stopped Louis XV moved to follow her. She jabbed her heel hard into his toe, smiled serenely and went back to her seat.

'It's strange seeing you in that costume,' said Sally.

'Oh really?'

'People can't seem to resist it.'

Ida leaned over and stroked the shiny satin. 'Mal insisted that I made my own,' she said.

The chandelier was swaying gently over the dancers. Betty put her hand to her head.

'I didn't expect to see it again,' went on Sally. 'Not after what happened.' She flicked ash into an empty champagne glass. 'At the moment of death . . .' Sally's words bubbled to the surface like gas through a swamp, '. . . the bowels contract. If she hadn't hung herself – '

'Who?' Ida picked the flowers one by one off her garland and shredded them into the melting ice cubes of the abandoned glasses.

'. . . the dress would have been ruined.'

Ida's tissue paper flowers dyed the water in slow, spreading stains.

'Who?' she repeated.

Betty nudged Sally who hiccuped. 'The lady who wore that dress last year.'

'Have you ever worn this dress, Sal?' asked Betty.

'Me?' Sally suddenly jerked into action. 'What would I be doing in that dress? I'd drown in it. Not hang. Drown.' She shrieked with laughter.

Ida dropped a red flower into Harry's beer. It turned a dull orange and wispy threads of colour crept through the glass like blood.

'She hanged herself?' asked Betty.

'Mm mm.' Sally beckoned for another drink. 'In her cabin.'

Betty was thinking of the horrible isolation of her windowless cabin and the red figure slowly revolving when Harry appeared at her elbow.

'Want to dance, Bet?'

'I don't feel well.' Betty shoved past him and out of the ballroom, her teeth clenched against the rising vomit. She felt the hateful slither of satin as she waited for the lift. The doors flew open. Betty stepped forward then recoiled as she saw a couple in a passionate embrace. She pressed the lowest button and stared blankly until the doors shut and they were carried below.

She tried the other lift and found herself between Abraham Lincoln and Cinderella who stood elaborately far apart, one to each side. Betty kept her eyes on the floor. Piggy in the middle. She sniffed. They weren't teenagers, for God's sake. Surely they could find somewhere a bit more private. The ride seemed to go on for ever. Cinderella's eyes smouldered. Let her wait, the bitch, thought Betty. As Abraham Lincoln pressed the 'hold' button for Betty to get out, she saw an inch of black skin between the white gloves and the white cuff.

Betty leaned weakly against the corridor wall. It wasn't that she wasn't broad-minded. She'd just never liked lifts. She tottered along to her cabin and lay on the bed.

She looked up at the ceiling and the central light. How in God's name could you hang yourself from a light socket? The only other possible fixtures were the wardrobe rail if you were a midget or the shower head which was adjustable, but not that adjustable. Betty lay and pondered upending the bed, until she discovered it was screwed to the floor. Sal was obviously quite wrong. Unless, oh no, unless it was murder.

Betty put her hands nervously up to her neck. She took a quick look at the carpet for blood stains. That was silly. Just because the woman had worn the same dress didn't mean she had occupied the same cabin. Anyway she'd hung herself, not been stabbed or shot.

It suddenly seemed dangerous to be down there on B deck, all alone. She'd have to get back.

Betty saw herself heading down the deserted corridor, like the heroine of some gangster movie, a tiny figure on a vast screen. Of course it wasn't so much the sight as the sound which lent drama to such a sequence. The minor chords first quiet and slow, then the long, gradual crescendo and accelerando to indicate the presence of danger and increase the rate of the heart beat.

She put her hands over her ears to shut out the sound. What was she, after all, but a plump, middle-aged woman in a ridiculous costume looking for her equally plump and middle-aged husband.

It was when she reached the end of the corridor that she heard the footsteps. Very slow footsteps coming down the uncarpeted stairs towards her. Betty looked at the lifts. They were both engaged. She flattened herself against the corridor wall as the footsteps came round the final bend in the stairs. Perhaps Thomas was in his pantry. Perhaps he would hear her scream.

Round the corner bobbed the black and white head of Mickey Mouse.

'Honey, am I glad to see you.' Betty flung her arms round his neck and wept with relief.

Mickey Mouse hugged her close an patted her on the back with his white gloves. She sobbed out the whole story on the way to the cabin where he again took her in his arms and his latex nose wuffled along the black lace of her corsage. Betty's bosom rose and fell like waves in a

303

hurricane. In her corset encrusted passion she truly became
Madame La Marquise de Pompadour.

The ship has anchored nose into the wind, bucking and
wallowing. Ophelia feels more and more queasy. Perhaps
she should try some food or drink. She opens a can of blood
hot Coca Cola and lets it trickle slowly down her throat.

Her head aches. She unties the pink net scarf and loosens
the curlers. Reties the scarf and applies some eau de
Cologne to her forehead and temples. It feels cool as it
evaporates. Ophelia tries to concentrate on the fresh clear
perfume, like flowers on an early morning after rain . . .

. . . and Granma's feet bare, toes splayed in the mud to
keep balance as she walks up the hill with her hips tilting
from side to side in crazy diagonals.

Ophelia sees the eyes of the men as they watch Granma
go through the village. She is happy to know that they
admire her as much as she does.

And Granma remembers the fathers of her children. She
loved them all. She smiles to herself when she thinks how
such little things, the look in a man's eye, the way he
walked or tilted his head as he spoke could be enough. But
she'd never sacrificed her independence to them. Not ever.
But all that was long ago.

Granma's breathing quickens. Her thighs stiffen. Startled,
Ophelia looks up, up into the caverns of Granma's nostrils.
Her head is pushed down roughly on to the lap again.

'Phelie,' she says. 'You know what they say?'

Phelie shakes her head and Granma takes a firmer grip
on the plait.

'They say, "Man on top and woman underneath like
foot on the ground and head up in the air." Well, it ain't
true. Don't you never forget that.'

* * *

Little Nell has less choice. When she is not obligingly spread-eagled like a rag doll she is set to work in that area where women are commonly believed to excel. The cooking. She feeds the fire and stirs the gruel and scours the pots as well as any Cinderella, and if the food is not exactly three-star she is as well off as the sea-going Devonians, which prevents her from acquiring the prison camp look that afflicts so many of her fellow slaves.

But so it is that Nell acquires three things on the voyage, a Christian name, syphilis and a baby, and she founds a line which passes through Horatio and George, Eugenia and Portia to Ophelia. Via Horatio comes the gene which roams at whim over all the colours of the spectrum, from the gleaming molasses of Eugenia and Portia to the glowing honey of Ophelia – though it must be said that some of the credit for this goes to Alice who kept alive through her daughters the tradition of total abstention from cocoa and coffee during pregnancy. Nor will it have been overlooked that there is a certain propensity among the womenfolk to fall for sailors. There is something fatally romantic about the sea.

Still at the ball, Mickey Mouse Harry is having a quick twist with another Nell, white as a lily. The music is fast and loud. It takes Harry back, not exactly to his youth but to when he felt youthful. The year when the firm gave him a new car and Betty was pregnant and they bought a new house in what was then a fashionable suburb of Rock City. He'd had no reason to suppose, as he drove along the highway with 'Let's twist again' blaring on the radio, that within so short a time all those dreams would fall about his ears. Betty in hospital, the kid living for a few days – a few days for Chrissakes, nowadays they'd surely have done something to save it – after which he'd got drunk and smashed up the car which had temporarily lost him his licence. And he was finished.

Harry danced grimly on, his eyes glued to the famous oranges, blaming his shortness of breath on the goddamn mouse head. He was quite relieved to be cut out by Charles II before the dance had ended.

As Betty was still not back he went into the bar and ordered a beer. On the stool next to his was Marilyn Monroe in the famous little white dress. Harry cast a critical eye. She looked perfect in every detail. Harry leant closer. 'Hi, gorgeous.'

Marilyn fluttered her weighty eyelashes in his direction.

'You like mice?' he asked.

'They don't bother me.' Marilyn's voice was pleasantly low and thick like black treacle.

'What'll you drink?'

'A beer.'

Harry was surprised. But then it was very hot.

'I can hold my liquor as well as any man,' drawled Marilyn.

Harry took out his handkerchief and mopped his Mickey Mouse forehead which did nothing to relieve the prickling of his skin inside the mask. He was dying for a smoke. A cigarette was not quite long enough to reach between the mask and his face. He tried a cigar. That was okay, but he'd only be able to smoke two thirds of it.

'Want to take a turn about the deck?' Marilyn looked him straight in the eye.

After his experiences of the day before on Sint Jan, Harry was ready for anything. He left the bar with Marilyn on his arm, feeling a million dollars. He was surprised by the curious looks they attracted, since Marilyn Monroe and Mickey Mouse were no more extraordinary as a couple than many others, and it was only when Marilyn whispered, 'Just wait here a minute,' and disappeared through the door of the men's room that Harry put two and two together. He moved with the speed he usually reserved for that vital point on the squash court and lolloped down the corridor with only one thought in his head. He must find Betty.

'You going back for the midnight buffet?' murmured Betty, lying on her bed with Mickey Mouse's plastic chin digging into her shoulder. She didn't mind, not one bit, even though it would probably leave a dent as red as her dress. 'It must be fifteen years . . .' she whispered caressing the plastic ears. She couldn't remember the last time, not to the exact day, but it was long before they moved into separate bedrooms. It had all been her fault. She had been quite wrong. In her crumpled satin she saw the rosy togetherness of the future.

There came a gentle knock at the door.

'Betty? You in there? It's me.' Betty froze. It was Harry's voice. Harry in the corridor.

'Betty, honey?'

Betty opened her mouth to scream. Mickey Mouse silenced her with a gloved hand.

Harry in the corridor fumbled with the lock. 'If you're in there, Bet, will you please open this goddamn door?'

Betty closed her eyes.

Mickey Mouse clambered off her. She heard him zip up his trousers.

As Harry's footsteps receded down the corridor, Betty heard the cabin door open and shut. She began to giggle hysterically then turned as red as her dress, sprinted for the bathroom and was violently sick in the toilet pan. The ship was tossing quite violently now. Betty steadied herself with one hand on the washbasin, the other on the shower cabinet.

Ophelia's candle is burning down. She takes out her nail file and polish, and peering, for the light is not good, grinds her nails to a delicate oval. Her head aches much as it would from an exhaust-clogged afternoon in Oxford Street or the stuffiness of an overcrowded cinema. The movement of the ship doesn't help either. Ophelia squeals and sucks her finger after a buck and a toss drive the tip of the metal file up underneath her cuticle. But at last the job is done. Ophelia leans back weakly and blows on the polish to dry it.

She is determined to look her best as she sets foot on American soil for the first time. Her eyelids are heavy and her head lolls, reminding her of the comment in the market place that too much learning makes the head too heavy for the neck.

The nail varnish topples off her knee and wakes her. The smell has become worse. When Ophelia reaches down and gropes around her feet for the small bottle, her fingers touch the slippery morass of the spilt slop bucket. She retches then vomits though there is little in her stomach except lukewarm Coca Cola . . .

Nell, in chains, slides easily back and forth on a lubricating layer of blood and mucus. For Nell has disgraced herself. Nell has contracted the flux and has been banished from the sailors' quarters and the cooking for reasons of nicety rather than hygiene. They find her presence offensive, so she finds herself once more in an environment where the indiscriminate depositing of excrement is accepted as perfectly natural.

The sailors, wearing rags over their faces in a vain attempt to keep out the stench, prove by a kick that Nell's second partner is well and truly dead. They take away her baby with all the kindness of farmers rearing their stock and the child is latched on to the breast of a nursing mother, who is placed in slightly more advantageous conditions directly below the hatch cover.

These are strong experiences for a young girl. In the jargon of today they may well be defined as traumatic. Nell will carry her scars to the grave and beyond.

* * *

'They saying to them poor black people,' says Granma, '"We bring you here and we save your souls, we giving you food and clothes so you ain't ignorant savages no more, so why you weeping?"'

Granma is on the last but one plait. Ophelia's eyes flicker open and shut as the voice comes and goes. Her left hand droops on to Granma's bare foot, scaly and rough as a hen's leg.

'Why you don' wear shoes?' she murmurs.

'Why you vex me with your questions?' rumbles Granma. 'I don't wear no shoes because I ain't use to them.'

'You wear them to town and to church.'

'Is different, child. Why I wasting good leather all over the house and garden, eh?' She feels about her lap for a rubber band. 'When I was a little child, I didn't have no shoes, Phelie.'

Granma's mind, as she approaches death, lives more in the past than in the present, and not the immediate past at that, but way, way back. Though she does not know it, she is immortalized in some children's encyclopedia as a 'magnificent young negress' whose image has been captured as she wades out to the banana boat with two stems of green fruit balanced on her head and her bare feet scoured by fine coral sand.

'You find the rubber band, Phelie?'

Ophelia feels with her fingers around the base of the chair. She finds nothing except the swept floorboards and a jagged splinter which stabs under her nail.

Granma removes the splinter with her teeth and sucks the wound. 'It better now,' she says. 'Everything done better.'

Betty hauled herself to her feet and sat on the edge of the bath. It was strangely quiet and seemed to be becoming hotter by the minute. A mosquito whined loud as the jets that shrieked across the sky above Rock City.

She wrung out her flannel in cold water and held it to her forehead. She would have taken off her wig, hot as a busby, if her fingers were not shaking so much that she couldn't find the pins.

She felt terrible. She wanted to find Harry, though she was not quite sure why. She could just hear him calling her a nymphomaniac pensioner when she'd always kept her thoughts under far tighter control than he had.

The heat was just terrible. She'd never liked the heat. Saunas. Things like that. Other people sweated and then swore they felt just wonderful. Not Betty. She felt like a piece of broiled pork. After a final dab of the flannel, she went back into the bedroom.

She was in the middle of slapping on puffs of powder fit to choke her, when the terrible thought occurred to her. She didn't know who the man was, but he knew exactly who she was, for she had taken off her butterfly face mask. Well, not exactly taken it off. It had got knocked off. And what if he came back? What if at that very moment he was actually creeping down the corridor? He must be a third class passenger otherwise what was he doing down on B deck in the first place? She was pleased to think back to the whisky on his breath. Maybe he would be too drunk to remember anything at all. She'd rushed him inside the cabin so fast he could hardly have registered the number on the door. But from now on, apart from Harry and Sam and Mal, she'd never be able to look another man in the face. Why couldn't Harry just have gone as a cowboy and then there wouldn't have been any mix-up at all?

Large crimson stains had appeared under Betty's armpits. The cabin was stifling. She just had to get out. Whatever the risks.

* * *

Harry had looked everywhere he could think of for Betty. He might have been avoiding her all evening at the ball, but hell, he liked to know where she was. When all else failed he returned to the cabin.

This time the lock turned easily enough. Betty's bed looked crumpled. She'd probably been down for a rest. She had no stamina, that was another of Betty's troubles. He could go on all night but Betty was a real early bird.

Inside the Mickey Mouse head Harry had a splitting headache. He'd hoped to find Betty so he could get the goddamn thing off. He got hold of both sides of the neck and tugged. It was no use. He picked up the telephone and rang room service. Thomas didn't answer. What helluva way was this to run a ship?

Harry hurled the receiver down. He could have wept with frustration. God, how he hated Mickey Mouse. He never wanted to see another Disney film as long as he lived.

He hurled himself out of the cabin and swept like a tornado along the corridor and upstairs. He would look for Betty on the compass deck. Where else could she be?

Betty flung herself behind the counter of a deserted coffee bar. Blackbeard was only a few paces behind, brandishing his cutlass and yelling, 'Avast there! Pillage and rape!'

She could not shake him off. If it hadn't been for his wooden leg she wouldn't have kept ahead for this long.

'Yo heave ho.' He stood in the doorway with the parrot bobbing on his shoulder.

Betty could see him reflected at least fifty times over in the mirror tiles. He looked slowly round the room, then took off his hat and mopped his forehead with the end of his beard. Even after he gave up and stomped out, Betty counted to fifty before she dared move.

The storm outside was fiercer now, but she welcomed it. She needed fresh air. She made her way towards the compass deck.

* * *

311

Nell, not the alabaster model but the flip side of the coin, is less fortunate. Her needs go unrecognized. Charles II, in whose reign the Habeas Corpus Act was passed, omitted to extend its benefits to other Nells in other places. There is a certain logic in this. Nell is a possession and not a person, and as such cannot call her body her own.

Let it not be thought that Nelly is without value. She is worth a certain number of gold pieces and the gold pieces must be carefully counted. At the end of the voyage Captain Brown will be called to account by his shareholders.

He can expect to lose fifty percent of his slaves without financial loss. He has learnt by experience not to expect a better rate than that, which he blames on a lack of personal attention to hygiene among his cargo. Very well. If they are not able to take better care of themselves, Father Henry will take the responsibility out of their hands. He orders salty showers to disinfect the sores, a good swilling down below decks and more dancing and singing in God's fresh air and sunshine.

Then a sail is spotted on the horizon. British or French, it is hard to tell. Down below decks go the slaves. Slam go the hatches. And Nell lies scarcely able to breathe, just one of eighty women in an area ten by three feet. The sailors cease to visit because they cannot see. It is too dark. There is not enough air for their candles to burn.

Harry's hopes of finding Betty up on the compass deck were strengthened when he caught sight of the flash of a scarlet skirt. Whoever it was, a man was following her. Harry followed too, using his arms to keep his balance, like a gorilla weaving through a bamboo thicket. His wife with another man?

As Betty stepped out on deck the wind took hold of the vast acreage of satin and flung her back against the doors, knocking all the breath from her body. Then as her lungs expanded again the implosion of air hit her like a dose of smelling salts.

Bent half double against the force of the hurricane, Betty made her way towards the metal staircase. It took all her strength to keep hold of the railings, and as her head rose above the level of the compass deck a sudden blast whipped the wig right off her head together with the hairpins, and chunks of scalp. She made a grab with her hands as the wig flew like a bishop's mitre above the dizzily swaying lights, before the squall knocked her sideways on to the deck. Above her, the ship's funnel tilted at crazy angles. On hands and knees she crawled round into its shelter and there was Harry, unmistakable in spite of the plastic head, with his shirt buttons undone and his belly bulging over the waistband of his trousers. And there was Thomas as well.

Harry was facing the funnel, leaning back against the railings with his feet braced against the deck and his head lowered like a bull towards the matador.

Betty struggled to her knees, then on to her feet. Harry in a fight? She just couldn't believe it. But Thomas, with one foot on the handrail level with Harry's hips, had Mickey Mouse by the ears. He was twisting the head from side to side, grinning horribly, while Harry bellowed with pain, audible even above the baying of the wind.

Beyond Thomas was the scarlet figure of a Spanish gypsy. The fairy lights gave a final epileptic twitch and went out. But Betty had seen enough to tell her exactly what the whole scene was about. Harry had seen the woman with Thomas and he had thought . . . Betty began to giggle. Harry defending her honour while she'd been downstairs with another Mickey Mouse, thinking it was him? Betty clasped her hands to her head and rolled with the motion of the ship.

Harry roared again. He had his hands now on Thomas's

shoulders and was pushing backwards with all his might. A sudden flare of moonlight unfurled across the sea like a carpet and caught the gleam of Thomas's laugh. He was enjoying himself in this combat with a man old enough to be his father.

Betty took off one of her shoes, and holding the toe of her stiletto with the heel projecting like a blade, she closed in on the two men.

In Europe the hurricane has attracted little interest. It will not hit the front page of any of the dailies.

Huntingdon and Gloria are in Paris. They sit at a table in the Folies Bergères and sip the last of their wine. They had caught a plane earlier in the day, when news of the hurricane first came through. The scenes at the airport had been horrific, with people fighting for seats.

On the same plane was his brother, the Minister of Education, on his way to attend to some pressing business in Brussels. He had his girlfriend with him. The four of them had had no difficulty in obtaining seats.

They were well away from Monday Island, scourged by a wild grey sea flecked with white like the fat on congealed gravy, where the Misses Simpson have lit a whole battery of candles in front of their statues. The deaf Miss Simpson sees the curtains toss and the blind Miss Simpson hears the wind roar. The youngest Miss Simpson clutches to her breast a silver medallion of the Virgin Mary. She pulls her sheet over her head and weeps and prays.

Jancis checks the sleeping boys. Nothing the wind can do seems to disturb their slumber. She puts her ear close to Napoleon's nostrils for he lies so still and she cannot hear his breathing above the wailing outside. She tucks the sheet close around Nelson's shoulders for fear that he will catch cold in the draught and checks the nails which hold down the shutters. Then she goes and sits with her old parents and recites the prayers for those at sea.

Up at Nelson's Look Out, Gladys stands on the verandah of her little wooden house like a captain on the prow of his storm-tossed ship and stares out into the darkness. She looks out towards the sea and all those countries she will never see. And she thinks about her niece Ophelia. Little Phelie done gone now. She feels that knowledge in the keening of the wind. In one hand, Gladys holds a candle, for the night is dark. With her other hand, Gladys shelters the fragile flame. The house rocks beneath her in the violence of the wind. She is pleased that her sons and Estelle are safe down in Sugar Bay with Portia. But she cannot leave. Her place is up here in her garden, among the banana trees that she and her mother and her grand-mother have tended with love.

As the candle flame flickers, Gladys draws it closer to herself. 'If God willing, tomorrow I go take the grapefruit to the deep water harbour.' But she knows in her mind that tomorrow there will be no grapefruit. That there will be no deep water harbour. That her lifetime's work will have come to nothing. Gladys suddenly feels old and tired. She is a grandmother many times over. She lets fall her guard from the candle and the flame is carried away by the demon wind.

Ophelia fights to be free of the suffocating darkness around her. But Granma holds her face between her knees as in a vice. Ophelia fights for breath, drums with her toes on the floor and with her fists on the thighs that have turned to steel against her. She hears her grandmother's voice.

'Don't make me vex, child.' For Granma is fitting the

last rubber band on the last plait. 'If I hurting you, child, is for your own good.'

But Ophelia has had enough. She wants out. She scrabbles with her hands at the ungiving steel, at the cold metal ribs. Ophelia, one of sixty in an area twelve by six. Nell would have envied her.

'Harry!' screamed Betty. The heel of her stiletto flashed in the moonlight. She brought it down hard on the arm of Harry's assailant, who spun round without releasing his grip on Mickey Mouse's ears.

Harry's head popped out from inside the plastic Mickey Mouse like a cork from a champagne bottle. Harry, still braced against the force of Thomas's pulling, jerked backwards. At that precise moment the ship gave one enormous roll. The deck dipped. With the angle of the slope and the force of the wind, Harry hadn't a chance.

The low railing caught him at hip level. He flung out his arms and screamed, but as the boat wallowed towards the trough, Harry was upended. His patent toes winked briefly, then another onslaught of cloud shuttered the moon and Harry was gone.

Ophelia's candle is burning low. Her fingers are clumsy, but she tilts it to drain off any accumulated wax around the wick, as if the gyrations of the ship would not already have done so. The candle goes out. She fumbles for a matchbox in her handbag, but her fingers no longer grip the match firmly enough to strike it. She cannot even feel it between her thumb and forefinger.

Ophelia like a fish out of water, mouth open, gulping and heaving, limbs flailing in an atmosphere which cannot sustain life, claws through the jabber of Spanish towards the door.

Granma's voice booms through her head, 'Remember child, you is all of we, Portia and your Daddy, me and your

Granddaddy, and George and Alice and Horatio and Bessie and Nell . . . '

But Ophelia isn't listening any more.

Betty locked her cabin door. She was glad that the cabin had no porthole in case Harry's face suddenly appeared upside down as he dived deeper and deeper into the sea, eyes goggling like a goldfish in a bowl. She poured herself a toothmug of gin. Then another. This, she told herself, was what she had been planning. She spread her little souvenirs all over Harry's bed. Stepped out of the scarlet dress and went into the bathroom. How she would have loved a bath, deep and perfumed. Her skin felt cold. Goosepimply. The next voyage would be different. State cabin, sunken bath, jacuzzi, the lot. She turned on the shower and roasted slowly beneath the gentle thrum of the water.

She would have to move house of course. She wouldn't stay in that dump a moment longer. Such a tragic figure she would be – first her baby, then her husband, she could hear them saying, even though the two events were twenty years apart.

Betty turned off the shower. Smothered herself in the talcum powder intended as a present for that nice woman from the supermarket and wrapped herself in an enormous fluffy towel. She poured another mug of gin. She could buy a thousand talcs tomorrow if she wanted.

Harry's razor on the glass shelf under the mirror caught her eye. She picked up two tissues, one pink and one yellow, and placed them on top of the razor which Harry never bothered to clean. She picked up the razor and dropped it in the bin, then blew the fuzz of bristles off the shelf. She giggled. It was the nearest she would come to scattering Harry's ashes.

'And the body was never found?'

'Of course it was a hurricane,' Betty heard them saying.

But she wouldn't give Thomas away. What was the point? It wouldn't bring Harry back, and he was such a nice lad. Pity about his girlfriend. Such a pretty girl but a bit over made up. Not that she'd liked to say so at the time.

Betty stepped away from the mirror. The lighting was harsh. It didn't show her at her best. Heard the voices again as she went back into the bedroom.

'Not even the satisfaction of a good funeral.'

'It's so important to grieve.'

'No use bottling it all up.'

Indeed not, thought Betty. She'd save all the tears for the press. She saw herself supported by Sam and Mal, flanked by Lou and Ida, as she tottered tearfully down the gangway.

Betty sat naked in front of the mirror with a glass of gin in her hand. Giggled and crossed her legs primly.

It was then that she heard the heavy footsteps in the corridor. Betty froze. The hairs on her arms and legs stuck out like a hedgehog's spines. As the first fist hammered on the door, Betty squeezed into the wardrobe, not at her end among the dresses, but at the other, among the suits and trousers where the smell of Harry was strongest. Where she could feel him all around her, even as she heard the key thrust into the lock.

Ophelia never heard the door open.

Postscript

A report that twenty-eight prostitutes had suffocated to death as they were shipped to the US Virgin Islands in a sealed container was confirmed yesterday by reliable sources ... (*The Times*, 22.4.85) [This container] was allegedly carrying electric dodgem cars for a United States Entertainment group ... *Le Matin* claims that the transfer of prostitutes by container from St Martin happens every fortnight with shippers charging between $800 and $1000 per girl. (*Sunday Times*, 21.4.85)